Nine

A Paninaro imprint

Cover design by Pat and Shan Wagner

A catalogue record for this book is available from the British Library

ISBN - 13: 978-1916088504

www.paninaropublishing.co.uk

"A great portrait of a seminal time for youth culture in the UK. A nostalgic must read for those who experienced it and an exciting and intriguing read for those that didn't."

Dean Cavanagh - Award winning screenwriter

"A punchy, authentic and recognisable trip down memory lane. Johnny Proctor captures the feeling of what it was truly like in early 90's Scotland when Acid House went toe to toe with football hooliganism."

Brad Welsh - Holyrood Gym and ex Hibs CCS

"Johnny Proctor encapsulates everything that was right and wrong about football hooliganism and Acid House. It evoked memories of how it felt like to be part of two scenes that co existed"

Anthony Donnelly - Founder and owner of Gio Goi

This book is dedicated to the early nineties warriors who threw punches on a Saturday afternoon and threw shapes on a Saturday night.

I sees you.

Twitter @johnnyroc73

Instagram @johnnyproctor90

Foreword

Johnny Proctor's novel encapsulates everything that was right and wrong about football hooliganism and Acid House. It evoked the memories of how it felt like to be part of two scenes that co existed, at times in the most conflicting of ways. In some ways it took me back to the days of standing in the vicinity of Old Trafford and Maine Road armed with craft knives and CS gas canisters waiting for the opposing team's main boys to have, what we'd waited all week, all year for. To cause carnage. It was all we had in our lives in terms of thrills and excitement.

Then Acid House and ecstasy gatecrashed proceedings and like Zico in the novel, one little pill was enough to change life forever. One yellow Californian sunrise given to me on match day was enough to alter things, permanently. One pill, one trip to Stuffed Olives had the effect on me where the next match I was akin to a Jehovah's Witness preaching to the rest of the boys with a big bag of smarties telling them to follow me, dressed in the maddest colours you could imagine, like the pied piper to the dance floor.

Next up was Liverpool, our biggest rivals yet instead of having a tear up in the back streets we arranged to have it with them on the dance floor in the underground club in Liverpool.

Johnny Proctor nails the feeling of anything being possible in those days. That if you wanted to achieve something it was a fresh canvas and that it was possible.

To highlight this. The "meet" in Liverpool was arranged with James Barton, who went on to form Cream, the first pill I was given was from one of the founder members of 808 State and my brother and I went on to create our own fashion label and one that cemented its place in Acid House history.

Acid House gave us the best days of our lives and Ninety takes you right back to the fresh, innocent and raw feelings of what it was like at the ground level of a scene that decades later still goes strong.

Anthony Donnelly - Gio Goi founder and owner.

Chapter 1.

'Re-fucking-wind' 'You paid HOW MUCH for a jacket?' I was stood there holding up my new CP Company coat for all the family. Until that very moment I had been feeling like William big balls about myself. It's not every day someone my age would spunk hundreds on a piece of immaculately crafted Italian designer gear such as this you understand? From the moment I walked out of Cruise Clothing right up until walking through the front door of my house, I'd been feeling that life was good, as good as it could get for a sixteen year old. It was the very exciting but also dangerous prospect of Aberdeen away the next day, and more importantly I'd be looking like a million fucking lira whatever capers I'd be getting up to in the land where sheep are statistically ninety seven percent more likely to be manhandled than anywhere else in Scotland. Now though? I felt taken down a few pegs.

I'd wanted it for quite some time and now after months worth of scheming I'd banked enough funds to add it to my inconsiderable wardrobe. I honestly can't wait til I can leave school and get a job. I'll need a fucking second wardrobe to handle all of the designer gear I'll be getting - CP, Fila, Stone Island, Adidas, Burberry, Lacoste, Tachini, a new pair of Stan Smiths as well as some Grand Slams and Forest Hills. I could go on. Anyway, the endorphins that had been flowing through me at the thought of how much respect I was going to get from the rest of the crew & what attention I would (hopefully) get from girls through this jacket, were sucked right out of me the moment my uncle heard how much money had been exchanged in return for this garment he was now sat in his armchair looking at.

'Son? You're standing there telling me that you've just went and spent the equivalent of what it costs to feed this entire house for the best part of two, possibly three months ON A FUCKING COAT?!?' The look on his face was a mixture of disbelief, disgust and delirium.

So many things I could've answered back to that outburst. Most based around the fact that it was my money. Money that I'd worked supremely hard to get in the one place at the one time and even then I imagine that there were several planets aligning to have helped make it happen. My money = no one else's fucking business. I resisted the urge though as I'd already clocked that he seemed to be quite a few cans into an afternoon session.

As young and inexperienced with life as I was I had already cracked onto the ways of just how impossible it is for someone sober to communicate with those under the influence of alcohol. I'd learned that life skill on the strength of all the weddings and birthday gatherings involving my family when all the elders ended up royally pished and I was still awake to witness the car crash. There always seems to be that little something that breaks the chain between both drunk and sober parties and things tend to get lost in translation. Through this I decided to pick my battle and take the lecture from him as he sat there holding court. Occasionally looking over at my auntie for nods of approval to assist with the point he was making.

'See when I was your age? Have you any idea how many things I could have bought for the price of that DP (I left it) or whatever it's called, jacket?'

I took a seat. Correctly assuming that this might take a while. Pair of shoes, tailored suit, trip to the pub, ticket for the cinema, fish supper. He kept going. Actually, he started to remind me about that Generation Game show when I was younger. Was waiting on him saying Breville toaster and cuddly toy in amongst his list. I started to switch off and was soon thinking of the imminent trip up north to Aberdeen for the United match, a topic that had dominated my week. I managed to pull myself back into the room just in time to hear his grand finale of 'and STILL have enough money left for my bus fare home' pointing his finger at me for emphasis.

'Bus fare home? I'm surprised you never bought a Lamborghini with some of your loose change' I said smiling back at him. Couldn't resist it and he took it the right way, calling me a cheeky wee bastard but in what I only ever detected as in an affectionate way. That's the good thing with my uncle Jimmy. He loves the patter. Really good with the banter likes. He'll dish it out but is always happy when he's getting it back in his direction too.

Once he'd calmed down a touch we sat and spoke for a while before I headed up to my room. I asked if he'd had any luck with the horses and who had been in the pub round at our local, The Central. The answer to both questions being 'no not much' although I'd have bet my newly purchased gear on the fact that he probably DID have luck at the bookies but wasn't letting on in front of my auntie. The first rule of gambling being NEVER admit to winning in front of the wife. Any male knows exactly why this is and whether they want to admit it or not every female will know too! One of the many nuggets of advice he had provided me during the three years I'd been staying with him and my Auntie Brenda. I won't bore you with all the details of why at sixteen years of age I was living with my auntie & uncle instead of mum and dad.

The short version being down to mum living abroad and my dad going for a packet of fags one time and not returning again, and by that I mean living a secret life as some Mr Big drug kingpin (not my words but those of The Sun no less) until he got himself busted and thrown in jail, never to be seen again. He was locked up when I was first year at high school. You can imagine what school was like the day after with it being all over the papers, fucking tabloids and everything. I heard he got out years later and now stays somewhere radge like Lima or Medellin which really wouldn't surprise me, well not now anyway.

To a kid it can be quite confusing to never see their dad again in such circumstances. For fucking ages I must've woken each day thinking that this would be the day that he would suddenly make an appearance again. As the years passed those thoughts became less and less until I reached the point where I didn't want to see him again anyway. I was in fact resentful towards even just the mention of him. On more than one occasion I'd told close family that if I was to ever see him again it would result in fisticuffs such was the feelings I now held when it came to Peter Duncan.

I suppose I was too young to really clock what was going on years ago but on the times that I actually did see him, which was once every blue moon, he was always driving a different sports car. A yellow Porsche 911 on one visit, a black Ferrari the next. Living the dream eh. Thinking back, the cunt seemed to have modelled himself on George Best. Ladies man, even had the same haircut as the ex Manchester United striker. Think George Best circa on the sofa with Terry Wogan when he told the nation that he liked screwing and that's my dad. Don't we all though, Georgie lad. Well, technically George Best has probably had sex more times today than I have in my life but in my defence I'm still finding my way in that particular arena.

I'd had that very same thought while walking back to Waverley to catch my train, speculating that this new CP jacket could well be the thing that would tip the equestrian scales in my favour. I bet it's going to be a right fanny magnet. I'll be doing more riding than Lester Piggot once out and about and I get myself seen in it whoa, ya fucker!

It would be getting its debut the next day on my away day to our bitter rivals, Aberdeen. Not that I'd be looking for my Nat King Cole up there likes. The only 'fucking' that would be the order of the day would be what Aberdeen Football Club would be, with a bit of luck, receiving out on the Pittodrie turf from Dundee United and what the ASC (Aberdeen Soccer Casuals) would be getting from our own team wherever those sheep shagging cunts would be happy to take it from what should be a healthy sized squad from Dundee. I'd only been running with the Utility Crew since last season but I'd noticed them inside and outside various stadiums across the country for the previous two, three years. Wreaking havoc all over the Scottish cities and towns, kitted out in the coolest of designer labels. And I wanted in.

Joining their team happened more by chance than design. Through my mum's chosen country of residence she was always bringing me tonnes of gear to wear from the boutiques over there in Madrid. Had me head to toe in Lacoste before even my tenth birthday had come around and I guess because of this upbringing I always did like my designer clothes.

Never saw too many people wearing the same labels as me though but was too young for that to even register. And then came what is, by some, internationally spoken as "The English Disease.' When it hit Scotland I was already going to the football week in week out with my cousin and his mates so immediately I noticed the sudden appearance of these gangs, who due to their clothes and haircuts stuck out like a sore thumb wherever they went. Mind you, when the first ever experience you have of casuals is when an opposing side's mob decides to alter the glazing situation of the pub that you're standing in as a twelve year old kid it's the kind of thing that can get your attention. Scared? You're fucking right I was scared. Who that age "wouldn't" be standing inside a Dundee boozer, The Three Barrels, drinking a can of coke and eating a bag of pickled onion Tudor crisps when a series of bricks come crashing through the windows, and then once free of glass you see around fifty angry looking men stood outside wanting to come in?! I wasn't just scared though and completely shaken by it. I was fascinated too in the way people are with horror films. I remember the bedlam inside the place. There was a couple of old jakeys, who didn't look like they'd be going to the game anyway, sat at the table by the big frosted glass window playing dominos who took a sore one from the bricks and rocks that had come through and into the pub. There was a mob of - what I would go on to class as "scarfers" - trying to mobilise to go out onto the street to confront the enemy while the Hibs casuals were trying to force their way past the bouncers and inside. In amongst this madness and seeing past my initial fear of these scary bastards getting into the pub and literally killing me and everyone in it, I had become transfixed with one of the Edinburgh lads outside looking in gesticulating in the most aggressive of ways I'd ever seen up to that moment in life.

It wasn't what he was doing that had caught my eye but what he was wearing. He had a red long sleeved Lacoste polo shirt on, the exact same as what I was standing there wearing that Saturday lunch time looking out at him. Then I noticed that one of his mates was sporting a Fila, Bjorn Borg polo shirt that I had back home. It wasn't hard for me to make the connection straight away that they all seemed to be wearing similar clothes and weirdly, similar clothes to me. From that one period of ten minutes of insanity inside and outside The Three Barrels and over the course of three seasons worth of seeing all kinds of naughty antics inside and outside Scotland's football stadiums, it was only a matter of time before I got involved in it all. Soon, a group similar to those mentalists from Edinburgh, started to be seen on match day when Dundee United were playing, also dressed like they were ready to step out on Centre Court at Wimbers.

Considering I was A. Still in my early teens B. Not even from Dundee as I was an out of town supporter traveling to each match. C. Going to the matches with my older cousin and D. Didn't know any of these 'casuals' who had sprung up from nowhere. I had no aspirations at all of being in any of these gangs going to the football to fight with others. As I got each year older though and due to my choice of what fashion to follow. There came problems most Saturdays when supporting my team. As the phenomenon of the casual movement grew I was forever getting myself into 'situations' purely through my gear I would wear traveling to the game each week. Then came Haymarket Station, Edinburgh and what was the defining moment.

I was fifteen by this point and trusted to go to the match on my own if my cousin wasn't going. With Edinburgh being only a short train ride away I decided to go on my own to a league cup semi at Tynecastle against Aberdeen. We were absolutely humped four nil but that wasn't the end to my shitty trip to the capital city. After the match I was back at Haymarket hoping to get myself on the first train out of there to hopefully avoid any of the inevitable fighting that by then I'd already associated train stations with on a Saturday afternoon in Scotland.

While sat there I noticed around half a dozen shifty looking boys standing on the other side of the train tracks looking over at me and pointing. I tried to do that 'not giving a flying fuck about them looking back at them and holding my gaze long but not too long' thing with them but it was getting clearly obvious that they were stood there talking about me. When they all left the platform they were standing looking at me from and disappeared from sight my paranoia levels were at a red coloured state of alert. Of course, a few moments later here they came marching along the platform I was sat on. I knew it wasn't going to be good whatever this exchange was going to provide, knew I couldn't run as the only options open were to go in their direction or head onto the tracks and disappear into the tunnel where for all I knew a train would be coming down so I just continued to sit and wait on them reaching me.

'Who ye with?' came the unmistakable Aberdonian accent. I'd been asked that same question before when on manoeuvres watching United away from home and like I'd always before, I played dumb.

'What do you mean who am I with?' I asked looking up from my seating position at what could be best described as half a dozen immaculately dressed menacing looking lads. You'd think their team going through to another cup final would have been enough to put them in a good mood but by the looks of their faces they had more work to do before their day out was done. I obviously wasn't going to ask but one of them looked to have taken a bit of a pasting at some point earlier in the day and this in itself quite possibly explained their heightened state they appeared to be in. I'm not sure why I never lied to them over the next question which was which team I supported. During those days I was an absolute statto when it came to football. Could've almost told you the preferred starting line up of Dukla Prague's reserve side back then so passing myself off as an Aberdeen fan would've been a piece of piss soaked cake.

I never though. As soon as I told him I was a United fan that was when the punches started to rain down on me from above. With natural instinct I managed to get myself up and off the bench in an attempt to at least defend myself in whatever way I could, quickly thinking of what all those heavyweight boxers would do when the fight was starting to go against them. Punches and kicks seemed to be coming from every direction with a few screams from fellow passengers sharing the same platform at the time providing the soundtrack to this little stramash. Self - preservation saw a few of the Aberdeen boys take a few punches and kicks back in their direction from me lashing out at them with no particular method or logic. Due to being surrounded, I never had the chance to see that there was another large group of hooligans bouncing down the platform towards us.

For the heinous crime of nothing more than me wearing a pair of Gazelles and an Adidas cagoule in addition to being a fan of the opposite team, my mutton molesting chums were so much in their element getting in as many digs to me as possible that they also didn't notice what was heading their way until it was too late and it was on them. In what was a welcome twist to proceedings they all went flying like bowling pins as the other gang wired into them.

I'm not ashamed to admit that in the heat of it all I dispensed a couple of timid kicks into the ribs of one of the Aberdonians who had fallen square in front of me while one member of the second group of casuals was kicking him in the head. For a brief second while we were lashing out at the guy on the ground we exchanged an almost knowing look. Mine's displayed thanks for turning up to save me from fuck knows what was to come while his one back at me can only be described as one of a person who's just found out that they've won the football pools after he's just hoovered up a gram of Ching. He looked ec-fucking-static. By now I was picking up Dundee accents from the second and much larger group who had fortunately came at the right time to save me and guessed that this had been the Utility boys now arriving back at the train station from Tynecastle. Whilst they may have saved myself they appeared to be having a whale of a time as they knocked the other lads around the Haymarket platform. Definitely a win win for us all.

After a couple of minutes it all seemed to have blown over. The Aberdeen boys doing a runner to all kinds of shouts and ironic cheers from the Dundee contingent still stood there. I reckon I had got through the past ten minutes or so on adrenaline and I was now for the first time finding myself taking the opportunity to catch my breath.

Stood there around all of this group of casuals who more than likely saved me from a real nasty beating from those sheep shagging cunts. The breather didn't last long in any case before.

'What the fuck are you still doing here ya fucking prick? You should be with your shitebag pals waiting round the fucking corner until we've got on our train so they can get the next one' - one of the Dundee boys shouted at me as he started to walk a touch menacingly towards me, giving it some growling action.

'Come fucking on,' I thought to myself. Surely I wasn't going to get a paggering from TWO different sets of football casuals WHILE SUPPORTING one of the teams they represented?! It never came to that.

'Leave the wee cunt alone, he's awright him' - The guy who had shared with me the most violent form of a threesome I could ever dream of with the Aberdeen boy, spoke up for me. He had one of those bowl cuts like the singer from The Inspiral Carpets and a wee light moustache that looked like he'd been trying to grow one but without much in the way of success. He seemed to have an air of menace and authority the way he was speaking to the others though so I was already pegged to the fact that this was one of the top boys in this team who had by now taken over the platform completely.

'How come? I've never fucking seen him in my life. We've just kicked fuck out of and subsequently ran Aberdeen's top boys from this platform and he's still here' - he said, still half - growling although appearing a little swayed by his mate's interruption. Stood there in what, for me, was a rather dated Nike Windrunner cagoule but it most definitely was neither the time nor the place to share such fashion tips with the chap.

'How come?' - Said the guy standing there with unwavering confidence. Pair of Stan Smiths on splattered in some fresh blood from the Aberdeen boy's face, obligatory jeans and an Adidas Ivan Lendl centre court sweater. That one piece of clobber which had already worked its way onto my "I can have both my Christmas and birthday at the same time' list. 'Because that wee bastard over there laid into Pagey from the ASC, right in front of my eyes. That sheep shagging bastard hit the fucking deck and the wee man was right in with the boot …. actually what's your name?' he asked me.

'Stevie, but my pals call me Zico' - I answered back like a shot still worried about if this was going to take a turn for the worse while still shaking over what had happened but trying not to show it.

'Well aye,' - Lendl continued - 'Pagey hit the platform and fucking Brazil's number 10 over there goes right in with the boot, game wee cunt. Of course, who widnae slash their own maw to get a chance to have it with Pagey so I went over and joined Zico by taking care of the rest of the so - called "top boy". Didnae look a top boy with someone who's probably no even legal aged to shag kicking fuck out of him' - To be fair, I was pretty sure that this guy in the Lendl top was remembering all of this with some kind of tinted spectacles having had the battle fever on for those five minutes or so. Aye, I gave this random guy a couple of kicks while he was on the ground because even with my low understanding of mathematics I could still estimate that he had had plenty fucking kicks and punches at me so, fair's fair you know?

Ivan Lendl, who I had began to sense was one of the higher ranking set of this crew, came over to talk to me, offering out a Regal King Size in my direction before he spoke. I "had" smoked before but didn't really enjoy it, didn't see the point of it to be honest but in that moment as a fifteen year old completely in fucking awe of this set of football casuals stood in front of me who had stormed in like the fucking S.A.S and saved my ham so aye, I accepted the fag from him.

'Fucking tell you what pal, I was at the front of our group running down the platform towards the ASC back there and I could see you taking a healthy amount of kicks and punches but you know what? You were giving some of them it back as well. Obviously you were getting loads more back in return but the fact that you gave some back?' - He lowered his voice for the next part as he looked around him. 'See half of the cunts behind me right now? They'd go all threatened hedgehog in that situation and curl up into a ball and hope for it to be over soon. So considering I just watched some top level Aberdeen faces setting about you I'm making an educated guess that you're not a red?' he asked while still appearing to size me up a little.

'Nah, I'm an Arab' - I replied, fishing out my match ticket to show him before adding that it had been a shite enough day as it was. I regretted doing it the second I did it and his response wasn't exactly sympathetic as he waved the sight of the ticket away in mild disgust.

One minute I appeared to be laying into one of the most feared football casuals in Scotland and the next I'm coughing up my match ticket like some cunt at school giving up his dinner money to the resident bully. I continued.

'Been going home and away since I was at primary school.'

'So what's with the gear then?' he asked while looking me up and down. 'If you're not running with anyone but you're going to be going to the fitba every Saturday you're going to end up in some trouble. Fucking hell! See if there had been no Aberdeen there on the platform earlier on I'd have been right fucking over to see where you were from. You stick out like a sore thumb in these crazy times we're living in, my man.' he said. I'm not exactly sure where I found my cockiness from in such a major stressful passage of time which technically had begun the moment Brian McGinley the referee had blown the whistle for the start of the match but the only answer I could come out with to that question was.

'Mate? I've been wearing this kind of gear when you were all wearing your Y cardigans and stay press trousers with Adidas Kicks, all of the mobs across Scotland have only now caught up with me but aye, it's making my life a fucking misery most weeks' - Taking in what I'd said for a few seconds that felt like minutes and had me worried I'd went too far with my jokey comment he burst out laughing.

'Fuck aye!! You're a mouthy wee prick but anyone who can set about the ASC and then still have enough cojones to play the wide boy with me for dessert is most definitely a good cunt in my book.'

From then until the train for Dundee via Fife arrived the two of us sat chatting about clothes and United. A few others from the crew came over to chat to Ivan who by then had introduced himself formally to me as 'Nora' with him introducing them to me as an when they came over. Finding out I was from Fife and not Dundee he called a couple of lads over especially upon hearing that small detail from me. Jumping the gun a little he announced me to them as the newest addition to the Fife squad that made up the Dundee Utility Crew.

One of the Fife boys I actually recognised although I'm not sure if it went both ways. I played against him in a fives tournament a couple of summers back. Cunt fucking should've remembered me considering I was the one who scored the two goals in the final to win the trophy for our team against his one. Weird to find though that after talking for a few moments I discover that we only stayed a few miles away from each other. Small world and all that. As the train approached the platform, Nora slipped me a card asking for me to give him a "call through the week" and with all the confusion of getting onto an already crowded train that had begun at Waverley I lost everyone in terms of who I'd already met by that point.

Once I got sat down on the train and began to take stock over all that had happened, the first thing that I noticed was that it felt like every single inch of my body was in the worst of pain. I hadn't even seen what damage the ASC had done to my face but judging by some of the looks I managed to catch in my direction from some fellow passengers in my carriage, it didn't look too promising. Beyond the fact that I had taken, without question, the worst hiding in my short life though I was sat there with a stupid smile on my face and, knowing I'd gotten through it without a trip to hospital, I was buzzing in ways I'd never experienced before. Maybe I'm just looking for an excuse when I say that at that time I didn't think I had the maturity to properly think through the pros and cons with getting involved in a violent gang who were partial to a whole list of crimes over the course of their day out at the match. I was always going to call Nora. Holding off until the Wednesday day before I did when in reality I could've called him that same night of the Aberdeen match.

He just struck me as an incredibly cool and sound lad. Was into everything I was in terms of clothes, music and obviously football team. It was the full set. I assumed that as, by the looks, the top man of the Utility Crew, he wouldn't have given two fucks about a younger guy like myself but he seemed to be actually interested in talking to me on both the day at Haymarket and then the phone call on the Wednesday. Asking questions to me, getting opinions, giving his, you know? Like I say, he came across as a chilled but engaging guy. As time would go on though I would really start to see what the man was capable of. I'd find out the other side he had to him. The one I wish I'd known about in advance.

After that midweek call, I was in. Arrangements were made for me to meet up with him and some others at The Snug, a boozer near the stadium for the home game on the following Saturday against Motherwell and the rest as they say was history. It's been almost a season I've been running with the Utility and I'd say I was as far in with them now as I'll ever be. It's been a wild ride and no mistake. I've had my cunt kicked in a few times, kicked a few others in myself. Have been home and away to most grounds in the Scottish Premier League and have always been there at roll call the next week on the Saturday morning. And this brings us back to 'tomorrow' morning and the trip to Aberdeen and why it had been dominating my thoughts. Since Haymarket, I'd never remotely been in the same postcode as the ASC and I have to admit I was fucking dying to meet them again after what had happened previously. Tomorrow I'd get my chance.

Chapter 2.

I almost never even made Aberdeen. As is the archetypal activities of your average Scottish sixteen year old, illegally procured alcohol had been the order of the day on the Friday night and as-per-fucking-always, farce ensued. Brycey, one of my 'through the week' mates of mine's, even if he is what I can only describe as a 'hun bastard' decided to pan a couple of windows of the local church as we were walking past it. 'FUCK THE POPE AND THE I R FUCKING A' he shouted as he lobbed some stones through the beautiful stain glass windows above the doorway.

Fucking idiot, I went mental at him. Through nothing other than some misguided sense of cause as a Glasgow Rangers supporter he, while six cans of Tennents in, thought it a good idea to stone a church. He's lucky I never fucking stoned HIM, Middle Eastern style. I pushed him and asked what the fuck he was doing. All bammed up through the drink and the messed up endorphins of what he'd just done in the name of the red hand Ulster, he pushed me back even harder which resulted in us going for a wee roll on the grass outside the front of the church. The area where you'd normally see families posing for photos at weddings and such like.

Oblivious, were still going at it when the police patrol car pulled up. By the time I clocked them standing over us it was well too late for any thoughts of running away. 'Fucking typical,' I thought to myself. Have been getting up to all sorts of 'bad behaviour' for the best part of the year plus on a Saturday and haven't been pinched one single time and here I am going to get huckled for fighting, not with some notorious fitba crew like the CCS or ASC but for swedging with my twat of a pal three minutes walking distance from my house at the end of the fucking night.

Having drunk less than Brycey I had a bit more about myself to try and at least speak to the two Fife Constabulary who were standing over us but who appeared to be in no apparent rush to put a stop to proceedings.

'Evening officer,' I said making no attempts to get up off the ground while The Ultimate Warrior there was finally releasing me from his death grip, himself now cottoning onto what was happening.

'So what's going on here then, Steven?' said a familiar face back to me. It's funny but I've always thought that Constable Munroe has always looked like Bruce Forsyth and as a result, every time I see him I always think 'Good Game Good Game' and pish myself laughing but there wasn't exactly much to laugh about there and then.

'Just a wee disagreement about Rangers and United that didn't know when to say when' I said - 'Aint that right, Brycey eh?' I put my arm around him. The two officers let me continue. 'Let's just agree to disagree right now that since Richard Gough is now a Rangers player he's a massive prick and be done with it!' Luckily Brycey followed my lead and laughed before telling me to fuck off but in a jokey all pals together kind of way. There was obviously still the issue of the two of us being underage drinkers right there in front of them in addition to the two broken windows right behind us, that may or may not have been clocked by the bods from Fife Cuntstabulary.

'I suppose none of you will be pressing charges?' asked Munroe's partner, this cunt with a tash that suggested he'd had pictures of Graeme Souness circa 1980 on his bedroom wall, and being honest, for someone that young he should've known better. Moustaches belong on porn stars and, well, Souness and that was pretty much it. Hadn't seen him before so he was an unknown quantity and one to watch for the next few minutes as far as I was concerned. I have to admit that I was well chuffed to have seen Munroe's face as him and I are cool with each other.

There's a lot of radges in the area and I'm not one of them so he always plays the game with me. Pragmatic, aye, that's the word. I learned it the other week in school in English where, unless I picked up the wrong end of the stick, means that you can kinda get a proper grip on what's going on around you instead of totally flapping all over the place and making an arse of yourself. All emotion stuff eh? Peaso, one of the guys in my class, thought he'd be the smart cunt by asking the teacher - 'So another way of putting pragmatic would be that you would find yourself completely fucked someway or other but would be able to accept it for why you were in that position' Ha ha aye, smart cunt danced his way down to detention after that.

Can't stand him anyway. He's a Hibs fan for one and I've kinda developed a dislike for all things Hibernian FC the past year due to some brutal meetings between us and their Capital City Service crew.

For the moment though, Munroe wasn't holding court. 'Nah, nae cherges, officer', Brycey found his voice with me nodding my head in agreement.

'Perfect' Officer Munroe said, moving to get back in the car. This, for me anyway, seemed the logical approach. It was Friday night and near chucking out time and it was a cast - iron, gold plated nailed - down fact that at this moment in time there was much more threats to society in the close vicinity than these two underage drinkers. I had fast learned through my Saturday afternoons that the police had to sometimes know the difference of taking things further or letting things go. I'd seen so many things happen right in front of the police that would normally land you right in the back of the van and a sleepover in a cell yet the police had turned the other eye.

Paradoxically I'd also seen some getting huckled for practically fuck all. Nora told me early doors when I started running with the Utility that some coppers would do all they could to avoid being on duty at the fitba and would pinch some poor unlucky cunt who was simply in the wrong place at the wrong time. Didn't really matter if they'd done anything or not. Their sole purpose being a reason for the officer to get away back to the station and away from where the real action was. Thing is, I didn't know that Munroe's partner was going to be a jobsworth of the highest order.

'Alex? You're not just going to leave these two alone for the rest of the night? They've clearly been drinking and it doesn't take an I.D check to tell me that they're not the legal age,' this other boy chips in as Munroe opens the car door.

You could tell that this new officer was gagging to get us in the back of the car and down to Aberhill station. If it hadn't been so dark I'm sure I'd have been able to see the erection that he had for the two of us. He appeared to have so much of a hard on, bromide wouldn't have been able to touch the bastard. 'I know what you're saying but they're hardly mortal the two of them are they?' Munroe said back to him. It was probably the first time in my life I'd actually felt feelings of respect for the police. One is making a play for lifting us and sticking us in the cells on an underage drinking charge while the other one is making a case for not.

'Not the point, not the point at all though is it? Officer Dickhead, not letting it lie replied back. 'How does it look if we've got people who have quite obviously committed a crime right in front of us and we just let them go? Hardly going to be a deterrent for them to not do it again'

'Look, mate, we're just on our way home for the night. Won't be anymore trouble from us' I tried to defuse things but was cut off by Munroe's pal - I say pal but I, as drunk as I was I could see that the two of them weren't exactly bosom buddies as far as work colleagues go. There seemed to be some uneasiness to their exchanges. I've never had a job before but fuck sitting in a car with someone you don't like for nine hours a day.

'You keep your trap shut, and I'm not your mate either' - I fucking hate when cunts say that when you call them mate. It's only a figure of speech at the end of the day. Not like I'm proposing to go out for a fucking drink and to take in a film or anything with the prick.

My insolence must've been the catalyst to escalate things as he instantly moved towards me, taking hold of my arm with a firm grip and pulling me up off my arse. I clocked Munroe shaking his head while his colleague had his back to him. Even if he was shaking his head in a disapproving way over how things had turned he was now making his way back from the car towards the three of us and specifically in the direction of Brycey. I figured that he was now left with no choice but to back up this fanny of an officer he was spending his Friday night with.

The only positive I was able to take from this was that nobody had yet mentioned the fact that the church was looking like it had suffered a few thousand of pounds worth of damage as this seemed to be exclusively about the underage drinking. Brycey wasn't exactly happy with this twist in proceedings and was in danger of turning it into something more serious than the likely slap on the wrist and our parents finding out about it that it looked like shaping up to be. I was more pragmatic (there's that word again) about it. We were underage and had been drinking all night. We were standing at the scene of a much more serious crime which had unbelievably been missed by the coppers. Things could've been far worse and at the end of the day if we hadn't been doing what we had we wouldn't be sat there in the back of the car like we were.

Brycey on the other hand was not in a frame of mind to view things with such twenty twenty vision, mouthing off at the two in the front of the car while I'm elbowing him in the ribs telling him to shut his fucking mouth before he made matters worse. I was obviously blaming the cunt for all of this and how he was the reason that our Friday night wasn't going to end with a badly cooked fish finger sandwich and a wank, courtesy of one of the many porno mags I'd siphoned off from my older cousin who had more porn in his room than Soho.

'Next stop, Methil' said the jobsworth looking round at us with a sickening self - satisfying grin. You could just tell that he was one of these pricks that wanted to get into the force for his own dickish reasons rather than the whole 'to protect and serve the community' that Munroe had always had an air of. He's old school though. Nah, this other guy was probably bullied when he was at school and wanted to take it out on others with him having the uniform on and the power that gave him. Probably wet the bed as well when he was younger, definitely looked the type. Before the car pulled away though a call came through on their radio. Couldn't quite make out all that had been said but I did make out something about Burt's Bar five minutes along the road and that there seemed to be some disturbance. This time it was Munroe looking back around at us and whilst he had a straight face I could still make out the smallest of smiles in his eyes when he said.

'Well, you pair of lucky wee bastards, it looks like you just won the lottery' getting out the car to come round to the back doors to let us out again. 'We need to get going.' The look on his partner's face was a picture, a picture of devastation crossed with embarrassment. Looked like he'd married a sex kitten right as she was about to turn into a cat as that VW Golf advert had said. It was beautiful!

I made sure to give him a wee wink when I was getting out of the car alongside a very much loaded. 'Hope you have a quick rest of your shift 'mate' - Now go catch some bad guys' with the emphasis well and truly on the term of endearment, mate. I tapped the roof of the car in that way people did when they were getting dropped off by someone.

Brycey and moi were almost back fighting with each other as the panda sped off. I couldn't resist having a dig at him over the fact through his lunacy we'd almost spent a night in the cells, that I wasn't impressed with his nonchalant blasé way he was acting as if it had been his plan all along that we'd have been spared the ordeal due to fuck knows what was happening along at Burt's Bar. The two of us argued all along the road until we parted ways. Walking down the hill towards my house I took the decision to stay away from the cunt for a while. Had he been the one to make me miss Aberdeen away I'd have been making it a permanent thing and no mistake.

My uncle was still sat up which had kinda put a spanner in my works. I always try to time my getting in when I've been drinking along with when him and my auntie are already in bed. They're not bad likes, I reckon my cuzz already took them through this when he was my age. I just can't be arsed with the lectures, especially when drunk. They never go down well when you've been drinking and more inclined to argue back. Most nights I would find myself hanging around at the end of the road until I would see all the lights in the house go out but after what had came before I just wanted myself in the house and out of harm's way. I hoped Jim would be passed out in his armchair by that point anyway. He wasn't though. I tried to go with the tried and tested barely pop my head round the living room door to say a quick hello to him but when he saw me he asked me through for a blether.

I wasn't really sure why he had MTV on the telly as that was about a million miles from all of his Perry Como that he always listened to but there was Seal on the telly singing on that Adamski tune, Killer. Good fucking song that as well, even if he looked a bit of a scary fucker. I'd been getting more and more into that type of music recently. Seemed really fresh and you could tell that there was some kind of movement happening when it came to dance music. I hadn't really been someone who had liked dance music until 1990. Ignorantly I'd always looked at dance music as disco, fucking John Travolta Saturday Night Fever crap and that had seemed all pretty lame to me as I was finding my way in the world with music and clothes etc.

Since starting high school I'd found myself falling in love with hip hop and with it being something that apart from the occasional tune was a type of music that wasn't mainstream and, like with how I was dressing, had a more exclusive feel to it and made me feel that I wasn't following any kind popular crowd. First gig I'd went to was Public Enemy at the Barrowlands in Glasgow. Blew my mind and after that night of watching Chuckie D and Flav, complete with his big stupid fucking clock round his neck there was no way back for me. Years earlier I'd gotten into the Beastie Boys but was too young to know what was what. Knew what I was doing when I stole that VW sign from my neighbour's car though. Got caught for that too, then again looking back I always was going to be caught. A Volkswagen loses a front emblem and two minutes later I'm walking about with one around me. Hardly an example of discretion. He still doesn't speak to me to this day even though I had to buy him a new one out of my pocket money. Fair enough I suppose.

Away from hip hop I was surprised to find myself getting into the whole 'Madchester' indie scene with what I called "guitar bands." I wasn't just blindly following new movements for the sake of it because The Face told me to or fuck all but I was definitely starting to see that I was getting into music that the majority of people didn't seem to be. You could always gauge that by what everyone was listening to at school, what band names everyone was writing on their jotters, that type of thing. I was definitely starting to have my head turned by what, in some quarters, was being called Acid House.

I didn't know the whole ins and outs of it at that point but knew drugs were a lot to do with it and I wasn't really into that side of things. I'd had my first toke of Hash at a Happy Mondays gig in Glasgow when I was fifteen, kinda liked it but I dunno? I had obviously had this misplaced idea that I'd be seeing wee green men after smoking it or something rather than the effect that it had in reality. That's what comes through reading tabloid newspapers though. Those fucking things don't seem to have a clue what they're writing about and even at an early age I could see that they weren't exactly bang on with what they were writing about. I could see that alone from reading the sports reports about United matches I'd been to where I'd often wonder if the reporter was even AT the fucking match?

My uncle was cool though about the fact that his nephew had evidently been drinking. This was Scotland after all, it's almost a rite of passage that you WILL drink before you get to eighteen. Fuck? How else would we be prepared for when we GOT to the legal age and when the REAL swally would begin? I'll never forget the very first time I had a drink at a girl from my class' birthday party and came back home drunk (three cans of Tennents, oh aye, triple can Dan so I was) he thought it was hilarious and looking back it must've been. Rather than do the sensible thing and creep in and get myself to bed before he noticed, full of nothing but deluded and drunken bravado I thought I could go through to the living room and sit and have a chat with him and he wouldn't notice. Worse still, as is the case after a drink you always want something to eat, anything. I'd went through to make something and thought it would be a good idea to cook some fish fingers and stick them on a sandwich. I brought the culinary delight back through to the living room to sit with him, took one bite of it and felt the sensation of my teeth crunching through ice before spitting it right back out. He's sat there pissing himself laughing.

'You ken that you're meant to cook the fucking things for fifteen minutes, pal, not two' he said once he'd stopped laughing. Fair enough although slightly ironic coming from someone who I doubt had cooked a meal in his life due to his doting and loving wife!

He was just wanting to know what I'd been up to while out so I went with the diplomatic answer of a couple of beers and playing the Sega up at a friends while keeping my fingers crossed that he wouldn't be running into Munroe at any point in the near future. Only sat with him for a few minutes as it was an early start the next morning. Would be for the both of us. He had work - I had Aberdeen. I said goodnight to him whistling the tune to 'The Northern Lights Of Aberdeen' as I went upstairs, stupidly waking up my auntie through my whistling. I was totally buzzing for the next day but knew I needed to go and get my head down for a few hours. It was going to be a day for the scrapbook and no mistake.

Could. Not. Fucking. Wait

Chapter 3.

I met up with the three other Fife Utility lads - Brewster, Carey & McGinn - at Kirkcaldy station nice and early for the 9.05 Inter City to Aberdeen. The plan being that the core members of the crew would be getting on and joining us when the train rolled into Dundee en route to Aberdeen.

'Fucking cool jacket son, must've set you back a bob or two' said Carey. 'Shame you won't be coming back down the road with it all in one piece' ominously adding with a smile on his face.

'Only thing I'll need to worry about is if my old dear will be able to get the blood from these sheep shagging bastards off it' I replied trying to come across as cocky as I could whilst inside knowing that the trip was going to be one of the most, if not THE most, dangerous of away days I'd ever had since joining The Utility. My Fife - based hooligan compadres looked like they'd all been making an effort for the occasion too. Brewster was sporting a brand new Stone Island jacket that must've cost the equivalent of every single item of clothing in my wardrobe put together. Same with Carey and McGinn with their own CP gear that looked new as I'd never seen them wearing before.

The thing was though, they were in their twenties and already working so adding to their wardrobe was a lot more easy than someone still at school. To be fair that in itself got me some extra kudos on occasion with the crew as I'd already had comments now and again over my gear I wore for someone so young. Actually had at times detected a bit of jealousy from some of the mob that I wasn't so close to who, without being big headed, weren't as good dressers as moi. The four of us stood on the platform waiting on the train arriving bantering about how last weeks home game against Hearts had went alongside sharing stories of how our respective Friday nights had turned out. The other three were already getting fired into their carry out that they had for the train. Not even nine and they're stood there with can in hand. I had to be sensible though. If I started drinking at that time of the morning and with the match kicking off at three, I wouldn't be seeing any fitba so I left them to it.

All of us in the crew who were underagers were never sure to even get into the pubs on away days wherever we were off to so drink wasn't as big a part of the day for us as it was for the elder members. We were nicknamed the 'baby crew' and due to our age we were often given our own duties to perform while the 'men' were sat in the pubs. This was mostly just doing a bit of 'spotting' and making sure that none of the other mobs would be able to sneak up on the designated pub undetected and catch the Utility with their pants down.

There wasn't much to that particular role although there was always an element of danger due to being on your Jack Jones in a strange city with no real knowledge of the location you were in and where the other mob might spring from. Wasn't rocket science though. The minute you saw the other team you'd tear it back to the pub to pass on the word, often being chased by the other team who would obviously want to get hold of you before you spoiled their plans for an ambush and the element of surprise they had planned.

On an awayday like this there is no denying the feeling amongst the troops that is one of a kid waking up on Christmas Day. The excitement mixed with anticipation of what lies ahead. The surprises to come and the 'presents' that are waiting to be opened up in the form of meeting up with the opposing crew. As we boarded the train, there was that unmistakable feeling that morning. I actually had Phil Collins pop into my head with his song 'I can feel it coming in the air tonight' as I took my seat with the other three. Kinda funny how stuff like that pops into your head, especially when it's a musical artist that you can't fucking stand and so much so that you'd be all for him having one of those Fatwa things placed on him like that writer did years back when he pissed off those religious chaps from the Middle East.

I'm not sure if Collins has done anything to offend muslims though likes but chances are he probably has as he offends every single cunt the moment he opens his mouth and sings. We were all buzzing, speculating on what was to come up in sheep town. Carey was going on about how he was hoping to reacquaint himself with a couple of ASC who had done him in a few months ago at a Stone Roses gig when he was waiting to get a beer. I of course had already met the ASC last season after the cup semi and alongside Hibs, had already developed a deep running dislike for all things Aberdeen Soccer Casuals. I'm not one who doesn't give credit where credit's due though. They're a capable and handy group of casuals. Always have good numbers. They were one of the first organised and dressed mobs to appear in Scotland. They dress well and are game as fuck when it was time to get down to the nitty fucking gritty. Then again so are we.

This was all too evident as the train started to pull to a stop at Dundee when I started to catch sight of all of the Utility Crew stood on the platform waiting to get on. It was a glorious sea of designer labels all along the platform merged with the famous tangerine and black colours of Dundee United that all of the 'scarfers' were wearing who were also on their way up to Pittodrie for the match. It might've been a cliche and certainly didn't suit the agenda of your tabloid journalist but us and all the others teams across Scotland had no interest whatsoever in fighting with other 'fans' and that was why we called them scarfers as they weren't going to the game to have it out with their like-minded ilk from the other team.

They were there purely to support their team, on what was their Saturday institution as a football fan. Wearing their team colours with pride by way of scarfs, hats, replica tops. Don't get me wrong, the Utility (well, the ones who actually supported United, of course) love United every bit as much as any of the other support base and no non violent fan could tell me that from the first whistle to the last they were supporting their team more passionately than I was. I just had other "motivations" when it came to my overall match day experience than theirs of a few pints and two points and a win for their football team.

Once our very healthy looking mob had got on board the train pulled off and within a few stops between we'd be in Aberdeen around lunch time giving us around three hours to get up to as much no good as possible before the match kicked off. Everyone was in high spirits and completely buzzing for their day trip. The carriage was rammed and it wasn't long before I had to give up my seat for one of the more so called important members of the firm. I understood the rules, didn't mean to say that I liked the fact that just because I was only sixteen I had to give my seat up for a thirty year old in Mad Dog from Fintry, but rule number one of running with a crew was that if someone called 'Mad Dog' wants your seat then it's probably a good idea that you comply.

I ended up standing for most of the journey along with a couple of lads from the Craigie area of the town. When we have a crew as big as we did it wasn't possible to ever know everyone and it was more during away matches that you'd have the opportunity to get to know a few new lads every now and again and this was one of those scenarios. One of them, who had introduced himself to me as Si, doing so by complimenting me on my new coat. I'd had quite a few comments on it by this point and was feeling well happy with myself over it. Had a wee laugh to myself over the paradox between yesterday's lecture from my uncle when I'd gotten back from Edinburgh and the kudos I was now getting a day later. We'd barely pulled out of Dundee station before Si was pulling a small wrap out of his pocket and dabbing a finger in before shoving it in his mouth. Aware of me watching him he instinctively ushered it in my direction.

'Want a wee dab, Zico?' he asked

Like I've said. I'm not exactly versed in the ways of the drug world and being honest I didn't even know "what" it was that he was shoving into his mouth.

'What is it like?' I replied still trying to work out if I was going to take it before I even knew what the fuck it was. I was already assuming that it couldn't have been cocaine as I'd seen enough films and TV shows to know the score with that.

'Just a wee bit Sulph, mate. Trust me, It'll put you in good shape for when we get up the road.'

"Sulph? What the fuck was Sulph?" I thought to myself? Only thing I could think of was 'sulphate' which had been something that had come up now and again in my chemistry class at school and speaking through experience, that didn't seem like something that you wanted to trifle with. Fucking hell! I was still getting over having a big sniff out of the Nitric Acid bottle after being dared by that radge bastard Pete Yule from Glenrothes. Jesus Christ, I saw stars for the rest of the day after that. The vacant look on my face must've been that obvious because before I could even say anything Si followed up his pitch with.

'Speed, toot toot, hurry the fuck up powder'

After that it was all down to a mix of peer pressure and the good old British tradition of accepting something through not wanting to appear rude. Didn't matter if I'd never tried it before OR me not having a clue what the effects would be after taking it. I accepted it from him, licked the tip of my finger and shoved it right into the wrap the powder was sat in and without hesitation shoved it in my mouth before handing it back to him. Tasted absolutely rank and I had the instant thought that it tasted like how my chemistry class smelled like. I didn't want to make an idiot of myself by asking him what would happen next and decided to let things take their own course. I never quite twigged at the time but it was pretty obvious really that for someone so young it was perfectly acceptable for me to not know what I was doing but that summed me up when with the Utility. Was always trying to make myself out as older beyond my years to fit in with everyone else.

'Good lad' Si smiled as he took his wrap back and stuck it away in his pocket. We were only just past the next stop, Broughty Ferry, before I started to feel this stuff coming on. Could feel my heart starting to speed up like I'd been chased by the police. Despite having only met this guy for the first time ten minutes before, I was talking the fucking lugs off him about everything and anything. The latest range of Adidas trainers, that fit bird who was Page Three in The Sun last Wednesday, why the Ewoks in Return of the Jedi were as evil as any Storm Trooper as well as the fact that Jabba the Hut and Bernard Manning had never been seen in the same room, how much of a doing the ASC were going to get once the Utility hit Aberdeen. No topic was off limits for me once that shit had entered my bloodstream. He just stood there pissing himself laughing at me and shaking his head.

'Good stuff eh?' he asked laughing while opening up what would be the first of many cans of Red Stripe that was sat in a Threshers bag. He handed me one which I gladly accepted.

'With that speed inside you the beer won't even touch the fucking sides' he added when handing me the can while pretty much confirming that he knew that I'd never had the drug in my life.

'That right, Aye?' I asked while opening the can which through the white with red stripe design, always makes me think about Peru and them humping Scotland at the World Cup in Argentina. 'Mate, what you've got here is a classic case of stone paper scissors and if that tin of Red Stripe is your scissors then this Speed is most definitely the fucking stone' he said patting the pocket where the speed was sitting in for emphasis. 'Trust me Zico, you'll be fucking raring to get stuck into those sheep bastards the minute you step off the train at Aberdeen with this stuff inside you.'

Chapter 4.

'I CAN'T READ AND I CAN'T WRITE BUT THAT DON'T REALLY MATTER CAUSE I SUPPORT ABERDEEN AND I CAN DRIVE A TRACTOR' sang the whole train carriage which was full of Utility Crew apart from a few random passengers who looked like they wished they were anywhere but there. Most of the windows were being banged by enthusiastic fists in time to the derogatory song that was always rolled out whenever United played our rivals from up the road. The media years back had invented the term "New Firm" in an attempt to manufacture a rivalry between Aberdeen and Dundee United in the same way that they had their "Old Firm," which, let's face it was all they were really interested in, especially considering the Scottish media were largely based in Glasgow.

Fans of both teams never came close to buying their synthetic fugazi rivalry and you'd have done well to ever find either set of fans describe the matches as the "New Firm Derby" which the media loved to call it when there was a game between the two. Fucking hell, how can a game of football be ever classed as a Derby when there's over sixty miles between the two teams? Truth be told, in a purely football sense Aberdeen fans seemed to attach more importance to it due to not actually having a city rival team to play against, but in a non-sporting sense and purely a potential for trouble one then yeah, this was as big as it would ever get and it was clear to see from the mood inside the train carriage as it pulled into Aberdeen Station.

The speed started to wear off around half an hour outside Aberdeen which saw Si produce that familiar wrap from his pocket to top us up. Which it most definitely did! I had all kinds of stuff running through me as we arrived and not just amphetamines. The usual nerves were starting to kick in which was a given for me. I always got them and as far as I was concerned if you didn't get nervous over the thought of effectively going to war then you really should stop to check your pulse to see if you were actually still alive.

The adrenaline was starting to flow through me also but nothing was coming close to touching the overwhelming feeling of simply just wanting to get off the fucking train and to just MOVE. I could feel it that standing still in a cramped train carriage like a sardine did not agree with the speed. I needed to march, fuck it, RUN. Didn't matter where exactly, I just wanted to put one foot in front of the other, shit? I could've run the London marathon at that point but was more than happy to substitute that for running the ASC all over their own patch. Well, so long as we caught them eventually. We sure as fuck never travelled all the way up here to engage in a ten thousand metre charity fun run.

Once the singing had come to a stop Nora started to speak up to all of the troops.

'Right, listen up. You all know the drill. The moment we step off the train there's going to be eyes on us from both the five o and some ASC spotters. Once we're off the train we're going to confuse the fuck out of them by splitting up. Half of you are coming with me and the rest of you are going with Walker but we're all meeting up at The Bobbin'

Walker, sat next to Nora, nodded his head and looked round us all to make sure that Nora's instructions had been understood. I'd never seen Nora so amped for an away day in my short time running with them all. He's normally right on the booze on a day like this but throughout the journey I'd not seen him touch so much as a drop which showed how serious he was taking things. Si had been bang on though on the subject of alcohol. I'd had four cans on the way up and normally that would have been enough to have given me a bit of a buzz but through the speed it had been like all I'd been drinking had been Dandelion and Burdock. Waste of fucking time even drinking them to be fair and all it had served was to have me feeling like I needed the mother of all pishes. Couldn't get near the toilets on the way up due to the combination of how rammed the carriage had been and the occasional chancers who hadn't paid for a train ticket and were hiding out in there trying to avoid the ticket collector.

Once we were off the train Nora's words of wisdom were proved astute. The hornies were waiting on us outside the station. Hardly inconspicuous in their fluorescent jackets and riot vans. The ASC not so much but they'd have been there somewhere, strategically placed to get a swatch at us to see what numbers we had brought up the road before reporting back to base, wherever that was. What was guaran-fucking-teed though was that we'd be doing all within our powers to find out where 'base' was. We walked out in a haphazard and staggered formation that to the untrained eye looked like this mob of soccer casuals were about the furthest thing from an 'organised crew.'

Half of us turned left and the others right when we got to the top of the stairs to leave the station. This obviously threw the coppers though as they didn't know how to deal with things. They didn't have enough manpower to split up and by the time they tried to take over they'd found the two separate groups already on their merry way. After the beer and the speed, I couldn't stop talking the biggest lot of shite you have ever heard. I mean, I KNEW I was saying it, KNEW how annoying it must have been but still couldn't stop myself. Didn't know if I liked the effect of speed or not and was seeing definite pros and cons to taking it. I could see why it would in all likeliness be on the list of banned substances for athletes at the Olympic Games and we all know how much those cunts love their narcotics as well.

All I'm saying is that if they got their hands on some of this stuff that Si had brought to the party today then they'd be well getting a cheeky wee dab into a wrap before it's time to go out and perform. I bet that was what Ben Johnson was getting down him before the hundred metres final a couple of years ago in Seoul! Tell you what though, the way I was feeling I reckoned I could've beaten Ben Johnson giving Carl Lewis a backy on a Kawasaki 250!

The walk to the pub was pretty much uneventful although what we'd lacked in excitement we were repaid in full when we eventually started to approach The Bobbin. Was kind of ironic, nay poetic, that the first hint we got that there was something going off was due to some of our chaperones from the Grampian Police who had escorted us along the way and were seen frantically talking into their walkie talkies before jumping in their van and speeding off in the direction of the pub. They couldn't have made it more obvious had they been handing out leaflets when we got off the train advising where the trouble was going to be. In what was nothing more than a natural reaction, no discussions, not even a look at each other, we all charged off down the road following the police van, which was disappearing down the street at Ben Johnson speed with blue lights and sirens, the lot.

The boozer was up ahead although had you not known this, the noise of shouting in addition to the police sirens were pretty much serving as a fucking beacon to us. We ran around the last corner ready to steam into, well that we did not know. Be prepared though as I learned in the Scouts, well, for the two weeks that I lasted after making the step up from the cubs after a distinguished 100% paedo-free experience. One swear word up in the big league and I was turfed out without even any kind of an appeal.

A Scottish chapter of the Boy Scouts really should revisit their rulebook though cause before they know it there'll be no cunt fucking going if they want to proceed with their zero tolerance to colourful language. Anyway, we fired round the corner to find complete carnage. Despite a heavy police presence and a semi successful attempt at a cordon, you had pockets of ASC and Nora's half of the team who had evidently made it to the pub before we did, going at it all over the place. Police were arresting heavily resisting hooligans from both sides with the boys in blue then coming under attack accordingly, letting their collars go in the process.

It was beautiful. Especially with the speed inside of me, my natural instinct was to just run right into a sensible area of the boxing up ahead but I paused for a second. I'd never seen such a full scale riot in my life with such numbers who wanted to hurt each other while having the police in between who weren't exactly that shy when it came to hurting others too. You had to have about six sets of eyes to take in all that was going on in front of you.

Just the mini situations that I clocked before I snapped out of being a spectator and turned participator. A couple of Utility were chasing this young ASC boy in a red Adidas trackie top, boy looked like he was shitting it the speed he was running (I'd still beat him in a race though, ye ken?) but the funny thing was that they chased the daft cunt right into the waiting arms of some policeman who was standing there like a Venus Flytrap version of a copper who scooped him up and marched him away. Afternoon over for him. Ironically if he'd stood and fought, probably taking a pasting but still, might have been the difference between getting lifted and spending the weekend in jail or still getting to see the game while wondering if your ribs actually were broken or that they'd be fine later on. Then again, my attentions were then brought straight over to "the other guy," the one who DOES stand there and fight. He's lying there wriggling like a crab that's ended up on its back and hasn't sussed that there's fuck all it can do now and the same rules applied to this ASC lad who has found himself unfortunate to have Nora on his case, booting him in the ribs and head in his Adidas Grand Slams in an almost hypnotic kind of tribal rhythm.

I'd never seen Nora in his element like this in my life but capturing him in that moment I was intrigued but more shocked than anything to see just how much pleasure he was taking out of what he was doing to the guy on the ground. He looked like he was having the time of his life, taking this by now defenceless Aberdonian one step closer to hospital, or even worse, with every kick. I couldn't watch it anymore as I began running towards everyone with the party still very much in full flow. I glanced over to the side of me and out of all of the madness I spotted Granty from Monifieth who was standing to the side pissing into an Asda bag. I still wonder to this day if he managed to launch that sick and twisted catapult of his own and whether it was a direct hit on his target or worse still, he hit one of our own boys.

I made straight for a gap in the police cordon where I could see one of our boys who was outnumbered by three to one and instinctively launched into this fucking stupid flying kick and punch into one of the ASC who were laying into the boy on the ground, couldn't even see who he was in amongst all that was going on. The Jackie Chan style flying assault I launched didn't go how I thought it would with my intended victim moving out the way right at the last second leaving me punching thin air. This gave him a chance to spin round and be ready for me before I'd even hit the ground, getting in a pinpoint kick high up into my ribs before I could even get my bearings. Normally a precision kick to a part of your body will have you paying the respect to the pain that you're experiencing but in a moment like that, adrenaline takes over. Face to face with each other, while his two mates continued to give it to the Utility boy on the ground, he started to do that whole bouncy-bouncy arms outstretched, trying to look menacing and not even coming close pose.

This confused me slightly, even for someone as wet behind the ears when it came to soccer violence. Surely we'd already crossed that 'verbals' point of our relationship? I'd come in flying like a ninja very much looking to cause him harm … he then actually connects with me. We were definitely past the posturing point. Knowing the longer I stayed on this side of the cordon I stood a good chance of getting lifted or outnumbered by the ASC so instead of meeting him in his dance I lunged towards him. The look on his face was a laughable mix of fear and surprise, as if he wasn't used to someone just going for it instead of going the tentative route of seeing how things were before deciding on a plan of action.

In a quick one-two I gave him what can only have been a sickening kick to the cojones following up with right hand punch, connecting like a fucking peach and putting him on his derrière while he was still trying to work out what had just happened. It just seemed like a wall of noise being there in amongst it all. Police sirens, dogs barking, a million and one swear words connected to all kinds of verbal threats that were being shouted towards one and all.

I fucking loved it if I'm being brutally gen.

Before the police got things in order I managed to get myself back onto the side that the Utility were stood on. Things were starting to calm down although this was more to do with the fact that the police were boxing us in and were now forcing us in the direction of the stadium while the ASC were being held back outside The Bobbin. The short walk to Pittodrie was filled with stories being excitedly exchanged between everyone over what had just taken place as well the most shittest attempt at some kind of a roll call from Nora. Not that I'd have been telling him as such, just nodded at him when he said my name. There was a few of our mob looking a bit worse for wear. Cuts and bruises and what ALWAYS hurts the most - ripped gear was all too visible but going by what I'd seen anyway it had very much been a case of 'You should've seen the other guy.'

It was when Nora had called out my name that from in amongst the crowd of faces the scariest of voices chipped in.

'Aye, there's the wee bastard - C'mere you for a minute'

Everyone looking at me as we keep our momentum on the way to the ground. It was Dawson, one of the old mob and to a sixteen year old he was like a fucking old man although in reality he was probably only around thirty or something. I'd never spoken to him before and apart from an occasional nod towards each other in the passing when on location away from Dundee, someone I'd had no dealings with. I just knew he was one of the top boys of the crew. I have to admit, I was more scared walking over to speak to him than I'd been running into a sea of coppers and Aberdeen Soccer Casuals.

Fuck knows what I'd done but I was about to find out as I made my way through a few lines of people to get to where he was. With a manic pair of eyes that made me think of those glasses and eyes on springs combination any self respecting joke shop would sell during the late seventies and early eighties, he instantly raised his hand which had me assuming the worst and that I was going to be on the receiving end of a slap from this elder statesmen of the Utility. Instead he put his arm around my neck and took me into a headlock before I could even grasp what he was about to do. He planted a big kiss on the top of my head while still holding me tight.

'See this wee bastard' See what he did while we were all scrapping back there?'

This was starting to get on top of me, I was starting to struggle to breathe and I was getting the impression that he wasn't aware of it as he played to the crowd, him almost dragging me along the road as we marched on.

'Only saw me outnumbered three to one during all of the fighting and steamed right into those sheep cunts to help me out'

With that he planted another kiss on the head and then released me mere seconds before I started punching, scratching and kicking for my life. In a man hug he pulled me close to him and whispered

'Nice work number ten' 'It's Zico right?' Dawson said to me.

I nodded more out of surprise that he knew who I was than giving him the affirmation of the answer to the question that he was asking.

'Nora's told me how game you are and today's the first of me seeing it for myself. Fucking im-presto young man' he said before releasing me back into the wild, dealing with all kinds of emotions after an interchange like that. I was relieved as I thought it was all going to go a different way, vindicated after putting on a good show during all of the naughtiness back outside The Bobbin and it actually being noticed by someone who mattered. When it's all going off I reckon everyone goes off into their own zone for two or three minutes and due to this sometimes things don't get noticed. Instead I only have to go and come to the rescue of one of the top boys … whilst not having a fucking clue WHO he was at the time! That little fact will have to be our little secret. As far as everyone there that day was concerned, I'd helped out Dawson who was in a bit of danger by the looks of things. He'd gotten out of said dangerous position. I helped it happen. End of story.

Sometimes you get dealt a good hand like I did today or you can be on the opposite side where you meet a psychopath like Nora on an away day and aye, you might well be willing to debate about the theory of being dealt a good hand. Nora had scared me for a few moments earlier though. The sight of just how violent he can be and how he seems to relish it, it kind of unsettled me seeing it as it's not what I'm about. Fuck, of course I go to the fitba each week HOPING to meet an opposition crew and engage in violent relations with them but there's definitely a limit to how violent I want it to be, not just for me but for everyone involved. It's only a bit of fun at the end of the day right?

The way I see it, being a football casual isn't anywhere near to being "all" about the violence. I'd say there's a way high percentage of cunts who are all about the clothes, wanting to look good, have people notice them, fronting about how cool they are when the reality is a fair percentage of them will be running at the very sniff of some actual action. It's like they're in love with the idea of being a casual just because it's the cool thing to do. Even then though I was clothes first casual second so I always think I can speak as some authority on it all even though I haven't even been with the crew for any real length of time. Hardly a fucking veteran, likes. I just don't want to be putting someone in hospital or have me end up in one either. I won't ever be slicing or dicing you with a knife because I will never carry one and if you do either of them to me with one then you sir, are a fucking wanker, a snake, a wrong un and one snide bastard to pull that kind of shit.

I wasn't prepared for the level of evil and the bloodlust that he had. I mean, his aura was basically fucking 'I'm going to kill someone or something' red! Despite all of those thoughts, after Dawson had told everyone about what I'd done. Nora made his way back towards us through the crowd to give me a hug followed up with a nod of the head. A nod from Nora though can speak volumes and whilst no words were spoken I knew what he was saying and considering how scary a person he could be and as I was starting to see, how could it ever be described as a bad thing to be on his good side???

Chapter 5.

'Mr Duncan, hello? Anyone in there?'

I became aware that I had completely zoned out of my Higher English class for, well how long was anyones guess. It was assumed that the only one who actually knew exactly how long I'd departed for was Mr Forbes, English teacher of St Andrews RC. He stood there in front of me clicking his fingers like those Spanish castanet things that I guarantee every single gran in Scotland has in her house taking pride of place on her cabinet alongside all of the family photos.

'Are you back in the room now participant?' he then asked noticing me beginning to return to the room once again. What the fuck was this? Now he was a Vegas hypnotist after his lame attempt at being Biff from that Michael J Fox film, Back to the Future. Well, I think that was what he was doing anyway. It was hard to tell considering I wasn't fully taking him in. It was difficult considering one second I was thinking back to the weekend and the absolute top buzz of the trip to Aberdeen and all of what came out of it and then the next. Dealing with my eccentric English teacher. Someone who on the whole I liked as he was a million miles from the by the numbers teachers in the sense that I had ever been used to.

No, Forbesy was "different" and he seemed to wear it like a badge of honour in ways which made him, at times, extremely hard work. I'm no teacher yet I think that the way it "should be" is that some of the pupils are meant to be extremely hard work, not the other way around. Total character though. Prone to hitting pupils on the head with a large wooden spoon when he was pissed off at them. I'd witnessed others in the class take a few healthy whacks from it but never had the pleasure myself. I'm not sure how he kept getting away with such a tactic to be honest as surely at least one of the 'victims' would've told their mum and dad. That's pure Medieval stuff!

There had always been an almost unwritten rule between myself and Mr Forbes. Kind of like, he could tell straight away that I was serious about getting my higher English qualification so he wasn't going to have a problem with me as a result. He was the teacher who introduced me to The Ramones and the works of Hunter S Thompson, which we're reading for class at the moment. The day he brought his record player in with "Rocket to Russia" an LP by this band called The Ramones. He told us to listen to it to feed off the energy from the music, said that it would increase our work tempo and inspire creativeness.

He really was off his tits at times but that day I just couldn't stop laughing over how loud this constant breakneck speed music was playing in the classroom that morning in our double period. It wasn't even my type of music but I thought it was brilliant. So raw and energetic and instantly catchy. Teachers from other classrooms kept coming in to make sure that the teacher was actually in there with the pupils because of the wall of noise spilling out into the corridor. A couple of the moshers from my class, sat there headbanging in their chairs while I and the rest of the class pissed ourselves laughing at them.

'I'm sorry Mr Forbes' I finally broke silence for fear of him slipping into another of his quick fire personas. 'I slipped off for a moment thinking of how much mixed emotions that hitchhiker would have went through in such a short space of time when Hunter S Thompson and his Attorney picked him up somewhere outside Barstow' 'The relief of finally being picked up in the lethal Californian desert sun and then onto the suspicion that maybe just maybe the people who had picked him up had something a bit odd about them all the way to the crippling fear and realisation that yes indeed, these two in the front of the car were maniacs of the highest order and that the new plan would now be to DEhitchike as soon as possible'

I was bluffing and bluffing like a pro if I do say so myself. I just knew that to show a bit of passion towards something that he was teaching us would be an easy way to have him in my back pocket. Thing is, it wasn't an act in "every" way. Aye, of course I came up with a subject to talk myself out of having my wooden spoon cherry popped but at the same time I was talking about a book he'd had us read (whether appropriate for fifteen and sixteen year old school kids, that's probably for the courts to decide) that I had really gotten into so it wasn't exactly hard to fein enthusiasm towards something he had been shoving down our throats for the past week.

He was impressed with the passion I'd shown and went off onto a rant over how works of art in whatever way could stir up such passion like how I had just displayed towards what was, in the scheme of things, a small bit part player in a much bigger story like the hitchhikers cameo appearance in the book was. Right after it seemed to look like the spoon wasn't coming out I had a quick cheeky look round to Stef. The two of us fucking hate each other and are always looking for ways to get something on the other, anything to see a bit of misfortune on their end. I'm not fussy I'd take whatever. Fucking knew that he would've been sat behind me with his fingers, legs, eyes, and arms crossed that I was getting the spoon.

'Not today' I mouthed back with him sat there with his coupon fucking tripping him, he could only hold eye contact for a second before it strayed again. He's too fucking stupid to talk himself out of a situation like that though. That's why he's a spoon veteran but has still never quite worked out how to avoid it either. The animosity between the two of us goes back to second year in P.E when we were playing fitba. We were having trials to see who would be getting selected to play for the school against other ones in the area. Pretty prestigious stuff, or so it's drummed into you at that age. As a result everyone was hyped up to try their luck at being picked.

I was lucky enough to get chosen to try out in what I had always seen as my preferred and natural position, right wing. Fucking adored Ralph Milne when I was a kid watching him for United and always modelled myself on him and from the age of eight I'd only ever wanted to play on the wing. Hugging the edge of the touchline, skinning the opposition full back and cutting in and creating havoc for the other team. So who was I up against at full back from the other team made up of eleven St Andrews players that day? Aye, that fucking Stefano wanker, eh?

Honestly? I fully appreciate that I could leave myself open to accusations of wearing rose tinted specs but I gave him a torrid time in the match, nutmegs the lot. I'd only ever seen him about school but he wasn't ever in my classes for those first couple of years and wasn't part of any of my network of friends in any way so I didn't really know him. Was going past him for fun, again and again, I also laid on a couple of goals and scored a complete rasper by cutting in past him and then his centre half before firing it right into the postage stamp. Left foot strike as well which was a collectors item as I'm as one footed as you can get. The trial was almost over and I thought I'd push on for one last attack.

Running down the wing, I knew that I was going to come up against some opposition from one of the midfielders as well as Stef further down the pitch. A drop of the shoulder saw the midfielder, can't remember his name, funny looking guy from Cupar with cock eyes, arghh It'll come to me in a minute as well! Sailed past him and the next thing I've got an Inter City 125 coming right at me in the form of Stef and the worst looking nasty two footed over the top challenge you've ever seen. Having no time to react to this, both of his feet came crashing into my leg. I heard and most definitely felt the snap of bone. Moments later I'm lying on the pitch in a crumpled heap screaming out in agony, the worst pain I'd ever felt in my life. Stef standing over me laughing. It was the stuff of Don Revie's Leeds United.

It didn't matter that on the way to hospital, Mr Welsh, our P.E teacher told me that I was the first name on his team sheet and had made it onto there on my first half performance alone. Due to Stef trying to settle a score that I didn't even know existed then aye, otherwise I'd have been in the team. Instead I had a broken leg and weeks ahead of pain and inconvenience. Things like that you don't forget and there's always been quite an edge to his and mines relationship now that we've been forced into the same class for one subject in what is going to be our last year at school before hitting the big bad world.

We've had a few "disagreements" in class since being thrown together but have always managed to just about know when to say when in a sense where we both know that one day our time will come. If anything it should all be about me getting revenge on his intentional broken leg two years ago. Some might say I should let that go as it was two years ago. I bet those that say that have never suffered a broken leg at the hands of some prick who actually meant to break it. Let's see how "understanding" they'd be then with a Vinnie Jones wannabe incoming like that?

Looking at the clock, I could see that we had around another half an hour left of class so I elected to egg Forbesy on by continuing to talk about Fear and Loathing and how it was impacting me on the revelation that it was possible to write in a completely different way, like Hunter S Thompson did, in a traveling guerrilla journalism mindset.

'EXCELLENT' Forbes shouted while walking over to his blackboard, picking up a piece of chalk and writing in capital letters on the blank board

TRAVELLING

GUERILLA

JOURNALISM

He was reacting like I'd just showed him the first ever wheel as opposed to what was nothing other than a throwaway comment to keep the conversation kettle boiling enough to get me through to the end of the period. He thought it was genius and was now asking the class to examine those three words put together while nodding in approval over in my direction. I was just getting lucky all over the place the past few days, finding fortune where I wasn't seeking it but all gratefully received none the less. We continued chatting about the book up until the bell went. Fuck, and now a period of Computing to take me up to lunch. I didn't even want to take it as a subject but I had to. I only came back for fifth year to get my Higher English but they weren't for allowing me to just come in for that and nothing else so I had to pick a few subjects I had no real interest in.

Mr McCallister, the computing studies teacher is one creepy fucker. I've heard he shags dogs which whether it's true or not is definitely something that will affect how you take to someone when you meet them for the first time. Probably an urban myth as you know how stupid kids can be with the stories that they perpetuate but once the stuff gets into your head it's hard to come back out again. It was that Denise Patterson, her wee brother and his pals were playing in the woods, wee bit sojay action, capture the flag and all that stuff and a few of them saw McCallister in the woods at it with a K9 but who knows eh? Thing is, I like the computer side of things but he's just an arrogant, smug prick who makes out that he's the only person in the world who knows how to fucking use one. He gives of the impression that he's come back from the future to teach the world and brought an Amstrad along with him. I've made a vow to myself to let out the whole dog thing in class with him when it's my last lesson. Just to see the reaction I get in a completely burning your bridges kind of way. I hope I do, I'll probably forget though and remember once it's too late and I'm on the bus home.

My mind wasn't on the period from minute one and I buried myself in the screen pretending to write some stupid code for a game that anyone with a decent console like a Sega Mega Drive or Super Nintendo wouldn't even play if they had a gun to their head. My mind was racing to lunch time and what business I needed to be taking care of.

I'd been having one of those "things" with Lisa Hopkins, one of the other girls from my year. A thing where the two of you aren't saying anything to each other but you can both tell that there's "something" going on that somehow feels different. A hard thing to even describe in words as it's more a sixth sense kind of deal. I hadn't experienced much of this before with girls but I could totally see and feel it with her.

The way our eyes were meeting when we'd come across each other in the halls or outside at break and then the reaction we had to that each time. She was from the same village as me too so it wasn't like she was an unknown quantity as such. I barely knew her but knew a lot more 'about' her. This had come to a head last Saturday night when I finally got back from Aberdeen and hungry, had made straight for the ABC Chinese restaurant to take something home with me in time for Match Of The Day.

Normally I'll eat all over the day, like anyone else but that speed I'd taken had left me without much of an appetite. I can't really argue of any accusation that I might have been a little "animated" when I was inside there waiting on my Special Fried Rice after my day of beer, speed and violence. Lisa and her mate Wendy were in there when I walked in and I, suddenly finding my voice with her, stood there talking away like we were old friends. Like most of the day, I couldn't remember half of the nonsense that I'd spoken to most people so the same applied to Lisa and her friend but what I did remember was that they appeared to laugh quite a lot. Whether that was with or at me. That was what I wanted to find out and was hoping to catch her over lunch to speak to her. See if I could gauge how she was with me after the speed addled drunken radge she'd bumped into at the weekend. If anything, I now had an in when it came to going up and speaking to her. Even if the "in" was an absolute OUT after Saturday night and I simply just didn't know it yet.

Chapter 6.

I walked up to her after lunch when she was standing outside the Modern Studies portacabin that was serving as a makeshift classroom. This excuse for a classroom was due to some cowboys through from the Weeg were taking the longest of time while appearing not to be doing visibly anything at all while fixing up some of the classrooms. They needed it. I'd thought they looked like they were from the fifties when I first saw them on my induction day.

I'd sat with Brizo and Callum, two of a very short list of people that by this point in my high school experience I could actually be bothered talking to and was willing to class as "friends." It's funny how you'll find yourself having friends for certain occasions like at school or something? During primary school I had a pal, Andy Wilson who was my "Subutteo pal" only fucking time we ever seen each other outside school was to play it. I never socialised with him in my life without it involving a game of carpet fitba. Same with going to see United, for a wee while and before the Utility stuff started I used to go to the games with this lad Jamie Thompson, again, never seen the cunt away from a match days.

Brizo and Callum were alright though but a world away from engaging in some of my outside school activities. Good lads, they didn't support Celtic for one, which was a rarity for my Roman Catholic school and more importantly, hated some of the boys that I wasn't exactly on Christmas card list terms with around the school. Decent enough reason to forge a friendship I say. As game as Dawson said I was it was always good planning to at least have some kind of allies in whatever situation. The past year and through my exploits at the weekend though, school had been elevated to nothing more than an inconvenience. Just give me the fucking higher English exam and pleasssssse release me let me go. My auntie always sings that song at New Year, proper pub singing style as well. Has to be seen to be believed and would bring a tear to a glass eye the level of performance she breaks out after a couple of drams.

The two of them fucked off for a fag before the next period leaving me on my own. I'd hoped to see her after lunch but when I did it was through pure chance (more of this lucky streak I'd been on?) She was one of the first pupils I saw when I left the dinner hall. Tidy wasn't the word for her when I assessed what was ahead of me as I walked in her direction. She looked round before I got to her and flashed me a big smile that caught me off guard but apparently contained the properties of that tractor beam that the Death Star in Star Wars was equipped with because once she flashed me that smile I was pulled right in with no control.

She was the best looking girl in the whole of the school, all the boys from first year to sixth would have agreed on that unanimously without question and her name was one you'd always hear getting spoken about in complimentary terms. Be that through the cute bob she had for a haircut, her big lips that you'd kiss for days given the chance right through to the fact that she'd obviously "developed" faster than a lot of other girls in her year and in fact more than some of the girls older than her. She was definitely the stuff of a schoolboys wet dreams.

The chances of me bottling it before getting to her were most definitely there but with her noticing me I had no real choice other than to prepare to dock at this beautiful Death Star in front of me. Heart beating like my first thirty minutes of meeting Si and his magic powder on Saturday morning. Suddenly everything I had planned to say to her was going flying right out my head, sucked out of me almost like the contents of an airplane when some daft cunt opens the door when it's thousands of feet above the ground.

Fucking stupid eh? I'm brave, or stupid enough to run into police and dangerous fitba casuals but nervous about talking to a girl?! Then again, Lisa Hopkins wasn't exactly your average girl. One of those diamonds in the dirt at school that's head and shoulders above any other girl and gets all of the attention. The type of girl that always ends up going out with someone who's already left school and levelled up to having their first job as well as a car.

Normally some cunt that no one has heard of from two towns away but eventually they invariably get outed as paedos. You see them in the Daily Record all the time, going into court with their hoods up and trying to hide their faces and all that. Apart from the fact that I fancied the fucking pants off Lisa I felt that purely on grounds of being a stand up guy, a friend if you will, I could save her from some torrid nights in the back seat of a Ford Escort Mark two with some nonce. Better she has some torrid ones in the cold and wet woodland of Beverage Park with me eh?!

'Awright, Lisa - How's your Monday going?' I said with a smile, aided by some alternate confidence that was flowing from me while inside my heart was going like the clappers. I almost fucked it before I finished speaking as for a nano second I'm sure my hand was moving in the direction of a handshake but I turned it into a scratch of my cheek. Close one though, likes.

'Good, well if you call a double period sat in front of McNulty good then yeah, I've had a luxurious experience. Brand new, Zico' She replied and unless I was getting carried away with myself, definitely looked like she was happy to be stood there talking to me. 'What about you?'

I just pulled a mock face while saying that it was all pish and I just wanted to get my higher done and get to Falkirk away from school once and for all.

I wasn't sure if there was an elephant in the room between us or not. That only happens when both people knows that the other one knows the score isn't it? This however was the classic case of boy (who has consumed many tins of lager and mixed with class A and B drugs) meets girl (who was guilty of nothing other than eating chips, cheese and curry sauce after nine at night) and with those polar opposites attracting last Saturday night we now had the game of her knowing how our exchange had went down and apart from remembering speaking to her and Wendy I could remember little else. She wasn't appearing off with me which was definitely a good start. I'm used to people being off with me because of something I've said or done but nah, the vibes were good this time around. Well, until.

'By the way, how smashed were you on Saturday night? I mean, I've seen you wrecked before on a Friday or a Saturday night but that was a gold star A++ performance' She said but in a good non judgmental way. No sneering or looking down her nose at me. It all seemed like just one of your normal 'Oh you should've seen you last night, state you were in' chats you'll have with your mates the morning after the night before. I was in a bit of a catch twenty two with it all though. I wanted to know if I'd made an arse of myself OR told her some blatant lie while trying to impress her and one that I may need to remember at a later date to back up BUT didn't want to admit that I was so out of it that I couldn't really remember what I'd said to her.

'Aye, it was like I thought I was Keith Richards with my rock and roll behaviour on Saturday' I replied going along with the joke 'Nah Leese, in reality it was a long day away to Aberdeen and having a few beers on the train journey home kinda zapped me.' I said this, placing blind faith in the fact that the majority of her drug experiences would have been while fingering herself to Miami Vice watching Don Johnson. The 'awwww poor baby' look she gave in response to my hard luck story was definitely encouraging though. And actually, 'this was going pretty good between the two of us' I thought to myself. She was habitually a bit stuck up in that way where a tidy looking girl begins to fool themselves into thinking they can behave that way on account of being better looking. Well that's the reputation she had for herself anyway.

Yet considering we spoke on Saturday and she's there right now having a laugh with me. This was definitely counting for something in my book and I had to keep it all going while conscious that we only had around five more minutes before the bell was going to go. Felt like I was on a fucking gameshow and put up against the clock. Will the contestant beat the clock and manage to ask the girl out and in doing so surely guarantee that he'll have his hole within the next fortnight or will he go home empty handed with tail between legs to many more dates with good old reliable Pamela?!

'What about you though? Haven't noticed you around the place at the weekend for ages until seeing you on Saturday. What's the score your end'? I asked an innocent question that was more loaded than the US Military who are currently lighting up Iraq right now. Something about Oil, well I thought so cause of Kuwait being involved. I watched the first night of it when it all kicked off. Was a pretty fucking good fireworks display if I'm rating it, which I'm not.

Haven't seen a war before though, well not in that way likes. You know? Live on telly watching it all go off like that. I fucking love when that happens on TV although it hardly ever does. I remember that time when I was at my nana's and I was watching the SAS abseiling and crashing through windows and blowing up some embassy in London. THAT was a good fucking day, can't remember what age I was but for the rest of the day I was acting like the SAS killing all these terrorists.

Kicking doors open and throwing tins of beans into the rooms pretending they were grenades. My nana wasn't too pleased if I recall. Told me I'd give her and my di a heart attack if I kept going.

Same goes for that time the Space Shuttle blew up. Was horrible likes, I was young but still old enough to know that everyone inside was dead. I sort of tailed off from the Iraq war after the first night. The Americans blew it, that first night of Desert Storm was what you would close off something with and milk the applause. Only they went with it to open the show. Strange move. Imagine The Stone Roses coming out and doing I am the Resurrection first at a gig?! I think Iraq aren't that good though and as far as army's go they're pretty pish. They keep talking about some kind of Elite Guard division that was going to take care of things and send the US and Brits packing, some right scary bastards, apparently. They've not been seen yet despite their country being taken apart so it was probably all a myth and they never existed in the first place.

I was basically looking for any intel on whether she was still seeing that boy from Burntisland, that prick with the Nova who never said cheers when I held the door of the off license open for him that time. Preferably I wanted to gain it from her before we had to go our separate ways for the day.

'Normally scooting around in the Nova are you not?' And BOOM … There we had it, the knock out blow leaving the opponent on the ropes.

'Who? With Grainger? Nah we split up a few weeks back. I've just been keeping myself quiet and stayed in the past few weekends and been studying for my Highers. He was a total prick in the end. I heard that he'd been shagging that Jackie Stanton when I was away to the U2 gig. Didn't even deny it when I said it to his face' She said in what was an absolute whirlwind of emotions that flickered as quickly as a strobe light. I was obviously happy to see that she was single again but a wee bit disturbed that with only a few minutes left this conversation was in danger of turning into a negative for her. The very last thing that I wanted her to be going away with having been talking to me. I'd grown in confidence through our micro chat and the nervous and sweaty mess who'd walked into it had been replaced by Joe fucking Smooth so I decided to just go for it, pull off a move that would either make my afternoon or see me fake a sickie and just go home for the day with my head hanging in shame.

'That's the thing with these guys and their cars, Lisa. No substance to them eh? Look at me. I spent more on a coat on Friday there than your ex probably would spend in clothes in a year. I mean, obviously when I'm old enough and get a job I'll have the car to go with but for now I'm happier to be looking good OUTSIDE a car.' She giggled at that and knowing the bell was going to go I quickly added

'Ok two questions before I head. One's serious and one's funny ..Which one do you want first?'

She looked intrigued by this shock proposition.

'Oooooh well it's always good to have funny follow something serious so yeah, give me the serious question first and then follow with the funny one'

'Right ...... Answer them at the same time then' I said tapping at my imaginary watch like a fitba player trying to draw the Ref's attention towards time wasting from the other team. 'If you're not up to anything this weekend you fancy doing something? Would be a laugh I think ... And question two ... Was I banging onto you on Saturday night about shagging sheep?'

She laughed out loud which was a good reaction to what I'd just hit her with, well, as long as it wasn't directed at my first question. By this point the bell was ringing for the first period after lunch but she managed to quickly answer before we had to get going to class.

'Yes, you mentioned shagging sheep so much that we all thought that you HAD shagged one, ok I'm joking. You did talk about sheep shaggers though.' How much of a tease was she? Answering question two first when she MUST'VE known that it had taken me a lot of balls to ask her the first one. 'And yeah I'm free this weekend so we'll do something if you like, sounds good. What do you fancy?'

My class was on the third floor and I was already looking like being late, I couldn't talk any longer so conveniently used this to my advantage by quickly answering.

'You' and laughed as I walked away like I fucking owned the school. Proper John Travolta strutting, likes. We agreed to talk later on and sort something out for Saturday night as we went our separate ways to try and catch the start of our periods. Lisa Hopkins .. Lisa-fucking-Hopkins. I'd just bagged a date with her and all I'd had to do was walk up to her and ask. You don't do that with her though. You pull up in some garishly and economically souped up Ford or Vauxhall car and she gets in like a prossie down Leith docks.

Actually "why" was I on my way to ANY fucking class? It dawned on me. I thought this was a call for a celebration and I wasn't going to find that in the next period of Modern Studies, a subject I wasn't giving a shit about as far as when the exams rolled around. Instead, I diverted to the nurses room, told her I'd brought up all of my lunch and that I'd been feeling weak and dizzy since and Bob's your aunties fella, I was sent home. One of the teachers ran me back as well, I was kind of pissed off about that as it meant having to keep up my act for around half an hour longer than I'd have liked.

The bus would've been fine for me likes but no, Mr Weston had to play the fucking hero. Wanted to talk the whole way back as well as we cruised in his Saab. I always thought that they were seriously bad bastard of cars. This was based on the fact that if a company can make fighter jets that military forces across the world would use then the cars must have a bit of some hot sauce added to them somewhere. The guy knows I'm not well, hence why he's finding himself driving me home but he's sat there trying to strike up a conversation from any angle he's thinking of. School, Fitba, TV. All subjects that I'd normally be able to weigh in with an option on but at this point? No. Not when I'm going for an Academy Award winning performance to bag a Monday afternoon off school.

'I'm really sorry Mr Weston, but I feel really tired after all my vomiting. Would you mind if I just had a wee sleep on the way back to my house?' I asked, instantly worrying that it had been too hammy.

'Oh, sure sure, of course Steven' He quickly replied with an air of someone who felt they'd done something wrong and were trying to show that they had meant no offence.

'I'll let you know when we get there, it's number ten you stay isn't it?'

'Aye' I replied without even opening my eyes or lifting my head up to look at him. I never slept one wink of the journey home but he wasn't to know that. Even if I wanted to have a small sleep I wouldn't have been able to anyway. I mean come on?! LISA HOPKINS!!

Chapter 7.

It had been a bit of an up and down week all in all. The high point being the procuring of a stolen pair of still in the box Diadora Borg Elites from Reasons, one of the junkies from up the scheme. He come by such a moniker due to the fact that he was a miserable bastard and there was this Ian Dury song called Reasons To Be Cheerful and I guess someone had made the connection between the two and the nickname stuck.

Technically the time to buy them had now already passed as they were considered a little dated but fuck that, they'd been my holy grail of trainers from day one and when a heroin addict offers you a pair of ninety pound trainers for the everything must go one day price of fifteen then who really is going to pass that up? I really don't understand the bad press that junkies get in this country? All this "they break into peoples houses" and "threatening the future of the kids" stuff? How can they ever be considered a stain on society when they have the ability of making high end designer gear affordable to the average teenager?

Of course, he started off at the asking price of fifty quid for them which I just laughed at him over. I wasn't by any means some expert on drug culture and in reality it had only been the previous week that I'd even taken a Class A drug for the very first time but one thing I DID know about drugs, or drug addicts at that, was that the minute they got their hands on some cash it was a case of go direct to your dealer and do not pass go! When we were haggling over the price I actually tried to make out that I was HELPING him by giving him less than he was asking for as he'd only be injecting it into him soon after. An opinion that he wasn't much in agreement with me over.

Judging by the state of the cunt he was in dire need of a fix and didn't really have much negotiating skills in him. Through his urgency at making the trade go through he folded and gave them up to me at fifteen pounds within minutes. That reminded me of that scene in the Monty Python film where Eric Idle's street vendor character wouldn't let the man buy something off him without any haggling taking place but aye fuck that, I was hardly going to engineer the situation where I'd have to pay more for them was I?

The low point of the week was without question getting caught having a wank in my bedroom by my auntie. Low point of my week? Low point of my life more to the fucking point. My cousin who still stayed with us had a massive pile of porno mags in his cupboard (more porn than Larry Flynt that boy) and every now and again I'd help myself to one. I'm not sure if he or anyone else knew I was doing it but I filled my boots likes and always stuck it back in his pile before he would get home from work. Anyway, I was lying there on my bed, looking at this photo spread of some Scandinavian looking bird. Her name, Fenella which I thought was a pretty radge name, if that actually was her real name of course.

It was new to me likes and that's why I remember it. I obviously never heard someone coming up the stairs, must've been getting too much into "Fenella" because I'm only a few more strokes away from ending proceedings when I then sensed the bedroom door opening. My auntie coming in with all my boxers and socks in her hand fresh from being washed and dried. It's hard to describe all that went on inside the three seconds, maybe two, I wasn't counting, that she was in the room. The fact I was shooting my load there and then only to find myself making eye contact with the closest of relatives? Sickening, absolutely the worst. I screamed for her to close the door while, laughably (although most definitely not for me) sat on the bed covering myself WITH the porno mag so I had Fenella and her big fucking tits and blonde hairy fanny on show for my auntie. Meanwhile, thankfully, hidden from her I was spunking all over myself and the outside pages of the glossy magazine. She thought this was all fucking comedy gold and laughed while entering into the obligatory auntie / mum saying … 'Oh It's nothing I've not seen bef..'

GET OUTTTT!!! I screamed with a panicky high pitched voice while my face felt so warm it was like I'd stuck it under the grill for ten minutes! She closed the door and left me to my world of pain that I was now in. My head was spinning and I actually felt like I could've been sick but luckily I managed to hold it down. Fucking Fenella STILL looking back at me as the porno sat on the bed with the outside pages sticky and now covering my bed sheet with spunk. It was a mess, literally. I didn't want to EVER leave the room again in my life but knew I'd have to at some point. One thing for certain was that she was going to tell my uncle and he was going to rip the piss out of me on a monumental scale. That much I already knew to be factual. It would take some ninth dan ninja skills to co exist in the same house whilst never actually bumping into him but I decided that I was up for that particular challenge.

Putting aside the fact that the foreseeable future was going to be socially awkward for me it was Saturday and I had an absolute topper of a day ahead. Fitba during the day and a date with Lisa at night when I got back to Fife. The match itself on Saturday was one of those rare occasions where you knew in advance that there wasn't going to be any trouble before during or after as it was Derby day. I know it should be obvious that if you're playing your same city rivals then you're going to want to kick the living shite out of the other mob and same with them but Dundee does things differently.

When we fight as the Utility Crew we do so as a mob made up FROM Dundee United AND Dundee FC. I didn't realise how unique it was, it was just how things were. So of course, the Dundee Derby was a day off from all the usual madness that Saturday afternoons would generally offer. Just a day to enjoy the match and the usual United win, and engage in some banter with the Dundee fans in a good natured way while having a few beers over the day.

Once that was over I was away to see the new Schwarzenegger film, Total Recall, with Lisa. There was a song I heard on the radio when I was at the doctors a few months ago with this guy singing 'oh it's such a perfect day I'm glad I spent it with you' nae idea who he or the band is but aye that pretty much describes my Saturday down to a tee. The season was pretty much finished. There was only a few more matches to play and that was that.

Didn't even matter who won or lost the match in terms of where the teams would finish in the league but try telling that to both sets of supporters come three and kick off. It's quite a depressing time when the fitba season ends. best part of two months with having to fill your time doing fuck knows what. Last year I probably filled the time with wanking in my room and playing fitba with my mates. If things went well with Lisa I could well be having a much different "pre season" this year.

One thing I absolutely knew was that I couldn't get drunk or take no magic powder this week to make me talk for hours at a ridiculous rate of knots. Needed to be on my best behaviour for what was coming at night time. I'd thought quite a bit about my amphetamine experience the week before going up to Aberdeen in the train though. It had been my first try of something considered much harder than Hash and apart from the feeling shit part the next day I'd actually enjoyed it, scarily so. I'd read all those scare stories in the Daily Record about how if you take drugs you'll end up dying or robbing old aged pensioners of their savings and, ehm, selling expensive pairs of stolen trainers for a fraction of the price due to being so desperate for a fix.

I read all of that propaganda and it had worked on me if I'm being honest and then a few years later I'm running around Aberdeen out of my tits getting fired into the other team in an against the odds fashion having the time of my life. I'd felt like I was able to talk more to some of the other boys that I didn't know, maybe a wee bit more confidence? I wasn't sure but one thing I "did" know was that it wouldn't be the last time I would dabble with Class A's again. Me and a few others were standing outside The Snug, up in the Hilltown area of Dundee, me concealing the fact that I had a bottle of Red Stripe from the police who were standing across the road when Nora came out. Spying me instantly, his face lighting up as he made his way over in my direction.

'Awright ya wee Brazilian bastard' he beamed back at me grabbing at my arm and, not realising his strength, almost pulling it out of its socket. 'Nasty Nora, how's it going?!' I said back hoping he was going to release my arm sometime soon and it still being attached to the rest of my body. 'Nasty Nora?' I like the sound of that he laughed with an evil smile letting go of me. Stood there in an, inexplicable ensemble but who was going to tell him? A pair of Adidas Arsenal tracksuit bottoms and a Boca Juniors top along with his trademark CP Company rucksack over him. Fuck knows what he kept inside it but I wasn't one for ever asking.

We all speculated what was inside it. Some said money as he didn't trust banks, others said drugs and that half of the gear that moved throughout Scotland were through him. I remember making a so called joke that went the way of a lead balloon when I suggested that Hitler's hidden gold might be inside it and a few around me, serious as fuck by the way, looked at me and said they'd never rule it out due to how connected and dangerous he was.

He certainly didn't look any kinds of dangerous stood there in front of me half an hour before the match. Big smile on his face as he's handing me a fag which as always I didn't want but took anyway. 'Good fucking performance last week, Zico' he started to talk shop. 'Don't think stuff like that doesn't get noticed, lad' he continued. I couldn't help but feel ten foot tall standing there hearing our top boy telling me this type of stuff. 'Ah man, I'm just one of those game cunts who won't let you down while they actually can't fight' I played it down.

Nora laughed already knowing what I was trying to pull. 'Nah, you can fight mate and as for you saying you're game? Most true thing any cunt has ever said in the history of the world, likes' He had the floor now and I was just going to have to stand and listen to it even though ideally I'd have been mobilising and getting myself down to the stadium for the match. 'Do you think over all the matches you've ran with us since you joined that we've not been watching how you do? Some get it when they join and take to it like the proverbial duck and others you see straight away that aye, they've got the clothes, they've got the look but as for being willing to fight in them? Different fucking matter.'

'As far as me and Dawson are concerned and that obviously means every cunt else in the mob, you're one of us now, none of this on the fringes stuff serving your time, we all know that when it comes to it, you're going to be there fighting for us' I wasn't prepared for this, I didn't know that I had even been on some kind of probation with them, apprenticeship even? I thought that I was in already and I could choose to be out just as easily. This talk he was giving me felt like it was official though. No medals, no diplomas, just a small nod and a wink from the head honcho in this crew of psychotic football hooligans.

We all had the rather sumptuous away day trip to Glasgow next week to play Rangers to look ahead to so as Nora and I said our goodbyes for the afternoon we agreed to catch up on the train through to Glasgow next Saturday. Despite not actually being IN the pub I'd managed to catch a few words with some of the crew and I'm not sure if this had all come down to my conversation with Nora but it had seemed like people were over talkative with me. Bumped into that mad fucker Si from the train, Doctor fucking Feelgood! That's what I called him when I saw him, 'Oh I've got something in my medicine cupboard for you my friend' he said ushering me round the side of the pub and out of the watching eyes of the coppers.

'How you doing anyway, Zico? Wasn't it?' he asked. 'Aye, bang on Si' I said confidently back when in reality you kinda notice names of people who will play a part in you experiencing something truly different like your first time taking a Class A drug. He looked impressed though as he opened his jacket and fished out a wee bag with some white powder in it. Straight away I knew I didn't want to be placed in the same situation as last week but didn't want to be rude to him either by not accepting anything he offered.

Oh well, just a cheeky wee one then I thought having had him twist my arm to take a dab. 'Same as last week?' I asked before fully complying with his insistence. 'Aye mate, ye cannae beat a wee bit toot toot on match day eh?' he replied and I really couldn't counter that for a statement. I'd only taken it the once and it had definitely enhanced my match day experience so who was I to argue? I told him about my big date later on and how I couldn't dab too much as I wanted to be on the same wavelength as her for the night rather than speeding out of my nut. He said it was cool but wanted to give me a wee bit for later on in case I wanted a wee top up.

In the most irresistibly chilling of ways I could see that the two of us were going to be friends in the best and worst possible of ways! Now that we weren't all hyped up in a train carriage destined for fuck knows what and instead, chilled outside a Dundee boozer before a guaranteed two points against our city rivals. Si and I were able to have a good chat with each other, aided and abetted by the amphetamine sulphate taking over the both of us. He told me a bit about himself and how he had been with the crew for a few years. We both admitted that we'd recognised each other on most match days and just hadn't spoken to one another until last week.

When you've got a mob of two hundred upwards most weeks it's not exactly conducive to producing much new introductions and conversations. Freakishly enough it had on occasion appeared that him and I had shared the same wardrobe only, and luckily, we never wore the same stuff the same week. One week I'd have a red Lacoste sweater on and the next he'd have it on. Another he'd be wearing his Tachini tracksuit and the next me. It was quite uncanny likes. One of those scenarios where some people will never see us in the same place at the same time and won't believe we both exist!

We walked down the five minute trip to Tannadice Park and ended up watching the game together on the terraces as United cruised to a 3-1 win, two from big Mixu Paatelainen and one from Kevin Gallacher. He fucking managed to convince me to take an extra wee dab at half time as he opened his jacket and invited my hand in. I did take some but not as much as he thought I had so as far as I was concerned I was going to be well set for the trip to the pictures later with Miss Hopkins. It actually felt really good to be able to go to a fitba match and not have the constant edge of feeling that you needed eyes in the back of your head looking for / being ready for trouble.

Not that I would have ever admitted it to anyone but given how the day had been. A few drinks, some drugs, chats with friends, good game of football with great atmosphere - I'd enjoyed it all much much more than any day I'd ever had running around fighting with other mobs. I made the most of it, four games out of something like thirty eight that there's not going to be a chance of fighting. I'm a complete hypocrite though because Derby day WAS so enjoyable knowing there was no fighting, just having a good time, as long as United won of course. YET I was already looking forward to all the chaos that next week in Glasgow was going to no doubt provide us all.

I did though take notice of the fact that I hadn't exactly been displeased over having a day with no violence. At the very least, I wouldn't have been looking to turn up to meeting Lisa with cuts and bruises over my face. This football casual side of me, I'm sure was not something that Lisa knew about. I stayed in too small a place to go shouting about my weekend recreational activities so even though as a sixteen year old my natural impulses were to tell one and all about some of my exciting experiences with football hooligans and drink and drugs. I had in reality told only a few close pals so there was no way she was going to know and at least for now I wanted to keep things that way.

Chapter 8.

I don't think I've ever deliberated over what to wear for any specific event of my life than when we were going to see Total Recall. It's one thing to be dressing up to go to the fitba alongside other similar dressers. That in itself can be the ultimate in posturing and one up man ship but going out on a fucking date and at that, not just "any" date? Different prop altogether. I once saw this advert on the telly that had said the first thing a woman notices about you is your shoes. Well if that's the case the woman in question better like Adidas otherwise I'm royally fucked! I've always been trainer daft since I was around twelve. I remember going to London that summer for the first time with a, for a kid, relative fistful of dollars to buy some clothes and once there the choice of trainers down there compared to Scotland blew my mind.

That summer won't be easily forgotten because some kid from Germany called Boris Becker rocked up at Wimbledon that summer as a teenager and won it and in some choice gear. Decked out in Ellesse and Puma. I bought a pair of Puma just like him down there thinking no one would be able to match me on them back in Scotland since I'd got them in "that London." Anyway, I scrubbed up decent enough for the date. Sensible if unadventurous choice of a Lacoste white polo shirt, Radio jeans and Stan Smiths. Aye, I completely played it safe. If there's one guarantee here it's that if somehow someone is reading this story in fifty years time it's that there's a small chance that they'll be wearing a Lacoste polo shirt and a pair of Stan Smiths while doing so. She obviously wasn't expecting me in a top hat and tails so I was sure I'd be passable.

I'd arranged to meet her at the bus stop before we headed into town. It was when I was on my way to the meeting point that it started to sink in. Previously if she had been going to see a film it would be sat in the front seat of a car driven by her boyfriend, not waiting on the 57a to come along. I'm not sure if it was still a bit of the speed floating around me but I shrugged off such thoughts with the knowledge that she knew in advance I didn't have a car and still accepted. In for a penny in for a pound as my Di would say and that was my thoughts on it. If she wouldn't want to see me again after tonight then it wouldn't have been for the want of trying on my part. I got there first at the bus stop which was fine, showed I was keen if anything.

Time started to wear on though as I stood there waiting on her. I kept looking up the road in the direction of where she lived but nope, no sign of her walking along. Constantly looking at my watch until the point that the 7.05pm bus was moments away from coming around the corner and she'd still not surfaced. 'Fucking knew it was too good to be true' I thought to myself, HER go out with me? I bet her and all her pals would all be pissing themselves laughing right now about it. The 7.05 did indeed come winging its way round the corner with no sign of Lisa so, being the only one stood at the bus stop I waved it on whilst cursing the fact that she had ruined my night. I could've still been in Dundee getting wrecked celebrating another Derby win with the boys and instead I'm stuck here not on the bus I needed to be to get myself into town for the start of the movie. 'What a wee bitch' Those words had barely left my lips and me taking a few steps away from the bus stop when I heard the peep of a horn from an oncoming car. Then it started flashing its lights at me.

That was enough to have me frozen on the spot as I awaited whatever and whoever was inside it as it got closer. First of all I looked at the driver but nope, didn't recognise him, an older guy who was looking back at me with an equally vacant stare. It was only when I looked to the side and by then having the chance to grab an even closer look as the car pulled up beside me. Lisa was in the passengers seat with an embarrassed look on her face whilst still managing a smile.

She quickly got out and ran up to me to apologise that we'd missed the bus but that her dad was going to run us in to town and how mortified she was that our date was starting out with her dad in tow. I was just relieved that she actually HAD wanted to go out with me for the night and actually so much so she was prepared to ask her dad for help in doing so! Maybe misguidedly but I took that as a compliment. And there was me worried about not having a car as well.

Lisa elected to sacrifice the shotgun seat she'd been sitting in by opening the back door and inviting me in before following me. It was only really then that the whole implications of it being the three of us together in the car began to hit home. Here we had a case of our first date not even having properly started and I was being introduced to the dad. Something I'd much rather have avoided, at least for a while if I'm being honest. Once we were all in he pulled off without having even looked round to acknowledge the new passenger in his car. 'Dad, this is Steven, Steven - Dad' Lisa said tentatively and completely straight faced even though she had never called me by my "Sunday" name in my life. As she introduced us to each other she subtly elbowed me to provoke a response from me. 'Alright Mr Hopkins? Pleased to meet you' I managed to get out. What I got back was in the same fitba stadium of a grunt and a meeting of our eyes via his interior mirror before he directed them back towards the road again. She flashed me a nervous smile that suggested a part of her was dying inside at how our night was starting off. With her dad looking very much like someone who wasn't up for a conversation in any shape or form, probably pissed off that instead of sitting with a drink in his hand watching Saturday night TV he was having to venture out to do taxi duties. Lisa and I talked in the back amongst ourselves while obviously still in earshot of the man in the front.

We discussed the film we were going to see and how we'd heard that some of the special effects were meant to be unbelievable, the likes never seen in a film before. Talked about school the past week, all kinds of safe small talk until we could be on our own and then feel semi close to being ourselves. She then asked me about the match earlier on and how it went. This seemingly doing the job of poking the bear in front with a stick and getting a reaction. 'What match have you been away to today?' came the voice from the front without him taking his eyes off the road. - 'I was up at the Dundee Derby today, Mr Hopkins', I'm an Arab so aye, had a decent day.'

Without warning he slammed on the breaks and stopped by the side of the road and turned round with a dead serious look on his coupon. 'AN ARAB???' 'No no no no no, I'm sorry princess but I'm not having you go out with one of THEM, I let a lot of things slide Lisa but not this.' He looked at her every bit as serious as how he'd looked at me. That's when I noticed the Rangers crest on his tracksuit bottoms but even then I still thought this was an extreme overreaction on his part. He can't be expecting the only men to date his daughter to turn out to be currant buns, surely not? Plus, at the end of the day, if I'd been a Celtic fan then I would have been able to kind of understand it although even to be able to do such a thing you have to try and "think" like a Rangers fan and that is not such an easy thing to do. I thought it was a complete overreaction, however he was about to school me in the lengths fitba passions and beliefs could stretch to.

I tried a half hearted laugh, to flush him out and get him to break character and give me an indication this was just a joke but nah he wasn't playing ball. The fucking madman had pretty much abandoned the car whilst doing this as well! Half the cars that were having to go around us were peeping their horns over the inconvenience of it all. 'Dad, no, please come on, just start the car and drop us off near the high street and we'll be out of your hair' Lisa pleaded with him - He wasn't for listening, instead going off on one about how Dundee United started off as called Dundee Hibernian and how the team was formed specifically for the Irish catholic community in Dundee. Due to this we were no better than Glasgow Celtic in his eyes and there was no way he was allowing his daughter to date a 'taig.'

If it hadn't been the case that this was completely fucking up my night and all those hopes I had at getting a crack of taking Lisa Hopkins out were evaporating right in front of me. Had it not been for those facts I could have almost congratulated him on his knowledge as I'd bet half the fucking United supporters didn't even know that. I at least had to try and save things despite the fact that due to "whose" father he was I was fifty fifty between feeling intimidated and letting him have a pass because I really wanted to make his daughter my girlfriend. Still had to say something though. I knew what audience I was playing to so wasn't afraid to sink to the lowest common denominator to reach him.

'Mr Hopkins? United don't have an agenda in that sense. We dropped the Hibernian around ten years later and made the club more inclusive than for just catholics, that's why we changed name and shirt colour, we dropped the name and we dropped the green shirts, end of story.' I looked at Lisa like I was going to receive backup when the reality of it was that she didn't have a fucking clue what I was talking about to her dad.

'Save your breath, pal ... Now get your arse out' He delivered the knock out blow. THAT was the moment where I was ready to flip, just tell the cunt what I thought of him and his bigoted views before getting out the car but, I don't know. I didn't ever have trouble with confrontation but in that moment I couldn't join the dots to have me in that frame of mind. Meekly I looked at Lisa and shrugged my shoulders, she looked well gutted which in that second I took as some kind of a perverse bonus. Silently I reached to open the door, swung it open and got my right leg out onto the ground ... Then came the laughter from the front.

'GET your stupid arse back in the car' He laughed back, shaking his head at the fact that I was actually getting out of it. He's looking round at Lisa by now saying how he can't believe that I was sucked in and believed him. She's looking like she wants the ground to swallow her up. I'm still half in half out the car feeling all kinds of emotions at the same time. I'm relieved that the date's still on, I'm pissed off at her dad's attempt at patter, which incidentally, he appeared to think he was the KING of, which he definitely wasn't.

To be fair, the second I'd gotten into the car, if he'd presented me with a legal document that needed my signature next to and titled 'Things I will put up with in order to date Lisa Hopkins' I'd have probably signed it but he was more about taking the surprise route. Given the fact that we were actually meant to be going to catch a film plus the additional fact that we were already late through missing the bus and now this brief interlude. I felt it best that I got back in the car and get us on our way again.

I took one for the team for the rest of the journey and as much as I wanted to sit chatting to Lisa I instead spoke to her dad about fitba. The one constant that two Scottish males that have been brought into contact with each other for the first time will always have together. I remember in the start of forth year and I got that Mr Baxter for English after Miss Peters had been caught shagging one of the pupils during a school trip to Bruges, made the papers and everything.

Well the first day Baxter took over I asked him, like I did with all teachers, which team they supported. I've always believed that this type of stuff can build a bit of a rapport with a teacher. Like, they're a person too, not a robot even if some days we look at them like they're one. Baxter's reply still chills me to the bone when I think about it as far as words coming out of another human beings mouth. 'I detest football' was what he said back after me cheerily asking him about his team. I didn't even know where to go after that so just turned around and went back to my desk. I'm not into fitba? Not much of a fan? Aye, all perfectly acceptable responses because not everyone is going to like the same thing but DETEST?! What the fuck did football ever do to Mr Baxter that he detests it?

I can't say that I'm a fan of Tiddlywinks but detest it? Anyway, no such problems with Mr Hopkins, even in the ten minutes of chit chat before he dropped us off it was evident that he was a complete bigot of a man with, as a Rangers fan and therefore following Scotlands best team, an air of arrogance and superiority. It had been seven years since we'd won the league / any trophy at all and he was happy to remind me of that whilst his own team were scooping the fucking lot. Funny though how despite him clearly being a man with such blinkered views I was happy to overlook them because of his daughter. Sometimes we just have to turn the other cheek eh? I mind my nana telling me that very same thing when I was getting kicked all over the place every game I played for my primary school team.

It kind of looked like Lisa was understanding this charm offensive I was on although I would make sure of telling her later on when we were on our own. Her dad eventually got to a suitable spot to drop us off on and I was left with the impression that despite how eventful the trip had all been, things seemed to be ending in a good place between all three of us. I was off for the night with his daughter and he was waving us on our way with a smile.

Once he'd pulled away and disappeared out of sight Lisa just wrapped her arms around my waist and kind of faked collapsing into me like she was about to sink to her knees, her face disappearing into my chest. Faking or not it still felt good having her arms around me so soon. If anything it at least showed she was in a good place and wasn't scared to show that she was comfy around me. It had taken us to exit the car for me to fully appreciate how cool yet beautiful she was with regards to what she'd chosen for the date. Standing there, her blonde bob immaculate with cute wee hair clasp to keep one side in place and dressed in what looked like a vintage sixties Lacoste women tennis players dress and a pair of Adidas Forest Hills. Fucking hell, between me in my Stans and Lacoste polo we'd be able to easily sneak in a quick game on centre court on the date if we so desired.

I tried to tease her by asking her if she'd come straight from the tennis court and she just batted that away by looking me up and down and asking me if tonight I was going with the 'When you've got the cinema at seven but the regional tennis championships at nine' look?! I actually think I fell in love with her right there and then! She was beautiful, smart, amazing sense of style and with comebacks like that funny with it as well. The two of us laughed before I continued on with the subject of her outfit and just how incredibly cool she looked and asked her where she copped the vintage Lacoste from. She told me that in her spare time she worked in a charity shop for a few hours to help her gran and one of the perks was being able to look through all the stuff that comes in before it goes on general sale. The moment she saw the tennis dress she'd pounced on it.

She complimented me on what I was wearing while I told her that due to how hot it was I was considering wearing a pair of shorts but that would've completed the look and I'd been as well bringing a fucking tennis racket and a few balls stuffed in my pocket with me which had her giggling. Walking to the cinema for our dual date with Arnie we went over the experience / ordeal of the journey into town. She apologised saying it was all her fault as she hadn't realised the time when she was getting ready.

When she finally noticed the time and knew she wasn't going to make the bus it took her an age to convince her dad to take us. She was praying that when they got there they'd see me on the road and if not they were going to follow the bus incase I'd got on it. She tried to say sorry on behalf of her da but I reminded her that none of us should ever have to say sorry for our dads, that's all on them.

I wasn't sure just how it would go, how it would feel to be in the situation where it was just the two of us for any length of time but the vibe had seemed to be good between us, natural likes. When we got to the cinema we ended up agreeing that I'd pay for our tickets while she bought all of our munchies and drink. Fair enough, I was expecting to pay for everything and with a looming trip through to the Weeg against Rangers the following Saturday this, financially, was all something I could've done without but this trip to the pictures was, in my mind, MORE important than a chance to go at it with the ICF on their own turf!

We took our seat up near the back, a cliche of an area in the cinema for a couple on a date however this was more due to the fact that we were late and the place was fucking hoaching. We were lucky to even get a ticket by the looks of things. Timed to perfection we took our seats right as the trailers were starting. The two of us juggling enough food to feed Ethiopia. Golden Wonder crisps, Minstrels, hot dogs, popcorn. We didn't need anywhere near as much but I think she'd felt the need to buy enough to come to the same amount of money as our tickets. I fucking love the trailers of films, it's like seeing lots of wee films before you get to see the main one you came to watch. Some good ones by the looks, those Gremlin cunts are back again in "The New Batch" I was a bit freaked out by them the first time around likes so would be swerving the next one but the trailer seemed alright, some funny scenes in it by the looks.

Then came the Diehard trailer and I almost lost my shit, grabbing Lisa's thigh through the excitement of seeing John McClane on screen. I didn't even know there was a part two coming and there it was …. and next month as well! Took me a few minutes before I even clocked what I'd done with her leg but she seemed wised up to the fact that I never took my eyes off the screen during the trailer and had seemed, for that moment at least, to be more interested in Bruce Willis than I was of her.

We talked amongst ourselves for a few of the next ones to come up, some Patrick Swayze film where it looked like he was actually dead in the movie but still trying to communicate with his wife. The other one had Tam Cruise driving round in some American style race car which to be fair I was out at Tam Cruise, can't stand that cunt if anyone's asking. It was the usual scenario when you're at the pictures where every time you think it's the last trailer BOOM another one comes after it.

That's when I heard Ray Liotta's words - 'As far back as I can remember I always wanted to be a gangster' and I had no choice but to break conversation for a moment with Lisa. This new Scorsese mafia film with Di Niro and Pesci looked unbelievable and apart from the few excited glimpses I shot at her I was transfixed at the screen for the ninety seconds the trailer lasted for. The moment it ended I immediately turned to her, smiling and took one of her hands in mine and asked 'So Lisa? What are you doing this "fall" and are you free for to come to see Goodfellas with me?'

She laughed back saying that she didn't like gangster films, too much violence and gore but that if I was willing to provide the entertainment like I'd been doing tonight then she'd love to come. So did this mean that she actually liked me and was having a good time? She'd been doing a lot of laughing and smiling, speaking a lot, there had been a lot of subtle arm and leg touches between each other? She'd definitely seemed comfortable the whole night, not withstanding the start of it where neither of us had been comfy, well apart from her dad I suppose. Surely all of this added up to all kinds of bonus rounds for later on with the two of us? As we continued chatting, the curtain down front extended itself outwards in that way it would when the film was about to start along with that usual BBFC classification message containing the age rating so taking that as our cue to shut our traps, the two of us got settled down for the film.

Chapter 9.

'So I assume that it's not actually possible for a woman to have three tits then' I jokingly asked Lisa as we sat in McDonalds discussing the complete mind fuck of a film we'd just been to see. 'Well tonight was the first time I'd ever seen one with three so I'm guessing not' she laughed back. It was a first for me as well. Pleasant surprise likes because who doesn't love tits so if there's three of them? Technically I hadn't had much experience with one breast never mind three and when I say that, I mean I'd copped a couple of feels over the past year and THAT was fucking it. Still, if women were to have three instead of two then automatically that would increase my chances, that's just common sense crossed with mathematics.

The film itself had been unbelievable, one of those movies that you watch and know you've not seen anything like it before. Big Arnie was, as always, running wild fucking lots of people up who were intending on fucking HIM up. Sack that for a job, you look at your things to do list at your work and you come across one saying kill Arnold Schwarzenegger, aye good luck with crossing that one off your list. This time though he was set in the future and ended up on Mars. The story was along the lines of him being just some normal cunt who had always dreamed of going to Mars so ended up paying some tech company to put a fake memory implant into him so he could see what Mars was like. All goes a bit tits up for him though. There was some crazy as fuck scenes in it likes and the special effects were out of this world, no pun intended, likes.

Lisa and I sat there blethering over a burger and chips. We'd both enjoyed the film and between us had almost sat there in Macky D's and replayed the whole movie we'd just watched with all our 'what about that part' and 'and when Arnie did thats.' That Sharon Stone was in it as well, she played his wife although as far as life partners go I'd say she left a lot to be desired and I'll leave it at that. She is tidy though, I bet the only teenage boys who haven't had fantasies about her are the ones who are going to be coming out as poofs in the next few years.

Eventually talk turned away from the film and back to us in general. What we were up to the next day, the exams that were looming in the coming weeks at school. I think by that point there wasn't any doubt that the night had been a success. We'd been laughing all through the night and had never been stuck for anything to talk about, none of those awkward silences that suck the life out of you. I'd wisely not tried anything on with her during the film. I know that's apparently the rules of every teenage boy who's taking a girl to the pictures but she was special.

I was trying to play the long game this time around. Of course, the pep talk I got from my cuzz before I left the house didn't exactly harm things. He waltzed into my bedroom when I was getting ready, the room already had a smell of the wee bit of aftershave I'd put on. I NEVER wore that shit, wasn't fucking shaving yet for starters but as I began to get nervous when getting ready I ended up spraying a wee bit on. He would've smelled that while seeing me doing my hair in the mirror, trying to get my middle parting just right when I saw the reflection of him behind me.

'Oooooooooh she must be special if you're putting on the poof juice, or should that be HE must be special' he ribbed me. 'Lis-a-fuck-ing-Hop-Kins' I said back with a smile slowing every single syllable down for effect. 'Jesus christ you're punching above your weight, Zico' he said with what appeared genuine amazement. I shooed that statement away and treated it with the contempt that it deserved. 'I mean, she could take her pick of most of the guys around this part of the world and she chooses you? She fucking deaf, dumb AND blind?' He laughed before admitting that he was happy for me and hoped it would go well. He passed on one bit of valuable information for me though before he went to get ready himself for the stag party he was off out on over in Edinburgh.

'Just don't make a schoolboy error on the first date that fucks your chances of a second one ok' - 'Like what?' I asked, genuinely wanting to hear what he had to say. 'Well don't be a dick, first of all if that's not already common sense to you' - 'Well I'm not a dick so that vastly reduces the chances of me acting like one' I said slightly defending myself over the outlandish thought of me being someone of dickish behaviour. He continued - 'Keep your hands to your fucking self, as well. I know she's a good looking lassie but the chances are most guys she's been out will have tried to get something off her on the first night, be different, you'll stick out to her that way, it'll show her that you're interested in her for more than just your nat king, slowly slowly catch a monkey my friend' At that he left the room telling me that any further nuggets of information would cost me a pint.

Lisa and I managed to stop talking long enough to clock that if we didn't hurry we were going to miss the last bus back home and without even discussing it, there was NO WAY we would be enlisting her dad to come get us, regardless if we didn't have enough money for a taxi. Luckily Adi Dassler had our backs. Had she been wearing heels we'd have missed it but due to the tennis shoes we got there to the bus stance as the doors were just closing while we shouted on the driver to open them again. It's a busy bus at the weekends and the bottom deck was full. Through our dramatic catching of the bus it felt like every pair of eyes on the bottom of the bus were looking at us.

I actually made out a couple of cunts that go to our school. The look on their coupons when they spied who I was with was priceless, as well as leaving me feeling pretty fucking good with myself. I've always hated getting on buses and having to go through that whole, you being the new person getting on so everyone is staring at you thing. The ones who are sat on their own, fucking shitting it that you're going to choose the seat beside them and are giving you the death stare as you walk up the aisle. Or even when you decide to try upstairs and find it's full and you have to come back down again to the bottom and sit beside one of those cunts that were giving you the don't you fucking dare sit here glare!

We managed to get two seats together upstairs but the chance of having a decent conversation was practically impossible due to the amount of radgeys on this last bus. The majority looking like they were heading back to their own areas in time for last orders at their local. I was right in the middle of trying to nail a second date with her when two men behind us started full on fighting with each other. I'd noticed something brewing between them even though they were actually traveling home together so had been keeping an eye and an ear on them. When you've seen as much fighting and trouble as I've had in such a short space of time you kind of develop a sixth sense for that type of shit before it happens. They were older guys likes, just your typical "mannies" from around here. Umbro polo shirts tucked into jeans with the obligatory Sambas on their feet. Tongues out, of course. They'd been arguing about how one wanted to go onto a club to extend their night while the other one didn't.

'Get yourself out ya fucking pussy, only half ten for fucks sake' One of the Samba twins aggressively said to his mate. 'I keep telling you, I'm playing fitba the mora morning, fucking Smirnoff cup final likes and you're wanting me out on the batter til fuck knows when? How me meant to do my midfield maestro thing when I'm still pished from the night before?' He tried to reason but you know what some drunks can be like. He kept pushing and pushing. 'Fucking Smirnoff cup final? Who gies a fuck about that shite? Yer making it out like it's the European Cup Final ya cunt, isnae fucking Juventus you're playing for, mon oot for a serious bevvy and get yerself a ride at the end of the night.'

Through the volume of the two of them Lisa and I were just sitting there looking at each other rolling our eyes in acceptance that we could do nothing about being caught in the crossfire of this pantomime that was taking place. Eventually it was a case of one insult dispensed too many as the one who was playing the next day had grabbed his "mate" by the back of the head and slammed it forward in a rage. Clearly he'd not thought this through though because by shoving his pals head in that direction it went right into the back of Lisa's knocking her forward. Her, screaming out at the fright and no doubt the pain this caused.

This of course now meant that I was going to have to become involved. Without any thought I cracked the fitba boy on the chin with a sucker punch, completely taking him by surprise. My assault coming while he was steadying himself for the retaliation from the boy beside him. He didn't know where to look as I was now considered a person of interest and on his radar. He raised his fists up as I went in for a second punch. I really wanted to check on Lisa but it wouldn't have taken a genius to work out that if I took my mind away from matters there then I was going to get clocked by him and never underestimating the unpredictable nature of someone drunk, potentially the two of them turning on me. There wouldn't be that particular issue to worry about.

'THIS CUNT'S MINES' The drunk lad now recovered from smacking his face into the back of my date stood up and in one movement brought his knee up right under his mates chin who was still sitting down in what was a schoolboy error if ever I'd seen one. It looked a right sore one he gave him likes, the kind that you ken that the other guy isn't going to come back with anything after it. My theory backed up by the fact no one heard from the boy for the rest of the journey.

Well actually that is a lie as he sat screaming his head off in agony for most of the journey while his pal kept telling him to shut his pus and for him to stick his Smirnoff cup appearance up his arse. Lisa was ok by this point, a bump on the head and more of a fright than anything else. Didn't stop me playing the concerned "boyfriend" though of course. Things went a little bit quiet between us for the rest of the journey but I reckoned it was all down to the fact that the bus ride had contained too much of an edge. I'll say one thing, at least we were consistent in that we had both an awkward trip there AND back from our date. Our stop couldn't come quick enough, just as it was approaching it looked like kicking off again between the two behind us.

The one who was nursing a potential broken jaw was now starting to realise that his cup final dreams were now over and he wasn't too chuffed at this epiphany. This two bob not even amateur cup final was obviously a big thing to him and now it was fucked. He was trying to talk but couldn't really get any words out as he could hardly move his jaw. It was pretty funny if I'm being honest going by the glimpses I caught of him. His pal was in no mood to put up with him though and was asking him if he wanted put on his arse again.

I wanted to get involved as I was still pissed off at what he'd done earlier but sensibly wanted to have matters at a more happy level with Lisa and I for when we were going to be saying our goodnights. I was already starting to get a bit paranoid over the fact that for a good few seconds I'd been sucked into a bit of violence when I was meant to be on a date and a big part of me was thinking that my "Saturday afternoon instinct" had almost certainly put a damper on things. I have no idea what I must've looked like when the red mist descended but Lisa had been sitting in the front row seat for it.

It wasn't until we got off the bus and made our way in the direction of her house after me, naturally, offering to walk her home, that she took the step of linking her arm through mines and thanking me for what I had done on the bus. 'Fucking YES' I screamed inside. 'I don't know?' I said 'It was just a natural reaction from me when I saw what I thought was you getting hurt, had to stick up for you' - 'Well not everyone would go on and punch someone more than twice his age so thank you .. Believe it or not, it was probably the most romantic thing anyone has ever done for me' I had her laughing over my suggestion of 'just wait until I actually learn HOW to be romantic and my love won't exclusively have to be displayed through the medium of violence.'

I'm not sure, weird the way things work but what took place on the bus was the catalyst for her to open up and show a different side to her than what I'd seen over the night. Sure she'd been funny, confident, interesting but here she was talking about me and the impression she'd been left with over the night. 'You're definitely different, Zico. Despite going to the pictures you never once tried to slip your hand where it wasn't wanted and yet will hook some guy in a heartbeat if he's threatening me' Lapping this up I egged her on by telling her that a guy like that is a keeper.

Smiling she replied 'I thought you played right midfield though' and without giving me a chance to reply, wrapped her arms around my neck and started to kiss me. Hands down it was the most brilliant thing to happen to me in my short lifetime. Fuck the feeling of buying a Stone Island jacket or securing a pair of Adidas that isn't available in Britain, forget the buzz of chasing the CCS all over Edinburgh and claiming the capital city as yours for the day. This was on a whole new level. She definitely seemed like she'd done a lot more kissing than I'd ever mustered since I got interested in girls but hey I'm a fast learner and was soon giving as good as I was getting.

When we finally came up for air, we just stood looking at each other smiling before both bursting out laughing then starting walking again, holding hands. Well, I say walking but it felt like I was riding on one of those hoverboards that Michael J Fox had in Back to the Future 2. It just felt so amazing and you wouldn't have been able to wipe the smile from my face if you'd set about me with a cleaver and a pair nunchucks. We soon got to Lisa's house and with the possibility that her mum or dad might be sneaking a look we played things safe and had a little peck and a cuddle before saying goodnight, thanking each other for a great night. Agreeing that we'd have to do something again soon and that if we didn't see each other over the Sunday we'd catch each other at school the day after.

I wasn't planning on going in much over the next week but I now had myself some extra motivation to go in on the Monday at least! She flashed me one more of those stunning smiles and then a wave before she disappeared into her house leaving me to jump onto my imaginary hoverboard again and get myself down the road. I couldn't help but think again about that Perfect Day song I'd heard in the docs. Within the space of less than twenty four hours I'd been elevated in my standing with the Dundee Utility Crew, had seen my team win the Derby (as always) and was looking like Lisa Hopkins and I might well be gearing up to be starting to go out with each other. This is the part where I wake up and find my cornflakes are all soggy, right?

Chapter 10.

ONE SHOE-YOU'VE ONLY GOT ONE SHOE-YOU'VE ONLY GOT ONE SHOE-YOU'VE ONLY GOT ONE SHOE .... The whole of the carriage was belting out to the tune of "Blue Moon" with the surreal sight of every one of the crew sitting or standing while holding up one of their trainers in the air. A colourful sea of Adidas, Reebok, Nike and Diadora. Fuck knows what anyone who was on the train who weren't with us was making of all of this. For us however, it was the most natural thing in the world for a day when we would find ourselves playing one of the teams from Glasgow. The inside joke being the regional inference that with them being from that area of Scotland they're all tinks with no money.

As much as the next man I always loved singing that, even if I still couldn't understand why a group of fans from a city like Dundee would be so quick to cast dispersion towards the dwellers of another city in such a way. From my hundreds of visits to the City of Discovery itself I had never suffered from any confusion that I had got on the wrong train and ended up in Monaco or Bora Bora. Spirits were high there in the carriage for the big day ahead as we headed through to 'The Weeg.' There were more cans in the carriage than you'd find inside Threshers and judging by the states of a good few of the lads there were Class A's being partaken also.

On that subject I was well up for getting my finger stuck in a wee baggie of that white go faster stuff but hadn't bumped into my man Si yet. I'd had a look for him but there was just too many of us crammed in there so I figured I'd maybe bump into him at some point once we got off at the other end. It wasn't lost on me that I'd had a wee dab two Saturdays in a row now and here was me actively WANTING to get myself my hat trick. I justified this to myself on the grounds that whilst there had been a wee pattern develop over the past few weeks, this had just been a Saturday thing. Hardly the stuff of addiction. I ended up thinking about Nasty Nick Cotton in Eastenders when he got addicted to Heroin and his mum, bless her, Dot, had to lock the cunt up in the house to stop him from going out and scoring. Soap operas pretty much had been my point of reference as far as drugs go, apart from scare stories in the tabloids likes. That and when Zammo in Grange Hill started dabbling with smack.

That's the thing though, every time you saw someone who was addicted to hard drugs it was always Heroin and as young and inexperienced as I was, that was never going to be an issue for me. If those programs and papers were to be believed, then the only cunts who were taking heroin weren't guys like me or anyone else on this train for that matter. They were all shady looking characters who didn't dress well and had nothing else in their life APART from drugs. To me, even then, drugs in my opinion looked like they could be something to enjoy and to help enhance what was already going on in life rather than actually BE your life. Aye, I bet that's what that poor cunt Zammo probably said as well.

There was quite a lot of excited chatter on the train as it made its way through to Glasgow. Mad thing is that on manoeuvres to the fitba, a lot of excitement that's generated is to do with the actual fitba itself but today was different in the sense that this was a match that we most likely weren't going to win. As a matter of fact, the vast majority of us weren't even fucking going to the game itself and were merely using it as a cover to go through and fight with the Inter City Firm. Ibrox Stadium, home of Glasgow Rangers was one of Scotlands biggest soccer grounds, holding almost fifty thousand but due to the fact that they had so many fucking glory hunters for fans, away teams would only receive around a couple of thousand tickets with the lions share going to the home supporters.

I say 'glory hunters' because when I started going to the United games as a kid, Rangers were absolutely shite and as is the norm with their fans, and to be fair most other teams fans, if things aren't going well lots of fans disappear like snow off a dyke. I knew they were a big team though purely cause of the fact that the papers wouldn't stop talking about them but back in those days they wouldn't even fill their own away allocation when they came to Dundee never mind filling out their massive stadium for every home game. Then things changed, they must've found some money from somewhere because they switched from being average at best to a team full of English and European internationalists. They even got Souness in as manager and it all went a bit mental after that.

I mind that first time they came to Tannadice after he'd arrived at Ibrox when their revolution had started. I walked into the ground and went to take my place near the segregation part of the ground, an area I always stood at as I loved the banter back and forward between both sets of fans. When I got there though it was to find that there were Rangers supporters in OUR part of the stadium. I was a couple of years away from getting myself involved with the Utility at that point but loved that day for how mental it all was, fights breaking out all over the place with United fans not exactly taking too kindly to the fact that the huns were in the same end as them.

Today though was absolutely ride all about the match itself. If we were able to give the Rangers mob a few things to think about for the rest of the weekend when they were sat in A & E then that was the ONLY result we'd be looking for out of the day. Of course, a wee sneaky win for United wouldn't have gone amiss either likes. I overheard a couple of guys I'd never seen before at a game talking about retribution for the fact that a couple of their mates got a right doing in The Three Barrels from some ICF the last league game in Dundee. Nora, who had made a point of getting me to sit with him and some of the top boys, was giving his reasons for why, despite how fucking nasty Hibs and Aberdeen were, the ICF were the Scottish crew he despised the most.

This was more to do with the fact that last year he had been ripped off in a drug deal by what would turn out to be, a couple of ICF lads. He'd apparently had a shotgun pulled out on him at the point of the transaction and was relieved of the pound of Soap Bar that had been sat in the boot of his car. Reason enough I suppose for having an agenda. I mean, I had various axes to grind with a couple of mobs, mainly Motherwell due to what happened after the match at Fir Park when they'd surprised us with an extra large mob that day and ran us all over the fucking place. I ended up being separated from the rest of the crew and only caught up with them again after receiving quite a doing from the "Saturday Service." I'd gotten myself penned in up some side street near the stadium. A pasting from the other side is simply a hazard of the job of a casual but the sick minky bastards stole my fucking trainers! I'd only bought them the week before, Gazelles, the purple ones as well that were more rare than rocking horse shit.

Had to walk back to the train station in my socks, wankers. It's moments like that where you can develop a grudge against others but that was only a pair of Gazelles. Nora looked like he'd lost more than a pair of trainers so aye, I could understand his issues he had with this particular group of hooligans. I almost pitied any ICF that he personally would come into contact with over the day. Nora wasn't exactly the discriminating kind.

This had been the first time I'd seen him since last week outside The Snug when he'd told me that I was "in" officially so him along with Dawson had been introducing me to some new faces I'd never clocked before on match duty. The two of them gushing with praise over this young one coming through the ranks who had proved how game he was in some of the most difficult of situations.' It had left me a bit embarrassed to be honest which was mixed with apprehension as I didn't want anyone who didn't even know me getting jealous from the start. You know how some can get? I know it sounds a bit mad as you can't ever compare the two scenarios but them singing my praises in front of everyone left me with with the kind of feeling that you get when the teacher gives you praise in front of the rest of the classroom. In one way you're happy they're doing it but sat there wishing they'd do it in private and away from the rest of the class.

Despite the buzz of the prospect of an away day in enemy territory that promised to be full of all kinds of drama, danger and excitement. I must've spent half of the journey thinking about "her." We'd seen each other every lunch time on the three days I'd went into school through the week. We'd take ourselves away down to the playing field and away from everyone else who would uninvitedly gatecrash our conversation. She had also came down to mines on the Wednesday night to sit up in my bedroom and chat, listen to music and engage in, what I'd learned from the local swimming pool rules and regs information board as "heavy petting."

She had asked if we could do something later on tonight once I got back from Glasgow, it was blowing my mind that in just over a week it had went from me nervously shuffling up to chance my luck and ask her out to HER asking ME! I'd explained that it was an away match and I wasn't exactly sure when I'd get back otherwise I'd say a definite yes and we'd left it that. In a play it by ear way way if I could find her when I got home then we'd do something the rest of the night, nothing set in stone likes. I knew though that there was a LOT to come before I found myself back home tonight, not that she knew this. All she knew was that I was going to watch my team through in The West.
Importantly she didn't know that I never even had a ticket for the match never mind the fact that my only reason for BEING in Glasgow was to roam the streets of Govan looking for fights. Even so I couldn't help but feel guilty over lying to her. It was mad but even after such a short space of time I felt like I was being out of order keeping this part of my life secret from her. This was evened out by the fact that had she

known this other side of me she wouldn't be interested in going out with someone like that so for the greater good it was better to keep it a secret which aye, is still nothing other than a euphemism for lying! The very last thing I wanted to do was risk losing her just when it looked like it might go somewhere. I must admit, when she mentioned doing something together on the Saturday night my first instinct was to sack the Rangers trip but that thought was brought to me by an angel sitting on my left shoulder. Soon though, I had a devil on my right one saying 'get a fucking grip, mate this is Rangers ICF for fucks sake.'

We'd arrived at Glasgow Central and then found our way onto the subway out to Govan. Seconds after getting off at Ibrox station, it all went a bit tits up. All the other high risk away trips I'd been on it had always been a case of the police having things in order and monitoring us from the word go but I'm not sure what happened on their part this time around. The moment we filed out of the subway station there wasn't a police officer to be seen as we found ourselves ambushed by a healthy sized team who by the looks had known we were going to be arriving on that particular train.

Spotters at Glasgow Central had inevitably put in a call to the boozer that the ICF had been drinking in. The ins and outs of that were aca-fucking-demic at that moment as we poked our head out of the station to find a shower of bricks and bottles coming down on us from a mob stood across the road. All I knew, in that moment was that they were raining down on us and it was getting a bit hairy. If it was scary for me then fuck knows how it felt for some of the random members of the public who just happened to be trying to exit Ibrox subway station at the same time as us. People like wifies with their kids just going about their normal Saturday afternoon stuff. It was poor form from the ICF, despicable, actually.

I'd watched some Channel 4 programme a few months before on soccer hooligans which was trying to say that there was a code of conduct with all casual firms where they would only fight each other and would never use weapons in a fight like knives. In my own experience that was all a fucking myth and never more true than in Glasgow, fucking bandit country. These cunts are a different breed through there and probably couldn't even spell code of conduct never mind follow one. What was going on outside the subway station was a timely reminder of that. I saw this woman with her kid who could've only been around four or five year old caught like rabbits between the headlamps of an oncoming Iveco.

Despite the fact that at that point it really was every man for themselves I ran up to them and shouted to the mum that she should head back into the station and give it fifteen minutes before coming back out again. She didn't know me from Adam but the fact I was telling her this mixed with me visibly being with all these other boys who had gotten off the same train as her she seemed to register that I knew what I was talking about. She turned back and disappeared in the opposite direction through the crowd of Utility who were pushing past her to get out into the action outside.

A group of our boys, head down, ran for it from the station across the road towards the ICF lads. I followed ducking and diving the missiles that were coming down, a bottle of Becks crashing at my feet which I knew had it connected somewhere else would have meant the end of my day there and then. The bottle assault soon stopped which was due to the fact that they had been coming purely from a young group of ICF who had bolted the moment they saw a team of Utility led by Nora running in their direction.

There was quite a lot of them likes but the sight of a much more mature group coming at them must've had their bottle going. I'd have done too, knowing how mental a group of boys were who were running at them. This made more sense as I'd have expected the main ICF to come and have it out with us toe to toe rather than the cowardly throwing of bottles and bricks that had greeted us. In my view though, that still hadn't reflected too well on the older Rangers boys that they'd shat out and sent their young boys down to meet us on our arrival.

We'd meet up with them soon enough to address that small matter of course, well, that was the plan anyway and hopefully only a matter of sooner rather than later. I'd still not seen one sign of any of Strathclyde Constabulary which given my experience of away trips was pretty strange but for us, it wasn't something to be complaining about. Most away days the police were up our arse the moment we arrived in their city so this was a pleasant surprise to be left to our own devices under enemy lines. Police aside, the question was, where about were these cunts that had sent some boys down to do a mans job? First up we'd needed to do an inventory check and see who was still fully functional after the extended warm welcome we'd arrived to find waiting for us.

Looking around, you could see that there had been a few casualties. I alone had seen a few of our boys sporting split heads, cuts and bruises from some who hadn't been so lucky when it came to what had been thrown at us. Some of them who would be off on their way in a taxi to Glasgow Southern General hospital instead of pressing on looking for the carnage that undoubtedly lay ahead.

Chapter 11.

I finally bumped into Si in the most comical of ways. I saw the trail blood on the ground in a drip drip drip way that led to some messed up cunt in a Burberry shirt sat on the kerb with hand pressed against his head, blood all over the place. His head, hands, shirt, the proverbial full house. As I approached in his direction he looked around at me which was when I noticed it was him. 'Fuck, man, you ok, Si?' Taken by surprise I asked which I instantly regretted as I'm looking at him drenched in blood, all over his head, hands and shirt. He looked a pretty fucking far way from being 'alright.' - 'Alright? He replied looking pretty pissed off with his lot.

You seen the state of this fucking shirt?' he said back while doing away with the pleasantries that would normally come when you see a friend out of the blue the way I'd come across him 'Only bought the fucking thing through the week and it's probably fucked now, fucking wee hun bastards.' I could see that he wasn't paying the respect to his injury as much as he should have been and instead was worried about his shirt that, yes, appeared to be past the point of no return. Without stopping to even reply I looked around and saw that there was a cafe a few doors down from where he sat and I ran past him and straight into and pleaded with the waitress that there was someone outside with a serious injury and needed something to stop the blood. She must've seen the desperation in my eyes as without any protest she rushed through to a room in the back and appeared with a towel for me and told me to keep it while following behind me as I rushed out the door and seeing the mob that was gathered outside, closing the door and locking it behind me.

I made my way back towards Si and handed him the towel to stick on his head which within minutes then began to show signs of blood soaking through it. 'Cheers man' he said with an appreciative look on his face as he sat there holding the towel tight against his head. 'I'd been hoping to bump into you mate although not under such circumstances' I said as I sat down beside him on the side of the road while watching an animated mob of Utility trying to regroup and mobilise themselves for what was now about to follow.

'Aye, I was on the same train as everyone but ended up in a carriage full of scarfers, it was packed so I just waited until we got to Central

Station before catching up with everyone' - 'Listen man, not wanting to be pissing on your bonfire here but you not thinking you should be on your way to the hossie right now?' I tried to reason with him. He really looked in a bad way. 'I'll go with you if you want likes' I showed my caring side as this was a big day in the life of a Utility boy but in the scheme of things making sure he was ok was way more important than running around Govan looking for trouble.

Despite all the shit he was dealing with right there in that moment he just laughed which left me feeling a bit stupid for showing the compassionate side to me. 'Behave Zico, we've got business to attend to' he replied as if he didn't have part of his brain sticking out of his head. 'Fair enough' it's not me who's got a split head right now I thought although still felt the decent thing would be to offer him my sun hat, one like Reni from The Stone Roses, to put on his head while certain in the knowledge it would never go back on my head again. He thanked me but refused, most likely for the same reason, knowing that it would be ruined in minutes. Since we were clear of that particular subject we sat talking while watching the animation of everyone else around us.

It was probably the worst timing but then again, ask my school teacher, my punctuality has never been what you could call impeccable, I handed Si a tenner. 'What's this for mate?' he genuinely asked me. 'That's for all the dabs the past few weeks' I said back and after a few seconds of thought he seemed to get it. 'I'm not looking for money, was just sharing with you as you would do with me if the roles were reversed. What? Can't give a mate a wee dab of speed no?' he laughed. I told him that I didn't want him to think I was some freeloader and that I'd always want to pay my way.

'Tell you what, Si. Going by my experience, if you've got any on you I'd get it into you post haste and that'll chase away the 'headache' that you're probably nursing right now' I added which brought a smile to his face. 'You've got a fucking point there, mate' he said as he popped his hand into the top pocket of his blood soaked checked shirt and in full view of anyone on the street produced a wrap and opened it up and took a dab before passing it in my direction. There was no second invitation required for me to stick my finger into as well before shoving it into my mouth without hesitation knowing, by now what would soon follow. Full steam a-fucking-head!

'This is all going to completely fuck my Saturday plans, fucking wee Weegie bastards, cause as mad as I am I still realise that I AM going to have to go to fucking casualty at some point tonight, this injury isn't one that's going to be fixed with vinegar and brown paper' - Si lamented. 'Oh aye, what are you up to tonight likes, mate, or 'meant' to be up to' I enquired. A lot of the interactions on match day with some of the other boys barely went that deep. I mean, I'd see these cunts every Saturday, have no idea what they get up to through the week never mind what they do on a Saturday once we all go our separate ways in the varied and unpredictable way that we all part ways post match. Would love to know all the wee stories that comes from how they spent their Saturday after the match. What capers they all get up to when away from the group.

'Was meant to be going up to Aberdeen to an Acid House party' he replied - 'Aberdeen?' I was surprised by that. Considering what we get up to on Saturday afternoons I wouldn't have thought it wise to be going on nights out on what otherwise would be enemy territory. He just laughed back at me while shaking his head in a show of disdain that I would later find for myself to be fully justified. 'Nah trust me it's cool at these things, man, I've never seen a fight yet at a party while I'd bet my last fucking rupee on me seeing one if I went out in Dundee when we get back to the station tonight within half an hour of setting foot back in the City of Discovery' - 'Haven't been to one, Si' I admitted 'I've clocked onto the fact that there's definitely something going on with the whole house music thing likes but don't know too much about it'

I continued before going on to tell him how I was still split between hip hop and the whole Manchester thing with the Roses, Mondays and the Inspirals. That was the thing though, even through being into the whole 'Madchester' scene I could tell there was some kind of cross over / shared ideal thing with house music since most indie twelve inches I bought would always have a remix from some house DJ. The Paul Oakenfold remix of Wrote For Luck from The Happy Mondays being one of my top tunes from the year before. I'd read in Melody Maker a quote about The Stone Roses album being the first 'Ecstasy rock' album, whatever the fuck that had actually meant. Same with all the gigs I'd been to in more recent times. You'd always have the warm up DJ playing a wee mix of dance and indie. Even if it was purely an indie band you were there to see.

Si being a few years older than me, he was way ahead on that front. I'm saying I like such and such a band and he's then telling me he saw them last year at The Venue in Edinburgh. I was saying how much I wished I'd been to Spike Island to see The Roses and not giving a fuck how bad the review was in the NME. Of course, he then replies. 'Me and a few of the other Utility boys went down to it. Fucking amazing, an unforgettable while UN-rememberable day. Couldn't hear a fucking thing from how far back we were by the way which pretty much defeats the purpose of going to a gig but fuck it, I can still say I was at Spike Island, Zico.' I had a mixture of jealousy and admiration for him.

I just sat there taking it all in while it appeared he'd already moved on from his trip to Widnes, or wherever the fuck Spike Island was located. 'Anyway, I'll have to give Pulsate a miss tonight which is just fucking shit, this DJ from down south is playing, I swear, this cunt, Carl Cox?, deejays with three decks' he said like I was meant to appreciate the significance of this, which I didn't. I could've sat there talking to him on the side the of the road for hours. I don't ever meet people like that in my everyday life so I'm always happy to talk for as long as we get the chance to.

Out of all of the Utility boys he's the one I'd kept an eye out for since Aberdeen, actually apart from the Fife boys who I've been training it up with each week there's not many regulars I'll talk to on match day. No sooner than the words 'You'll need to come to one of the parties with me mate and see for yourself, I know you're into your other music but trust me, come to one with me and see what you're saying a couple of hours into it.' Almost rudely, the cry went up from Nora, drawing our attention as well as everyone else.

'THESE ICF WANKERS ARE ALL DRINKING AT THE KING WILLIAM, OBVIOUSLY NOT IN A MOOD FOR COMING LOOKING FOR US SO LETS GO AND FUCKING PAY THEM A WEE VISIT' He shouted to what looked like a good hundred and fifty of us standing around. I of course had no fucking clue where the pub, The King William was but someone must've as we all set off on a course down the busy street. It's moments like that where you feel like you're a giant. Walking in a group like that miles from home and seeing the place come to a stand still with everyone looking at you. Nothing beats an awayday, nothing. I still couldn't believe that the police presence had been absolutely zero but then again this was Glasgow. Chances were there were so many other crimes being committed around the city that they weren't bothering about soccer casuals and were going to let them sort it out amongst themselves. Boys will be boys and all that. One theory I had was that because Dundee United only get a few thousand tickets the police wouldn't have been too concerned about looking out for them, forty eight thousand Rangers fans to contend with over the day is probably top of the pops in their main concerns when there's a game on at Ibrox.

It had always fascinated me. That moment on a Saturday afternoon when you knew you were minutes away from a potentially dangerous situation. You've got some that as they walk along that street who are stoney silent, visibly psyching themselves up for what's about to come and making sure they don't shite when 'that' moment arrives. Then you've got Simon, his shirt by now, ironically, looking like the fucking Rangers captain, Terry Butcher when he played for England last year against Sweden when by the time he left the pitch he looked like he'd been in The Texas Chainsaw Massacre. Blood dripping all over the place, speeding out his tits telling me all kinds of tales from these illegal parties while in all seriousness should be heading anywhere BUT in the direction of a fight.

I was never one of those silent psyching himself types though. I saw that whole 'what or who's going to be around this corner' side of things as curious and intriguing rather than scary. I think that was why I must've stuck out to everyone in the crew, or the ones who mattered at least. Life growing up hadn't exactly been by the numbers in the sense that most other kids with their mum and dad and two other siblings and all of that. I'd had to roll with so many punches over the years it had been like I'd gone up against a tag team of Ali, Frazier, Bruno and marvellous Marvin fucking Hagler. Through all of this, by this point in life I'd developed a right case of not giving a fuckness and I guess it had its advantages like when it came to being a hoolie.

Chapter 12.

Be careful what you wish for. That's the expression isn't it? A saying never more applicable for when we were getting kicked all over the place outside The King William by, what was a pretty fucking good sized ICF mob although these snake bastards moved the goalposts on us. We had turned the corner to see them up ahead congregating outside the boozer. Upon making them out, Nora and Dawson turned round to everyone to gee them all up. 'COME ON THEN UTILITY, UNLEASH HELL YA CUNTS' Dawson shouted to everyone as he bounced up and down on the spot like he was on a trampoline. A stoney faced Nora then chipped in, with a bit of a sneer and chilling tone 'And it goes without saying, no fucking runners' before he turned round and started to jog down the street with everyone else following.

As we got closer I could see that the ICF were boasting a much bigger mob than I ever would have imagined going by previous meetings with them. Weirdly my bottle almost went there and then when the thought entered my mind that we were running towards such numbers. Actually, looking at what we were running towards it was nothing short of lunacy. As we got closer still I was starting to clock some of the clothes that they were wearing and that's when I sussed that it wasn't just going to be a case of casual on casual here. These bastards had all the typical mannies from the pub alongside them who'd no doubt had a few drinks and weren't slow in being up for a fight with the so called opposite fans.

I could say that this was against the rules but then again, what WERE the rules? You had to be prepared for anything, cunts can be unpredictable, especially fucking Weegies. Aye, I'm sure when someone pulls a knife on you and you tell them that it's against the rules they'll then swiftly apologise before putting their knife back in their pocket, rolling their sleeves up and squaring up to you fist to fist. Code or no code all I knew was that we were now full scale running down the road towards a healthy sized mob who appeared to have already known we were on our way.

About a dozen of them were holding pool cues and I could see that some others were already starting to pick up some tables and chairs that were positioned outside of the pub. Having the advantage of being drinking outside a watering hole they weren't short on bottles of beer either and with us almost at them by now they weren't shy in sending them our way. When I saw them flying through the air I quickly pulled my hood up on my coat, thinking that if I was going to get one smashed on my head then that might be the difference between a head gash or not, and kept running with my head down until all the bottles had landed and smashed.

Once we got face to face with each other it was a fight like I'd never seen before and truth be told, had that been my first experience fighting for the Utility then it would have been my fucking last! Normally there's always x amount of lads in a mob whose arse will drop and when that happens the other group automatically has the upper hand. Not here. If it had been an actual fitba match then it would be described as a 'cup tie' … Two teams who aren't going to give an inch against each other. It was just a sea of jinking, dancing and toppling bodies all over the place with an intimidating and expletive filled soundtrack playing over top of it.

I didn't run but have to admit I was placed on the back foot. Everywhere I looked there was some cunt kicking the living shit out of someone else. Tools were being aimlessly used, the pub had been emptied of its pool cues and were making perfect weapons to brutal effect. This being Glasgow also which is the blade capital of Scotland, there was also the very real risk of one of these sly bastards pulling one out on you, something that sickeningly I'd find out later on that they had.

To be fair, had we been able to retreat and get ourselves to fuck we might well have done but once it all kicked off we ended up surrounded, completely ambushed likes. Nowhere to run to baby, nowhere to hide. With that we had no choice but to stand our ground and quite literally fight for our lives or else we'd have been in some proper trouble. While I was standing there on edge, looking for my next target I must've paused too long because some cunt in a Stone Island, King Billy of orange coloured (of course) jacket came at me from the side, cracking the butt end of a pool cue across my head knocking me to the ground. The kicks followed, into multiple parts of my body from more than one ICF. Self preservation kicked in and all I could do was curl up into a ball. I'd been in that position before and always fought back but there was too many of them. All I could do was pray that it didn't continue for too long, reasoning that in these moments no one gets carte blanch in terms of time before something else comes along to interrupt them. It had seemed like minutes the kicks had been going into me but was probably thirty seconds tops before they stopped. Each one had felt more painful than the one previous. I can't really class it as much fun.

I cautiously released my arms from over my head and opened my eyes to see the cunt in the orange Stone Island on his arse with Si jumping up and down on his head. It was actually quite intense to see and for a few seconds I felt sorry for the guy until I remembered that he wasn't exactly scrupulous when it came to trying to take my head off with a pool cue. Si was some boy likes, most probably suffering from some kind of head trauma from earlier yet there he is, like a kid in a candy store. Well that was until two ICF came along, shoving him off their mate and started firing into Si accordingly.

I tried to get up but what must've been from the pool cue, when I stood up I got a shooting pain through my head that felt like it was going to explode. This leading to me ending up back on my arse again. Before I could even get a chance to process it all I took a vicious boot to the face from some, what must've been, fifty plus year old man in a Rangers shell suit, sending me spark out on the deck.

I came round to the sight of a couple of Utility who I half recognised but didn't know to talk to, crouching over me, one slapping my face trying to get me to come round. 'Come on mate, filth are on their way' one of them said urgently - I could hear the sound of police sirens getting closer. 'Where the fuck were they when we needed them' I thought to myself then instantly shook my head over the fact I'd even thought such an unlikely thing in the first place. They helped me up to my feet but Jesus, I was in a bad way. I could barely open one eye as it had puffed up from the kick from the cunt in the shell suit. My head was throbbing from the blow from the pool cue but looking round me there were scores of Utility who had taken the same punishment, some far worse than me.

The ICF and their support act had moved back over towards the outside of the pub but were fucking revelling in the fact that they'd without question 'done us.' We didn't fucking run though and if these cunts had any shred of decency, something, which I wouldn't stick a single pound on at the bookies by the way. They'd recognise the fact that we stood and went for it with them even when we knew we were in a bad spot. Moral victory my friend, well that's what we'd all tell ourselves when traveling home licking our wounds over how badly wrong it had all went.

I had never seen us take such a pasting in my life, actually I'd never seen us GIVE out such a beating either. This had been on another planet as far as Saturday afternoon violence. Savage, vicious, unforgiving and I'm going to admit fucking terrifying. A side to casual life that I'd never experienced it and had shaken me up a bit. Not that I was going to be outwardly admitting that to anyone, of course. Once it had passed and the police now on the scene making a show of separating both groups in what was a classic example of someone shutting the stable door while their horse was miles down the road. Our bravado could kick in again, well, kind of. A quick scan around us and the state we'd been reduced to was like the scene of after one of those battles back in the day between Scotland and England. Bannockburn, Culloden and all that stuff. Men nursing wounds, aches and pains all over the place. Some in need of a trip to hospital, others with the type of injury that would largely be walked off by the time we got marching again towards the subway station.

The plan "had" been to see if we could meet the ICF before the match .... go for a few drinks during the ninety minutes and then see if we could get at them again after full time but the prospect of that happening was completely fucked now. Walking away from The King William with the jeers and laughter spewing in our direction from all those blue nosed cunts outside it, I went looking for Si. I had suddenly got the flashback of the last time I'd seen him when he'd disappeared, set on by a couple of ICF. Didn't take long for me to spy that distinctive and boy now, bespoke Burberry check. Walking along, trying to smoke a fag with a burst mouth covered in blood, one of his eyes starting to swell up a cracker.

When he saw me moving between a few others to get over to him, casual as fuck and like he'd just been out for an afternoon stroll in the park he simply smiled and issued a friendly 'alright?' in my direction. Once he saw me up closer though? 'Fucks sake, Zico you look like you've seen better days, brother' Looking me up and down, hood still up while the fabric has been ripped at the neck, eye looking like I've done twelve rounds at Caesars Palace, jeans covered in the dirt of the street, the suede of my Adidas Hamburgs looking like a herd of elephants had paraded all over them. 'Aye well, Si, it would be a lot easier to see better days if i could see out of both fucking eyes, mate' I replied laughing at the irony of the statement. 'And anyway? Have you seen the fucking nick of you? Fucking Terry Butcher stood there in what used to be a Burberry shirt, commenting on the state of me is some pot and kettle stuff' Looking down at his shirt and general state of him he couldn't help but offer a wry smile back.

'Right anyway, we're getting you to a hospital, you obviously need stitches on your head, maybe I can get some cunt to open this eye for me when we're there, two for one likes' I asserted, despite the fact I didn't exactly feel like I was in any position to be assertive with Si. He waved me away in a 'yeah yeah yeah, in a while' kind of fashion saying that he was going to wait until he got back to Dundee and would get a taxi up to to Ninewells and get it looked at before he went home. He figured that he'd rather sit for (most likely) hours in an accident and emergency room a lot nearer to home than have to get a train back home at god knows what time on his own.

Understanding that way of thinking I dropped the subject once and for all. Confirming that I wouldn't be bothering with my eye, hardly accident and emergency worthy although from a vague look at myself in a shop window I'd passed, I already knew my family were going to go mental when they saw me on my return home. Then there was Lisa and I knew that was going to go either of two ways. She would either look on me as trouble and best to steer clear of or I was going to cop some serious sympathy from her over the next week or so. As we walked I heard Nora's raised voice a wee bit up ahead so left Si talking to a couple of the lads from Fintry while I moved up ahead to catch him. Taking one look at me he just smiled 'respect young Jedi' he said before giving me a huge bear hug. 'FUCKING SEE THIS' he shouted for everyone while pointing at me 'WEE BASTARD ISN'T EVEN OUT OF SCHOOL YET AND LOOK AT THE LICKING HE TOOK FOR US RATHER THAN RUN, THIS IS WHAT WE'RE ALL ABOUT, FUCKING THIS.'

It looked like he was off on some fucking motivational speech but as soon as he entered into it he stopped again and turned back to me. 'Fucking sore one today though, Zico' he said which would've had more effect and impact were it not for the fact that he did not have one single hair out of place. How was that even possible considering what we'd all had to deal with for those ten frantic and volatile minutes? 'No going to lie, mate. We were meant to be sticking around until later but fucking hell, look around you. Nah, let's just get ourselves back, circle the wagons and we'll be ready for these cunts next year. The season's about done so it's time to put our feet up, rest and recuperate and be fresh for the challenge next season' It could almost have been a quote, found in that nights Evening Telegraph coming from Jim McLean, the United manager after full time following, what would turn out to be, a comprehensive 4-1 defeat to Rangers over the next few hours.

After what I'd faced outside The King William and the battle scars I was now carrying afterwards. The end of the season honestly couldn't come quick enough for me.

Chapter 13.

I don't think that you really can ever really prepare for losing your virginity. How can you when you have basically no point of reference to work with? I thought that it would be no harder than a case of having watched a porn film then just copying what you've seen and putting it into practice. Life doesn't work like that though does it? Fuck, if that was the case everyone would be able to watch Diego Maradona play fitba and then go out onto the pitch themselves and copy the little Argentinian magician.

It had been a subject that after the first month of dating, Lisa and I had started to speak about. Obviously I'd decided to steer clear of trying to get something off her in the first few dates. Aye, most of that had been driven by not wanting to chase her away too soon. There was an element though of me being nervous about it all too. Without mentioning it to me I think that she had started to pick up on it. Considering she'd most likely expected me to be trying to get into her pants from the first night and then weeks later still nothing? It was probably something that was beginning to stick out for her. Fuck? Maybe she had even started to take it personally?! That it had been a sign that possibly I wasn't that into her?

I can't really speak for anyone else round about my age of course but I had so much worries attached to it all. What if I didn't do it right? What if I COULDN'T do it? Would she laugh at me? Maybe she'd think my cock was too small? What if I ended up putting it in the wrong fucking hole by accident? The list of worries were endless.

Lisa being the confident type in general had outright asked me if I was a virgin one night when we were lying there talking on her bed, kissing and cuddling. Of course I lied, who the hell admits to being a virgin? I'd been too embarrassed to say otherwise but I was most likely fooling nobody. She admitted to me that she'd had sex a couple of times but well, that was a couple of times more than moi. I admit I was a wee bit gutted that she'd already lost her virginity before me. As unrealistic as it was for me to think that way considering she'd been running around with guys with their own cars. I'd kind of held out some hope for the Hollywood fairy story where two teenagers in love were going to pop their cherry together. The scenario where they would both learn along with each other. It was something that had actually affected me for a couple of days until I managed to get past it.

The two of us had done nothing more than dry runs up in her bedroom, always stopping from going any further due to her mum and dad being downstairs. As far as a natural progression for two people going out with each other though it was something that was going to have to happen, sooner or later. I almost make it sound like a chore like doing the dishes or something but I really don't mean it that way. A more accurate way for how I felt about it would be to liken it to a band about to go off on a world tour. They're possibly a little nervous about that first gig and how it will go while knowing that once they get that initial one out of the way things will become more natural from that point on.

One night through the week I'd been up at hers to chill and watch a video. Somehow her dad had managed to get a pirated copy of Die Hard 2 (which hadn't even been out at the cinema yet) from someone at his work so we planned to watch it up in her room. It was a complete farce though, it looked like someone had shot it while sitting inside a cinema. Most of the time you could see peoples heads bobbing around in front of the screen. At one point you weren't able to see ANY of the film because of two people walking past on their way to buy a fucking ice cream! We gave up in the end as it wasn't worth watching. Instead, we stuck on some Eric B & Rakim and lay chatting.

That's when she broke the news that on the coming Saturday her mum and dad were going out during the night to some wedding. Some girl that Vera, Lisa's mum, worked beside was getting married so Bob and her had been invited to the reception in the evening. I can't even quantify into words how cute and bashful Lisa was while telling me this while trying not to overtly say what opportunity this house to ourselves was going to present to the both of us.

I picked up on what she was getting at after a few moments and when I did I started to fill with the most eclectic mixture of feelings that went from excitement to happiness then onto relief which soon turned to dread before back to excitement again.

At no point did she or I blatantly come right out and say that we'd take this golden opportunity of alone time to 'do it' … Neither of us really had to. It was obvious.

'With mum and dad being out all night and us having the house to ourselves I was just wondering if you …… wanted to come up here Saturday night?'

The way she said it to me and the look on her face as she done so? The pause between "you" and "wanted." I heard her loud and clear. Despite not being someone who is backwards at coming forwards she still said it in such a shy and innocent way. Almost as if she thought there would be a chance that I would say no to her.

The Saturday afternoon I had been a bag of nerves. Actually, from the moment I woke that morning the very FIRST thing that popped into my head had been the fact that by the end of the day I would no longer be a virgin. It was a thought that stayed with me all day long. I travelled up to Dundee for the match as always but my mind wasn't remotely close to being in tune with running around looking to batter the fuck out of some other mob of casuals.

Luckily it wasn't exactly a day that promised such anyway. We were playing Dunfermline Athletic, not a side that was renowned for having any kind of reputable crew to speak of. Well, not in my opinion anyway. I know they've had their problems with Hibs but then again, who hasn't? By around two there had been no sign of any from their side having even travelled to Dundee. The spotters down at the station had come up with zilch when it came to the few trains that had arrived with their fans from Fife. The same with the supporters buses that had arrived in the city. Apart from a few hundred fans all decked out in club merchandise like fucking Christmas trees there was no sign of anyone. It looked like we had the day off. This suited me fine if not the rest of the boys who had felt robbed of a day of the obligatory violence.

I went and watched the match like any other supporter in what was nothing other than a routine 3-0 victory against a side that we are generally expected to take care of when playing them. I'd taken a bit of good natured banter from some the boys in the crew when asking one of them if they could get me some johnnies from the machine situated in the toilets inside The Snug.

'Oh aye? Feeling lucky today are you?' Dawson said when he overheard me asking Hunter to get me some as I handed him the money. Nora catching onto this shouted louder than I really appreciated 'Nah, he's just wanting some balloons to play with, gonnae stick one over your head and blow it up, aye?'

I could feel my face starting to turn scarlet at this sensitive and unwanted attention and without really thinking lurched right onto the defensive.

'Nah mate, I've got a date with your mum tonight. Didn't she tell you that you've to get yourself something from the chippy for your tea tonight since she's going to be too busy to cook'

It was out before I even realised and I instantly regretted saying it. Being cheeky to Nora was not something I'd been a stranger to. Jesus, the first time I met him or even knew who he was or what a dangerous individual he could be I had been like that to him. I think in a certain way he actually admired that but making a comment about his mum, in front of others, I felt was probably too far. Everyone else stood around drinking immediately burst out laughing, he didn't. If the look he flashed me was anything to go by then it told me that he would be having a word at some point about it. Actually if looks could kill then I'd have surely died there on the spot. Dying a virgin!

On the train journey back down the road I barely said a word to Brewster, Carey and McGinn. I was completely miles away. Wondering to myself how Lisa was feeling on her end. Was she as nervous as I was? Excited? Fearful? Of course, it was something "to" look forward to. Something that two people with feelings towards each other "should" be excited about. Fear of the unknown can do certain things to a person though.

You could've cut the atmosphere with a knife when she closed the door behind us when I arrived at her house that evening. We'd been nothing other than completely cool with each other since we'd started going out together. This felt different. I don't know what I looked like but I could see straight away that she appeared nervous around me. Unlike every other time visiting her house, instead of heading straight up to her bedroom she took me through to the living room. An area of the house that apart from that first night of me visiting when she brought me through to say hello to her parents, I'd barely seen much of. She already had a glass of wine poured for herself and a bottle of Becks sat there waiting for me arriving.

We sat talking about how our day had been. I told her how the football had went while she took me through what she'd been up to which had been a trip into town with a friend to buy make up and go for a spot of lunch. It was obvious that we had other things on our mind however. Half an hour in though and we had both began to loosen up a little. Alcohol always does that. Such a leveller! I'd sank the bottle of German beer in no time and noticing this she was straight through to the kitchen to get me another.

Once she came back through with another beer for me I'd barely had a sip of it before we'd started to kiss each other a little and, not unlike any other time up in her bedroom, began to let our hands wander. It was then that, from somewhere, I managed to find enough confidence to suggest that maybe we should head up to her bedroom to get more comfortable. Gah, what a fucking cliche it was and in truth was something I'd seen in about a hundred films and TV shows before. Nothing more than a template like cliche but in that moment it was all that I had.

She smiled back and agreed that yes maybe going upstairs would be the best idea before we started to get ourselves settled downstairs. Taking my hand she got up from the sofa and led me upstairs. Once her bedroom door closed behind us I started to kiss her again while running my hands up and down the sides of her body, occasionally slightly grabbing her arse but without any kind of confidence whatsoever. The kissing started to become more deeper and frantic and in doing so I could feel things starting to stir down below. This was something that I celebrated privately in my thoughts as one of the fears that I'd held was that I was going to be too nervous to even get a fucking hard on.

As we progressed, this led to her taking the bull by the horns and removing her jeans while her top half remained fully clothed. I done the opposite by gingerly taking off my t shirt. I wasn't sure if I was meant to follow her lead by taking off my jeans first too but had been too nervous about doing so. Before long though all our clothes were lying in a heap on the floor. The two of us fully naked. With this it had seemed to signal a race for us to get ourselves under her duvet as quick as humanly possible. We barely even got a chance to fully see each other in such a vulnerable state of undress before we had found the relative safety of underneath the sheets.

Her naked body against mines felt fucking amazing though and I could feel that just having her pressed tight to me was making me even harder than before when we had both been dressed. We lay there kissing frantically with our hands running all over each other. With more confidence, which had seemed to come from somewhere I started to fondle her tits and reaching round grabbing at her bare arse. Soon I felt her hand tentatively rubbing against my cock. It had been the first time that I'd ever felt anyone touch it other than myself and I thought for one worrying moment that I was going to come there and then when I felt her hand take a grip of it. Since she had "went there" I decided that I should reciprocate this by moving my hand between her legs and began to rub her fanny with a couple of fingertips.

She moaned slightly when I started doing this which I took only as a good sign. That I was doing something right at least. Our tongues danced around each other as our hands continued to do their own thing. That was when, unintentionally I found a couple of my fingers sliding inside of her. She felt wet inside, really wet. Nice and warm and as far as I knew, ready for what was meant to come next.

My mind was racing by that point but I managed to rein things in a little.

Before we went any further I stopped kissing and touching her and instead just looked straight into her eyes in a way that I don't think I'd ever done with anyone before in such a sincere way and asked 'Are you ready?'

'Yes, Stevie. Please … I'm ready. I want this' she replied smiling before kissing me again deeper than at any point she'd ever done since we had started going out.

Just as I was about to begin, it then hit me … THE FUCKING CONDOM! In amongst everything I had completely forgotten all about the three pack of Durex "ribbed for her pleasure" that were still sitting in the pocket of my jeans that had been purchased from the Dundee boozer earlier on. I was worried that with us coming so far I was then about to upset the whole rhythm and order of things. Having to stop again to get back out of bed and go looking for my jeans to find the fucking things. I didn't really have any other choice though.

'Two ticks' I excitedly said before quickly leaving her for a second to go get them. This I admit "did" alter things slightly because in the time that it took for me to go and get them from my jeans, open the box and grab one out of the three pack I could feel my hardness starting to dip again. Ripping open the foil to remove that oily, greasy piece of rubber I could feel things dipping even further once more which had me apologising to her that now I "wasn't" ready. She told me not to worry and to come cuddle with her again and in no time things had went back to how they were before. Some of my earlier inhibitions had clearly disappeared because from being intentionally hidden under her duvet I was now kneeling on her bed in clear view of her while trying to put on the condom.

Trying, being the most of appropriate words because kneeling there I found that I wasn't sure which WAY I was meant to put the fucking thing on. It looked the same either side and with that I reckoned I had a half and half chance of putting it on correctly.

I can only guess that she had already had previous experience with them because lying there looking at me with one hand still hidden under the duvet which I took to mean that she was touching herself. She giggled but not in a nasty way and said 'Let me.' The way her eyes looked at me as she took in what I looked like as I towered above her was just so very fucking sexy. I'd started the evening with feelings of embarrassment in terms of letting her see me without my clothes on and yet now the way she was looking at me had me feeling completely at ease.

She took the condom from me and without hesitation placed it over the end of my cock and rolled it all the way down. I had worried that the thing would be loose on me but as she pulled it downwards it felt nice and tight like it had been designed by some Saville Row tailor to fit me and only me.

Lying back down again and with that cheeky confident smile I loved so much, she asked the same question that I'd initially put to her.

'Ready?'

I guess I'd been a little TOO ready because no sooner had we started than it was over again. Two minutes tops before I had came. Talk about an, Well, it's an unfortunate way to word it but, anticlimax. If that was my thoughts then fuck knows what Lisa had been thinking!

I had so many emotions through those two minutes though. Embarrassment over how quickly I had lasted ... Something that I quickly put down to AND across to Lisa over how excited I had been. Relief that I was now no longer a fucking virgin! Extreme pleasure over what it had felt like to ejaculate inside her and how much more different it had been to simple masturbating. This though was mixed with almost an anticlimactic feel of, after so many years of wondering and building up to having sex of ... Is that it? It really was such a compendium of thoughts and feelings to have. Still though, it was something that I was way glad to have done and one that I was already looking forward to trying again.

Which the two of us did again. Later that night after we'd had a few more drinks. The second time around was about a hundred fucking times better possibly even more. It had been almost like the first time had just been a dress rehearsal, while ironically "undressed," and the second time was the REAL thing.

I couldn't help but feel that the first time I had been a major disappointment to her but it had been evident from the look on her face and the sounds emitting from her that the second time Lisa had enjoyed so much more. As did I to be fair.

I headed down the road that night with a hop skip and jump like a fucking olympian with one of life's major boxes now ticked off. NOT. A. FUCKING. VIRGIN. ANYMORE.

Put that in your pipe and smoke it!! Yaaaaaaaaaaas

Chapter 14.

2 Months later …..

I really had no words of distinction that came anywhere close to fittingly describing how it was for me when I felt it all clicking into place. The combination of the music and recreational narcotics was like nothing ever experienced. I felt like everyone around me was beautiful, fresh, unharmed. Weirdly unspoiled. Like I knew every singe person around me and had no hesitation in flashing them a smile whenever we would make eye contact. It felt like the air around me was the cleanest I'd ever breathed in my entire life, kind of like we were all in a space and time that no one else in the world was living in. Only us.

We were there, on earth but in a completely out of world like place at the same time. I'd lost all track of my bearings a while back but it must've been around four, maybe five in the morning as I could see the sky getting lighter. Despite this, I'd never felt more awake, so alive. Stood in a farmers field, somewhere in Ayrshire, alongside which for all I know was around three to five thousand others. Massive strobe lights going off all over the place, dry ice drifting through us all like some soldier had thrown a smoke bomb into the mix, proper Vietnam stuff. A sea of smiles and happy faces all around me in a display of unity that I didn't know could ever exist between a large group of people.

The music, which at the start of the night had not been even close to being on my day to day of listening to, and the effect it had on me over the night and how it had made me feel at times? All of this, whatever "this" actually was because nothing could have been as good as it had been. It all added up to my epiphany that this hadn't been just "one of those nights" where you have a good time and then think, 'aye, I'd like to do this again sometime.' This felt worlds away compared to that standard feeling when you've had a top night somewhere doing just doing the standard things and stuff. This felt like one of those moments where people first heard The Beatles or The Sex Pistols.

When they were first blessed with Rappers Delight by The Sugar Hill Gang. To me it was like a new part of life had opened up to me within the space of a night. Almost like I'd discovered that there was an extra door inside my mind that until then I'd never bothered to open. Even 'different' didn't do it justice. The best way I can describe it is that by sixteen years old you think that you've seen it all in life, know about everything out there only one night you experience something that you didn't even look for because you never knew existed only to find out that actually, it does and it turns out to be only one of the most amazing and exciting things to ever enter your life. Well, times that all by a fucking hundred and you're still not even close but you're getting there.

The whole night, and morning had been, well I'm not quite sure. Was it a personal revolution or maybe an evolution, both? What was absolutely positively undeniable was that I'd felt 'something' a shift of sorts that I wasn't even able to fathom out because it was unlike anything I'd ever experienced. All I DID know was that there was not going to be any brief period of reflection on the impact of it all. I was absolutely smitten.

It had been a cracking summer. Pre season when it came to fitba so no United matches which equalled no fighting in any shape or form. If anything, it had been a summer of love. Lisa and I had really fallen right into each other and with no match day duties to worry about we'd spent most weekends together. Had almost been inseparable at times. If you'd have told me that before our first date, I'd have laughed in your face before calling you a taxi to take you up to Stratheden Mental Hospital to share a ward with Fife's finest nutjobs.

It had also been the summer of the exam results which I admit had come as a mixed bag on my part. Failed chemistry, badly which I thought was the height of irony considering I'd been getting really into my "chemicals" right around the time that I sat the standard grade test. Absolutely pissed my higher English though which out of the six exams I sat was the one I wanted to do well in the most. Couldn't help but love that fact that I got an A while writing about a day out at the fitba with the rest of the crew. I'd been sat the task of writing about a time I felt scared in my life so had ended up writing about an away day at Easter Road when United were paying Hibs in a midweek cup game.

I might be wrong but I'd hazard a guess that there couldn't have been too many exam submissions based around a violent encounter between two sets of soccer casuals. The rest of the results were so so, Social Studies had been a breeze even if I didn't even know what I was going to be able to do with such a qualification. Failed miserably at Food & Nutrition which to be fair wasn't a surprise considering I couldn't cook to fucking save my life. I only chose the fucking subject because it was going to be either that or History and there was a good chance I would get Mr Jenkins as my teacher. With him being a proper cunt of a teacher and all, I wasn't in the mood for rolling the dice so went with the cooking.

Lisa, the egghead that she is sailed every single one she took, bagging A's and B's over the six subjects that she sat. Evidently not just a pretty face that lassie. I was happy for her, she'd put the work in and got her reward. Me on the other hand had fucked about for most of school and had only really started to take it serious when it was too late like the hare in that hare and the tortoise story. All my own fault to be fair, if I'd had one report card saying I just needed to apply myself more because I was smart enough I'd had a million. Never listened though. Lisa on the other hand was now all set up for another year of school when the summer was over while that was me, gone and out into the big bad world.

Admittedly I'd not spent much of the summer actually "trying" to find a job for myself apart from a few enquiries here and there. A relative was a manager in the building trade and had told me that if I was interested there was an apprentice plumbers job coming up at some point in his department that he thought would be perfect for me. Get yourself a trade they all say eh? I guess through that knowledge it had taken the edge off my whole job seeking vibe, leaving me just to enjoy the summer, which I'd been making a decent stab out of doing. There had just been a good feeling about the country in general. The weather had been good which is anything but a fucking given in Scotland when it comes to summer. New exciting bands and styles of music were making their mark and changing some peoples attitudes accordingly. I don't know if it was all in the mind through it no longer "being" the eighties but it actually "felt" like it wasn't the decade anymore.

It had even been a World Cup year with Italia 90 which saw Scotland do reverting to type by playing three games before being pumped out and finding themselves back home before the players postcards had arrived to their families. As far as Scots go we also had the very real scare that England were going to get to the final until they lost to

Germany in the semi. That was a bit too close for comfort though. Fucking hell, as long as I can remember growing up. When World Cup year rolled around all we got rammed down our throat from the BBC and ITV was about England winning it in 1966 which Jesus Christ was so long ago you'd think the cunts would drop it by now so the LAST thing anyone in Scotland wanted or needed was England to go and win the fucking thing again.

Anyway, we'd been left to breathe again when Chris Waddle skied his kick in the dramatic penalty shootout in the semi final. Kicked the ball so far and wide it's probably still circling the globe right now. Was a great tournament though, some cool as fuck tops on some of the countries. My out and out favourite had been the Adidas one worn by the Germans which between you and I I'd have loved to have bought for myself but try and imagine wearing a fucking German top in front of your old Grandad? Mines would've ripped it off my back and thrown it in the fire if he'd clocked me in one. The war might've been a long time ago now but feelings still run deep you know? I don't think people my age fully appreciate what all those old hoors did for us.

I hadn't had any contact whatsoever with any of the Utility boys since the season had finished. No real reason to I suppose. I knew a group of them were all heading over to Amsterdam for a week of debauchery during the pre season. Nora had invited me along but something like that was never going to be a goer for me with the budget I was operating under. Good of him to ask likes and was a reminder where I stood with them that it was even put to me. I'd wondered over the summer how that had went.

Didn't know much about Amsterdam other than the obvious that everyone knows being the prostitutes and drugs, and tulips of course! The mind boggled though how they would all have gotten on over there with that combination of entertainment on offer. I think they were going to go to an Ajax pre season friendly when they were there to try and strike up some kind of an alliance with their group of casuals which might well have come in handy for the up and coming season's European campaign. We'd drawn the German side Cologne in the UEFA Cup and with Holland being next door to Germany it might well have meant some much needed back up to call on as from what I gather Holland and Germany are every bit as bad as Scotland and England when it comes to rivalry. Proper Ike & Tina stuff.

I'd been enjoying the break from all the thug side of things and while, like any other fitba supporter, had been missing the matches each week. I hadn't been missing the fighting side of things. Don't get me wrong, I loved it as much as the next man but it had all gotten too intense towards the end of the season. That trip through to Govan when we got our arses handed to us was too much and the chance to recharge the batteries was a welcomed one.

It was around mid July one evening when out of the blue, sitting up in my bedroom playing Streets of Rage on the Mega Drive my Auntie shouted upstairs to me that someone was on the phone. Wrongly assuming that it was Lisa calling for a chat which I always found bittersweet because I loved speaking to her but not so much doing so while sat in the living room with the family listening. I found that there was no such thing as a private chat under those circumstances. Still though I always told myself that there was a time I'd have donated my left ball to Hitler to have been able to have Lisa Hopkins call me so couldn't really complain that much. Walking into the living room I made for the phone while asking her in a taking for granted way if it was Lisa.

'No, it's some laddie, Simon he says' she answered before turning back to watch the TV. Her and my uncle were sat watching Coronation Street, an institution in the house, well for them anyway and if there was one thing I knew it was NOT to disturb them during it so I already knew that someone calling during it would have been an inconvenience. An inconvenience in the sense that they'd be wanting to eavesdrop on the conversation, especially since this was a person they didn't know on the phone, but wouldn't be able to listen to me without missing out on what was being said on the telly. For a split second I didn't even know who "Simon" was but before picking up the receiver the lightbulb went on that it was Si. We'd exchanged numbers near the end of the season but hadn't actually called one another yet.

'What's happening, Si?' I asked, genuinely happy to hear from him. There was so many things I wanted to and could've said to him but ninety nine percent of it involved subjects that I'd rather not have voiced while beside family so played it safe. 'Not much, Zeec, bored out of my tits without the fitba being on just now' he replied back. 'Aye, same here, can't come back quick enough' I agreed. 'Listen, man, what you up to this Saturday night?' He asked, doing away with the pleasantries and cutting right to the chase. 'Emmm not much I don't think, just doing something with my girlfriend, likes' I said, intrigued by where this was going and what his intentions were.

'Well, Shan and I are heading through to an allnighter somewhere on the West Coast on Saturday, going to be a top night and I wanted to see if you fancied coming through with us, mate' - I knew we'd spoken about it previously back in Glasgow about the whole indie and house music links but I'd not really thought about it too much more than the few days following the Rangers match. I wasn't exactly moving in the same circles as those who were part of this secret society of party people and there certainly wasn't any of these allnighters going on in my own backyard so yeah, it hadn't really been something that was much of an issue to me. I was initially hesitant to accept and told him I didn't know and asked if I could think about it for a few days leading up to the Saturday.

Si wasn't for taking no for an answer though in that way that your friends can be like when they're trying to persuade you to do something. 'Look, you trust me right? You and I have been through the fucking trenches together, Zico' as we strayed into the territory of conversation that I wasn't going to be able to reciprocate while within earshot of my folks. 'Well, no denying that, Si' I said diplomatically in an attempt at answering him but not going down the road of talking about it any more in depth. 'Well then, that's sorted, I'll give you a bell on Saturday morning to sort the plans out' he laughed before saying he had to go, barely giving me a chance to even say anything before he hung up again leaving me stood there with the receiver still in my hand trying to process how he had just managed to persuade me. Well, if you could call it that as I couldn't remember at any point actually saying fucking yes to him!

Of course, I was now going to have to pitch this to Lisa which that alone was quite possibly going to be a hard sell depending on how I pitched it to her and that was the thing. I didn't know HOW to.

This was something so far removed from anything either of the two of us had indulged in since starting to go out. There was no point of reference I even had to give her. While both still being under the legal drinking age we'd still managed to go out a few times to a couple of pubs that were known in the area for being lax with underage drinkers so long as they were close to passing for eighteen years old. We had already broken ground with that but this was an entirely proposition altogether. To ensure I had all facts in hand I called Si back later on that night to ask him a few questions about Saturday so I would be equipped for when the inevitable questions were fired back at me from Lisa.

He told me that it was a big all night party on a disused farm somewhere in Ayrshire although he couldn't give me much more intel on that side of things. With this all being very much under the radar of the authorities, most of the details were being kept back until nearer the time to insure that no information would end up in the hands of the police. This in itself made perfect sense once explained to me, it also provided me with a small buzz knowing how exclusive and illegal it was. He told me that the rumours were that Fabio & Grooverider (whoever the fuck they were) had been booked and that the night was going to be the best yet since Acid House had hit Scotland.

I asked if it would be cool to bring Lisa as I wouldn't be able to go otherwise and Si said this actually suited as his girlfriend, Shan, would have another girl to talk to over the night about 'whatever shite girls talk about'. Apart from what I felt was stating the obvious having now learned it was outdoors and all night long he reminded me that we'd need to have some warm clothing for later on in the morning but apart from that there really wasn't that much to tell me in advance.

He'd left me intrigued about it all, I'll give him that and it had been all I'd thought of over the night. Part of the attraction to it was actually the prospect of having a night out with him as the two of us seemed to get each other in ways that surpassed just being in the same group of football hooligans. The thought of hooking up but without the added edge of there being violence around the corner appealed. I just had the less than small matter of bringing it up with Lisa to see if I could get her on board. I mean? Girls like to be wined and dined, treated like they're a princess, put your coat down on a puddle to stop them from getting their shoes wet and all of that shite don't they? Instead she was going to be taken on a night out that involved standing in a field all night until sunrise, listening to music she didn't understand in a setting where the chances were she might bump into a cow or a sheep in the toilets, if there even WAS toilets.

'So let me get this straight, Stevie? You want the two of us to to go across to the other side of Scotland to stay up all night and hang around in a farmers field listening to all that bleepy music?' She appeared far from convinced. 'Well, considering that there's thousands all over Britain doing the very same thing, babe I have to imagine that there's a lot more to it than just that. I totally get what you're saying, how mental does it even sound to spend a night in a field but the fact some people are, it kind of leaves me a wee bit curious to find out WHY?'

I hit her back with a beauty of a reply, tapping into Lisa's psyche of hating it when someone knew something that she didn't. In these cases she automatically would then try to find out. I say "Lisa's psyche" but that was just birds in general, nosey bastards, the lot of them! I could see the cogs turning inside her head. Like me she had no real way to imagine what it would be like, had nicks to help guide her in the direction of being able to make a decision apart from her curiosity. Then came the questions, most involving what the party would be like, what other girls wore there, could we buy drink there or would we have to take some with us, with it being a field would there be toilets, all questions I had no answer to.

She then started asking about Si, who he was and why I'd never mentioned him before until this out of the blue proposition. Almost fucking tripped myself up as well by answering that he was in the same crew as me. 'Crew?' What crew?' She asked before I managed to save things by explaining the Dundee United supporters, putting it across that all the supporters fell under the same umbrella of sorts. Lisa, knowing ride all about fitba wasn't going to question such a thing. I told her that him and I had seen each other on a lot of away trips and one day got chatting on the train and had been pals ever since in the sense of a weekend pal only due to how far away he stayed. Added that his girlfriend was going too so it could be like some double date.

She asked if she could take a while to think about it but she needn't have bothered as I already knew she'd be going by the time I kissed her goodnight at her front door.

Saturday's plans had dominated the next few days, was never off the fucking phone to Si to the point that I was starting to worry that he was beginning to regret asking me in the first place. Most of the calls were because Lisa was asking more questions before the night arrived which he, being someone in the same position before he'd went to one, understood completely. The question about what to wear, while coming from her was actually a pretty valid question. The past couple of years had taught me that to go somewhere else in Scotland wearing the type of gear I did, could cause a problem depending on who you bumped into and considering we were going to the West Coast who the fuck knows who you would potentially come across there.

'Well tell her not to wear a dress and heels for fucking starters, Zico' he laughed down the phone while stating the obvious before going on to give me the low down of what the dress code was for these things ..there wasn't one! 'I know this sounds the exact opposite of the way you and I normally live and how labels are everything to us but at these parties no one gives a fuck what anyone's got on, no judging at all. Take me, look at what you'll see me on our Saturday capers with the Utility? Well the last night I was at I wore a pair of Air Jordan shorts, a hoodie and a battered pair of Adidas ZX450'S on, looked a fucking mink whilst not caring one jot about it either.

Never mind the fact that yeah, he did sound like he was seriously dressed down for the boy that I would imagine going on a night out but I was more taken aback by the shorts side of things. 'Weren't you fucking freezing all night in a pair of shorts?' I had to ask. Despite this being over the phone I could actually sense him shaking his head at me after that question. 'Just trust me on this mate,' everything that you might think is all a bit radio rental about this will all make sense when you're there on Saturday.'

Chapter 15.

I could barely sleep the night before through the excitement. I was at that stage in life where I was enthusiastically trying out new things in all ways. I'd been to gigs, started to experiment with alcohol and drugs, experimenting with sex. Both feet firmly in that period of not quite being a fully fledged adult but nowhere near to being considered a bairn anymore by the family and my peers.

I was taking to this new life of freedom where I was able to make my own choices like a duck to water but this outdoor Acid House party could well be the most new and left field of experiences, I thought to myself as I lay there tossing and turning in bed.

I was wondering about how Lisa was feeling on her side, I knew that she was excited about it. This, a complete hundred and eighty degree flip from how she was initially when I first asked her if she'd like to go. The two of us had went into town for her to get something new to wear for it. After me taking her through the dress code that really wasn't a dress code at all it didn't take her long to decide how she wanted to attend her first all nighter.

Soon she was dragging me along with her to go shopping which I admit I hardly needed my arm twisted since I wanted to look for a few potential things to wear myself. I came back with the paradoxical mix of a pair of baggy Gio Goi shorts and a new Adidas cagoule figuring it might come in handy if it rained during the night. Yes, while i was also wearing shorts! My bottom half going to the beach while my top half is going for a walk up Salsbury Crags. Lisa, also getting exactly what she set out to buy, a figure hugging black catsuit which, having modelled it for me in the shop, looked unbelievable on her. She reckoned a catsuit and a pair of Adidas Superstars on her feet would be just the ticket for this type of deal and looking as amazing as she did I could not argue. That was one of the things I loved about her though, she had the ability to look shit hot whatever she would wear. She could be wearing her jammies and a pair of Kicker boots, a Tom Weir woolly hat and still make it work.

One recurring thought that I hadn't shifted since agreeing to go had been the subject of drugs. Obviously Simon and myself had a shared interest in them since the day we met in the train carriage going to

Aberdeen and had indulged in every match we seen each other since but from what he'd told me. Drugs were a much ingrained part in these gatherings and went hand in hand with the music itself. The music apart, it's clearly obvious through basic common sense that if people are staying up all night and dancing for around twelve hours then they're most likely shopping at the same pharmacy as Ben Johnson.

I assumed, through Si I'd get a chance to stick my finger into his obligatory bag of powder or something but what about Lisa? We'd never really spoken about drugs. I'd been so focussed on not doing or saying anything that would potentially drive her away in the very early days of us starting to see each other. I had conveniently neglected to mention to her that I was a soccer casual and had been experimenting with speed and smoking Hash. How was it going to go down if I ended up out my nut at the rave and that being Lisa's introduction to the "other side" of me that was developing? I'm really one of those cross that bridge when I get to it types so trusted in the fact that it would all work out, somehow.

I eventually dropped off with one final thought following me turning to check the time on my bedside clock. 2.47AM the red LED digits glowed back at me ..... 'What the fuck will life be like in twenty four hours time?' my final thought.

The day had dragged in while waiting on Si coming to collect us both. I couldn't concentrate on fuck all, struggled to start a meal never mind finish one although one of the things that he had mentioned more than once like it was super important was to get a good meal inside me for the night ahead. He had told me to tell Lisa too which I did while receiving a reply of 'Who does he think he is? My mum?!' The local pub team were playing a friendly against The Crown from Burntisland up at Central Park so I took a trip up there to kill some hours and get a laugh in the way you only get while watching twenty two overweight untalented men masquerading as soccer players out on a pitch. Cento, Kif, Davie Lessels and Rab Prenton were stood near the halfway line watching so I stood having a blether with them. Hearing their tales of what they'd been up to the night before.

Where they'd been drinking, who they'd been shagging. Most of them were already half pished after starting drinking again by lunch time. Cento was taking major pelters from the rest over the fact that he fell asleep in the corner of The Royal down in Leven while everyone else had upped and left him there. Passed out with about twenty beer mats, an ashtray, an empty packet of Benson & Hedges and half a pint of special balanced on his head and a cock drawn in lipstick on his forehead with a tampon hanging out his mouth while they all went to The Caley for another drink. Rab Prenton was in the middle of asking me if I'm coming out with them for a swally after the match.

Before I could answer him, The Crown's number six, this fat guy who despite the game only having kicked off a few minutes previously, looked like he was blowing out his arse so much that his complexion was taking on the form of a beetroot. He looked like one of the Ribena men from the drinks commercial. This number six has taken out Deek McConnville, knee height, almost surgically removing his left peg, a right bad one.

This resulted in Harry Ferguson the team captain running over and grabbing this beetroot face cunts throat and pinning him to the ground. Cue bedlam. Both sets of players waded in, engaging in private wee scuffles and pushing sessions but it was all handbags really. The same shite you see in the professional games too, all fronting from players who know that there's no chance they're going to get a pasting from the other player, not with all the fans and TV cameras watching likes.

Once it all got broken up Deek was still lying on the deck in agony in a crumpled up mess with the quote unquote team doctor attending to him with the Ralgex and magic sponge. The referee who, unless I'm mistaken should always be neutral with a sense for the impartial but here instead, was a guy I see all the fucking time sat in The Central drinking is standing there with the red card out. He held it up to the fat number six who was still trying to get his breath back after Harry almost asphyxiating him.

Ribena man looked almost relieved to get sent off judging by the look on his face as he exited the pitch to various laughs and jeers from the smattering of what spectators were stood watching. He'd only played ten minutes tops and was borderline heart attack plus one of the opposing players had tried to strangle him, that's no way to spend a Saturday afternoon is it?! Once it died down Rab and I got back to our conversation that had been so rudely interrupted by the brief melee. 'Nah I'm off to Ayrshire tonight' I said before then fielding the questions that would follow from saying something random like that. Ayrshire not exactly being widely viewed as the mecca of fun times at the weekend.

He looked at me like I was a fucking alien by the time he'd taken on board where I was going and for what purposes before inevitably bringing the others into it. 'Heard where this cunt's going tonight' Rab said with loud intention and once sure of an audience, continued. 'He's driving two and a half hours to stand in a field listening to some cunt playing records, not bands or fuck all by the way, just a fucking DJ, and will be there til the mora morning, eight-o-fucking clock in the morning?! You'll be doing the walk off shame home from some slut's house Kif and this daft cunt will be standing in a fucking field' 'I worry about you, Zico' Rab Lessells chipped in shaking his head. I took it well, telling them that they'd all be doing it in a years time when I had moved onto something else again. That, a bold statement from me considering technically, I didn't know what I was really talking about myself.

'I very much doubt that, mate' wee Kif laughed back 'As if I'm going to swap a pint and being sat in a comfy seat inside a pub with the jukebox for tunes for some farmers field!' I only stayed for the first half of the game as I had to start looking at getting ready for Si picking us up although technically what I was wearing I could have probably managed to throw on had I woken to find my house on fire. Kif and I had ended up having a decent chat about the up and coming Happy Mondays gig where he asked if I was interested in going along with him and a couple of others. Sound boy, Kif, likes.

I used to hang around with him during the summer holidays when we were a few years younger and palled about for a while and now is, what I could best describe as one of those mates, acquaintances who you don't see all the time but you're always cool with each other when you do. We'd moved over towards the pavilion to smoke a joint away from everyone else. Away from the others ears, he'd dropped his bravado from earlier and was genuinely interested in what this Acid House scene was about which I could only say I didn't know myself but would be able to tell him everything the next time I bumped into him.

With him being as into all of this Manchester scene as I, the one example I gave him that I knew he'd appreciate was that it would be similar to the legendary Manchester club, The Hacienda only outdoors in a field. That only served to increase his interest. He passed me the joint again and told me to keep it for my walk back down the road before he made his way over towards the rest of them by the touchline, pausing for a moment to remind me to catch him through the week.

I'd arranged with them to pick Lisa and I up on the main road going through the village as this had been key to not blowing the two cover stories that we'd told our parents. Wisely recognising that by telling them that we were going to be up all night across the other side of the country, an interrogation would duly follow. Instead we both went with the cover story of going on a night out locally and staying at a friends house. When Lisa and I were walking along the road, I saw a blue Vauxhall Nova up ahead parked by the side of the road and assumed that it was Si and his girlfriend.

Didn't have a clue what type of car he drove but it was sat exactly where I'd told him to get us so it wasn't hard to put two and two together. Even though I thought it practically impossible, Lisa was looking even more hot than she had in the dressing rooms at Next when she'd given me a quick glimpse. I on the other hand had felt seriously underdressed for supposedly going out on a big night out. My Air Max I had on my plates?

They'd last seen action when I was doing Mrs Walkers garden from a few doors down before the summer when trying to scrape enough funds together for my CP Company coat. That's how important I now viewed a piece of footwear that they'd been relegated to gardening wear yet here I was going on a night out with them on. It was almost liberating in a strange way actually. I'd become such a designer label snob over the past few years through running with the Utility that it had gotten to the point where I was close to defining not just myself but anyone else I'd come into contact purely through the labels they would choose to wear.

As we approached the car from the back, both Si, and Shan must've spied us getting closer as both doors opened with them both getting out to welcome us. His girlfriend Shan looked really attractive in one of those eat nothing for a week but smoke eighty fags a day to compensate super models that you see on Milan catwalks kind of ways. Fuck, she was thin though, absolutely nothing of her and looked like she'd have to run around in the shower just to get wet. She had on a pretty peculiar get up of what looked like a swimsuit with a pair of tights underneath along with Air Jordan basketball boots.

Well I thought peculiar anyway but then again, what really did I know? Despite the fact that she'd never set eyes on either Lisa or moi before in her life she was still standing there with a big smile for the two of us. As was Si although I'd seen that smile many times before. 'Mr and Mrs Duncan, so glad you could make it' he said looking at the two of us which instantly had Lisa laughing at having been described as my wife,'Didn't I warn you about him?' I said to her, loud enough for him to hear. We went through a quick burst of introductions with each other before getting into the car and setting off. Shan, making sure that I knew I was to get in the front alongside her man ensuring that her and Lisa could sit in the back and get to know each other on the long drive through.

'Next stop, the Moon' Si announced to everyone as he turned the ignition in what appeared to be a line that Shan appreciated more than Lisa and I. The car had that familiar Cannabis smell perforating through it, shit, even if I had no sense of smell it would've only taken a quick look at what was passing as his "eyes." for a visual confirmation. They were probably only open at a quarter although fuck knows what that was doing for his visibility of the road in front of him. We could have only been on the journey for half an hour or so and you'd have thought the four of us were old friends, the car full of excited chatter in what was such a natural connection.

Half the time, two different conversations going on at once. One in the backseat between the girls and then the alternative one in the front between Si and myself. They were discussing where Lisa got her black catsuit and how Shan didn't think that she herself had the body to wear something like that. In return Lisa's commenting on HER outfit for the night and how she's never seen anyone in her life mix such a random assortment of clothes and end up looking as cool and original as Shan is.

Up in front we're going over what new players have come to United in the summer and which ones have departed. The World Cup that had just passed, England blowing it and in the process producing much source of entertainment. I'm sure there's a German word for it. They taught me it at school but I can't r member what it is now. I'm sure it begins with an S though. The up and coming Autumn Winter range of

CP Company coats that were weeks away from dropping amongst clothes in general. The topics rattled through, and that was WITHOUT even dipping into any wraps of white powder.

Si moved onto a certain trip to Amsterdam involving some of our mutual friends which upon hearing only left me all the more happy that I hadn't taken Nora's invitation up and went with them. According to him, the group were in the infamous Red Light District drinking all day and had bumped into a stag party of some cockneys. A group of lads who'd had a bunch of Chelsea Headhunters in tow. Apparently "words" were exchanged in The Old Sailor and it took some seriously cool heads to avoid it all kicking off inside between the two groups. One of them moved on to another boozer and that should've been that only, they all bumped into each other again a few hours later in another bar. They were, of course, a few more hours into drinking by this time and I guess it was inevitable that there would be some scuffles.

Then dropping all hints of a smile went on to tell me that Nora had taken a chair and cracked it over one of the Chelsea boy's heads and knocked him spark out out, sending him flying into the canal to the side of them.The English boy almost drowned since he was fucking clueless he was even in there. The mad thing was that due to all of the wee mini fights that had been going on around, the only person who had actually seen him go into the water had been Nora. Turned out that despite him being the one who'd fucking put him IN the canal it was Nora who ended up jumping in to save him when he noticed that the cockney wasn't coming up for air. It was only when the two soaking wet figures emerged from water that the rest of them all stopped fighting.

This cockney cunt is standing there telling his mates that this Scottish boy had just saved his life. They all went out for a drink together after that and the end result is that we've now got ourselves an alliance between The Utility and Chelsea Headhunters. They're going to come up through the season to help us against Hibs or Aberdeen and we're all invited down there for a game to sample a bit of soccer hooliganism in England in return. Si's telling me this, smiling again now that he's past the part of the English boy almost dying. Sitting there driving with a look on his face like all his Christmases have come at once. 'I mean, fucking Chelsea Headhunters for fuck sake, those sheep bastards are going to shit bricks when they find out about this.'

I'm sat there hoping like fuck that this is not a conversation that the two girls in the back are also listening to, for obvious reasons. However, when he took a pause, the first thing I heard was 'So this girl comes into the toilets right, and I swear you should've seen the state of her' coming from Shan. I looked towards Lisa but she didn't notice as was so into Shans conversation, sat there with a smile on her face. I could see that the two of them looked to be hitting it off together. They'd barely even spoken two words to us the whole journey and we were past Glasgow by this point with not much more miles left of the trip.

We'd tackled the whole me toking revelation earlier on when almost simultaneously, Si and Shan had both sparked one up. Shan seeing her boyfriend lighting one up and immediately saying that her and Lisa would have one between them in the back to save everybody having to pass one back and forward so much. Lisa and I instantly gave each other a look, mines a fake one of 'what do we do here' - her one was real but I quickly mouthed the words 'Fuck It' to her and we both smiled before going back to our separate conversation again. She's just a fucking cool girl though Lisa, never had a toke in her life and is sat there talking away, joint in her hand and looking like she's done it all of her life no coughing or spluttering or fuck all. I'd actually sneaked a cheeky few puffs earlier on in the car but having sneakily checked behind me, she hadn't noticed.

This public show of Lisa and I, apparently, trying it for the first time was just what I'd needed. Then again, considering what I'd kept from her in our short relationship, who knows? Maybe she'd been smoking it for years?! Now going through Ayrshire by this point, Si asked me what time it was and when informed that it was the back of eight he said we'd need to stop at the next town and look for a phone box somewhere. It was now getting near the time where he'd need to put in a call to find out which exact direction we were meant to be heading towards.

We'd hardly discussed the night ahead over the journey but now that it was getting closer the excitement in the car was starting to build. Knowing Lisa, she, by this point probably knew more about illegal parties than anyone who's even been to one! Si mentioning having to make a call for the next directions was all I needed for it all to become a bit more real to me. I mean, how much of a buzz was this? Here we were, going to something that was so secret that even the people going to it didn't initially know where the fuck it was.

It didn't take a genius to see that on one side you'd have a nightclub or some kind of establishment in the entertainment industry that would go out of its way to spend money to make sure everyone knew about them and where they were. Yet on this side we had something that didn't require any ads in the newspapers, no publicity to make sure the paying customer will be aware of or indeed want to go. Details so sparse that there wasn't even any kind of hint as to where the party IS until the last minute. Despite all of this there still appeared masses of people willing to jump through all of these consumer unfriendly hoops such was their desperation to go!

He eventually stopped in a town called New Cumnock to find a phone box as well as buy some provisions that would come in handy over the night. It all seemed a bit "wrong" to me in terms of all the stuff he came back with and handed over to Shan to put it in the back. We were, after all, going out for a night of fun, not a hiking expedition. In the short time I'd been chancing my luck getting into pubs for a night out, the only preparations I'd need to put in place would be to make sure I had a few cans to drink before going out to the pub and money for when out as well the much required funds to get me home at the end of the night.

Instead, here he was with a shopping bag that had all sorts of random stuff in it like bottles of water, about twenty packs of chewing gum, an insane amount of packets of Regal Kingsize, a wee tub of Vics Vaporub and bottle of Olbas Oil. I never said a word likes but it was a pretty bizarre array of stuff he'd returned with. It was when he'd popped back out to make the phone call that Shan started to bring up the night ahead with me. 'So, Zico, are you getting excited?' she asked with the biggest of smiles on her face. She was absolutely beaming and despite edging towards the skeletal she just seemed to have this beautiful healthy aura about her, you could tell how excited she was herself about it. 'Well, aye' I said in a less convincing fashion which I felt instantly, made me look like I was almost lying with the way I'd answered. I felt I had to quickly clarify. 'I'm looking forward to it but I just don't have a clue what it's going to be like if that makes sense? I've been to a few gigs likes but I kinda know that this isn't going to be like one of them so that leaves me no further forward'

'Look, I'm saying this to the BOTH of you' Shan replied, looking at me and putting her skinny arm around Lisa's back and squeezing the side of her, pulling her closer. 'This is going to completely blow you away, after a couple of hours of you being in there and getting used to it I'm going to come and ask you if I was right or if I was right' - The weird thing is that the way she'd been speaking about it had been the exact same as Si, not exactly word for word but similar stuff yet I couldn't help but notice that both of them had said it with the most wide of eyes and full of sincerity. Delivered by the two of them in a way that even if it wasn't true you could tell that they at least "believed" it to be so.

He came jogging back down the street with that trademark grin on his face before jumping back into the car and turning to everyone. 'Right, Dalleagles Farm, the old cunt in the chippy told me that it's only two or three miles back down the road we've just came, or in that general direction anyway, it's cool we're going to start bumping into quite a bit of traffic in a wee while anyway so we'll find it no problems.' Shan clapped her hands like a dolphin at Seaworld while looking like she was going to spontaneously combust at the news. I reached over to Lisa and grabbed her hand, squeezed it then held it for a few seconds while we exchanged a brief look with each other that, for me at least, felt like a mixture of excitement and nervousness. She just gave me an adorable confident look back that I knew was her masking whatever uncertainties she was suffering from.

Si hadn't been wrong about the traffic. A road that we'd come down maybe three quarters of an hour before which, had it not been for a couple of tractors would have been traffic free was now resembling an inner city rush hour. 'Well, Zico my son, all we need to do now is follow the leader and its mission a-fucking-complished and by the way, I hope one of you lot will be able to remember the way back home tomorrow because I might find it a little tricky.' Always the joker, I could tell that he said this though in a way that I only ever took as the ultimate in seriousness. 'Should've left a fucking breadcrumb trail eh?' I said back remembering some story from when I was younger that I couldn't remember the details otherwise I'd have referenced a bit more of it.

It wouldn't have mattered anyway because he was so hyped up by this point that he was already onto something else. All the cars had stopped and didn't look like moving which prompted him to get out to see what was happening. Next something seemed to catch his eye or ear as he was now launching himself up onto his bonnet and then upwards again onto the roof of the Nova. I thought the cunt was going to come through the roof when he started to jump up and down shouting 'OVER THERE, YA FUCKING BEAUTY!'

I got out to see what was going on, completely ignoring the fact that with the car being a three door both girls were trapped in the back and not able to get out and investigate things for themselves. Something which would've seriously pissed the two of them off I'll bet. Si's still on the roof pointing west saying to others who had also gotten out of their cars where the party was. I got myself up onto the roof to see for myself and sure enough, a few miles down the road there was the glow of the lights and lasers and now that I was out the car I could hear the music, well what sounded like some heavy bass, like the ground was rumbling if that even makes sense. Couldn't help but think that if that was how loud it was from here then what the fuck was it going to be like over there?

The, what was now, convoy soon found their way on the right track and it was only around twenty minutes before we were pulling into a field where some guy was standing there in a fluorescent yellow vest holding one of those glow sticks like you see someone on the tarmac telling airplanes where to park. Finding a spot, he pulled in and came to a stop in what looked like a makeshift car park that was filling up fast. 'Right, we're probably going to have a bit of a hike so we best check we've got everything before we set off as once we're on our way we're not going to want to double back.' Shan said to us, already zipping on her hoody before even tackling getting out the back.

'I was just about to tell them that' Si laughed back while taking out a fag and lighting it before passing them round. It was weird but not in a bad way, even the innocuous things that Si or Shan would share was said in a way that you could tell there was so much more to it. Like you could tell there was a story behind it from another event that they'd been to or something to that effect. It left the impression that these two knew stuff that I or Lisa didn't and this I was totally cool with also had me naturally eager to find out for myself.

When we left the car the first thing that hit me was the music. Here I was in the middle of fucking nowhere, it was still light but entering that part where the sun was already on the way down for the night and I could hear this music playing, loud, very. I couldn't see where the party was but finding it wasn't exactly going to be what I would consider a challenge. I'd watched a film through the week where some slick Manhattan lawyer, sorry, attorney, was telling everyone else to follow the money. Well this was simply a case of follow the music.

Along with what looked liked hundreds of others we headed in its direction. As we walked, chatting amongst the four of us and some excited randoms who would strike up mini conversations along the way, Si looked specifically at Shan and said with a should we shouldn't we look on his face, 'You think it's time, babe?' - 'Yeah I'd say so, Simon, get those little fuckers out' she replied with a naughty like look on her face, like she was up to no good, doing something bad but taking extreme pleasure out of doing so. He apparently hadn't needed much in the way of motivation with him fishing out a clear small zip locked bag with some white pills in them "before" his girlfriend had even finished the sentence, classic Si.

Now this was a different proposition. I'd become familiar with sharing his bag of speed on match days, had smoked tonnes of Hash with him but pills? Nope, never seen him with them at the fitba. He emptied some of them out into his hand and fished one out and passed it to Shan who had already located one of the bottles of water in the rucksack she had over her shoulders. Without any hesitation she stuck it in her mouth and drank it down with a swig of Evian. Si then taking the bottle from her and doing the same. Which then left Lisa and I standing there. 'Here you go Zeec' He said passing me one and thrusting it into my hand 'That there is your golden ticket to the dream factory and I am Willie fucking Wonka, here you too, Leeze' He reached his hand out to Lisa to give it to her.

'Ummmm, I'm not really' she got out before Shan butted in 'Honestly Lisa, I'd never taken drugs in my life before coming to my first allnighter and look at me, look how excited I am to be coming here, see how quickly I necked that Eckie the moment it was in my hand? You'll find there is a pretty good reason for that, It's the best fucking feeling you're ever going to have in your life.' There wasn't a question that I didn't want to take it but I didn't want to throw my hat into the ring until I saw which way the wind was going to blow with Lisa. If I'd taken mines straight away that, I felt, would only have put more pressure onto her which would've been a bit of a shitty thing to do.

'Are things like that not addictive' Lisa tentatively asked which immediately I saw as her not saying no initially. A scenario which I knew would've been a possibility. 'No not at all' Shan continued, 'I've only ever taken Eckies at these nights, it's way more than just about the drug, it's like the music only truly works with the drug and the drug only works with the music, it's a hard thing to explain but in a short while you're going to know for yourself, Si and I are going to look after the two of you, you know?!' She offered some reassurance to us. I decided to take over.

'Right, we'll take it at the exact same time on the count of three' I said to Lisa in some fake as fuck way that suggested that I was a little nervous about taking them. 'We all take it now we're all going to be going up at the same time and will look out for each other' Si chipped in while crouched down trying to find one of the joints he had stuffed into his socks. We all stopped while I gave Lisa a cuddle and whispered in her ear that we should just go for it and that we'd be in good experienced company to help us through it if we needed. Adding that the two of us didn't know but that 'tonight could be the best night of our lives.'

Cautiously she agreed so with the two of us standing there with a bottle of water each the other two counted us down from three and without any hesitation both downed what we'd learn a few minutes later to be a "White Dove" which we were informed would take around thirty to forty five minutes before lift off. Full of intrigue, trepidation and excitement I continued through the field. The music getting louder and louder until we could hear what sounded like a cockney accent shouting over the top of a high pitched piano 'HANDS IN THE FUCKING AIR, LETS SEE HOW YOU DO THIS, SCOTLAND BRING THE NOISE.'

It was close, so close actually that after having went down a small dip we found ourselves heading upwards again. When we got to the top, there it was. It didn't even look possible, fields and fields of what really looked like nothing apart from one section with a sea of people congregating, moving into shapes together, lights going all over the place, strobes, lasers, all types of shit flashing on and off. I'd started to hold Lisa's hand ten minutes previously as we walked in its direction. We were both feeling the need to be tethered to each other while waiting on, well, whatever it was that was heading our way.

When we got down there we found a long line of everyone waiting to get in. Every now and again some mean looking boy in a black bomber jacket with some kind of karate symbol on the back would walk up and down the line with a Rottweiler on a lead, checking everyone out for whatever he needed to before walking back towards the entrance again. As we stood there with the line going down I could swear I felt something inside of me. Almost like it rushed over me and was gone again although I wasn't sure if that was just my imagination. It felt like a warm rush traveling up my back and right over the top of my head before evaporating again. I looked round at Si and Shan who were standing there sharing a joint while smiling and without speaking nodding their heads to the sound of the music beyond the entrance that everyone was filing past and into.

'How you feeling?' I asked Lisa, giving her a tender kiss on the cheek - 'I felt like something was going on around five minutes ago but nah, nothing really' - 'Aye, me too, just the now, almost felt like, you know when you get the feeling and people say that someone has walked over your grave? Well that's what I got but in a completely different way' I responded, feeling like I knew what she was meaning without her actually describing it any real or clear way.

'That's the start of the rushes, mate' Si moved his way into what had been, what I thought, a quiet few words between each other while him and his girl were doing their own thing. He took one last toke and passed me the joint saying that we needed to get it finished before we got close to the bouncers. 'What you've just had a glimpse of isn't even on the same planet in terms of what is heading your way, mate. I'm fucking jealous of you two that this is your first time to experience it all. Lucky bastards!'

Lisa and I polished off the rest of the joint between us. I had noticed that I felt like my heart had started to beat a touch faster and the feel of each toke had the effect of clashing against what was going fast inside me and had a nice comforting feeling to it, like it was calming me exactly when I needed it. Lisa tossed the roach to the floor just as the entrance came into our line of vision. There was around half a dozen guys in the same bomber jackets all standing around waving everyone in. Further down another two Rottweilers at the front which I thought was as excessive as it was novel to me going anywhere for a night out. I'd learn later on that the reason for the scary dogs wasn't so much to do with people going in but to keep the police out as had been the case on previous nights over the past year.

When we got face to face with them all, I was definitely feeling something. Like a happy tingle that felt like when you wake up for the day and have lots to look forward to in it but, with this, had an added edge to it. I'd noticed over the course of us standing in the line to get in that there had been a definite change from feeling completely normal to "did I just feel that happen to me there" right through to nope I can DEFINITELY feel something happening. Like when you see those NASA rockets taking off to do fuck knows what up there in space and that ground control boy is giving it all of that "T Minus ten seconds" stuff and as he counts down you can see the rocket starting to show signs that it's getting itself ready for lift off, smoke flying out the side. Then the rocket boosters kick in then the suddenly the egghead is at T minus one second and BOOM.

Well, standing there talking away to everyone I'd say I was T Minus ten but by the time I got to the front of the line I must've been down to T Minus five seconds, minimum because I just felt, well, different, pleasantly so but absolutely nothing compared to Si's usual white powder effect. Conversation between Lisa and I had been attempted but moments away from getting in we were just standing with the most stupid of smiles looking back at each other. When it came to getting in all I wanted was a text book entry and then we could really see what this was all about. The bouncers weren't even asking for to see tickets by the time we got to the front and instead were just waving people past. Such was the amount of bodies they had to get through the doors before shutting them again for the night. Obviously it wasn't as easy for me, it never fucking is though.

The bouncer waved me past, some guy in a crew cut, decked in black from head to toe including some twenty four holer Doc Martins. He looked me up and down and waved me past only to grab my shoulder as I was on my way in. Looking down at me again he pointed to my Gio Goi shorts and decided to tell me how he was friends with "Anthony & Chris" from Manchester, who owned the label. I didn't have a fucking clue who he was on about, I just thought it was a cool brand, doesn't have to mean I know the mother's maiden name of the owner of the label. Here I was though dealing with what Si classed as "coming up" for the first time in my life and just needed to get inside without any drama or interruption. Noticing that Lisa was now inside and standing by herself I managed to stammer something along the lines of 'Anthony and Chris? Absolute fucking legends, the pair of them, mate' which seemed to go down well with him as he flashed me what looked like a knowing smile and reached out his hand and grabbed my by now, clammy hand tight and wished me a good night before moving his gaze back to those still streaming through.

I was in.

I looked across the sky and saw that the sun was completely gone and the moon and stars were now out. I don't know? It felt symbolic in a way that I couldn't explain. They had come out to play and so had we, thousands of us. This was me just starting for the night, looking like a complete twat with a Berghaus wooly hat on my head, a joggers Adidas cagoule, pair of shorts to offset the above and my gardeners Air Max yet slowly, slowly I was starting to feel like I was king of the world with sense of fashion or style the absolute last thing in my mind.

Chapter 16.

Standing there waiting on Zico getting past that bouncer for what seemed like an age I could feel it running through me. It? Perhaps not "it" but definitely something. Despite it being effectively night by then I could feel myself burning up but yet still kind of shivering if that even makes sense but that's what it was like. My palms were so sweaty it was as if I'd dipped them in a sink with water in it. With me not knowing what to expect from the pill that Zico's friend, Si had given me, how the hell was I supposed to know if it was working or not?

There seemed to be a change though. Definitely a shift in mood and in feeling, even from the relatively short time since we had stepped out of the car and went for a walk through the fields. I wasn't really sure about taking it, actually was downright scared but didn't want to show it in front of Zico and his friends though having just met them hours earlier. They had all put me at ease just enough to let me drop my guard and just go for it.

I wouldn't say that I was anti drugs but nether had I shown any interest in taking them either. I suspect that Zico HAS though, he was oblivious to it but on the drive through I noticed Si passing him a joint that had been lit and there was none of this trying to talk Zico round to have a smoke of it, no protestations or questions from him. He simply reached his hand out and took it from him and smoked it like it was the most natural thing. I know him enough though to know that while he's probably smoked Hash he hadn't taken Ecstasy until the same night as me. Well either that or he's a pretty good actor. I could tell he was a wee bit different as we stood waiting to get in. He seemed a little nervous, was talking complete shite, even more than he usually does. I could see that he was starting to burn up a wee bit too, sweat had covered his forehead despite the fact that technically it was already starting to get a bit chilly with it being the back of nine.

Waiting around for the other three I had a really pleasant tingle that seemed to be covering me but all surging and pulsating towards my head that left me a little light headed. It felt divine but equally, like I might have to take a seat for a second before my legs gave way on me. It seemed like parts of me was going faster than some of my other vitals, almost like what happens to your head when you stand up too quick. Untying my coat from around my waste I placed it on the ground and sat down, crossing my legs as I watched everyone file past me. While sitting there I lost count of the amount of people who walked past whilst flashing me a quick smile or a hello, the occasional squeeze of my shoulder from someone walking past and reaching out to me. I just sat giving everyone a smile back. I don't think I could have wiped it from my face if I'd tried. I just felt so incredibly happy.

When Stevie, along with the other two finally appeared my way it was all in the eyes between us. Upon spying me through the crowd he had the biggest grin on his face which I saw and raised him a Cheshire cat one back. It was when our eyes locked though, it felt like a moment where we spoke hundreds of words between each other without actually opening our mouths. He could see that the Ecstasy had started to work on me and equally I could see that it was the exact same for him. He jokingly put an imaginary gun to his head and pulled the trigger to indicate that he felt like his head had been blown off which was a pretty decent analogy for someone who, and speaking through the same shared experience, at that moment probably felt like his mind had been strapped to a rocket ship that was on its way to leaving earths atmosphere.

Shan, with eyes the size of a fifty pence piece ran over and knelt down in front of me and came in for a big cuddle which actually felt amazing, way more than a hug could or ever should. I'm not joking, it felt like the best cuddle anyone in the world had ever given me in my life. I always compliment Zico on how good his hugs are but this was in a completely different league. I hugged her back every bit as much, I didn't want it to ever end. While we embraced I got this sudden shooting feeling that ran right up the back of my neck and made the hairs on my head stand on end like there was some kind of energy that was inside me and flowing out through my hair.

This stuff was good but I managed to notice that it was still coming on stronger and stronger, how much longer "would" the going up part last? Every film I've ever seen with drugs had always involved someone smoking pot or taking cocaine and heroin and as far as the films portrayed, the people smoke a joint and are high instantly after. They snort some Cocaine and look like they can instantly run through walls and Heroin? I haven't seen much of that but the times I have? They seem to plunge the needle into themselves and they're under the influence straight away. Ecstasy wasn't like that. It was quite sneaky in that way, actually.

From the moment I took it I was expecting an instant effect which saw me constantly checking my watch to see how many minutes had passed only for me to get to the stage of getting sick of looking at the time and actually questioning if I'd been given a dud. It reminded me of the fifth of November and how you are always warned not to return back to the firework that you've lit. Reaching the point of questioning if I had a dud THAT'S when I started to feel something. Sat there on the ground looking up at the three of them with what I can only imagine to be a stupid glazed smile I tried to talk and it all came out wrong. It didn't feel like it was actually me that was speaking such was this amazing disconnect between one part of my brain and the other. I tried again and fared much better second time around.

'YOU TWO are baaaaad' I said smiling back at Si & Shan, who were standing there giggling. Him smiling back with his arm around her neck - 'Oh an unhappy customer is it?' he said trying to adopt a serious look on his face and failing badly. 'Yes, you and your other half have had me taking drugs for the first time in my life and are the cause of me sat here right now in the middle of a field in some kind of weird and wonderful state of mind while questioning if I'm going to be able to stand, where do I make a complaint?' I said, just finishing the last part as I was about to run out of breath. My heart was racing so fast.

'You know, babe? Normally someone who is wishing to make a complaint about something don't ever do so while having a grin like yours on their face. I'm not saying NOT to complain likes, Lisa but maybe you should rethink your strategy because no one's going to take you seriously with a smile like that on your face, and I haven't even mentioned your fucking eyes at this point by the way' Zico said in his usual dry way. 'Well if you're talking eyes then you best keep your thoughts to yourself until you've seen your own ones, honey' I replied letting him know that despite what he was seeing in me he was neglecting to think that maybe just maybe he wasn't looking too composed on his side either, which he wasn't.

'Right, we getting into this madhouse then or what' Shan said impatiently, starting to dance to the rhythmic beat that was filling the cool night air as she stood around while I remained seated, still looking back up from the ground at them. She held one hand down to me and Zico took the other and between them they got me back to my feet again. The head rush I got from being propelled back up almost had me on my behind again of course but Si, clearly of faster reactions than my "gallant gent" of a boyfriend saw the danger and caught me from falling back. After that I was good.

Shan, led the way in some manic hybrid of dancing and walking with us following like she was the pied piper of Hamelin. We made in the direction of this big rusty old metal shed that you'd see farmers keeping all their cows in or that kind of thing. There was lots of people mingling all over the outside of it too. Pockets of people all doing their own thing, some dancing, some sitting on the ground talking to them, most of those on the ground dancing without worrying themselves about the practicalities like moving their feet or legs.

I was finding it a challenge to hold onto any kind of thought for more than a second at a time before losing it again and was automatically onto something completely random and different. What a cool top that girl over there has on - that shed we're heading towards is going to smell so so bad - is that Jack Your Body I can hear the DJ playing? - I need to ask Stevie how "he's" feeling right now, he looks really wrecked - where's the toilets I think I need to poop -these rushes (?) are getting stronger and stronger - is that someone from my class over there?. I lurched from one thought to another with none of them even close to being anything remotely related to the one before.

I assumed it was the same for Zico judging by the amount of random nonsense that was coming out of his mouth every time he opened it. He definitely wasn't aware of it but kept repeating things seemingly forgetting he'd just said the exact same thing minutes before. He had us all in stitches though with his reactions to what his first E was feeling like. Si and Shan looked like they were taking some extra bit of joy in seeing Zico and I taking it for the first time. After his earlier comment about 'next stop the Moon' (which incidentally now felt a LOT more meaningful than it had been in the car back at the start of the journey) Stevie, said to Si 'You weren't joking about us going to the Moon were you, mate?' and without warning my embarrassment of a boyfriend then started singing that Rocket Ship song by Queen, even pretended to be walking about with the microphone stand like Freddie Mercury.

I almost ended up with a sore head through laughing at him. I'd never found myself so far out of my comfort zone yet feeling so at one with myself. This all despite the fact that god knows what was all going off inside me. The intermittent waves that were coming over me, the like I didn't know existed but when sampled felt so weirdly natural. I could never have imagined that I would find paradise in a Scottish farmers field yet here I was, palm trees excluded.

We entered what was the completely rammed full shed. It's funny but once inside the first impression I had was one of like I'd walked into one of those evangelist sermons you see in America. Almost the whole of the shed were standing there with their hands in the air, screaming, shouting, cheering. All completely under the control of the DJ and this other guy walking about in front of him with the microphone that Si had called the 'MC.'

This was nowhere near like the few concerts I'd been to like Bros and New Kids on the Block where it was simply a case of everyone all going there to have a good time with their own friends. This was the polar opposite, I hadn't been in there that long but was already left with the impression that every single person in there were 'together.' The feeling of unity inside there was so powerful it smacked you in the face. Everywhere I looked it wouldn't take long to find another party goer smiling, nodding or winking back at me like we'd already met and despite not knowing them, each time I'd automatically smile back.

There was just so many happy faces all over and that alone left ME happier as a result. While it might've been surreal to see so many people all standing with their hands in the air like I was looking at, it was even more novel to see them, almost in sync drop them again and then start to do their own thing again as they started to dance. The minute the piano stopped on the record it was almost like it was the signal for them to just go crazy. It was like nothing I had ever have witnessed before.

Without even realising it, I started dancing too. I'd always been conditioned, through youth club and school discos and the like, to dance with a partner or in most cases, with my friends. You didn't dance on your own, people would just laugh at you if you'd done that. Not inside there. I never even thought to look towards the other three. I just instinctively started moving to this (what was a) new genre of music I was experiencing but in that precise moment was the best and most impacting music I'd ever heard. And I've listened to The Beatles as well.

With the Wheel of Fortune style thought pattern I was dealing with I eventually rested on one that involved Stevie. I looked to the side and he was dancing too, badly but bless him, he wasn't a dancer but there he was, grooving his little heart out. In amongst the darkness and occasional flash of lasers he still seemed to notice that I was looking at him and looked back at me. He stopped for a second and moved closer to me.

'Whoooaaahhhhh ya fucker, NO. FUCKING. WORDS to describe how amazing this is' He yelled into my ear in a way that was ear drum troubling. His eyes were so big that they reminded me of that Total Recall film we'd went to see a few months ago. The part when that guy ended up outside the safe zone on Mars and his eyes started popping out his head. Zico's were like that only a bit smaller, thank god! His grin was the size of which I'd never seen since I watched Batman with Jack Nicholson playing The Joker. He looked the same Zico but yet unexplainably, different.

'How you feeling, babe? You enjoying it? Personally I don't want to ever drink again in my life, where's the need when there's pills like this about!!' It was pretty clear my boyfriend was enthused by it all. I'd never seen him as happy in the short time we'd been going out but then again this and what we were doing was not relative to "normal" life. As out of my mind that I was I still realised that everything that was going on inside and out was still synthetic when matched up against day to day life. Then again, that's why every one was here, to "escape the normal."

'I feel amazing' I beamed back at him 'I'm really glad we came now although, like you I don't think I can really find any words right now to capture how I'm "feeling" I then, remembering the hug I got from Shan, opened my arms out with Zico mimicking me as we went in for the mother of all clinches, and kisses. The combination of feeling his body against me, his arms wrapped around and his lips against mines while another of those special piano breaks boomed out of the giant speakers was enough to completely finish me off.

I knew that this was the one moment in my life where I had never felt so happy and so content and who knows maybe I'll never feel that way again. If that ends up to be the case I'll still feel blessed to have had "that" moment. I'd already fallen for Zico, over a month ago but I swear, seeing that smile and those eyes when he looked at me and how it felt to be touched by him. I fell in love with him all over again right there. Caressing the side of my face so tenderly he gave me another short kiss before, once again with the increased sound levels, shouted in my ear 'I FUCKING LOVE YOU!!' before grabbing both of my hands and holding them up in the air while he started dancing again.

I almost cried right there over the feeling it had left me with. This Ecstasy was emotionally powerful stuff and it hadn't taken me long to see just exactly why it had earned the name that it went by. I honestly believed that it had the potential to change the world as I looked around witnessing its impact on such a large gathering of people.

People get me all wrong, because I started hanging around with boys with cars when I was fourteen I ended up with that kind of a reputation. In reality though I'm more than happy to be with someone like Zico when they have the ability to make me feel the way that he does. Despite not even having his provincial license never mind a car, Stevie has made me feel the most happy, valued, special girl out of any boyfriends I've had since going up to High School and, being there in that cow shed while feeling like I'd travelled to another dimension. It meant the absolute world to me that he was the one right there beside me to share in it. The knowledge that we were making such a beautiful memory together made me smile so very much. Inside and out.

I eventually reached a point where I no longer felt like I was strapped to Saturn five and my head state had now levelled itself out. I lost track of time a while back but I estimated that it must've taken a good hour and a half before I stopped feeling like I was on an upwards trajectory. I could now go about the night free of any nagging concerns about the whole drug taking thing. I done pretty excellently if I do say so myself, at my exams so I'd like to think that I know a thing or two about a thing or two.

With that I had been able to work out that this E seemed to have a long upwards trajectory so by basic reasoning would have something similar while you were high and then a similar amount of time on the descent. For now though I could simply just enjoy it all. Shan and I went off to find what toilet facilities there were around the field, leaving Zico and Si looking like the Marx Brothers trying to make a joint between them in the dark. Thinking, knowing actually, that by the time we returned they'd STILL be trying to get that same spliff together.

On our travels, Shan and I bumped into these girls from Saltcoats, Abby & Hana. Absolute nutters but the best kind, really friendly and chatty girls. Hana asked Shan and I three questions in a row like we were in some role playing fantasy where you meet some wizard or gatekeeper who will only let you pass if you answer their three questions. What's your name? Where you from? What've you had? It was three questions I would be asked more than once over the night but the first time was definitely a novelty to me. On answering the third question this produced some excitement on their side. 'you two have had Doves tonight?' Abby, this really pretty, glowing girl with a smile that you couldn't help smile back at, really petite with long hair, said in a raised voice while jumping up and down like some kid that just got told they're getting the day off school. 'PLEASE tell me that you have some more' Hana, who was almost a carbon copy of her friend, said along with the most pretend saddest puppy dog eyes you'll ever see.

'Well, we still have some more but need them to see us through to eight' Shan replied with genuine and sincere regret on her face. Obviously wanting to help these girls out but without cutting off her own nose in doing so. Abby started to look in her handbag while interrupting Hana who was about to say something herself back to Shan. 'Well what would you say if I was to offer you a NEW YORKER back in return for a Dove' She brought her bag of pills out in time to go along with what she was saying, dangling the bag of red pills right in front of Shans face.

Shan was quite excited about this unexpected development which led to an agreeable transaction which saw the swapping of some pills between them. Her reasoning being that it only took one look at Abby and Hana to know that the pills were amazing so, felt that her and I should mix it up with a different pill for our next one of the night. 'Next one' I thought. I never considered there being a next one but for Shan it looked like it was nothing more than a formality.

'Here, Lisa, you need to get a massage from Abby' Hana said before popping the white pill into her mouth no more than a couple of seconds after being handed it by Shan. I'm not sure what I had in mind for my Saturday night but it most definitely wasn't standing in a makeshift toilet in the middle of a field with strange girls offering me a massage. 'Oh you DEFINITELY need to get one from me' Abby said persuasively with an adorable wicked smile. 'I've been told I have the hands of a magician' she said as they both laughed with a knowing look between them. I complied as was in too good a mood to disagree with anyone, preferring to go with the flow of the night as long as I felt good about it.

I stood, hands down on the sink facing the mirror while Abby moved up behind me and placed her hands over my shoulders. Even the feel of her thumbs digging into me was giving me rushes and tingles all over my body and I knew she was only just getting started on me. 'This could well be one of the best decisions I've ever made,' I thought to myself standing there feeling her hands rub, dig and press all over me. No part of my upper body was spared including my head. Digging her nails into my scalp she ran her long fingernails all over my head which had me involuntarily moaning as she moved them over my head.

I've never been attracted to girls, I know there's a few in my year at school who are beginning to get a little confused in terms of who they like, girls or boys but I'm not in any much doubt on that front. The way this other girl was making me feel though? Wow, just wow. She was producing moans from me that I'd only ever previously let out when alone in the house for a while when mum and dad are out and I masturbate but here was someone just with their hands on my head making me feel the same way. When she drew her nails all the way down the back of my head and then continued down my neck and back I had a mini orgasm. I tried to stop it, I tried to think about something else other than how good the feel of her nails on me was. I was powerless to resist it. Some things just can't be stopped. You can't cheat science.

'OH MY FUCKIN GODDDDDDDDD' I screamed out throwing my head back while Shan and the two Saltcoats girls burst out laughing. I turned round, and gave Abby a big hug before telling her that her hands had orgasmic qualities which turned out not to be the first time she'd heard that and given my experience, not something I wasn't going to doubt. 'I call them the Orgasmatrons' Abby said laughing while holding both hands up for effect.

The four of us ended up sitting down in the field and chatting absolute nonsense that had us in fits of giggles, probably losing an hour or more in the process. A timescale that Zico or Si would've probably not even noticed given the state they were in when we disappeared. Abby and Hana eventually left to go back towards the shed, leaving Shan and I still sat and in the process of taking one of the New Yorkers before heading back in ourselves. While fishing around in her bag for the pills Shan and I continued chatting about everything and anything.

'Zico seems really sound, nice guy and I'm not saying that cause I'm on an Eckie!' Shan said. 'You been together long?' - 'Just over a couple of months, almost three' I replied, briefly reflecting on how much had changed in those two plus months and where I was now, right at that exact moment in time. 'Same with your man, he's such a friendly, funny and warm guy.' I replied. It felt like it was a little forced in terms of, she'd said something nice about my boyfriend and now as a result I was saying something similar back but in reality Si WAS an extremely likeable guy and to see him and Zico together they were like a double act. I could see how and why they were good pals. 'Yeah, Simon's a great guy, loves me to death, really looks after me and is just someone you really can't not like. I don't like what he gets up to every Saturday though of course and have told him so but I'm hoping that through time he's going to phase that part of his life out.'

I'd be a liar if I was to say that I wasn't interested in all of this "What he gets up to on a Saturday" stuff that Shan was hinting at. 'As long as I'm not poking my nose in where it's not wanted, what do you mean about every Saturday? A great guy is a great guy, they don't take a day off, no?' I said, half worrying that I was exposing myself for how wrecked I was by asking a question that I possibly already knew the answer to. 'Well, I'm meaning at the football? Dundee United? You definitely know what I mean It's probably just the Eckies, darling' Shan said handing me over the pill as she swigged from a bottle of water taking hers. 'It's easy to forget even the most obvious things when you're skied on a pill like these Doves, I was talking about the casuals, Si, Zico and everyone that goes to the matches?'

I had just unbelievably, taken a second E so I admittedly maybe wasn't thinking the clearest I'd ever done but from what I could see she was saying that my man was one of those football hooligans that you see on the TV and read about in the papers. I'd watched some BBC Scotland documentary on how they were taking over the Scottish game and causing fights and lots of trouble. I really couldn't see it as far as Zico was concerned but she seemed to know that Si was which in turn made me question how they knew each other and were as friendly as they appeared to be. Then there was the scars and puffed out eye he had on the Sunday I seen him following his trip to Glasgow months back when he said he'd fallen down the stairs at the train station after a few beers?

I could've, and normally would have, stormed right back to that shed to find him and ask him if he was in some gang that got into fights but sensibly, I decided to park it until another time. I was having too good a night. I was enjoying this feeling I had too much to risk ruining what had effectively been the best night of my life over what may have been nothing more than me misunderstanding something someone else has said because I was out my bloody tree. We decided to have a quick joint while waiting on our New Yorkers coming on, which, to give Shan credit, she knocked up in next to no time. Watching her do so, I smiled as I pondered whether Si and Zico got there in the end with their one or had just given up altogether.

Chapter 17.

Everything had changed for me by the time Si pulled gingerly out of the field at the punishing hour of ten in the morning. It had been an adventure, an expedition, a departure of state and mind. I mean, I always thought it would be good but in one of those normal ways that you get when you go out with your friends. Shroom though? This allnighter of Acid House? Nope, it went way past being "enjoyable." I'd never had an experience in my life where, as it was actually still taking place I had been able to appreciate it as life defining to me. Even while sky high on three different types of Eckies I still managed to pluck out a solid and productive thought such as how "important" this felt as I stood there sampling this alternative side to having a good time. This "society" that lies under the radar of the nearly every one else.

The last record the DJ played, as I was helpfully informed later by Simon as being "Anthem" by N-Joi, was spun just before nine o clock. Considering everyone had been there all night it had been heavily impacting to see the energetic and enthusiastic reaction the second they heard the opening lyrics. The woman singing something about being in love from what I could make out. Almost everyone inside that shed apart from the uneducated like myself singing along. The whole place went off like a bomb once the beat kicked in. The high pitch singing scream from her doing things to me that a mere singing voice really should not have been capable of. It was a moment that moved me. Fittingly spiritual considering it was now Sunday morning and almost time for the doors of all the churches across the country to open for Sunday service.

Regardless of the hour of day and the circumstances, the tune seemed to saturate everything and everyone inside that shed. With the sun being up hours ago, this was all taking place in complete daylight. A crowd that had, for many hours, been shielded by the dark, were now entirely visible and to look around and see so many people. All so full on up, for it and happy, insanely. Maybe it's a bad analogy but when in the few times I've managed to get myself into a nightclub I've always noticed a bit of a sinister edge to the end of the night.

You've got a building full of people who have been drinking alcohol all night long. Some have spilled others drinks accidentally, some have chatted up a girl that someone else had their eye on, that guy who accidentally bumped into the other one in the toilets and led to piss being accidentally sprayed on trousers. Lots of personal agendas that have festered over the night only to come out at the end before everyone goes for a kebab then head home. I sensed it every single time and possibly perversely and hypocritically I never quite liked that feeling of knowing something was going to go off. In the middle of this farm with the DJ spinning the last song of the morning? Not even close to having any threats of end of the night, well, morning violence.

The opposite if anything. By the time that last song had ended I had engaged in so many mini conversations with random people over the night that once it was all over and done with I'd have forgotten half of the people I met. All it took was a wee smile in someones direction and brief nonsense filled conversations would soon follow. I spoke to people from all over Scotland and Northern England. Those Geordies are mad fuckers but like I said to one of them at some point in the night, they're barely English the Newcastle people, just ended up being born on the wrong side of the border but still as good as being Scottish. Then again I'm biased with the Geordies as I used to love that Auf Wiedersehen Pet show when it was on. Fucking adored that show, that big OZ boy was funny as fuck, proper character. Wouldn't want to share a hut with him though, mind.

One of these Newcastle lads was carrying this "thing" about with him, kinda like a big fat german sausage (apart from it was made of rubber) that you put round your neck and it vibrated. I resisted at first on account of it looking quite fucking dodgy and I had this idea that they were taking the piss out of me for a joke to put it on. They wouldn't give up though and it was only after Si had a go of it and I saw the look on his coupon.

That's all I needed to be impatiently waiting on a shot after him. The feeling it produced was one of those types of things you can't even begin to describe. It like, sent lots of vibrations running up my neck but then it spread into my chest and up into my head until the vibrations changed to a kind of explosion which almost decapitated me. Fuck knows what my face was like when I handed it back to the boy from The Toon because he just laughed as he took it from me while saying a 'fucking TOLD YOU'

Out of all the hours we were in there I think I must've lost about a good six of them through a mixture of dancing and sitting talking to others. I honestly thought there might be an element of snobbishness from some towards me because they'd never seen me there before at one of those nights. With it still being a secret sub culture that was flourishing out of everyone else's line of vision I felt like it would be some kind of deal where everyone knew each other. Once I saw it all for myself and how big it was though, I knew this had been a stupid theory in any case.

I met lots of cool people over the night with such an eclectic range of conversations. The best example I could give on that was later on in the morning. I was sitting outside the cowshed just catching my breath from the chaos that was still taking place inside, watching the sun come up. A boy I'd never seen before in my life came up to me asking if I had a lighter he could borrow. Ironically I shouldn't have, what with me not being a smoker as such.

I DID have one on me though as the last joint I'd smoked with Si, wrecked as I was I kept forgetting I even had it in my hand. It kept going out as a result and he got pissed off with me repeatedly asking him for a light again so just gave me his clipper until I'd finished the joint. Delighted, the guy pulled out a packet of Embassy and took two out, handing me one whilst understandably having me down as a smoker. I took one anyway. Over the night I had found that I enjoyed the feel of a joint or a cigarette while on E. There had just been something I hadn't been able to put my finger on about how good it felt when you took a long draw of either.

With the sun being in the early stages of coming up it must've been around six and it was by then that you were really starting to see which people had been putting away copious amounts of drugs over the night. You would see some people who while obviously had taken something, now looked like they were nothing more than tired. Others though, having lost the protection of the dark, were really showing themselves out to be something quite special. I say that, fully appreciating the fact that the sight of me may well have been enough to draw comment from others in a similar way.

Three pills over the course of the night. One White Dove, a New Yorker and I forgot the name of the third one approximately five seconds after being told. Three pills over the night and morning had left me in quite the head state. For some reason, without me feeling anywhere close to being cold my teeth had began to chitter and no matter what I tried they wouldn't stop. They reminded me of those wind up teeth that you used to get in joke shops that after being set to go would travel across the table. Merry Molars or whatever the fuck they were called.

If it wasn't my teeth that was chittering then it was my jaw, which over the night had taken on its own separate persona. It was going so far to the side it almost needed its own postcode. I found it would be swinging like a gate left open in the wind, couldn't fucking keep it under control to save my life.

I completely got why Si had bought so much chewing gum for over the night. If anything just to be able to give your jaw something constructive to focus on! Whilst I wasn't as high as I'd been over the course of the night I could still feel a lot going on inside. It now felt like my body was getting back to normal again. My head though? Nope, absolute nonsense going on up top. My eyesight was completely trashed, I was seeing double for one thing and had held many conversations with people while covering one eye with my hand.

It was a couple of hours earlier that I had the other three laughing and shaking their heads at me when I was standing trying to light a joint but through the double vision, I kept trying to light the one that wasn't actually there. It wasn't even just double vision. I was finding it difficult to judge distances and through this, once I settled on which of the two joints I was seeing was the real one I then went and destroyed the fucking thing by misjudging lighting the end of it, or where I thought the end of it was. Instead, I sparked the lighter up, halfway ALONG the joint and underneath which set it on fire. Aye, they weren't fucking laughing at that part though.

I wasn't equipped for any kind of conversation, couldn't hold on to any kind of topic in my mind for too long before I'd forget again. I'd descended into the standard of memory that even a goldfish would mock someone over. This guy who'd come over to me for a light was even past where the state I was in. He had a similar wooly mountain hat on like mines, which I have to say that by seven in the morning had proved a master stroke to have brought with me, a long sleeved t shirt that looked like a bucket of water had been poured over him such was the amount of sweating he'd been doing in it. The whole time he stood chatting to me he could not stop moving his head in time to the muted sounds filtering over from the shed across the field.

I got the impression that even if the DJ was to stop the record right there and then, this guy would still have continued to nod his head. We must've looked a right pair of twats to any onlookers. He's dancing to practically nothing while I'm stood with one eye covered while talking to him. I briefly thought of that "winners don't do drugs" slogan that had began to pop up on some of the video games I'd play in the arcades. The short conversation we shared itself though was just crackers. We took each other through the same three questions I'd been asked all night long when meeting someone new. When he told me where he came from I saw that he lived close to me, small world and all that.

When I told him where I was from I expected a similar reaction back. instead I got a blank look from him as he asked me where that was?! That only served to blow my mind and then further again when I asked him, while assuming, if he was new to the area. He told me that he'd lived there all his life. Anything I tried to tell him that would hopefully spark a glimmer of recognition simply didn't get through to him although it probably didn't help that i kept forgetting names of places, shops and anything I felt might've helped jog his memory. For some reason though it was frustrating the fuck out of me because there was no way that he didn't know where I lived and that he probably passed through it every single fucking week!

It felt like, you know when you have one of those dreams? When you're fighting but you can't hit the other cunt and it gets you so frustrated that you wake up all pissed off about it? That's exactly how I was feeling. I just wanted him to say that he knew where I was talking about. Even if he was fucking lying, I'd have been happy! It's like you trying to tell me that you don't know where your garden shed is out the back of your house, I know you're talking pish and that you know where it is. I think I eventually started to annoy him with it though, thats what I sensed anyway but it really was a confusing time by then, all things considered, not just for me but for a lot of people in that field.

I was still "happy," and wouldn't have wanted to be anywhere else in the world but I was no longer feeling the invincible and untouchable way that I'd felt for most of the night. I had the sense that normality was now forcing its way back into my world while at the same time my brain was resisting saying 'not just yet, just a little taste.' It was just so so much to take in. What I'd experienced, the feeling that it had brought me, how in a matter of hours I was now questioning so much about life. The kids will always search for a way to rebel, to forge their own identity. It's probably why I ended up running with the Utility Crew. To show everyone that I'm not going to grow up like them.

With the mixture of Ecstasy, the location, the impact of the music and the sheer togetherness that I'd felt along with all the others who were there sharing it with me. I felt that I'd found a new form of cultural expression that could only have been how the Mods and the Rockers, the Punks and Skinheads had felt. Something exciting, breathtaking, exhilarating and the sense that doing it alongside so many others. It was almost like you knew you were part of something that you would remember for the rest of your life. And as far as expressing and rebelling, this one night had left me more rich and fulfilled than all of the capers on match day I'd been involved in put together.

The guy from along the road who I'm not even going to pretend to know that I remembered his name, he eventually gave me another fag, that I didn't want. He popped another in his mouth and once again asked for the use of the clipper before lighting up, giving me a handshake and a mini hug before heading off in search of his friends. He was only gone a few minutes and I then had a couple of lads, round about my age standing talking to me as we shared a joint that one of them had been smoking as they headed over my way.

Was mad as fuck but it turned out the two of them were Hibs casuals with the CCS. This came up in a completely non threatening or intimidating way as we chatted. I feel I have to say that because generally most casuals are going to mention that they ARE a casual for the glory (in their own worlds) of people knowing it. No, it came up in the way that the three of us were sat there trying to put into words what discovering all night house parties meant. It wasn't just me who was so heavily impacted by all of this, everyone was. It's like they all knew how unique and special a thing they were helping create, be a part of and felt privileged accordingly.

As we sat there, I mentioned that with it being my first time I had been blown away with the atmosphere, just how warm and friendly I'd found it from the minute I'd walked in. How it's completely the opposite of what I'd been led to believe, "going out in Scotland" was and how people were supposedly conditioned to act. A matter of hours in a field in Ayrshire had broken down all kinds of preconceptions that I may have had about that side of things.

'That, personally is my favourite part about allnighters' said one of them, a thin as a rake looking guy with, and I'm not sure if this was a product of what his night had involved, but cheeks drawn in like he was sucking on them, a face whiter than a polar bear with sunken eyes, it was possibly the MDMA but I thought he looked like that painting "The Scream." Only one where Edvard Munch has added the exact same middle parting haircut as mines. His one completely stuck to his head through sweat. 'It's kinda mad though, ironic likes, in the sense that I just breathe the friendliness in through all my pours in here and am automatically the same back with everyone yet if you were to bump into me in the wrong place at the wrong time on a Saturday afternoon then I might not be as friendly.' As the words came out I, more slower than normal, realised that I was sat there talking to another casual but from another mob entirely and one I had potentially came across previously in some shape or form.

My brain told me to play dumb. The problem being, round about that time of the morning I WAS dumb, too dumb to even follow instructions from my brain. 'Who do you run with' I asked him casually. The words escaping before I even knew I'd said them. The two of them, both looked towards me instantly with a pleased yet surprised look on their faces. 'CCS' replied the other one who had decided to stop opening his eyes completely whilst still nodding his head to the muffled beats traveling across the field. He was still holding conversation easy enough likes but for whatever reason wasn't opening his eyes for anyone or anything.

'We travelled through with Brad, he's overseeing the security side of things tonight so he got us in for SFA' the other one added. It didn't go unnoticed the way he'd dropped the name in assuming I'd recognise it, which I did. He was without a doubt referring to Brad Welsh. A name known to all of us in the Utility. Synonymous with the CCS and someone whose rep most certainly went before him. Started off as one of the top boys in the Hibs Baby Crew and as far as the history of Scottish fitba hooliganism, already had his place in the folklore cemented. This boy was fighting with opposing casuals at the age of thirteen or fourteen which made me look like a late bloomer by comparison. I wouldn't know him from Adam although I'm positive we'd have been in the same post code as each other when Hibs and United had been playing.

'What about you?' He continued. I wasn't sure if they thought I was a casual too purely through me sussing him out or not but I really wasn't in any frame of mind for composed and measured thinking. The pills had stripped me of a lot of things that I was only really beginning to notice by that point of the morning. I didn't really have the mental capacity to deal with rational thinking and something like being able to keep cards close to my chest was an impossibility.

'Dundee Utility' I answered in a matter of fact way I never, ever thought I would be able to while in the presence of members of Edinburgh's infamous Capital City Service. Yet it was all good, one of them rolled another joint and we all sat laughing, sharing match day stories as well as reminiscing about some tussles between The Utility and The CCS. It made no sense the whole conversation and who was engaging in it yet there we were, the apparent best of friends. I guess that moment summed up the whole friendly community vibe that had engulfed the whole field we were in.

If you can have members of the Utility and CCS sitting joking together then there's definitely something magical in the air. It reminded me about that time the British Army played the Germans at football on Christmas Day, like actually stopped the fucking war for a game before going back to killing each other again the day after. I'd learned about that from some Paul McCartney song although I'm not really sure if the story had all just been romanticised for maximum effect.

The drive back home was a much much quieter affair compared to the boisterous excitement that had filled the car on the way through. While all trying to remain in conversation with each other in Si's Nova I think we were all in our own comedown worlds. All just so incredibly tired, drained, defeated BUT our head's were still full of way too much strong chemicals to just clear themselves entirely and let us sleep.

I'd noticed a few hallucinations in the car as well as indescribable moments such as me for a second forgetting where I was sitting and thought I was on my way to school for the morning, aye, nothing that strange! We all tried to keep in the game though, primarily as he, who had ended up taking five pills over the night, required supervision at all times in terms of trying to drive without crashing the car and killing everyone inside it. Then again, when the supervision is coming from three other people with a combined Ecstasy intake of nine pills over twelve hours then that's where it all became a little dangerous. Who was there to supervise the supervisors I ask?

We made it back home in one piece. it had been a hard journey though but hats off to Si for managing it. I'm not sure I'd have been able to, even if I'd have been able to drive. Looking around the car and then at myself in the mirror inside the sun visor it was clear this was a car full of people who just needed their alone time now, to not have to speak to any other member of the human race for the next twelve to twenty four hours and just find their way back down to earth while relaxing. My eyes were just so unnaturally large, I'd never seen the likes. I know people had commented on them over the night but I'd had no idea they were "that" bad. I cringed at the thought of trying to sleep with them as from what I could see there was no fucking way that my eye lids were going to be able to stretch over those bad boys anytime soon. It was only when seeing them for the first time that I realised that there might have been a problem when coming face to face with the family.

I could have easily went on a ten minute speech to Si and Shan about how grateful I was for them to take Lisa and I with us, how it had been the best night of my life and my urgency to do it all over again as soon as there was another party. The quiet vibe in the car though, it was almost like words weren't required. We'd all experienced it, we all knew how amazing it had been. It was like it didn't need said and would be words wasted.

We all said our goodbyes which included an ill timed comment from him about the United pre season friendly next weekend against Millwall and how he was hoping they'd bring a mob up from London which I clocked Lisa noticing too and for a second I'm sure I saw her face change. 'Always good to test yourself against English opposition' I said back in a way that could easily be put down to a comment that was nothing other than in a sporting sense. As spaced as he was he seemed to get what I was doing.

His car sped off into the distance before disappearing completely while Lisa and I stood rooted to the spot while she searched for her eyedrops that were scattered along with the other seventy five things in her bag. Once we started moving, every single step was a task. The pavement underneath my feet felt strange after being stood in a field for so long although I concede, the Eckies probably had something to do with it too. I can only imagine what I must've looked like the way I was walking. Something along the lines of a spaceman walking on the moon with those big steps.

The thought of having to walk all the way up to Lisa's house then back in the opposite direction home was not exactly a pleasing one. I struck lucky when it dawned on her that she was meant to have been staying at her friends over night so it would've looked suspicious if I had been seen with her. She also, and at least one person was thinking straight out of us, reminded me that by now it was almost lunch time so lots of people were going to be out and about so maybe it would be best we just headed both home, asserting that her mum or dad could drive past in the car any second. We both looked every inch like two people who had been up for more than twenty four hours and had spent the night in a field. The key between then and getting home to the relative safety of our bedrooms was to avoid contact with any human beings. ESPECIALLY the ones of the parent and or guardian variety.

She definitely had a point so we gave each other a cuddle that once started I didn't want it to end. Oh to have been able to go back to her bed and the two of us just collapsing into it together sleeping away the day. Sunday night would have normally been a night we'd see each other but given the circumstances it was inevitable that we were both due to crash and burn and when we did, who knows how long we'd be out for so agreed to see each other the next day. Her face was just so cute the way she thanked me for taking her and that she couldn't wait to do it again before planting a simple peck on my cheek and starting on her way home.

This left me with a paranoid thoughts filled walk home while worrying about what was going to happen when I walked through the door. I'd stopped going to church the minute I could but yet in that walk down the hill I found myself trying to remember my Hail Marys and Our Fathers that I used to recite. Unsurprisingly for a boy who would have struggled to have been able to tell you what he'd had for his dinner the night before. I was not able to remember anything more than a couple of lines of each prayer. Not sure if they worked or not but when I turned the corner to enter my street I instantly noticed that my uncles car wasn't sat outside which could only have been a good sign.

I slowly and carefully turned the door handle .. locked. That was positive sign number two. It took me almost a week to actually put my key into the lock, some of my attempts were pitiful, truly embarrassing, a fucking toddler could have found the keyhole quicker. Eventually I struck gold and managed to get myself in. My mind had me as some stealthy ninja warrior entering a building on a kill mission but I'm betting the reality of it all was a lot different. I needn't have bothered anyway, I was still doing this cat burglar creeping stuff when I noticed a hand written note with a tenner beside it sat on the kitchen bunker.

Steven

We've went out for the day for a drive along the coast and then our tea later on so won't be back until evening. £10 for you to get yourself something for your tea x

I'm not sure if there really is a god or not but on a day like that Sunday, with the state that my mind was in and what my appearance was like. All I could've ever wished for would have been some privacy and I'd effectively now been given my own house for the day AND with the added bonus of pocketing a cheeky tenner to myself because unbeknown to my auntie, the way I was feeling on my return from Ayrshire I didn't think I'd be eating anything until the Tuesday, at the earliest.

Chapter 18.

Saturday had taken quite a bit in getting over and recovering from. While the Sunday had been more of an inconvenience than anything else with me just wanting sleep while being a million miles from actually being able to do so. I'd finally managed some late on the Monday morning where by then, was approaching having been awake for a full forty eight hours. Most of the day found me with a body drained of any kind of being and a head that was having a hard time in appreciating what was actually going on inside of it. I tried to watch films and TV shows but couldn't concentrate on them.

I'd find myself focusing on a silly thing like a persons haircut or garment of clothing only to find that I'd have missed five minutes dialogue of what was going on, me staring blankly at the screen like a zombie while my train of thought was going from station to station. Tried to play my Sega but that was a waste of fucking time too as my reactions weren't anywhere close to being up for playing video games. I can hardly follow the puck on NHL 89 under normal circumstances so, unsurprisingly on a Class A drug comedown it was practically impossible to play. Had to pretend I was crashed when my auntie and uncle came back as I just didn't have a conversation in me, well definitely not with them anyway. I figured that by the Monday everything would be all back to normal and I'd be safe again.

I was right and I was wrong about the Monday. Right in the sense that aye, my eyes would be back to normal size and aye the Eckies would have worn off. Me thinking that everything would be all rosy again for me, wrong! No one warned me about the depression that would follow how good Saturday night had been. Fuck, I was depressed. Snapping at people, not wanting to do anything or speak to anyone, with the exception of Lisa. Seeing her made things better, well, a touch. That's how low I was feeling.

I fired up to hers for a while after tea. When her mum opened the door she, looking exasperated, said to me 'thank god your here Steven because if you can't put a smile on her face today then we're all in trouble, oh is she snappy today.' Vera was brand new, had really taken to me since I'd started coming up to the house, always wanted me round for tea with the family. She looked kinda like that Bet Lynch who was behind the bar in Coronation Street, fucking loads of hair, must've taken her to employ a structural engineer to help put it up in the morning and stay up. I once asked her if she had to walk on her knees when when entering doors which she pure lapped up. I headed upstairs and Lisa looked exactly like I was feeling.

We sat down on her bed and talked over how the past day had been since we'd last seen each other. She told me that today she couldn't stop crying over stupid little things and that her emotions had been out of control. I couldn't help but nod my head in appreciation with her when she told me that she was having a hard time dealing with how she felt on Saturday and where she was in comparison to her Monday. I think the fact that someone is saying that can only serve to highlight just "how" special a night they'd had.

I told her I felt the same but had actually spoken to Si about it and he told me that Monday's were notoriously hard to handle after an allnighter. He'd said that Tuesday would be better and by Wednesday we'd be back to normal. I'd been hungover before and felt like I was dying the next day but I never thought that the baggage that would come with going to an Acid House party would last for days. And even so, when I questioned myself as to whether it had been worth it or not all I got back was a resounding YES. Even as shit as I felt, one of my constant thoughts was that I could not wait until the next time rolled around.

Lisa felt the same and we sat chatting about when we'd get to another one together. Soon as fucking possible was the answer! Between the pair of us we'd heard some whispers over Saturday night that there was one in a few weeks near Inverness but nothing more than that. Si would keep us informed, no worries on that score. I think though that there on the Monday night, Lisa and moi would have felt a LOT better if we'd been given an exact date for when we could go. We swapped some stories from over the time we'd been in Shroom over the Saturday night and most of Sunday morning.

There was so much the two of us had forgotten about since leaving the party. Some things I wished had stayed in the forgotten zone. Like me doing a fucking Freddie Mercury impression for them all while I was off my tits. Well fuck them anyway cause I WAS on a rocket ship on its way to Mars and I WAS having a good time! 'Forget Freddie though, I never knew Zico was quite the dancer' she teased me - 'Aye, neither did I, you think that the E might've had something to do with it?' I said dryly.

'Well they say that it can make a white man dance, and you're white so, might be possible' She replied with the first big smile I'd seen since inside Shroom. I loved that smile so much and as many aspects of my Saturday night that I loved, seeing her so smiley and happy all night was the best thing of all for me. For most of the night her eyes resembled stars and she had such a glow to her. She looked "healthy," ironically so. She'd expressed a lot of love my way in and around that cow shed. Which she got back double from me. The Ecstasy though, over the night had allowed Lisa and I to share some of our most deep and inner thoughts about each other.

I'd never felt so free, willing and able to tell another person exactly how I felt way deep inside of me and that night she appeared to be the very same. It's not what I'd been used to, after all, that's what the adults do, right? With their "feelings" and all of that. She told me how happy I made her. On my side I'm sat telling her that single handedly she had altered how I felt, thought and acted. How she had changed things for me, personally. That through her I wanted to be a better person and how no one had given me inspiration like that before in my life. I was a young man heading towards adulthood doing all he could to avoid doing so because at the end of the day, who really "wants" to be mature and have responsibilities and all of that boring stuff? Lisa though? She made me want to grow up and become a man, her man.

The paradox of us holding such a deep, meaningful and more specifically, adult conversation while on her side she sat chewing gum so fast you'd have thought that she had been stuck on fast forward with a remote control for a video recorder. This done while I sat covering one eye, my free hand making shapes in the air with a neon yellow glow stick, the kind that cunts use when they're in trouble stranded on boats or on mountains. The paradox wasn't lost on me. All of those thoughts had been inside me once I'd started falling for Lisa and long before we got to the farm.

The idea of me being able to find a way to get them out and tell her though seemed outlandish to me. I'm not saying that E was a truth drug but what I will say is that it appeared to remove certain barriers and leave you as open a person as you could ever possibly be. Almost blissfully vulnerable to what might come out your mouth. As high as I undoubtedly was though it was experienced while at times I felt that I was operating with a brain that had been upgraded while also having the ability to see the world with a fresh pair of eyes. When I say this I do not just mean when on the drug exclusively.

Following leaving and eventually getting some me time alone with my thoughts I had done a fair bit of reflecting. Deep stuff that I'd never found myself doing in my life. What I was doing with my life, what did I "want" to do with it. Where did I want to go in the next few vital years before I became eighteen. In doing so one subject kept coming back to me again and again. The Dundee Utility Crew and was this something I really wanted to be doing with my life? I faced the fact that it was for certain only a matter of time before I ended up huckled by the police, or worse. Just say, and against all the odds. I was to manage to avoid a criminal record for violent behaviour or an extended stay in hospital. Deep inside, suddenly I was giving serious thoughts over if it was something I really wanted to do anymore. Whether it was now a part of life that needed left behind.

Over the summer break, the mentally scarring ill fated trip to Glasgow near the end of the season had revisited my thoughts quite a few times. I'd never have admitted it to anyone else but that day gave me a bit of a fright, when we turned that corner and saw how many there was of them, I'd never felt so scared in my life when I saw position I was in. If I'd decided to run from the ICF, my "friends" and Nora for certain, from the Utility would have probably put me in hospital themselves. Despite all of the madness that I'd sampled most weeks since starting to run with the casuals it had been that trip through to The Weeg that day which had been a wake up. Even so, it hadn't been any kind of catalyst for me to entertain any kind of thoughts of removing myself from my Saturday afternoon fun and games.

One single pill, ok three, while surrounded by the most friendly and vibrant people I'd ever met in my life while taking in a new form of music that had instantly felt more than just music to me. I found my reason that I hadn't even known that I was looking for.

I was so comfy lying there just snuggling into Lisa and could easily have just spent the rest of the night with my arms around her, passed out. We'd not yet managed to work out an unplanned/completely planned overnight stay yet but had discussed it and were going to test it out one night soon. It's not like I would have been seen as a one night stand in the eyes of Lisa's parents but still, it was a bit of a liberty to be doing it at anytime without her parents consent. I won't imagine I'm going to be too fucking chuffed if decades from now my daughter's boyfriend is sleeping in the same bed as her under my roof at sixteen so I can't image Lisa's dad, Bob would be happy as Larry at such news.

I hope he's not one of those gun nuts that keeps them in the shed, a shed that no one else gets into. Firearms just waiting there for a special occasion, like someone shagging his daughter while he lies in bed through the other bedroom. Good enough reason to lock and load, I can't help but concede.

I reluctantly got myself together to head down the road. Due to my messed up sleeping patterns I "should've" been ready for sleep but was far from achieving it. It was a really sticky humid night. One of those types where despite living in Scotland which isn't exactly known for high temperatures, you need to sleep above your sheets. It got too much for me, plus, never mind the heat. I'd been sleeping at irregular hours so my head was completely fried. I decided to roll a joint around five in the morning or so and go outside for a walk along the beach across from my house.

It was still dark with the moon out but you could tell by the colour of the sky that it was soon going to start getting lighter. The cool breeze that I found down by the water after all of the humidity filled tossing and turning I'd done lying in bed in that hot room was an absolute god send. At such an early part of the morning the only sounds to be heard were that of the waves coming into the shore, and the seagulls. The fucking seagulls. Without a doubt THE worst thing about living by the sea is those flying pricks. They scare the fuck out of me. As far as animals go, they're game as fuck. They don't mind going toe to toe with humans and I think that's the part that gets me with them. Can't rule them out having a pop at you, especially if you've got food. Fucking scavenging cunts.

My Auntie told me that a couple of them had attacked old Mrs Stewart who lives next to the Co-Op a few weeks ago. Absolute dicks. Luckily they're not so bothered about getting their beaks round a joint so never took an interest in me as I shared the beach with them.

I'd borrowed one of Si's tapes that were in the car on Sunday morning before he dropped Lisa and I off. Written on the sticker on the side of it was the words 'Nicky Holloway / Ibiza.' Before leaving the house I'd remembered to pop it into my Walkman so decided to have a wee listen to it, reasoning that at the very least it would get rid of the seagull noises. The DJ skills of Nicky Holloway was well impressive, almost more of the same stuff from Saturday night but a wee bit slower. Every single song on it just some happy piano stuff, quite a few of them with vocals over top which going by what my ears had been assaulted by at Shroom, hadn't been so common.

With it beginning to get a bit lighter, visibility was starting to get better and spying quite a large sized rock I walked over and sat down on it, staring out over the water towards Edinburgh although the dark was still obscuring the capital city from my vision. What I was looking at mixed with the music and in addition to the spliff, it all just felt so tranquil. Stupid, I know but at that moment I felt like I was the only person in the world.

I left the beach just as the sun was starting to come up. Could've sat there longer but I knew I had to get back in the house and up to bed before the folks were all getting up for work. Simply couldn't be arsed going through the whole explaining to them why I was coming through the door at seven on a Tuesday morning when they were going in the opposite direction. Since Sunday when I'd arrived home I'd done almost everything I could to avoid the rest of the house, figuring I'd best get this whole comedown stuff out of the way before I returned to humanity once again.

Chapter 19.

'Alright ya wee Fife bastard, just checking yer still alive and ready for duty against these English cunts tomorrow' The unmistakably perma aggressive tones of Nora roared down the phone at me. It was the first time I'd heard it in months. I was surprised over the reason that he was calling though. It's not like he'd ever done that for any other game. Truth was I'd mulled over the Millwall match all week long and right there and then with him outright asking me if I'd be there it threw me and I fucking shat the bed.

I wanted to tell him that I wasn't sure and was still to decide but instead I stammered back with an in no way convincing 'Fuck aye, Millwall? Wouldn't miss that for the world, mate' - 'Aye just as fucking well, Zico. I'll not fuck you about here, tomorrow isn't going to be a dance around the maypole. These cunts are respected all over England, their team might be shite but their hooligans are fucking primo. We're going to need a good crew repping so I'm just phoning round a few boys tonight to get an idea who's all going to be there, cunts are on holiday just now so some of the team won't be there.'

Fucking great, not only had I confirmed that I'm going to be there looking to fight some scary creme de la creme of hooligans but now I was being told that the ranks were going to be somewhat depleted.

He went on to tell me all about what had happened in Amsterdam, which Si had already filled me in on at the weekend. I tried to tell Nora at the start but he didn't seem too impressed at the fact I was robbing him of the chance to tell the story about how mental, yet compassionate he had been with the Chelsea boy and how we were now officially linked with the Headhunters. I wouldn't have dared say it of course but I was standing there in my living room thinking to myself 'well where the fuck are these Headhunters tomorrow then considering we're playing one of their cross city rivals?' I'd have thought that they would've jumped at the chance to have a swedge with Millwall, especially with it being under the radar of all the London coppers who they'd undoubtedly have been known to.

'Some fucking place, Amsterdam though, Zico. Fucking heaven on earth, heaven .. on .. earth' I could tell how excited he was through the enthusiasm he was putting into each and every single word. 'Aye, I'd love to go someday' I feebly replied safe in the knowledge that all I wanted to say about the city I couldn't due to the folks listening in. 'Was out ma fucking tree on the strongest grass you've ever seen, away shagging prostitutes down the Red Light District that were like fucking MODELS, every one of them' 'Keats from Monifieth? Ken him?'

For easiness sake I said yes even though I only vaguely knew who he was. 'He thought he was Billy fucking big time and hired two hookers at the same time, had to pay them a shit load to agree to it, should've seen the fucking smile on his coupon when he walked back into The Bulldog and joined us afterwards though, couldn't fucking wipe it from his face all day, likes.' All I could do was offer inconspicuous standard 'no ways' and 'that's mentals' and things like that without really contributing to the conversation in any meaningful way.

'Right then, Zeec, meet us up at The Snug about lunchtime, if plans change I'll give you a call tomorrow morning' he said once he'd taken me through the Amsterdam tales. Just as I was about to hang up I heard him shouting through the phone 'OH OH OH ZICO' I was close to actually putting the receiver down right before I heard him, that's how loud the cunt was. I put it back up to my ear 'Aye' I said, letting him know he'd caught me before I'd hung up. 'You might want to take a taxi or bus up to Dundee tomorrow by the way, mate.'

Fucking taxi I was thinking to myself, he does realise I'm sixteen with barely two pennies to rub together? Before I could say anything back he continued 'Chances are a lot of Millwall will be coming over to Dundee by train from Edinburgh and considering every fucking train you get over here every week comes from that direction, you're playing Russian Roulette by what train you get on tomorrow morning' - I thanked him for the heads up as the last thing I needed was to share a train carriage with some bad bastards from London Town who would more than likely see to it that I wouldn't be able to walk back off the train by the time it had arrived in Dundee.

The fact that I'd spent the whole week with Saturday even up for consideration in my private thoughts spoke volumes because I know for a fact that the Zico from last season would have been like a kid before his birthday over the prospect of taking on a serious mob like Millwall. Have to admit I know practically fuck all about the team themselves as they've always been in lower leagues and hardly ever likely to be on Match of the Day on BBC or The Big Match on a Sunday afternoon on ITV.

The reputation of their hooligans goes before them though. First time I ever took notice of them was when I was back in first year at high school, maybe second year? I remember lying in my bedroom watching the highlights from a midweek FA cup tie where they were away to Luton Town. All through the match there were hooligans trying to get on the pitch. I'm sure the ref was going to take the players off the pitch in the first half because of it all. Anyway Luton won and when the final whistle blew it all went fucking nuts after that. Millwall were ripping up seats from the stands and lobbing them at the police until they got tired of that and all piled onto the pitch and started chasing the coppers all over the fucking shop.

Everyone was talking about it the next day at school. Only time I've ever seen the filth running scared like that from casuals. I'd seen them running from the striking miners years back when all that stuff was going on but had never seen them chased from fitba hooligans before. Cunts with alsatians running for their lives. Too mad likes. Everybody knew about Millwall after that and now we were getting a chance to go up against them. Like I said, a meet like that should've been, for me, the holy grail, the fucking ultimate. That's the thing though, it wasn't feeling that way.

I'd told Nora that I'd be there. That was the only fact of the matter but yet, inside I still gave consideration to me not appearing. I figured I'd make up some flimsy excuse for my non appearance if need be. Put on the spot the way that I had been with Nora I didn't feel like there was any option open to me for saying to him that I wouldn't be going. I've never had a problem with him since the day we met but I'm not stupid either. I knew how dangerous he was and what he's capable of. I've seen it with my own eyes and lets just say I wouldn't want to be classed as an enemy by him.

Volatile isn't the word. I seen him grab a Celtic supporter and when I say supporter I mean a scarfer, just someone there to watch their team and not bother anyone, nothing remotely like a fucking casual. Anyway, Nora grabbed this boy from behind and shoved his head right through a bakers plate glass window, Baynes I think. Fucking blood everywhere, made me sick just seeing the mess he'd left the guy in. The reason? Primarily United had been humped 5-1 by Celtic and this boy n the hoops had 'looked at him.'

That was just one example of what i'd seen him do on a Saturday. The whispers were from some in the crew that away from the matches he was involved in drug distribution along with some gangsters, right serious characters that don't fuck about. All in all, he was a person that you really wanted to have onside as the alternative isn't something you'd even want to have to consider.

It was a small worry to me that for the first time since becoming a casual, I was now having second thoughts although that wasn't where the worry was presenting itself. I'd never thought about the implications of one day actually NOT wanting to be one so hadn't really thought about what it would be like stopping with regards to some of the other guys in the crew and how they'd take it. The fact that I appeared to be in Nora's little black book showed I definitely was thought of when it came to who made up the team on a Saturday.

There was Si too, I'd started to really value our friendship and if I was to stop with the fighting on a Saturday would that then mean an end to him and I as pals? I fucking hoped not just when he'd introduced me to Acid House and it's all I'd thought about since sampling it. I never considered any kind of downsides to joining the Utility back when I did. The only downside is that you're probably going to take a paggering every now and again but it's not really a downside, just a simple fact and one that if seen as a problem by someone would've probably stopped them from even becoming a hoolie in the first place.

'Who was that?' Uncle Jimmy asked without taking his eyes off the telly and the program he was sat watching. I'd been clocking it while speaking to Nora. I'd never seen it before but it looked like ordinary members of the public were dressing up to look like and sing like famous artists. James seemed to be into it likes. 'Just one of ma mates that goes to United games asking if I'm going up to Tannadice for the game' - 'You're wasting your money going up to see that rubbish' He baited me, or at least that's how I initially took it until he carried on.

'Pre season friendlies are nothing more than a training session for both teams. They're no worried about performances or even winning the game, It's all about getting their fitness up to scratch. You'd be as well saving your money for when the season starts properly and the games actually mean something.' He had a point, actually. I told him that I was going to sleep on it and decide tomorrow morning. Aware of the fact that he'd have just heard me on the phone saying that I was going to Nora I followed up by telling him that I'd just said yes to my mate as I couldn't be bothered having him on my case as I didn't have the time.

'So what's this you're watching? I've not seen it before?' I changed the subject swiftly and taking advantage over the fact that it was the break and that giving me more chance in him actually answering me. Normally if he's into something and you try to talk, he grabs the remote and makes a point of turning the volume up but if it's on the adverts he's happy enough to have a bit back and forth with you.

'Stars in their Eyes, tonight's the first one' he told me. 'Some good singers on it, you want to have seen the boy that just done Meatloaf before you came downstairs. Wasn't just the voice, looked the spitting image of him as well' Before I could really answer him it had come back on for the second half. That scouser, Matthew Kelly was welcoming everyone back apparently, before announcing the next contestant, Wendy from Milton Keynes onto the stage.

Watching her walk up to speak to him my first thought was that she couldn't have been imitating any star because she didn't look like anyone I'd ever seen before. Felt a bit stupid when I then heard Kelly ask her. 'So Wendy who are you going to be tonight?' and her answering back 'Tonight Matthew I'm going to be Debbie Harry.' She disappeared and then when the doors opened again she's standing there all done up to look like the Blondie singer. Had to sit down for a moment to watch her, sucked right in so I was. She done Tide is High, no fucking joke, if I'd shut my eyes I could've sworn it WAS Debbie Harry who was on the telly. 'She's no bad' I said to my uncle as we sat and watched her 'Aye, still not as good as the Meatloaf boy though, he's winning this, have no fears about that' He insisted.

Completely out of character for me, I stayed sitting and watched the rest of the show with him, my auntie joining us after coming through from the kitchen with a pot of tea and a plate of custard creams for the two of them. He was right, the Meatloaf impersonator won. (Which my uncle fucking loved, flashing me and my Auntie a knowing "told you so" look before smiling and turning back to the TV proud as punch) He got to perform the song again to close the show after being announced as the winner. I think he goes through to the final along with the winners from each week, not too sure though.

Next up according to the STV voice over guy was Coronation Street and most definitely my signal to depart. I needed to get ready to meet Lisa in any case. It was a nice night outside so we were going to get a wee carry out from Paul's and head up the park to have a drink, away from anyone else hanging around outside. I would never ever blow her out and mess her about at the last minute but following Nora's call I now knew I had plenty to be thinking about ahead of Saturday morning. I suddenly felt like I'd been placed in a no win situation. If I don't go then I'd most likely have to face some consequences for it. If I do go, then, Millwall, just Millwall.

Chapter 20.

'What you fahking sayin to it now you little Jock cunt?' This skinhead
in a white Fred Perry polo shirt spat as he pinned me against the inside
of the train door with the majority of the carriage looking on. Some
women were screaming at the sight of him holding a knife inches from
my face, so close to me that I couldn't really see it but believe me, I
knew it was there. Understandably I wasn't exactly in the most chilled
of minds due to how this situation had escalated.

If there's one thing I know about soccer hooligans that come out of
London is that they're not exactly against using blades on others. And
reverting to type, here was one pulling a blade out on me for pretty
much fuck all. How close it was to my face coupled with the
unpredictable movements of the train meant that I knew I was
potentially moments away from having my face carved open,
regardless if all he was doing was trying to give me a scare or not.

'I wasn't saying anything in the first place, never mind now' I pleaded
but not in some whiny shitting myself way. Simply just trying to
diffuse the situation, if possible. 'I was only having a bit banter with
your mate over there about our teams and next thing I know you've
come from nowhere with your chib out' - 'You've changed you're
fahking tune haven't you' he replied, his manic eyes ironically were a
good comparison of mines inside that cow shed the week before. I
genuinely didn't have a fucking clue what I was meant to have done to
merit a blade coming out.

Well first of all, aye, I decided to go to the game after all. Still wasn't
sure if I wanted to make the trip to Dundee even by the next morning
but after weighing up all the pros and cons of it all I decided that I'd
go. Doing so with only a few minutes to spare before the train arrived.
The only reason I'd decided to go was down to the thought of what
implications there might be through telling Nora I would go only for
me not to show. That and the fact that a wee percentage of me was
worried that it would be a good day against such a tough opposing
mob and I'd have regretted it if I'd missed it then had to hear all the
stories second hand.

Secondly, I had completely ignored Nora's advice about my mode of
transport and ended up not only taking the train but due to where I

was when I took the decision to go. I got on the train two stops earlier than the rest of the Fife members of the crew, if they were even going that day at all. When I'd got on the carriage I instantly felt a few stares in my direction from a select amount of particular dodgy looking characters. A lot of them weren't even the best of dressers from as far as I got a chance to see but I could still tell they had an air of menace about them. 'WE ARE MILLWALL SUPER MILLWALL NO ONE LIKE US WE DON'T CARE' a few of them a bit down the carriage piped up to the same tune as that Rod Stewart song, Sailing.

The song then traveling all the way down via the cockneys that were littered throughout the carriage. Just my fucking luck! The same carriage as them, they've already clocked me before the train doors have even closed and now I was faced with a journey all the way up to Dundee in their company. I just wanted to keep my head down and avoid them but it was never going to happen. I thought about moving through to the next carriage but looking through the window to it there seemed to be even more of them assembled in that one so there was no real point of transferring from one to the other. Maybe it was just my paranoia but even though I was consistently looking at something other than one of them, I could feel eyes on me staring in my direction hoping that I was going to look back at them.

I had the thought of getting off at the next station but to do so would have meant I'd have had to sack match day completely as I didn't have the funds for the extra train fare so it was all or nothing with this one. I was standing there praying that Brewster, Carey and McGinn would be getting on a few stops on from me. Not that it would have made the slightest bit of difference anyway in terms of numbers against all the Londoners.

It might've inflamed things if anything. While staring at the toes of my Borg Elites for what must've been a good five minutes I was taken out of my hypnotic state by a loud 'OI MATE, YOU A DUNDEE SUPPORTER?' Ah the classic mistake made by someone from outside Scotland. They say Dundee but when they say that they mean Dundee 'United' not Dundee FC who ARE called Dundee.

Ask any United fan about it and they'll tell you that it does their head in. Probably does Dundee fans heads in too but I couldn't really give a fuck about how they feel. They should take it as a compliment if anything to have their name linked with a better team even if it is by mistake. Normally when someone says that to me I'll snap their head off or be wide and say no I don't support 'Dundee' until they realise what I mean by that.

This guy asking? I wasn't so much up for giving him that much of a lecture. He knew who he meant, I knew who he meant but even so, I couldn't resist a slight nudge so with him and all the others around him staring back, waiting for a response I replied 'well, Dundee United, aye' - 'Fahking Dundee, Dundee United whatever you fahking amateurs call yourself … You're fucking shit anyway' the rest of them cackled before joining in. Some pointing aggressively, others coming out with the stereotypical standard insults the English always hit us Scots with. Haggis eating cunt, skirt wearing prick, you fucking jock wanker … and many more.

I was a bit pissed off by it all because I was now put in a situation with them. The train journey was fucking ages away from pulling in to Dundee and if I didn't give them a bit back I was going to be walked all over during the journey. As bad as they were I'd noticed that they weren't being dicks with any of the other passengers on the carriage. There was no coincidence that I'd stuck out to them through the clothes I was wearing which wouldn't have been any different to what the casuals were all wearing down in London.

The fat guy with the middle parting, that was a weird choice of hairstyle when you had as much spots on your forehead as him, and had what looked like a Millwall home shirt on. I'd clocked it earlier on. Was trying not to stare at it for too long but I didn't recognise what make the top was. You know? We have Adidas which is top drawer as far as fitba teams go, other teams have Umbro as well but then the really wee teams all have some radge wee company making their shirts. One that no one has even heard of. That shirt alone told me how insignificant they were as a team.

Fat boy stood there well pleased with himself and waiting on a response back. I know that by answering cunts like that you're only playing into their hands. That's exactly what they're looking for and to ignore them would frustrate the fuck out of them. I'm not really that good though at biting my tongue though, never have been. No matter what might happen as a result. I simply couldn't stand there and watch all of them stand there telling me that my team is shit when they're supporting MILLWALL? Fuck that.

'You sure, pal?' I replied friendly enough and was cut off before I could continue. 'Course I'm fahking sure, All you Jock teams are fucking rank' He was getting fired into a tin of Carlsberg and going by the rest of the tins that were in a carrier bag at his feet he was already on the sesh for the day. I couldn't really read him. There were more casual looking guys, although still not that up to scratch in the sense that your average Scottish casual would be seen wearing.

They stood surrounding him and the way they'd all been eyeballing me I knew that at the drop of a hat they could and would steam in. It's times like that where you wish there was a phone on the train and not just one at each station. I'd have called The Snug and alerted the boys about where they needed to be when the train got to Dundee. This guy who wasn't a casual but being the biggest prick of all I was willing to just put down to being a wee bit drunk as well as a smug English twat in general. I couldn't help but engage.

'Was just asking if you were sure since it as only a couple of years ago that my team was in the Uefa cup final, beating Barcelona home and away on the way to the final. Only way you'll see Europe is if you go to Magaluf on your summer holidays, pal.' Some of them never took my comedic genius in the way that it had been intended though. 'Check this little wide cahnt' I heard from one of them but I wasn't breaking my stare at the boy in the team shirt.

He was fuming but hadn't found a comeback to me so I kept going. I'd got it into my head that I'd get more respect from them if I stood my ground. I thought by doing it with a bit of humour then it wouldn't give them a chance to mistake my tone with them. Some of them "got it" and I knew they'd not be a problem from then on. I tried to continue my charm offensive on the others. 'Not being funny, pal but if someone is going to tell me that my team is shit I'd really be looking for them to be someone like a Bayern Munich or Manchester United fan, not a supporter of a team who plays in the …' I genuinely did not know the league that Millwall played in down in England but it made it all the more fitting when I then had to say 'Actually, what league are you even in, mate?'

I didn't get much time to gauge any responses from what I said because in a flash this guy with the skinhead just lunged at me pulling a knife out of his pocket, so quickly I thought there was only going to be one outcome. I could hear protests from some of his mates who were behind him. 'Cahm on Lefty, leave the kid alone' - 'Put the fahking blade away and behave yourself, the little cahnt is just giving it some lip.'

'Think you're fahking smart do yer?' I'm looking at him but also past and around him hoping that some of the others were going to pull him back again but apart from all of the comments they were putting in his direction they weren't for moving. 'Look mate I was just having a bit of a laugh with your man over there in the blue top. I'm not here looking for any' He cut in moving the blade closer to me 'I AINT YER FAHKING MATE.' - 'Seriously, what's with these pricks that take this mate stuff so seriously' I thought to myself despite the fact that there was obviously something more urgent that needed attending to? He brought the sharp tip even closer to my face again. I assumed that half of the carriage had been watching this take place because as the knife moved closer to me I heard a few screams and gasps from some girls close by.

A good half dozen of his group are shouting at him. I'm "trying" to talk some sense into him but it's hard to really find a flow of constant words when you have the tip of a knife pressed gently against and menacingly traveling along and under your eye. When he started doing this that's when I knew that he wasn't going to stab me and he was just being a total fanny about it. 'He'd have stabbed me by now if he was going to' I told myself.

I just wanted him to end his charade and fucking pronto because one bump of the train carriage and I'd be losing an eye as things stood. Seemed like an eternity but he eventually took it away from my face but slowly took it over to my cheek and with how sharp this chib was of his he had managed to intentionally nick the top of my cheek sending a small trickle of blood down my face. Noticing this he gave me one last sneer before taking the knife away and breaking into some freaky laughter and putting both hands up into the air like he was hearing a fucking piano break on an E!

A couple of other Millwall lads came over to speak to me for the last bit of the journey, surprisingly both casuals. Initially they came over to apologise for the maniac that was their friend. I said that I wouldn't be surprised if there were police waiting on him at Dundee if the driver had heard about it going on in the train. They just looked at me like I was stupid which left me with the impression that this mob get up to all kinds of shit like that and most of the time they're getting away with it.

They were asking me about if there was going to be casuals from 'Dundee' who would be there to fight them. I do a lot of stupid things at times but even I wasn't stupid enough to stand there and tell them that I was one of the Dundee crew so cautiously told them that I wasn't the person to ask a question like that.

I informed them that through going to the games I'd seen the casuals outside and inside the ground but that they didn't really seem like they had too big a crew and that there was nothing for a famous mob like Millwall to worry about, especially with this being a meaningless pre season match. I couldn't help but take advantage of the situation I was in so a wee white lie like that to these lunatics from London might've helped put them off their guard a little when it came to taking us on.

With me being stood by the doors I got the fuck off the train post haste the second they opened when it pulled to a stop in Dundee. I figured with such a healthy sized mob it would take them a few minutes to get their bearings and thought that alone might give me enough time to make it to the phone boxes outside at the entrance to the station and put in a quick call to The Snug. Instead of Nora coming to the phone it instead, was Dawson. 'Aye, who's this?' - 'It's Zico listen man cause I don't have time. I've just been on the train with a big mob of Millwall. They just got off a minute ago so are going to be down here in the city centre for a wee while at least. I've had a bit of bother with them so need to make myself scarce as they'll be here the now' I said with urgency.

'Listen, wee man' he replied while trying to fight against the noise of everyone stood drinking in the pub. 'Can you do one thing for me, when you put the phone down try to get as much distance from them as you can but still keep them in view. Don't let them out of your fucking sight, you hear me.?' 'You'll be that far away from them that even if they see you they won't chase after you.' He was employing me to play spotter. You see them at every away trip, you can tell they're casuals by one look at them but with them being only one or two of them you know they're not there for a box, always keeping their distance so much you won't catch them if you tried to so you don't even bother.

It didn't take a brain surgeon to work out that they would head into the city centre towards the boozers then eventually head up to the ground via the Hilltown part of the city, although we all pronounced it as "Hulltoon". It's the route any fans would take from the city centre. Due to the rushed phone call I had with Dawson I wasn't sure what plan he was without question putting into action but if I was sure of anything there was a mob already marching from The Snug and on its way down the hill. Predictably, Millwall ended up congregating at The Trades Bar. A decent sized team of them stood outside with pints in their hands. I'm not sure if they'd noticed me or not but I was able to stand at a distance without any hint of trouble my way.

It gave me time to think about things for the first time since setting foot on the train. I hadn't even been sure about going and look at all that had happened since I'd chosen to. Almost stabbed and now I was scouting what was meant to be Britains most psychotic gang of football hooligans. It was a weird feeling that I was almost ashamed at myself. That for the past week I had been doing a bit of genuine soul searching and had come to terms with the fact that I wanted to move away from all of it and move on with my life. The moment I had that first reservation about being a casual THAT was when I should've ended it all, taken the decision and rolled with whatever consequences it might've brought. Instead I'd hummed and hahd leading to this and how easily I'd managed to slip right back into it within the space of a train journey.

Soon the Utility lads were going to appear, and a lot of them, well hopefully as far as any Utility were concerned. A skeleton staff really wasn't going to cut it with these maniacs. It wasn't going to be pretty whatever the size of crew that was on the way down the hill and something I wasn't exactly looking forward to, having had a taste of how some of these Millwall lads went about things.

Chapter 21.

'We need to talk' - The four words that someone NEVER wants to hear from their girlfriend, wife, boss or parents yet here was these same ill fated words coming from Lisa as we walked through into her bedroom. And I knew "exactly" what it was she wanted to talk to me about. The look on her face when she opened the door and saw how messed up my face was told me all I needed to know. I had stitches on my forehead and my right eye was so bruised and swollen that I couldn't open it at all.

Hours before, some mad bastard from London had opened my forehead up with the corner of a metal chair and when I went down, followed up and done some renovating of my right eye via an extremely painful kick to the face. And now hours later, still suffering the aftershocks of what had been a tough afternoon to be a soccer casual I was now having to go through the other kind of pain other than physical. Mental, the kind of pain that is way more worse than the physical version.

During the day we'd well and truly had our tatties from the Millwall boys. We knew they had quite a few in the way of numbers with them but well, this was "our" city so we were going to defend it. That much was a given. Nora was right about a less than full squad for us as well which was ominous on our part when we ran into them as they stood drinking outside The Trades. What it resulted in was complete carnage. The pub, situated right across the road from Dundee's biggest and most busy shopping centre, this taking place on a Saturday afternoon.

As we fired into what was already a healthy sized team of them standing outside drinking in the sun they showed that they were ready to go at the drop of a hat. As they watched us get close to them they all started lobbing their pint glasses at us. Some of our boys took a sore one from the missiles, likes. No fucking wonder either! THEN almost as many of them came steaming out from inside the pub after getting word of that was going on outside. Families out shopping for the day who happened to be unfortunate enough to be caught on that side of the street went running for cover while others who were already on the other side of the street stood watching the show.

It was just a melee, shit going on all over the place but always in close proximity. It was handy that most of them were quite mouthy cunts as I could then peg where I needed to be keeping my eye on. I never done that too well though apparently as I had unfortunately managed to overlook the boy throwing the chair at me. With it coming from the side and catching me by surprise I still don't know who threw it at me and never will. I delayed my reaction for a second and that was enough for the punch to connect. Catching me on the side temple and sending me down.

It was all a bit of a blur after that for the next minute or so. There was definitely more than one person laying the boot into my curled up body. I obviously didn't do a good enough job in covering up my face because in a now you see it now you don't kind of deal I saw one blue and yellow Reebok Royale in my line of vision and the next it was smashing its way into my cheekbone and eye socket. I thought he had kicked my right eye back into my head such was the force I felt it when it crashed against me.

Something must've distracted them because that was the last kick I felt. By the time I was able to get myself together it didn't look as mad as it had previously. It was now the two groups standing aping each other but with a bit of distance between them. I could only see out of my left eye and felt like my ribcage had been caved in. It was only when I tried to get myself back up on two feet that I noticed the blood that was on the ground, and on my white Ralph Lauren polo shirt.

I felt around my eye and then looked at my hand but there was no trace. I'd been so preoccupied with the kick to the face that I'd forgotten all about the chair to the head which had been the start of my troubles. When I then checked my head I thought I was going to be sick when I felt a finger tip running across my forehead and then sinking INSIDE the torn skin. When I brought my hand back down, the fingertip was covered in blood.

Due to this, instead of going to see what would no doubt be a meaningless and boring match between United and their low level English opponents I spent the rest of the afternoon sat inside Accident & Emergency at Ninewells. Getting my head stitched up again. I wasn't the only casual in there that afternoon either. It said it all though that everyone I saw in there were Utility. Not one single Cockney accent to be heard. I'm not even sure what happened the rest of the afternoon with our boys and Millwall although if there's one thing I know about Nora is that he would've taken it hard what had happened before the match. In his home city. Unless the police were on top of things following what had happened in the city centre he would have been leading the rest of the team into fuck knows what kind of fresh hell after the match.

The final whistle was more or less ready to blow when I was getting myself on the 4.45 to Edinburgh. No fucking way was I going back for more. I shouldn't have fucking even went in the first place and was angry at myself for doing so. I had my doubts and should've listened to them but instead I did go and from minute one onwards it was a fucking nightmare. And "now" I had to deal with family and even more importantly, Lisa. It really wasn't shaping up to be a night for the scrapbook, that I already knew.

With the train being the one before all the fans would be getting after the match it was like a ghost town inside my carriage. Sat there at a table with four seats on my own, which suited me as I had a lot to be thinking about. I knew the state of my face and the fact that I was in pain simply through breathing was going to play a major part in mines and Lisa's night. We weren't going out or anything and had just planned a night in her room. Some quality time, a good film, pizza delivery and a wee "cuddle" on her bed.

The first thing to enter my head was to tell her that I'd been jumped by some Millwall fans. Due to their notoriety as hoolies that story alone, I felt, was plausible and something that would hold weight under questioning. As easy as I could have probably gotten away with that excuse it didn't feel right to me. I love the girl and the thought of lying to her then continuing to lie wasn't something I had been happy about. I'd felt that this trip had been one too many for me and that was me now done. End of the fucking line. I'm not saying that because I got my head kicked in either. Maybe I am but I don't think so. Regardless, I was done and sat there on the train I couldn't have given a fuck if Nora, Dawson, even Si were to say that I chucked it because I got completely rinsed by what is commonly regarded as the elite of football hooligans. Those wee pills I'd taken at Shroom were a million times more responsible for my decision than that blue and fluorescent yellow Reebok running shoe.

No, lying to Lisa wasn't the way I wanted to go. I wanted to tell her where I was in my life and what I wanted to be doing with it. One thing being to not run around with a gang that results in me looking like the fucking elephant man. My timing couldn't have been more off though. It "had been" something I'd wanted to speak to her about but now it was going to look like I was only opening up to her because my own face had been opened up. I wanted to tell her how it had been a major part of my life for a few years but that I now felt differently about it and wanted out before I ended up in trouble. Excuses and stories this time just wouldn't do.

Dealing with the folks at home was exactly as I thought it would be. I had my auntie on one side fussing over me, she actually went to the fridge and brought back a sirloin steak for me to put over my eye. I seriously only thought that stuff happened in Hanna Barbera cartoons! While she was doing this I'm taking a lecture from Jimmy over the fact that he'd told me not to bother going to the match at all. I wanted to remind him that his reasons for me not going didn't exactly have him down as a clairvoyant with regards to what actually happened to me. After they were both done with their separate performances I went up to my room, telling them that I needed a wee lie down before I got ready to go up to Lisa's. I really shouldn't have went to sleep because I woke up in ten times more pain than I'd been in before I slept.

I needed to raid my uncles medicine cabinet before I was even in a position to get myself ready. That's one good thing about my uncle, amongst many. Due to an injury he did to his arm a while back he'd been sorted out with some heavy duty pain killers, fucking things that could put a rhino to sleep! He wouldn't take them though due to how spaced they made him feel. I was a bit more unscrupulous when it came to them though and necked a couple with a glass of water while I sat on the edge of my bed contemplating the task it was going to be for me to get myself ready, walk the fifteen minutes up to my girlfriends and then after all of that. Have to sit and have what was going to be an awkward talk and one that for all I knew might see me a single man by the end of the night.

I was immediately thrown a little off guard by Lisa's reaction when she opened the door to me. I'm not saying I was expecting to be showered with a thousand kisses when she saw me but knowing her like I do, I at least expected her to react with one of empathy and a show of support. Instead, when she saw me it more resembled, I don't know?

Despondence. I had this weird feeling that when she saw me with part of my face caved in it was almost like it wasn't a surprise to her. No, 'are you alrights' or anything in that ballpark. Just a look of disappointment crossed with a weird kind of acceptance before closing the door behind me and heading upstair leaving me to follow her.

Before I could even utter a word, she started to let rip at me. 'I know what you get up to, Stevie .. You think I don't but I do' - Those words alone gave me a sinking feeling in my stomach. She seemed super emotional and I could already see a tear in her eye from the initial few words that she'd came out with. 'I worked it out last week when I saw you around Si and had some chats with Shan. I didn't want to believe it though, wanted to put it down to me being wrecked on the E. I thought you deserved the benefit of the doubt but here you are one week later walking through my door looking and walking like you slipped on your arse while doing the Pamplona bull run.'

'I know you might not believe me here, babe but before us even having this chat tonight I'd already decided I was done with it all. This whole week I've been thinking about what I'm doing with life and decided that it was a part of it that I wanted to leave behind' - With it being the absolute truth I delivered it with what was nothing less than confidence and sincerity. 'SO WHY THE FUCK DID YOU GO TODAY THEN??' Exasperated by what she could have only seen as an excuse from me, her voice was now up a few notches.

'Believe me, it's a long story and I want to tell you all about it, Lisa' I only ever said her actual name when I was serious about something and she knew it, almost calming down through hearing her own name spoken. 'We're talking here about a part of life that you've never had any access to in yours apart from maybe read about it in the papers so there's stuff I need to tell you about and I think, or hope at least, that you'll understand things a bit better by the time I'm done' By now she'd joined me in sitting on the bed and I took her hand as I spoke, rubbing my thumb up and down her palm, taking the tip and trailing it over the lines in her hands.

I took her through the hows and the whys of me finding myself in a position of while being a stand up boyfriend who had been nothing other than good to her, I had my other side to me. She seemed to get it the way I had explained it to her. I told her that while yes, I was going to games in the day time and dating her at night, I had started to question it near the end of the season and that the break, all the summer I'd spent with her and then last week at Shroom and the powerful impact that it had had on me. It had all changed, I had changed.

She asked why I'd went to the Millwall match while feeling the opposite. I told her about the scary proposition that is Nora and how he'd called me, put me on the spot and I'd shat it because of him being the type of person who has that effect on people. Someone that you can't really say no to. 'Because of being scared of his reaction if I'd said I wasn't going I ended up going, last minute decision by the way. From the moment I got on the train I had a knife against my face, chair opening up my head and a kick to my eye socket.

I'm annoyed at myself, didn't "want" to go .. went, and now look at the state of me. I'm not expecting you to know, but these guys from London today are the worst there is' I ranted and couldn't be stopped 'Half of them London gangsters, fucking Krays and all that stuff' I couldn't help but embellish it all, safe in the knowledge she knew the square route of fuck all about the reputations of someone like a soccer hooligan crew from England. For the first time in the night i saw the hallmarks of her sympathetic face showing.

'So you're really finished with it, Zico? This is important to me. I really like what we've got here with each other but I can't have you coming home like this every Saturday either. To be brutally honest it's not what I'm looking for in a boyfriend. I look at Shan, she's with Si KNOWING that he's a casual and STILL goes out with him. Shits herself every Saturday when he goes away to wherever, I don't want or need that.' What a difference a week can make I was sat there thinking to myself.

Last Saturday we found ourselves, MDMA assisted, pouring out our feelings towards each other and how much the L word had been used and now fast forward a week and we're now having our most serious and also, adult like talk. 'I can't do that to you, babe' I replied my eyes never leaving hers. 'When I met you, it made me question things because I didn't like not telling you about it, hated the fact that I was leading a bit of a double life and that both of them could never come into contact with one another. You made me think twice about it all and then look at last week and all that we experienced in that field? Seeing how much better life is when you're in an environment of peace and good vibes and how much at odds it all is compared to what goes on when the fitba season is on. She was staring intently, just listening and absorbing every word I had for her.

When I finally took a pause Lisa found her voice again. 'So what now then?' A simple question, had I known what it specifically meant of course. In that moment that question could've been what now between her and I? - What now in terms of me being a casual? - What now for the rest of the night or even what topping were we going to get on the pizza later on? I took a chance and guessed that she was referring to me and my Dundonian friends. 'Well it's going to be a bit of a sticky one for me. On match days we generally meet up at the same pub before doing what we do so what happens next is that I don't go any fucking where near The Snug before a United match' - 'Well that will be simple enough' she said like that was all I needed to worry about, case closed. Case NOT fucking closed though because there was the not so small part involving me still wanting to go and watch my team BUT them also not exactly playing at a stadium that is ever going to be compared in size with the Nou Camp or Old Trafford and in fact, having a fan base of less than ten thousand at every home game.

There was a high chance that avoiding The Snug or not, it was still possible that I would bump into The Utility in or around the ground at some point. Those chances only increasing on away trips due to the small traveling support to places such as Motherwell, Kilmarnock or Hearts. Once again, Lisa thought the solution to it all was obvious and staring me in the face. 'Well just don't go to the matches, it's easy.' To me though? I understood each and every word she said to me but it was the placement of each word she'd chosen to make up a sentence that sounded like she was telling me that I shouldn't go to the football, THAT was the confusing part.

Not go to watch my team? To suggest such a thing was nothing short of sacrilege and I was surprised that she hadn't been smited there and then on the spot for such a display of blasphemy. I explained to her that if you're talking what came first the chicken or the egg then going to watch your fitba team most definitely came before being a soccer hooligan. You were only there "because" of the team. And with that there was no fucking way I was stopping going to games. ' Bu bu bu bbbbbbut' She stopped me with that pout and eyes combination that I can't ever say no to. Something she was well aware of.

By the time that particular conversation was done I felt like she'd done one of those Obi Wan Kenobi Jedi mind tricks because I'd soon agreed not to go for at least the first couple of games to see what the lay of the land was going to be. I tried not to show it to her but I was gutted about it. Doesn't matter what team you support and how good or bad you did the season before. The couple of months break does you the world of good and you're ready to go again for the next ten months. Optimism restored again and by the time the first match is kicking off you're champing at the bit for a game of competitive fitba. Instead, here I was resigned to the fact that I wouldn't be there on the opening day of the season against Motherwell. More than likely was going to miss the away match in Aberdeen too. Then again, even I was ready to admit to myself that Aberdeen away was maybe one best sat out considering the circumstances.

At the end of the night the two of us were in a good place once more. I knew this when she managed to start asking if I'd bumped into Si (aye, in amongst getting hospitalised) and if there was any word on the party up in Inverness. Actually I hadn't seen him but that's not to say he wasn't there. With Dawson telling me to sit tight in the vicinity of the Millwall boys I never got the chance to see what faces were kicking around up at The Snug. I only really saw The Utility for the first time when they were upon me, running along the high street towards Millwall and by that point it was go time. Next thing I'm in a taxi for Ninewells so aye, he could've been there but I never seen him if he had been. I told her that I'd give him a call after the weekend to see the score. 'What's he going to say to you when you tell him that you're giving up the casuals?' she asked. A question that I really didn't know the answer to.

'File that under a bridge that will be crossed when I come to it' I said as honestly as I could. I was holding various doubts and fears about what indeed came next. Nora's reaction, Si's reaction, what it now might mean in relation to what things would be like when just trying to follow my team. All questions that couldn't be answered there and then so I changed the subject. Wanting more than anything for us to salvage the rest of the night. 'So, we ordering this pizza or not, I'm Hank Marvin here' I said putting my arms around her and testing the water by planting a kiss on her cheek.

Chapter 22.

Match day and the opening game of the season killed me. I'd been going to the fitba since I was eight years old, was such a big part of my life. Ate, slept and breathed it yet here I was. First real United match of the season and I'm lying in my bedroom listening to updates on BBC Radio Scotland. It just wasn't right, likes. Not fucking normal. We got off to a win to kickstart the season. Fucking Alex Cleland was the scorer in a 1-0 win against Motherwell?! I hope they fucking drug tested the cunt afterwards cause he's the very LAST player I'd expect to be scoring the winning goal in a match for us. Still, a win's a win though.

Naturally I'd spent most of the afternoon thinking about what was going on "off" the park every bit as much as what was going on out on it. Motherwell were a good crew of casuals. Were one of the original ones in Scotland as far as I was aware and they knew the score when it came to dressing. Game cunts as well. Especially with it being the first day of the season they'd have came through mob handed. That's the thing, I don't just mean Scotland here but there's something special about the first day of the football season.

An almost magical, outburst of optimism. All the kids and scarfers, decked out in the new shirts for the season. I used to love that as well, counting the days until the new top was released. Well, that was until I reached the point of someone who wouldn't wear a team shirt to the match if he was paid to. That first day optimism only lasts for a short time for most fans though. It's only when, as the season goes on, the enjoyment gets drained from you as you watch your team suffer from sickening defeat after defeat. Casuals are no different, first day of the season they're ready to go so I had no doubt the city of Dundee would have seen some tasty confrontations at some points over the day.

I thought about if anyone had noticed that I wasn't there to take part in it all. In a perfect world then aye, for me it would have been the case that I never even entered anyones consciousness over the whole day as they went about their business. Deep down, and without being arrogant or anything, I was of the opinion that Si, at least would have noticed my absence. We were all heading up north next Saturday for the next all nighter so I was going to be speaking to him soon enough anyway to make the arrangements. I'd still not even really assembled a plan on how I was going to tell him about me stopping with the Saturday capers. I decided that the best bet would be to just not appear for the Motherwell fun and then see what followed after that. It wasn't so much a plan than me just burying my head in the sand like an Ostrich and hoping that it would all sort itself out.

For the first time in so long I couldn't even remember I wasn't seeing Lisa on a Saturday night. She was going out with her pals through to Dunfermline. Some sixteenth birthday party in a masonic hall or something. She asked me if I wanted to go but it was asked in that way when someone does so in courtesy when actually fucking praying that you're going to stay no. I was cool with it. We all need our space and to do things with our pals so I was happy to assist her and say she should go with her friends.

It actually had left me stuck for what to do though on my side. I was desperately rooked due to having to keep my money back for the party up north so wasn't like I had a bottomless pit of cash to help me find something to do either. Accepting my fate for the night and that I'd not be going further than anywhere that was a stones throw from my house I headed out to get some cans thinking I'd have a couple of drinks in the house watching telly before going out later on and see if anyone was kicking about and up to no good. Anything but me sitting in The Central by the end of the night. If you're under thirty and are spending your Saturday night in there then you're doing life wrong. I say that though but would never rule out me doing just that. You really have run out of options if that's where you are Saturday night though but then again .. Options wasn't exactly something I was overflowing with.

When I was standing in Paul's looking at the beers that were sat in the fridge wondering whether to go for Becks or Budvar, Brycey walked in. Hadn't seen him much over the summer, actually. He was decked out in his Rangers top and was carrying his scarf in his hand, fucking Christmas tree that he is. I figured that was him just off the supporters bus back from Ibrox after the huns match. 'Alright Brycey, lad just back from the game?' I asked in that way when cunts ask a question but already know the answer to it. So much so that I never even gave him the chance to answer me before asking him what the score was. This was also something I already knew the answer to but with me knowing that Rangers had suffered an opening day shock defeat to

Hearts I knew I would take a bit of enjoyment out of his reaction to that. Have to admit, I love the reactions of Rangers and Celtic fans when their team gets beaten. Both of them seem to share this fantasy that they should win every single match that they play and they lose the fucking plot on the occasions that they DO get beaten. It's either the ref was a mason or he was a fenian, never the fact that the other team might just have been better on the day. More conspiracies than Watergate those cunts.

'Fucking two nil against Hearts' he spat back at me. 'Oh aye? Who scored for you likes?' I couldn't resist it, feigning my ignorance. - 'Naw, two nil to THEM, fucking disgrace by the way. Three stonewall penalties knocked back in the second half alone. Tosh McKinlay near enough fucking caught the ball from a shot and what does the ref do? Fucking waves play on. - 'Oh well, it's a marathon not a sprint, mate. No one wins or loses the league on the first day' I dished out the meaningless sentiments to him.

'Wee win for us up at Tannadice today' I added which I knew would only escalate his mood. 'Fucking Mo Johnston missed two sitters as well, useless catholic wanker' Brycey continued, either conveniently ignoring the fact United had won or still stuck in the seethe of going back over the afternoons events, I couldn't decide which. 'Aye well get a swally inside you pronto, you look like you need it' I laughed while I decided to opt for the Budvar.

Once we'd both paid for our carry outs, the two of us stood outside talking away over a beer. I asked him what his plans were and he told me that he was having a quiet one, just going down to The Central for a few drinks and that I should meet him down there. I agreed that I'd probably pop my head in for a couple of drinks later on but couldn't end up going into town or anything (something that had I been the owner of a house I'd have calmly bet it on him wanting to do) and that I was keeping my money tight until next week. Fucking hell, trying to take him through the whole house music - illegal parties - E's thing was like trying to teach rocket science to a sloth.

By the time we went our separate ways I'm sure he hadn't really understood what I was going on about. Brycey's your type of guy who doesn't quite get music. For him, the only music that ever exists for him at any period of time is the forty songs that potentially will be played on the radio due to them being what's in the charts. Never buys his own albums, just listens to Atlantic 252. Half the songs he likes he doesn't know what the singers look like or where they're from. Complete ignorance on that side of things so to try and get him to understand that a specific type of music held such power for people in the important way that it did like Acid House?

It felt like I was pissing into the wind. It had been a hard few weeks on that side of things following Shroom. All I wanted to do was talk to people about it. Enthusiastically tell them just how life changing an experience I'd had but there was a lack of people that I knew would 'get it.' I knew that to most all I'd do would come across as some mentalist talking about dancing in a field all night long to strange electronic music.

I'd went up to Kif's house through the week after Shroom as arranged and he was mesmerised by what I was telling him. Hung onto every single one of my words but that had been an exception to the rule. Frustrating as fuck so it was. I wanted to scream from the rooftops just how tremendous house music and MDMA was but I had no audience to do so. There really was only that certain type of person that you felt that you could tell. That would "get it." The type of individual that you felt you could trust with such intel. Those type of people were in very short supply.

One thing it had all affected immediately was my ability to look at a Saturday night doing anything other than that as less than ordinary. Despite the fact that his team had been beaten, Brycey looked genuinely happy with his lot that the rest of the night was going to involve drinking at the local pub where, on my part, I was already cringing over the fact that I would more than likely end up doing the same thing as him. We went off in different directions agreeing to catch up later for a few. I went back down the road and gave Si a call.

I called him thinking that he wasn't going to be in at that time. Thought he'd still be in Dundee up to god knows what so was surprised when his dad told me to hang on a second when I asked if he was in.

'How's it going Zico? You alright pal?' he came on the phone sounding genuinely concerned - 'Aye all good, Si' I said completely missing his reason for concern. 'What was the score with you today then? Noticed you weren't there, I wasn't the only one either. I heard Nora and

Dawson asking a few of the heads if they'd seen you' As every word spilled from him it felt like my heart was sinking in the way a rollercoaster will do to you as it makes its drop.

'Not been feeling well the past couple of days, Si' I lied on the spot with a spur of the moment excuse. I wasn't ready for telling him that I was binning going with them to games so at least for now was going to avoid that conversation as long as I possibly could. 'Been in my bed for the past two days, haven't eaten a fucking thing, wouldn't have been able to make it to the top of the road to get the bus to the train station never mind run about Dundee chasing Motherwell all over the place' I said in, caught in my lie, was nothing other than common sense that I couldn't have been there.

'Fair enough, Zeec but Nora wasn't exactly chuffed so best you know from me, eh mate' There was that concerned tone again but even more emphatic than the way he started the call. He'd confirmed EVERY fear that I had held about me just going missing in action. I felt absolutely gutted, presented with the knowledge that none of this was simply "over" and that surely now there would be something to follow. I tried to mask this by changing the subject to next week and the all nighter. He wasn't ready for moving on to that though. Preferring to tell me about what had happened during the day against Motherwell and how the Utility didn't exactly have it all their own way over the day and how that had left Nora in a fucker of a bad mood and several people paid the price for it.

Apparently he'd slapped a few Utility boys around for absolutely fuck all, threatened to glass the two of them when they were all drinking at Frews Bar after the game. Apparently Motherwell had brought a rather large amount of hooligans through with them and had split up into different groups so whilst at no part of the day did they really give our boys a doing they still had other groups causing a bit of havoc with not much Utility around in attendance. The Three Barrels got all of its windows put in while the Utility were down at the train station waiting to ambush the 'Motherwell Saturday Service' before they'd even left the platform. It hadn't really reflected well on the Utility that Motherwell had snuck in undetected.

As he told me all of this there was the definite feeling that he was telling me it all as one of his own and to another casual. I, on the other hand was sat there listening to him, easily able to imagine it all through all of my own experiences but doing so with the novelty of it feeling, to me, like a soccer hooligan telling stories to one who isn't one. He just didn't know it, yet.

I eventually got him changing the subject to us going up to The Highlands. I heard his mood lift and him light up once he was focused on the delights that surely awaited us in the land of the Loch Ness Monster. 'Aye, Shan and me are set, you two as well, pal?' - 'Do you know a catholic that lives in The Vatican?' I replied before the words had even left his mouth. 'Nice one' he laughed 'One thing though' he paused. 'Since we're going in the opposite direction next week we'll not be able to pick you up, think you and Lisa can get yourself up to Dundee and we'll get you there?'

Shan was apparently sorting the pills out during the week from a guy at her work. Red Playboys, which he seemed excited about specifically while I was just excited about the prospect of taking one, or more! We left it at that, agreed that I'd give him a shout on Friday night about it but both coming to the conclusion that with the long drive up north it would mean that we wouldn't get to the Aberdeen away match, which was convenient for me. He said that was him staying in for the night as he was driving his mum and dad to Glasgow airport around half three in the morning which meant he couldn't get drunk so following a day of mindless violence he was spending a Saturday night watching telly with his parents! The irony was not lost.

I left him to it and went upstairs to my room with my Budvars to see if there was anything worth watching. Caught the start of some documentary on UFO's on BBC 2, fucking nice one! I haven't seen any UFO myself likes but believe that they exist, same with aliens, well who else is going to be flying the things? I'm not an expert on all of that stuff but for the universe which is so huge it actually hurts my head when I think about it, it would be pretty mental to sit here and say that we're the only planet that has life on it.

The documentary was decent, lost a whole hour lying on my bed and watching it. Not sure what I'd do if I came face to face with a UFO or an alien likes. I wonder if they wear Adidas? That would be funny as fuck, going at it with an alien! I wouldn't fancy my chances against them likes. Who needs to worry about Stanley Knives when you're up against cunts who can control you by lighting up their fingertip and pointing it at you? The Mars solar system service or the Saturn

Headhunters or something. They're wearing some intergalactic special edition Stan Smiths that you've got no chance of copping on Planet Earth while they're trying to steal your Stone Island jersey since they hardly get shipments up there on Mars and are still wearing the Autumn Winter collection from 1981! Too mad.

I eventually tanned all of my Budvars and left myself with no choice other than to head around to The Central to meet up with Brycey. Well, if I wanted to keep drinking that was, which I did. Once you start, the tendency is to keep drinking until you either run out of money or stamina. I popped my head into the living room before leaving, actually asked Jimmy if he fancied coming round to The Central with me for a wee drink. Could see I'd struck a chord with him as he sat up in his seat, ears pricking up and everything. The look on his face was most definitely one of enthusiasm. One look towards my auntie seemed to have dampened any spirits he was momentarily holding for going out though as he slumped back in his easy chair and told me to have a good night. Said I was only going for a couple so would probably be back before he was away up the stairs for the night. Famous last words though, eh?

Had to nip back within seconds of closing the front door as I had to ask him to tape Match of the Day for me which, due to him watching the telly he waved me away in a dismissive fashion when I tried to tell him. He's some boy. I couldn't resist being a wide-o back though so went through to the kitchen, grabbed the wee pad of post it notes we used for reminders to stick on the fridge. Wrote in capitals - TAPE MATCH OF THE F****** DAY FUR ME ... Walked back through and stuck it to the remote control for the TV. Safest place to put something you want him to find is right there bar none.

The Central public house is not exactly what I would call the last bastion of fun and exciting times. Anyone with a shred of ambition in their lives for what they wanted out of a night would not be hanging around there any time after eight and it was with that mindset that I approached the entrance, pulling the door back and instead of seeing half a dozen men propping up the bar and little else I, instead, walked into the madness that was Tam Cluny, a man in his sixties who was a regular there, standing with a burning copy of The Sun in his hand. Waving it like a torch and singing along to Billy Joel's "We Didn't Start The Fire." that was playing on the jukebox. The bar staff freaking out over the fact that actually he fucking HAD started the fire and the whole pub was in danger of going up along with it.

People were making a grab for it which was only making him swerve his arm to avoid them, sending small pieces of burning paper flying in all directions. 'WE DIDN'T START THE FIIIIIRE IT WAS ALWAYS BURNING SINCE THE WORLDS BEEN TURNING' Brycey, who still hadn't changed out of his Rangers top and had, by the state of him, just went straight to the pub. He's by the side of Cluny egging him on by singing the chorus along with him. It was pretty funny likes. It ended up with Tam getting lobbed out for the night from Wattie the owner, telling him that he was banned for a week. He's protesting like he's been hard done by instead of taking on board the fact that he, to be brutally fair, did come close to setting a boozer on fire with his creative use of a prop as he enjoyed some music while incredibly and fabulously inebriated.

Worked out a treat as I was able to get the seat at the bar alongside Brycey, that Tam Cluny, aka 'The Clunatic' had timely vacated for me. 'What was all that about?' I asked him still trying to get to grips with what I'd walked in on. 'Not sure' Brycey, looking like he'd definitely sank a few by then said all a bit non plussed by it all. 'Song came on the jukie and he reach over and grabbed the paper from behind the bar and took a lighter to it.' 'Aye all normal stuff for a Saturday night then' I laughed back. The two of us had a decent chat, actually. Hadn't been for a drink since that night when he panned the church windows in although that alone wasn't the reason for such inactivity between the two of us. I'd have been a hypocrite of the highest order if i was to disown a mate for doing something like that considering some of the shit I get up to. Well, "used" to get up to. Changed man and all that eh?

As had been easily predicted, he ended up wanting to get me to go into town. Telling me that there was only half an hour until the doors closed at Manhattans (fucking stupid name for a nightclub in a small Scottish town if you ask me by the way) and we'd need to get there before then if we wanted to extend our nights drinking by another few hours. I reminded him that one, I wasn't going anywhere as I needed to keep my coin for next weeks festivities and two he wasn't getting into a nightclub anyway dressed in a Rangers top no matter how drunk and deluded he was.

Even if I was wrong on point number two, wearing either old firm shirt when out drinking was never a scenario that was going to end well for anyone on a Saturday night. There's no talking to Rangers fans though, especially when they're full of peave. The arrogance and hubris just seeps out of them. He wasn't for listening and despite my words of wisdom he was soon asking Wattie to call a taxi for "us."

I sank the last of my pint and decided to leave him to it. There wasn't a chance that he was going to change my mind but you know how drunk folk can be when they don't want to take no for an answer, proper nippy. I knew he'd get to that stage, he was already in that post code as it was so I told him I was going for a pish and then swiftly ducked out the side door leading out into the street and took the short walk back round to my house for the night.

I knew Brycey would have been pissed off by the time his penny dropped that I'd baled on him but also knew that by tomorrow he'd have forgotten all about it. If he managed to get himself into Manhattans with that Rangers top on then he was going to have much more important things to worry about than where his mate had disappeared to. Guaranteed.

Chapter 23.

First it started with the phone calls. It was obvious that someone was there on the other end of the line but remaining silent apart from their breathing. The sound of that alone though was disturbing. This shit went on for the best part of a couple of weeks. Every single night there would be at least one phone call but most nights more than that. I'd seen stuff like that happen on the telly to people but never thought it would be as creepy in a psychological way as it was. Thing is, it was probably more of a mind fuck for me through being ninety nine point fucking nine percent sure that I knew who was making the calls.

A few weeks before that, Nora and I had exchanged words. Well, that would be a wee bit disingenuous way to put it as he was the one doing most of the talking. It had been the absolute worst timing in the world when we did. It was the Monday that followed Rave On The Loch and after what had been a monumental night where the four of us repeated our capers from the month before.

The only difference being a farmers field had been swapped for a spot down on the banks of Loch Ness. Eckies, house music, lasers, mountains and the Loch Ness fucking Monster! What's not to like about that for a combination eh? Like last time out I had three pills over the night only, unlike the last time we had mixed them with a stupid and potentially dangerous amount of Whizz. Through that I knew that I wasn't going to sleep on the Sunday night so didn't even bother trying. Of course, by the Monday I was a complete car crash of a human being.

By the Sunday night I was sat in my room still nodding my head to imaginary beats that were in my head only. The one comfort that I was able to take was that I still had not began to feel the effects of the comedown although as much as a novice that I was I still realised that when it arrived it was going to be catastrophic. It would be so ugly that it would make The Mona Lisa look like fucking Michelle Pfeiffer by comparison.

By the Monday afternoon I was still scarily alert, and confused. I'd last slept on the Friday night and was getting close to seventy two hours since going to bed. Aye, confused. Isn't that what they do to terrorists when interrogating them? Stop them from sleeping, to fuck with their heads? I could relate with that only it hadn't taken the CIA to fuck with my head. I'd managed that all by myself. Which didn't exactly put me in good stead for a phone call from Nora. Without question the very last person that I could have done with talking to.

Everyone else was out at work and I was desperately trying everything I could to get myself into a position where I could find some peace and tranquility. I was genuinely starting to panic thinking that this was it for me now. I wouldn't sleep ever again due to the amount of Class A's that I'd taken. That I'd went through some kind of looking glass without any way back again. Welcome to your new life. I'd "borrowed" one of my Cuzz's magazines and had three tugs over the day to try and relax me but nope. They'd been more than a chore than anything else. One thing I'd learned early on was that these chemicals, and whatever the hell was inside them, did absolutely fuck all for a man as far as the size of their cock. I'm not sure if this is a thing or not with other guys as I'd been too embarrassed to ask Si about it but every time I'd taken a Class A drug I'd ended up with severe shrinkage down below. Like I'd been out in the sea down the beach for a swim for fucks sake.

There had actually been a moment over the night up in Loch Ness where I had been standing doing a piss in the mens when this couple came in. I looked round having heard a girls voice and clocking me she immediately apologised and said that she wasn't looking. 'Look all you want' I joked to her, 'you won't fucking see anything anyway.' So aye, because of that it was an absolute farce, trying to force myself to have a wank. I wasn't even trying because I was in the mood as such but simply because I thought it might expand a bit of energy.

It didn't work so I gave up, not after leaving a blister on my dick (I never knew that was possible) and went outside to the back garden to have a joint. I heard the phone ringing inside the house but standing there as mentally deranged and sleep deprived as I found myself, my initial reaction was .. Leave it, they'll call back whoever they are. After about a minute or so, still stood out the back puffing away, the phone continued to ring and ring.

The amount of time it had rang for by this point was way over what a regular caller would hold on for. It either gets answered or it doesn't, simple. Just the general rule that anyone making a phone call will follow. It kept ringing and ringing though and by doing so managed to reduce the enjoyment of the spliff. Each toke I relished less and less. The sound of the constant ringing gatecrashing what should have otherwise been a chilled and serene setting. The fact that it kept going and wouldn't stop was also something that my drug induced paranoia was more than ready to jump all over and feed off.

Who calls someone else and doesn't hang up after three minutes? 'Wait though ... Maybe there's a serious reason for the call and THAT'S why the caller isn't hanging up' I started to think? Maybe it's an emergency? What if it was Jimmy or Brenda and they know I'm home and am likely completely dingying the phone because I can't be bothered getting up to answer it? What if this is one of those serious calls that someone "should" be answering and will possibly regret for the rest of their life if they don't?

To a normal person the obvious case would've been that they would have answered the phone straight away and in turn finished the call in a quicker time that it had taken me to stand listening to the phone ringing for all those minutes. In my defence all I can really say on such a subject is that most normal people don't ever stay up for more than two days after taking copious amounts of narcotics. Lets see them do run of the mill things like answering phones after coming down from pills and fuck knows what powder! Then we'll see how smart they fucking are then eh? Whoever was on the other end wasn't hanging up, it was at the point of just being stupid now.

I'd taken the decision that on the grounds of me really not wanting to speak to anyone in the state that I was in, answering it would kind of break that whole speaking to people rule. I would just stay outside for a few minutes more and smoke the rest of the joint before going back in. IF it was still ringing by the time I went back inside, then I'd answer it. Face up to the 'your auntie's had an accident at work and has been rushed to hospital' or the 'would you like to buy some double glazing' right through to the random calls our house would get from companies thinking that we were a fruit and veg supplier a couple of miles away due to us having a similar phone number with only one digit different. Once, just to be a wee dick, I some man from this restaurant rattle off a massive order to me. Carrots, tomatoes, aubergines, leeks the fucking lot. Once he'd finished speaking I asked the guy on the other end of the line if that was the whole order to which he confirmed it was. That's when I informed him that he'd called the wrong number.

I done this in front of my uncle, it was quite telling that he displayed so much pride in me for that call. Get through my exams as good as can be? Meh, he's non plussed. Take the piss out of some poor random cunt who's just trying to do his job though and you're king amongst men for my uncle and I love him all the more for it. He's right into his wee pranks as well you see? Some of the patter he dishes out to these poor office staff drones that have the misfortune of his telephone number to call on their list for the day is comedy gold.

Wasn't just phone calls though with him either. When we were out in the car together one time when I was a kid we saw a hitchhiker stood by the side of the road so he pulled over. Turning round I could see the big smile on the boy's face as he started running towards our car. It was only when I saw his hand reaching for the back door handle when Jimmy, put his foot on the accelerator and sent us driving off, forty or fifty yards away before stopping again. Rolled the window down in his Vauxhall Viva and popped his head out and said to the guy that he was only mucking around and to get in. Of course, when the boy got there and went to get in. Uncle pulled away again. Pishing himself laughing as he did.

It still ranks as one of the funniest things I've ever seen, actually. Half of my amusement being his reaction to what he was doing with this poor guy outside who just wanted a lift somewhere and had probably been stood there for hours. He was already degrading himself in the first place by hitchhiking and now he had someone making him a focal point of their fun due to his own misfortune. For our mixture of reasons we laughed all the way home that day. Gotta love my uncle. They broke the mould when he was made, without question.

'What fucking took you? Fucks sake' - This was definitely not a cold calling salesperson. There really isn't much to be gained with such a sales pitch. That was my first thought upon answering the phone. I'd done all I could to avoid answering it. All of the mini targets I'd set for things to happen before I'd answer the call had come and gone. Even then I had started adding new ones to it in the equivalent of someone losing a coin toss and seeking a stay of execution pleading double or quits.

Instead of going straight into the living room and picking up the phone I went UPSTAIRS to the toilet, wasted another few minutes up there before going back down. A couple of times, momentarily the phone would stop ringing which would make me breathe a sigh of relief only for it to then immediately start again.

Out of all my speculation on who could be so insistent that their call be answered I never even considered that it would be Nora and as far as my mind was at that moment I really could not have ever imagined a worse phone call to be taking. I thought to just hang up as soon as I heard his voice but as drug addled as I was I still had enough marbles to know that it wouldn't have solved anything and would've been pointless. If he had taken the best part of ten minutes solid trying to get me to answer his call how was he going to react upon hearing my voice giving him the confirmation that I was actually there. Hanging up on him was never going to be the magic wand that I would so very much have liked it to have been.

'That you, Nora?' I stalled for time as I tried to prepare myself for what I was certain was not going to be too much of a pleasurable experience, not there, not then, not anytime actually. - 'Course it's fucking me, who else did you think it was?' It wasn't hard to detect his tone of being not in the best of moods. 'Alright Nora, what's happening mate' I know it was futile but tried to at least get off on the right foot. 'Don't you fucking give me the what's happening mates, Zeec, what's been going on the past few weeks? Last I seen of you was you spark out with some Millwall boys all over you, haven't seen you since.

Expected you last week on the first day of the season and DEFINITELY assumed you'd be at Aberdeen on Saturday there, you know the fucking score when it comes to those sheep cunts. So, where the fuck were you? You can't just decide to come when you want, or if you're a bit shook by what happened against those cockney cunts and you don't want to appear because you're a shitebag, doesn't fucking work like that, did you not read your handbook when you joined?' He launched into his outburst letting me know just who was in control of this conversation although technically I hadn't even really had a chance to speak yet. 'Well?' He gatecrashed the silence that had followed. 'No denying we took a right sore one from Millwall before the game that day but I was trying to get us all in the one place to regroup and ambush Millwall back at the train station before they left Dundee again. You were conspicuous by your fucking absence, what was the story?'

Completely on autopilot I hit him with a truth crossed with a lie. First of all calling upon the truth part with me having to go to hospital following the encounter with the London boys and then threw in a mini lie that I was stuck in Ninewells until around eight at night. Not getting out until so late had left me with no point of going back into the city centre to look for anyone as most would have been gone by then.

'Oh aye, well what about Motherwell last week? First fucking game of the season, Zico, EVERY CUNT shows face for that one' - 'Was wiped out for days with some virus. Could barely get out of my bed to walk to the bathroom. Had to get the doctor to come out to the house due to how high my fever was, wasn't fucking nice, Nora mate' I pleaded while completely lying my arse off but elected to continue with the lie that I'd already told Si to keep some kind of consistency up.

I figured that possibly he had already mentioned to Nora in all innocence during a conversation. He was like a dog with a bone though, When I had one answer to a question of his .. he'd just ask me another more penetrating question, with the threatening tone increasing each time he spoke back to me.

'Aberdeen at the weekend then? Wedding? Dog ate your bank card? Slept in? Stuck in traffic and missed the train? What's your excuse?' Then it fell silent again with the floor apparently open for me to speak. This was when I decided that I had to stop lying, just tell him the truth. Even if he didn't like it he could hardly reach down the phone and strangle me like some Bugs Bunny cartoon or something. It didn't stop me from speaking to him while wincing with one eye almost closed as if I was anticipating a punch in my direction when I told him that I couldn't make the sheep meet at the weekend because I was going to Rave On The Loch.

I told him that I would've missed it if I'd went to Aberdeen with the rest of the crew. In my mind, the way it had been delivered was one of maturity where I felt that I'd managed to put my point across in a measured way that the other person would be able to see logic in. My sleep deprived mind however had completely disregarded the prior knowledge I had on just "who" I was speaking to. A man that was at times bereft of all kinds of reasoning. Being told that I had chosen a night of taking drugs and dancing in The Highlands over representing his Utility Crew on match day against the ASC was not something that he was in agreement with me over.

He bawled me out for a good five minutes with not one word spoken from me in return. 'Who do you think you are you little prick?' he launched into it, his tone having seamlessly switched to one I'd never heard him talk to me in although one I'd heard him use on occasion when talking about some members of the opposite mobs. 'Do you think that you can just decide that you're not running with us anymore? Is that it?' He asked with no intention whatsoever of actually letting me answer his rhetoric. 'Doesn't fucking work that way my friend and if that's the impression that you're under then you're fucking deluded. Only way you leave the fucking Utility is if and when I say so. You don't get to choose, just like how you joined, you joined because I said you fucking could' - 'Awwww come on man there no need for' I found some balls and tried to say my bit but he wasn't for allowing me.

'Shove your no needs up your fucking hoop, you don't get to choose what's happening here, dick' I was stood there almost shaking, head spinning at these implications that were hitting me in the face as hard as a punch or a kick from the person on the other end of the line with me. 'It's Celtic on Saturday, we both know that the CSC always bring a large crew with them so it's going to be on and I'll expect you there at The Snug usual time.'

He then paused for a second before ominously adding 'If you're not there, then … I'll have to deal with that as and when' And with that he was gone. Phone slammed down leaving me stood there trying to process everything. I'd been put right into what was the epitome of a catch twenty two. I comply with Nora's "orders" and I'll lose Lisa .. Comply with Lisa's ultimatum and well, if the phone call was anything to go by something bad was going to happen. I just didn't know what but really had no interest in finding out either.

Going by the way he'd been with me I couldn't even guarantee my safety even if I DID decide to show face again in his company. Even putting all of that aside. I'd be the first to admit that even if there was no Lisa for me to be worrying about I "still" wouldn't have been up for joining with the rest of the boys in Dundee. That ship sailed for me the moment I chose to go down the road of expanding my horizons and sample Ecstasy and Acid House.

With me having only days before experienced my next dose of Scotlands best kept secret of a party scene, I'd had my fix again and was happy as Larry and his brother Barry. Well had been happy until that phone call of course. The second party had been a case of more of the same but yet different. I guess you only get that first time where it blows you away to such a degree. That initial feeling of FUCKING HELL THIS IS ACTUALLY A THING that you can't help but feel when that first pill hits you while you're standing somewhere surreal surrounded by all of those kindred spirits.

That's a one time gig but what that is then replaced by is the fact that you DO know what lies ahead in the night and the fact you possess that inside info has its own merits to enjoy. I fucking swear, the whole of Saturday before we left to go up north my guts were churning. butterflies in my tummy and that. Filled with a nervous excitement of sorts. I'd never tell Lisa this but that feeling I describe is the exact same feeling I had the day of our first date when we went to the cinema. Yet here I was getting it again only not from a person in any shape or form. It had been a right cracking night, and morning and by the time it was over and we began the long drive back to the East Coast from The Highlands I was nothing other than pulled further and further into this whole new culture. Lisa too, who not holding any of her previous apprehensions over what Ecstasy would be like, was able to just let herself go from minute one of us getting in there.

Following Nora's call I did what I do best, I decided to worry about it later on. I still needed to find sleep and if I was sat worrying about what was going to happen with the whole Utility side of things then it was never going to arrive. When the Saturday of the Celtic match rolled around, my head was absolutely bursting with it all. I knew I couldn't go but also knew that would ensure there would be more shit to follow as a result.

I'd had a brief chat with Si about it at Rave on the Loch but we were both pretty wrecked and I'm not sure if I was making too much sense to him. When I diplomatically told him that I was thinking about knocking the casuals on a Saturday on the head for a while he responded with a cautious 'You think that's wise?' It wasn't a long chat though so I never learned what he meant by questioning if my thoughts were wise or not. In that moment with how good I was feeling I really didn't want to know what he meant by that.

Inevitably I took what I regarded as the only choice available to me and stayed home and listened to the match on the radio. Trying to concentrate on what the commentator was saying while doing all I could to stop the thoughts that were taking over as I imagined the exact moment when it had dawned on Nora that despite his threatening phone call I still hadn't appeared. What his reaction had been? What plans he would now have when it came to yours truly. I'd made my choice so had to deal with the paranoia that it was now going to bring. Basically from around two o clock onwards I had started to sit there in fear of the phone ringing for if it was going to be him on the other end.

My wellbeing decreased even further when Celtic scored an injury time winner, that Polish defender they have that you'd need to be a world Scrabble champion to speak or write his name, aye he scored with a header. Fucking Celtic always score last minute winners against other teams. Does my head in, I bet their fans love it though. No better feeling than a last minute winner in a fitba game. Even a last minute equaliser, leaves you feeling like you've won the match! So aye, anger notorious leading East Coast soccer casual, check. Find your team sickeningly lose the match in an agonising fashion, check. All in all an afternoon I could've done without.

I was scared for the phone ringing but that particular call didn't come. It got to just past a week and I had begun to do that typical human being thing of slipping into a comfort zone and gradually starting to forget about things. It was about that time where I was getting back into being in a good place when that first phone call came. After my first hello when I answered it I got nothing back, just breathing. As you do, I said hello again but still no one spoke back. I tried one last time in case it was maybe a bad line or something to that effect.

I was still met with a wall of silence however so, resisting the urge to be a bit lippy with whoever it was on the other end I put the phone down on them. I'd only taken one step away from the phone when it rang again. I picked it up and offered a half hearted hello, already assuming that it was going to be the same person. Still breathing with zero in the way of words for me. I didn't even bother with a second hello that time.

I half expected the phone to ring for a third time when I walked away but it stayed silent as I disappeared up into my room to sit there and think of nothing but the fact that it might ring again. No one else was in the house at the time which was handy as there would be a high chance that some prank caller would seriously stress my auntie and uncle out so it was just as well that it was me who had answered it. That would've been fine had it not been for the fact that the "prank" calls went on to continue night after night.

I answered some, so did my folks. It was horrible to see how upset they got just from a few times of them answering. They were in the process of speaking to British Telecom about going x directory to stop these calls when suddenly they started to dry up. Every night became every other night until they trailed off completely. We'd enjoyed two whole days of non calls and that was when that silver BMW started to show up. Parking a wee bit up the road from my house. I started to see it a lot from my bedroom window, just parked there, with two people sat in the front, it was always parked too far away for me to see if it was men or women inside but there was always the both of them sat there.

The first two nights I clocked it parked there. It literally sat there for hours at a time. Any time I'd get up off my bed for something I'd have a wee look out and it seemed to always be there. Of course, I never saw the connection that the car was only parked there for so long outside my house because I was "inside" it.

Chapter 24.

I had never felt so ill equipped for an alarm clock going off than that morning when it woke me from the deepest of sleeps. I'd watched a show a wee while ago about the human body and apparently there's all these different stages of sleep that we're in. I must've been in the most far gone state you can get in when I was woken by those piercing beep beep beeps. How shit I was feeling at such an obscene time of the morning actually felt almost symbolic in a sense as to what I'd gotten myself roped into.

Of course, no one had put a gun to my head when I had accepted the offer to help out at the local bakery in an attempt to get myself some extra roubles. As far as I could see, my future ahead saw lots of partying in random locations and lots of drugs to go with. Through that, if I was to have that vision of the future ahead become reality then I would need to step up to the plate as it definitely was no time to go hiding. Money doesn't grow on trees as I'd been told constantly by family members while growing up.

Still though, why did I accept an offer of summer work which would see me having to get up at four fucking AM in the morning? My official start time was six likes but with there not being any public transport at that time of the day I had to walk there each morning. Well I say each morning but that would risk misleading you into some kind of fantasy of me reluctantly getting up day after day and dragging myself along the road on an hour long walk every morning. That would though, be a false impression you would be left with of me. I didn't stick around for long. One week, actually. One week too fucking many.

My uncle knew the manager along there at Perry's Bakery. He initially and without my knowledge was speaking to him in the bookies one Saturday. During the conversation between the two of them he asked the gaffer along there about the possibility of any work for me. Like I'd wanted to be a fucking baker as well eh? Personally I think Uncle Jimmy's motivation for finding me a job was more about getting me out the house and making sure I wasn't going to be one of those, just left school and hanging about the house like a bad smell types. A case of that way more than it was helping me find my perfect vocation.

Which was never going to be as a fucking master baker. Masturbator more like.

Even if I was allowed to get up at any time in the morning THEN have the warehouse teleported to me each day, I'd still be knocking it back. I can't even make toast without burning it and they're wanting me to make fucking savouries and cakes? Jesus! That very first morning though? Tough fucking gig and no mistake. It felt like I'd worked a double shift and that was just the commute from my house to the bakery before getting started. Was well weird, on the walk along, no cars passing, no people around at all. Made me think of that Ghost Town song. It was almost like I was in one of those post apocalypse films and I was one of the unlucky ones (in that they're left to clear up the shit and start again) who had survived. Eventually though, about half way to the warehouse I came across another person but fuck me, they were far from normal.

Walking along the kind of no mans land that separates East Wemyss and Buckhaven, no houses, no fuck all apart from fields and a tight wee path for mugs like me who don't have any other mode of transport other than their two legs. On my way along there I started to see another figure heading in my direction. My eyesight isn't the best so it took a while for me to be able to focus enough on who or what was oncoming. When I was able to get a proper look I then saw that it was an older man. No disrespect to him but he clearly looked like a tramp.

He looked fucking bizarre, actually. Was clearly dirty looking yet was wearing a suit, shirt, tie the lot but the trousers and blazer had rips all over them. His hair, reminded me of Beetlejuice the way it was going up into the air. He was pushing a bike, my first reaction was that he was a lucky bastard to have one as that's exactly the thing I was needing myself. I figured he must've had a puncture and that was why he was pushing it but as we got face to face with one another on this path you couldn't swing a cat around on, I saw the reason for why he wasn't riding it. He had every available part of the frame with sacks of coal draped over it.

There was quite a bit of uneasiness between the two of us as we negotiated our way past each other. It was so early in the morning and the way I saw it, we were both not expecting to see or deal with anyone else on our journey but yet here we were. My uneasiness was through how eccentric he looked and if he was some radge serial killer he could easily have done away with me there on the road with nothing remotely like a witness to be found, well, apart from sheep. I'm not daft though, I could see by the look on his face while carrying all this coal that he had the appearance of someone who had just been busted.

I actually couldn't have given a fuck about the coal although I spent most of the walk thinking about where he'd got the fucking stuff from because there was no mines in the area as such. I just offered him a quick 'awright pal?' as I passed him and we, for a nano second, locked eyes. He grunted back at me while looking at anything he possibly could other than directly at me. As it was to turn out, I'd see him the next again day in what was almost an instant replay between us, then the day after. This cunt was stealing coal from somewhere each morning when everyone else was asleep, that much was obvious.

As each morning passed however I became more and more intrigued by what he was up to. What was he doing with it and where was he storing it. Most of all though, where was he getting it all from? He obviously had a nice wee gig going whatever he was up to but now I knew too. On the Friday and what I'd already decided was going to be my last day, when I, once again, met him on the road. Knowing that I wasn't going to be walking this path again in my life at such an obscene hour of the day, I had to ask him.

'Oi, pal, I've seen you every single morning this week. What's the score with the coal? He stopped, It was actually the first time that I was able to get a real good look at him while he was stood still. He was one of a kind that was for fucking sure. He looked like a combination of Beetlejuice and that Argentina manager years ago that chain smoked on the touchline, Cesar Menotti I think. His face so thin he could've almost passed as someone balls deep in their Ecstasy honeymoon period. The fact that he'd stopped gave me a bit of hope that he was about to reveal a few secrets about this operation of his.

'None of your fucking business, kid' he replied in what was not an accent I was anticipating. I heard the words he sad but barely. It was like he was Irish but it was different from how they speak at the same time. I actually laughed back at him. Was laughing at the fact that for the past five days I'd worked myself up to try and find out what he was up to and then when I finally did that was his response?

Of course, I couldn't help but be a bit of a prick back at him before he moved on, especially knowing that I wasn't going to see him again anyway. 'Aye no worries auld yin, one thing though? Since it's clearly obvious that you come back this road each morning with your chorie goods you'd maybe want to think about rotating different times and different routes. You wouldn't want to be coming along here one morning at say, I don't know? Half five in the morning and you find a couple of coppers waiting there for you.'

'What's that meant to mean?' He said, his self confidence in swatting away some young cunt gone in a second. - 'I'll leave you to try and work it out, I need to get myself to work' I winked at him before turning my back and carrying on. I can be a bit of a fanny like that, admittedly.

The early morning journey aside, the work at the bakery was what I envisaged hell to be like. If that is what working is going to be like then I'm really not sure what I'm going to do with my life. Working with a bunch of people who in their own individual ways were absolute goons while doing a job that a fucking toddler could do as some kind of activity at nursery? Nah, not for me. The staff there who actually did that as a living? I'd almost feel sorry for them were it not for the fact that they were all, largely complete wankers, boring dicks. Take out a couple of guys who seemed to be sound but I never got to work beside. I admit that a lot of my "low" opinions held on the staff of Perry's Bakery was down to their conduct on the Friday when it was announced that I was leaving and the whole unpleasantness that it brought my way.

Between that day and the Monday when I'd started though I was made to do such taxing duties like, well, you know how you get gingerbread men? And how they have buttons going down the front of them with smarties or some equivalent sweetie? Well I had the all important job of putting the buttons on them. Apple turnovers? I was the fudd who turned them over. Then there was the manual jobs like being on hand for when the deliveries came in.

Weirdly enough, in all of my short years I'd never had to lift a big industrial sized bag of flour in my life, or when coming at me thick and fast on some conveyor belt system. I didn't much care for it to tell you the truth. This had me putting my fucking back out that morning on what was only day two for me. An event that led to me going home early.

The gaffer, Drysdale wasn't too impressed and I didn't think he even believed me but I wasn't taking any of his pish so went home anyway. Actually, the only duty that I did enjoy there was when I got put on the donut machine, making sure it was topped up with batter. Mindless and dull work but any donuts that didn't come out the correct shape and size you KNOW I was fucking swiping them for myself!

By the Thursday I knew I'd had enough so figured I'd work the Friday and at least pocket my full weeks worth of wages. Told Drysdale the news first thing when I went in on the Friday morning. He was a right wee rat faced prick this gaffer. Wee thin pencil moustache like you'd see those gangsters with the pin stripe suits and tommy guns. He was giving me all of the 'I was only doing your uncle a favour and that's the thanks that I get back' when I told him. Not that I was giving a fuck about quitting a job that I hadn't even asked for in the first place.

I told him that the job wasn't for me and that I should be doing something that I like. I never name dropped anyone but told him that half of his staff in the place didn't want to be there either but were now trapped. Weighed down by real life commitments like mortgages and car payments. He sort of sneered at that and told me that I had a lot to learn about life and that if I thought the only work I would end up doing would be something that I actually "enjoyed" then good luck to me.

It didn't take long for word to get round the place that it was my last day and that was when I started to get some snide wee comments in my direction. All alluding to what happens to people on their last day in there. Some nonsense about them getting stripped and smeared in about a hundred different food products, jam, icing, flour, hundreds and thousands, the fucking lot. This particular guy, Bobby Tait, one creepy fucker of a man and that was my impression after five minutes in his company on the Monday when I started. Bobby was telling me with a bit of a disturbing smile on his face that after work when they all grabbed me he was going to shove a glass bottle of Irn Bru up my arse. I mean, the whole stripping someone naked and covering them in food seemed pretty suspect to me anyway but then he's talking about inserting inanimate objects into my bottom. Not a fucking chance, mate. Fucking bottle would be going over his napper before it went anywhere near my derriere.

With around five minutes left until we were all finished for the week those around me were getting quite animated over what was happening at three. It's fair to say the work floor was not one of harmony between all staff. They were quite jovial where on my side I was giving a lot of them some verbals back calling them weird creepy cunts and such like. I'm not sure if I was meant to play along with this and take it like a man but well, I wasn't one, yet.

My very first reaction was to just duck out a few minutes early and get myself to fuck but due to my temporary work situation I was to pick up my wages from Drysdale in his office at finishing time. Instead, I went with Plan B which was to disappear to the toilets before three then hide out until everyone else had left. They weren't chuffed when it dawned on them that I wasn't going to go along with their nonsense. I'd barely even worked there and they thought they could treat me like someone who had been beside them for years. Like one of the team. Someone who was "one of them" and if there was any thing that was for sure it was most definitely was not one of 'them.'

A few soon came bursting into the bathroom to find me locked in the cubicle. Shaking the door so much I thought it was about to come loose from the hinges.

'Get your fucking arse out here ya wee prick'

'Aye, we're wanting to get to the pub, stop your fucking about'

'Come on Stevie, it's tradition, mate. Just what we do in here, likes'

Came three separate voices ranging from angry to annoyed to simply plain delusional. I stood on the toilet itself so I could hang over the top of the cubicle and talk to them.

'Fuck you, after what you said you wanted to "do" to my arse there's no way I'm bringing it out for you'

'The pub's going to be on last orders tonight and you'll still be waiting on me coming out of here'

'Fuck your tradition, you're making out like I've worked beside you all for years and we're all best buddies. I still don't even know your name for fucks sake and you think I'll be cool about you stripping me and covering me in fucking jam?'

I answered each of them in the order they had shouted to me.

'I tell you what though? You're all a right special level of weirdos though, I'll give you that. Right up there with the best of them likes.' I continued.

This was met with all kinds of abuse back from them, like I fucking cared. Sticks and stones boys, sticks and stones. Regardless, the situation hadn't changed. I was still in the cubicle and they couldn't do a thing about it apart from breaking the door down which I knew they wouldn't be doing. They eventually left but even then when they did it wasn't like I was just going to follow thirty seconds behind them. I had the paranoia filled thoughts of, had they really went or were they all waiting outside for me showing my face? It was ludicrous but I started scanning the toilets for any kind of weapon I could use. Last day at work in my first ever job and I'm looking for a weapon to help fight my way out the place. There's just something so beautifully worrying about that thought.

It actually took Drysdale to come in looking for me before I eventually left the cubicle. Even when he told me everyone had gone home and he was needing me out so he could lock the place up for the weekend, I didn't believe him. It was only when he then threw over a wee brown envelope into the cubicle to me and said that my wages wouldn't be much use to me if I was locked inside the warehouse all weekend that I decided to end the madness and go home.

I can't say that the whole week was a complete wash out because there I was on a Friday afternoon with sixty notes in my pocket but as far as the whole work side of things. It wasn't a week that I would ever wish to repeat again. And wouldn't be. In some ways though a large glass soft drink bottle being shoved up my arse by a stranger would have been preferable to the earache I got from my Uncle Jimmy when I told him on the Friday as we sat having tea that I'd chucked it in.

The mother of all lectures followed where I was told some of the rules of life and apparently, one of them is that all of us have to do stuff that we don't like. I tried to joke by saying that I was way ahead of him as I'd been going to school for years and it's not like I was dancing a jig each morning when I left the house to catch the bus there. As tough as it was having to sit there and listen to him I'd have taken that as being the worst part of what had been a success of a shitey day. There was FAR worse in the cards for me before the day was done however.

Walking up to Lisa's early in the evening, minding my own business I was in a world of my own thinking about the night out we all had planned next week over in Edinburgh. Instead of any elaborate illegal parties we were going to a club called Pure which was effectively the same thing as the outdoor events only inside a club with a legal license.

This again, would be a chance to experience something different so I was understandably very much up for it. Basically, if it was a chance to get a wee bit of MDMA inside me while listening to house and be with like minded souls then I, I was in. Stuck in a daydream walking along the street I never noticed that there had been a car creeping slowly along the road behind. It was only when it pulled up alongside me that I was even aware of its presence. As I glanced to the side, it was with first of all surprise immediately then followed by a sickening sense of realisation that left the worst feeling in the pit of my stomach.

Chapter 25.

The silver BMW matched me for what must've been ten unnerving, creepy seconds or so. Each step I took it crawled deliberately alongside with me. When I'd first looked to the side and seen it there not to mention the glare I was getting from a menacing looking chap in the passengers seat, the penny eventually dropped. It had been ME that it had sat waiting on for all those days outside my house. I anticipated that the passengers window was going to go down or even the door opening but nope. It just kept crawling blatantly along as I walked. The man in the passengers seat staring back at me, never taking his eyes off me in fact. This I know as I wasn't taking my eyes off HIM or the car in general. His eyes piercing whilst his face remained emotionless.

I think the fact that they were driving alongside me in such an overtly and purposely menacing way but without actually doing anything further than that was what I found the most unsettling about it all. I hadn't had a chance to really see who was behind the wheel but the passenger alone was a proper man likes, must've been in his early forties. He had that whole Brylcreamed slick back thing going on. Beard that looked like it was there by design rather than someone who hadn't just shaved for a while.

Fuck knows what I must've looked like to him as I was a fucking jungle inside my head with all kinds of thoughts running through it. I couldn't see anything that was going to constitute as good coming out of this situation and until I found out which direction it was going to go on I was never going to be close to being descried as at ease.

Just when I thought that something was going to happen. It didn't. With an unnerving and arrogant sneer, he looked me up and down one last time before looking back towards the driver and saying something to them. Without warning the car then sped off past me. I was still flicking through the different scenarios of what had just happened as I continued along the road when a couple of minutes later I saw what looked like the same car coming back in my direction, at speed. I'm not ashamed to say that the sight of it on my horizon again and traveling so fast along the road worried me. The very first instinct was one of self preservation and me running but there wasn't any place for me to go. No nooks or crannies tits and fannies. No side roads, no friendly houses, fuck all. I was completely exposed.

The speed they were tearing along the road at in any case meant running would have been a waste of time. My stupid pride overruled everything inside me regardless. Imagine if they were going at that speed but it was completely unrelated to me and they just happened to be going that way only to see me run from them? How embarrassing would that have been? You can take the boy out of the Utility but you can't take Utility out the boy eh? I was fooling myself. Cars don't just pull up beside you in such an intimidating way for no reason.

When it got close enough for me to be able to look inside I could see the cunt with the beard pointing over to me. This, leading to the car swerving over onto the other side off the road to block me off. Both doors swinging open before the vehicle had barely even screeched to a stop. It was proper rabbit in the headlights time for me because THEN would have been the fucking time to run with them both being outside the car and not traveling at the speed of sound as before. I froze though.

Finding myself rooted to the spot long enough to see the driver who looked like one of those Russian Spetznaz bouncers from Shroom with the crewcut and scar on the coupon, discreetly open the side of his jacket to show he was carrying some kind of a gun inside a brown leather carry holster belt. It's mad the things that run though your mind in these moments. Aye, I could see the gun but it was the brown leather holster that had me thinking of a leather pouch that you pour Sangria into that my auntie had brought back from a holiday in Lloret de Mar years ago.

'Get. Fucking. In' He said, deliberately pausing between each word. Despite looking like he was from deepest Volgograd he delivered his ominous "invitation" in the broadest of Weegie accents. 'You sit with him in the back' He looked to his side to the other man with the beard. Without speaking he nodded and walked over to grab me. I made a bit of an arse of myself by at first trying to resist him grabbing onto me before remembering about the gun which soon had me complying.

'What's all this about boys?' I genuinely asked them as I was marched over to the back of the car and shoved into it. Fuck me, I wouldn't wish a scenario like that on my worst enemy but if they did have to go through similar then I'd be asking them about the ridiculous amount of thoughts they had to contend with when it was taking place. I was doing a quick mental search for what I'd possibly done to anyone in Glasgow to have scary cunts with guns on my case. I came up with nicks, nada fuck all. Aye of course, I'd had my scraps with the Rangers ICF as well as their Celtic counterparts from across the city but it's not like I was a known casual, well didn't think so anyway. That's why I was so surprised by the whole Nora placing so much importance on me as one of the main lads in the crew.

Apart from the whole casual side of things, the only time I've really come into contact with Glaswegians had been on holiday. Sharing the same planes to Spain, and hotels. They're ok in moderation I suppose, without an equal when it comes to patter. That aside, my internal search function I'd performed had come up with absolutely ride all of a reason for me to be on the wrong side of a pair of formidable looking gangsters from The West.

They definitely weren't casuals anyway. Their dress sense was about the polar opposite of your average Scottish fitba hooligan. Leather jackets and jeans and shoes with a gap enough so that you could see the white socks they were both wearing , dripping in gold the pair of them as well. Sovereign rings and chunky chains around their necks. They stank of thinking that they needed to dress a certain way due to their niche line of work.

'Well budge up then ya fucking wee bawbag' The bearded boy said to me all nippy like as he shoved me across the back seat towards the inside of the door. 'Everybody in?' The driver said looking round to check that all was in order and that he was good for pulling away. I'm probably sat there with my pus tripping me while his mate playfully patted me on the shoulder and said 'aye, all mates together' before the two of them laughed and the car moved off.

I'm not really sure what the score with these cunts was in terms of did they know where they were or not because the first thing we did was a three point turn sending us back in the direction they'd went in when I'd seen them earlier. Got to hand it to myself, I thought having some psychotic Millwall fan holding a knife to my face on an unpredictably moving train was probably gong to be the most dangerous thing that would happen to me in my life but within a matter of weeks here I was topping it, big fucking time.

'Look, any chhhh h h chance one of you can tell me what the fuck is going on here' Shit, where did that stutter come from I thought to myself. I don't stutter, the only time I've stuttered was when slagging Eddie Heavy Head back when I was at school. His stutter was pretty bad likes, of course he got the pish taken out of him about it. Most who done it will no doubt regret it years later once they mature a bit, me included. 'n n nnnnnno w w wwwwwwe wwwwwonnnnn't' Beard cunt said to me while the driver started chuckling away in the front. 'Let's just say you've stepped on the wrong fucking toes, pal' My friend sat babysitting me in the back followed up in his grating nasally accent.

'I've not done fuck all to anyone' I pleaded. By that point I was officially shitting myself. I'd never seen a gun in my life before, apart from on telly and here I am with two beasts of men telling me that I've done something to merit them paying me a visit. You'd be fucking scared as well and don't even try to tell me you wouldn't! 'Oh but you have, Zico' The boy in the front said as he concentrated on the road, taking a turn that I noticed was for Lower Methil. He knew what he was doing when he called me by my name and I picked up on that straight away.

The chances of this being a case of some kind of mistaken identity now reduced to minus one hundred. I didn't even know what to say back. The two of them were in complete control and it probably wouldn't have mattered "what" I'd said to them as we sat there. 'You're a hard man to catch up with by the way, I tell you. One more day and Joe there was ready for just going into your house and dragging you out of there himself' He continued. 'Fucking was anaw' the man beside me agreed. 'You think I've got time to waste coming through from Glasgow looking for wee dicks like you night after fucking night?' He asked me. Not sure if he was being rhetorical or not but I answered his question with my question 'If you told me why you're even looking for me maybe I'd be able to answer your question.'

I knew the area, most likely better than they did so I was following where we were driving to as we travelled and soon we were pulling into the docks which as far as a venue for a gangland execution goes was fucking textbook, couldn't fault them for a location. He eventually parked up out in a secluded spot beside the water. There wasn't another car or person around as far as I could see. Turning the ignition off he looked round at me. Maybe it was just my sheer sense of desperation and looking for "any" kind of sign to cling onto but I thought I seen a glimmer of almost sympathy when he looked at me and asked 'You ready then?'

I couldn't believe that this was actually happening. Was it? It seemed like it definitely was but at the same time how could it be?! This was what happened to people who were making cameo appearances in The Bill on STV. The reality that I was seeing here was that yes, it was for real. More than that, it apparently was being taken as assumed that I knew what was going on here as there was not much in the way of details being provided. 'Ready?' I thought. 'I don't even know why I'm sat in the back of your car, mate? You're asking me if I'm ready to take a bullet in the back of the head which I'm not sure if anyone would ever be ready for something like that but I guess it might help a person get some kind of closure or acceptance on it if they at least knew why.'

'Aye fair enough I've had a few battles with boys from your side of the country on match day but if anything, I've taken more sore ones when doing it than they did, fucking hard bastards from Glasgow likes, game as fuck, should've seen it before the game at Ibrox near the end of the season, got our cunts kicked all over Govan, right bad one likes' - Once I started speaking I couldn't stop. I wasn't exactly finding any kind of life altering meaningful words to help change this position I was in but I just kept talking and talking all the same.

'Look pal, one of our business associates called in a favour and asked us to come and take care of you. He must really have a hard on for you though wee man because he wouldn't have been so quick to call in a favour with us normally, you should take it as a compliment.' My sitter in the back offered me some extra information but if he thought that I was going to take a compliment that I had managed to engineer a situation that had led to some dangerous killers(?) being on my case then aye. I wasn't likely to be seeing the compliment tucked away in that.

As I sat there processing, Joe reached over my lap and pulled the interior handle of the door to open it. Ready or not, he'd answered that whole will I get out the car to have my brains blown out question for me. I got out the car, my legs almost buckling from underneath me. It's weird but as I found myself standing there on the docks, I was hearing every sound around, taking them all in, in an instinctive way almost like my senses knew I'd not hear them again. The irony of how beautiful seagulls sounded right there and then was not lost on me. The sound of the waves was more amazing than any song I'd ever heard. Of course, not all sounds can be beautiful though and I'd class a Weegie accent telling you to walk with him while he's holding a gun in his hand as one that goes in the category of not so pleasant.

They marched me over to the end of a pier that extended out onto the River Forth. Reaching the end, the driver, pointing the gun at me, told me to turn my back and get on my knees. This, in a fucked up way gave me a wee bit of hope to cling onto which is fucking stupid when you think about it. A guy has you under his control, a gun in his hand and he's now told you to get on your knees. That's a case of goodnight Vienna right there but with my frazzled brain that had taken on its fair share of Eckies over the summer I somehow managed to find hope due to all the TV shows and films I'd see where someone had a gun on them in such a way.

I'd say more often than not something else happens before the trigger is pulled. Police arrive, always with seconds to spare and the bad guys get taken out by some crack firearms squad in ski masks. When I stop though for a moment, if I'd actually taken a second to think about the calibre of the local police who have been known to take a couple of days to come and see you when you've had your house broken into. Had I done that I would not have even began to hold any kind of hope that they would be coming to the rescue.

'What's his name? Before you do this at least tell me his fucking name' My anger was now starting to spill out of me, if I got angry at them what might they do? Kill me? 'I'll haunt the fucking prick for the rest of his days' I said which actually made one of them giggle. 'It's fucking Nora, you mean you genuinely didn't know?' This seemed to come from the driver with the gun pointed at me but was said with genuine surprise and sincerity.

'Mate, I never thought it was him because for fucks sake I ran with the team for a couple of years and decided to give it up. He's a scary cunt likes so I knew he wasn't going to take it too well but seriously? You two showing up from through in The Weeg with guns? Nah, never thought it was Nora. I'm not being funny here boys but do you not think that being executed gangland style doesn't exactly fit the crime of stopping running with a gang of fitba hoolies. Wee bit excessive if you ask me'

'The wee man's got a point though' I could tell this came from Joe with the beard as his nasally accent had already made it onto my list of most annoying noises ever.

'Aye I know he does, Joe but a favour is a fucking favour, plus we've got our rep to think about. Imagine what it would look like if people found out that we'd went back on our word? Look at all the alternative things we could be doing to pay Nora back but instead he has us taking out some poor wee sapp, better for us .. if not for him, admittedly'

The fact that the two of them had, what looked like, entered into some debate was at least something. Doubt, doubt would be what potentially would keep me alive by now. Sadly though the one in charge was the one who was firmly in the lets do away with Zico camp.

'Right let's do this then' He said before Joe had a chance to respond. I felt the gun begin pressing into the back of my head, initially with so much force it pushed the whole of my head forward before I regained my composure. Well, as much composure as someone could possibly have in such times. Staring out across the sea I found myself focusing on the Bass Rock over the water in North Berwick. The things that go through your mind in such a moment?

What I should've been thinking of was things like Lisa and my family, bemoan the fact that I never got a chance to really get started with Acid House and see what it would go on to become. Would United ever win the league again? Another thing I'd never find out. I thought of none of those things though, just this big fucking stupid rock. I remarked to myself that I'd never been to North Berwick in my life, would see the Bass Rock every day but never from that side of the water and for some reason this felt important to me there and then. The reality of course being that I couldn't have given two fucks about the rock. In that moment though it was right in my line of vision and the last thing I was going to see. It felt like one of the fucking seven wonders of the world to me. Fuck your Taj Mahal.

This almost trance like state that I'd taken myself away to was crudely broken by the sound of the steel of the gun, cocking itself back. The sound of that "click" instantly sending me into a bit of a wobble. I started to tremble, uncontrollably. I wanted to stop, wanted to at least die with some kind of dignity but I couldn't help it. Fucking hell, I wasn't even old enough to rent Scarface from the video shop yet here I was being asked to handle a situation like this. Sensing I had a second to spare, if that. I found a wee bit of bravado, managing to speak up enough to ask them to tell Nora from me that I was going to make the rest of his life a living hell from beyond the grave. I'm really not sure where I was getting all of this me being a ghost nonsense from but I wasn't for dropping it.

Then came another click, different from the one where he'd cocked the trigger back. I was still there. Could still hear the seagulls, still smelling the seaweed with open eyes looking over the Forth.

'You can tell him yourself .... if you're brave enough, Zico, lad' The gunman one said, taking it away from the back of my head for the first time since I'd first sunk to my knees. The two of them bursting out in laughter. I plucked up enough courage to look around and see him stepping away from me and moving towards Joe who'd sat on the bonnet of the BMW laughing back at his mate. I'm still on my knees looking at them, not wanting to tempt fate and ask if they're not going through with it but from what I saw it looked promisingly to be the case.

'Look wee man, Nora's big on respect isn't he and what you've done he's unfortunately taken badly. Fucking speaks highly about you as well, that's the thing. Said he was bringing you up through the ranks. You were going to take over from him one day. The boy thinks you saying you'll pass is a slap in the face for him and aw that, he's not taken it well. You've made a bit of an arse out of him in front of everyone else from what I heard' The other guy starts to tell me as he sits down on the bonnet along with Joe as he sparks up a fag, briefly stopping to ask if I wanted one.

Ummm I've just been taken up to what I thought was my last second alive only to get a reprieve? Aye I'll take a fucking fag, and some drugs and alcohol as well ya cunt! I nodded my head so he lit the one he had in his hand and then threw it over in my direction leaving me to pick it up off the ground before gratefully sucking on it. Best fucking cigarette ever by the way and no mistake. If cigarettes tasted as good as that one in that moment. I reckon the world would have maybe five or six future generations left before the whole planet had croaked from cancer.

'He wanted to give you a fright over this whole you going against him thing and employed us'

'Well accept my commendations on a job well done, the pair of you' I nervously laughed while setting about smoking the cigarette in a Guinness record breaking time.

'There is one thing though wee man' Joe said in what sounded like an ominous caveat. 'You're banned from Tannadice, banned from away matches as well. In fact, put the City of Dundee down as a no go zone, no passes there for you my friend. Trust me, if you do and then you get spotted then we're going to have to come back through again and Nora really will be the least of your worries by then'

The time for me to be pissed off about the whole implications about that really was for later on when I was on my own, safe and away from gun totting Glaswegians but even then I was devastated over this news. Aye fair enough, I 'was' grateful over the fact that they were just fucking about and had not actually intended to shoot me but well, now I was alive still and finding myself told that I couldn't go to see my fitba team anymore. They might have well as shot me.

I planned to live a long and fruitful life and one of the vital components of that was surely going to include going home and away to support my team. The wee break alone since the start of the season had been killing me and I was looking forward to getting back once the whole Utility thing had died down. Now? Here I was being told that I could "never" go back to Tannadice Park?

I nodded back at him doing just about enough to let him know I understood the message he was delivering. He ushered me back up off my knees 'Come on' motioning for me to get up and come back over to them. I'd heard about that Stockholm syndrome thing you get with hostages and their captors and aye, I know it was way too soon for me to have that. Seeing them sat on the bonnet having a smoke all casual like, asking me to come back over I felt they weren't that bad after all. All they had to do was not plug me then toss me over into the Forth for the jellyfish to snack on, simple. I found some cojones to ask for another fag. Standing there with them I could've smoked twenty Regal King Size at the same fucking time if they were put in front of me, fucking easy.

'The kid's bound to be in a fucking tailspin right now' Joe remarked to the other one while taking a fag out, lighting it and then throwing it over without looking at me. - 'Oh aye, Joe, you never forget the first time you get a gun pulled on you, mind what Walker Campbell from The Gorbals did when it happened to him? Cunt shat himself didn't he?' - Joe laughed away at the memory of this man I don't and hopefully will never know who lost control of their bowels when presented with a gun pointed at them.

'Aye I'm in a fucking tailspin alright, one minute I'm on my way to my birds to have a Saturday night of watching a film, having a Chinese takeaway and as always trying to convince her to have sex with me while her mum and dad sit downstairs and the next I've got a gun at my head down the docks' I managed to laugh at myself at the sheer plot twist that my night ended up taking.
They both laughed at me. It was a weird feeling but despite everything that had gone on I'd been left with the feeling that they almost liked me. It was confusing to say the least.

'Anyway, we need to get going so come on ya wee cunt, back in the fucking car' The crewcut one said to me. That's when I realised these two were actually going to drop me back off again. Fucking unpredictable pair of boys I'll tell you? They more than intimate that they're going to execute you then end up driving you back home like a fucking black cab. This in itself was quite fortunate as I had not one single penny towards bus money home due to being unexpectedly snatched in the way that I'd been. Every cloud.

Chapter 26.

I never told Lisa about what happened, how the fuck could I? Weeks back I turn up at her door with pieces of me hanging off courtesy of the Millwall boys. We had that open and honest chat where I said enough was enough and that I was going to keep my nose clean from any trouble. Me professing that I was choosing to turn over a new leaf? I could hardly go in there and give it the whole oh how was your day? Oh me? Well half an hour ago two big bastards abducted me and held a gun to my head down at Methil docks.

Hardly the type of conversation two teenagers would normally be having in a small Scottish village. That would've went down like a lead balloon had i told her and that would've probably been enough for her to end it with me so aye, schtump likes. I wouldn't have seen her for dust, understandably. She knew something was up with me though. I'm not the best poker player and that's putting it kindly but I managed to pass it off. Putting it down to all the shit earlier on at work and then the blowback I got from James when he found out I'd jacked it in when he got back home.

Even I knew I wasn't being my normal talkative jokey way with her but I couldn't pull myself out of it. It was impossible for me not to keep thinking of the sound of that trigger being cocked back. It was something that would give me nightmares about for a long time to follow. As far as messages go though? Nora managed to deliver it better than Royal Mail Special Delivery and it was very much a case of message received on my end. This whole being banned from going to the matches thing though was as impacting on me as a gun pressed to the back of my head had been. You can't take a mans fucking football team away from him, poor form, likes.

Fuck knows what it's like for those fans who occasionally have to put up with their team going into liquidation cope, must be an absolute nightmare. I have this theory about fitba where I reckon that your team is the first thing growing up that teaches you what it's like to love someone or something. All the good times and the bad times, the happiness, the deep hurt. To extend that way of thinking, if you're then told that you can't see them again that's the equivalent of splitting up with the love of your life or losing a loved one through death. It might seem a bit melodramatic to some, that but if that's the way you look at it then you simply don't understand the sport. Simple as that.

Perhaps I was deluding myself but even though my message had been delivered in such a dramatic and scary way, I still thought there might be ways for me to still go to the fitba. Considering I'd run major risks in bumping into the Utility at every single game home or away. A platform here, a train carriage there, an away match where there's not as many united supporters and the chances of seeing someone else vastly increased. I'd already went through a few potential ways around this so called ban. First thing I thought of was going there in disguise, absolutely not a stitch of casual clothes, wear a scarf and a wooly hat like all the other Christmas trees. The like that don't ever attract the eye of a casual.

I was thinking of a pair of glasses and fake beard combo and that's when I knew I was getting carried away with myself. Fucking hell, next I'll be wearing one of those things you get at the joke shop which is a pair of glasses and a fake nose attached to it like that Groucho Marx. One other option I thought of was to actually give Nora a phone to try and have some words with him. Clear the air, apologise (which in itself I wasn't too hot on considering the move he'd pulled on me) explain myself and see if he'd call off this fucking Fatwa that was placed on me. Never thought I'd feel like I was a kindred spirit with that Salman Rushdie although I'm assuming he'd still be up for a swap with me if he got the chance.

Our next match was away to St Mirren through in Paisley, someone once told me that, you know that paisley pattern design you see on ties and scarfs? Well that was designed through in Paisley. Not sure if it's true or not but aye, good on them if they did. Couldn't see me wanting to go in any case so I tried not to think too much about that side of things. The game after that was at home to Dunfermline so I aimed to have a plan of action in place before that game, even if I hadn't a fucking clue what that plan was going to be, not even remotely.

Apart from all the soccer related problems I had to deal with I was just keeping my head down and immersing myself into this new scene that I now felt completely part of. The triple assault of how much I was hooked by house music that had me wanting to listen to and find out about more and more, the impact that Ecstasy had on me and I'm not just talking about for the short hours that I was under its influence. Thirdly, the new friends I'd made at the events I'd been to.

It was a full on assault that completely fucked my head in the best of ways. On the nights I didn't see Lisa they were spent either listening to house music or talking on the phone about it to one of the friends I'd met at events and had swapped numbers with. Ecstasy is some drug likes, the way it can have you feeling like you're really connecting with someone else, a total bond even though you've just met them fifteen minutes before. A drug that has you giving out your phone number to pretty much anyone due to you thinking that they're your new best friend after exchanging a few words.

The first time someone called the house it was a boy from down in the Borders, Lawro. It was a touch embarrassing because I couldn't remember who he was when he called but I done that thing where you don't know but you try your best not to let them know it. He mentioned that we'd swapped numbers after chatting for half an hour in the chill out zone up in Loch Ness but aye, must've blanked out that one I'm afraid. I'm sure I'll recognise him when I see him at the next party wherever it is. Sound boy though and someone who had been going for a good six months before me. He was really knowledgable about the scene. People like that, and Si I absolutely loved listening to and learning from. I just wanted to find out as much about the scene as I could and as quickly as I could. Names of bands or producers, record labels. Who the top deejays were to be looking out for. Total immersion.

It seemed pretty ironic but I found that so many of the people making the records weren't even from the UK, yet when played over here the crowd goes mental to it? To learn that house music originated in America blew my mind as it was what I thought of as the least likely thing to come out of America, Germany aye with their Kraftwerk and that but America? Nah. I always see America and music as some boy in a big stetson hat and cowboy boots playing a steel guitar country and western style. That or some rock star with hair flying all over the place on stage at some American fitba stadium belting out some rock with woman on folks shoulders getting their tits out. Aerosmith, Bon Jovi that kind of stuff. Bleepy electronic music to be listened to by teenagers out of their heads in the middle of the night outside in a tent? I wouldn't have thought so. Never the less, god bless America all the same. Us Europeans owe them, big.

It really did speak volumes for the community spirit that the house music illegal party scene had though here in Scotland. Just by going out I was making new friends here there and everywhere that had me speaking on the phone and even a few times, meeting up with outside and away from the parties themselves. Spoke a few times with this mad cunt called Obi from Arbroath and he eventually took a drive down to meet up with me for a smoke when out in his car.

The more I spoke to these other people the more I was seeing that it wasn't just me whose life had been completely turned upside down by this musical and cultural revolution. It was fucking brilliant if I'm being honest, like we were part of some underground society. A party sub branch of the masons or something. Without the whole trying to catch the greased up pig or whatever they get up to behind closed doors.

The passion that we all held for the scene was like something I'd never seen people share before. It was such a refreshing thing. The closest I can think of is when you're on the terracing and it's a crucial match, your team scores a goal and suddenly it doesn't fucking matter who you went to the game with because for a few seconds you're all as one, hugging and smiling. That's only for a few seconds though. This felt much much more.

I spoke to Si, midweek in the build up to the usual four of us going through to Pure in Edinburgh on the Friday. I so badly wanted to speak to him about what Nora had done but as always was stuck in the living room along with the family. I did for a few paranoid seconds earlier on in the week consider the fact that he already knew what Nora had set in motion for me but dismissed it as quickly as I thought of it.

I reasoned that had he known what was headed my way he'd have at the very least put in a call to me to warn me in advance. When I spoke to him on the phone though there was no indication of anything to contradict that. He was absolutely hyper about Pure, kept saying how much it would blow me away. Experiencing what I'd already done so far I was already thinking that there wasn't much more new to see, just more of the same which I'd have all too agreeable with.

'So when will we see you back on foot patrol on match day then' he asked hopefully, finally breaking away from talking about Pure and what kind of pills he had for us.

'Aye, there's stuff I need to tell you about that side of things but can't just now' I responded in what was the definition of cagey. The 'can't just now' part was enough for my uncles ears to prick up and he had a wee glance my way. Fucking ears like a hawk, him. Makes out he's fixed exclusively on the telly but is hearing every single word of the conversation. Not fooling anyone! Understandably it has made having various phone calls almost impossible to conduct since I started going out and taking Class A's. I need to be developing a new form of code for these phone calls. Morse or if I stutter twice that means pills, three times for speed. Something like that.

'I'll tell you about it on Friday night, mate' I said in a final kind of way. Si, picked up on my tone and left it at that. He continued to talk about Utility matters however. Telling me that he was going to St Mirren on the Saturday "after" Pure and how he was just going to get dropped off in Dundee in the morning on the way back from Edinburgh.

I was dong the maths in my head as the words spilled from his mouth. Unless I wasn't hearing properly I was sure he'd told me that after a night and morning of taking pills and fuck knows what else. He then, without having had any sleep, would go on to have an afternoon of fighting some West Coast fitba casuals. I'd always thought the mob from Paisley had a really cool name, LSD. Short for "Love Street Division" which came from the name of their team's ground. Without incriminating myself in the room I told him that it wasn't even possible what he was suggesting. I could well have reminded him about the fact that his mind would be reduced to absolute mush and that he wouldn't have enough strength to punch his way out of a wet paper bag. I didn't exactly need to though so left it.

'Don't you worry about a thing sweet Zico' He sang back at me in the tune of a song I recognised but don't have the first clue who sings it. Some soul group I think. 'You underestimate the power of speed paste my friend, I take too much of it I'll be still awake for the Scottish cup final in May that we're going to be in, most likely against one of the ugly sisters from Glasgow' I just laughed back at him and told him I'd believe him on Saturday morning when I seen the state of him once Pure was over.

He told me that there would be CCS there on Friday night as well but that it would all be cool. As long as we weren't dicks to anyone then they'd be fine with us too. Mad how, as I'd already seen for myself, different crews of casuals were at the same nights and not fighting each other. I wouldn't have believed it had I not had That blether with those Hibs lads that night at Shroom without any hint of it turning nasty.

I couldn't help but think that part of Si's insistence on going to the game on the Saturday after being full of narcotics and partying until the sun came up was more due to Nora than anything else. I couldn't really blame him if that "was" the case, obviously.

Chapter 27.

Whoah ya fucker, Si wasn't joking. Pure was outrageously good. A completely different experience from all of the out in the middle of nowhere and wait until an hour before it starts before knowing where you're even going type of deals I'd become accustomed to. This was a fully licensed, no need to worry about the coppers ending the night, club. Just off Princess Street in the city centre. The four of us took the train through on the Friday night and it must've taken about five minutes walk and we were there taking our place in the line to get in.

The place itself looked like nothing from the outside and, well, wasn't much on the 'inside' either but fuck me, what a mad house of a place. A venue that took no prisoners, no easy way out for those that just want to sit in a field talking shite for hours on end, nowhere to go on that front apart from through the front door and back outside. It was dark, it was deep it was hotter than the fucking sun and reminded me of the one and only time I had been in a sauna in Loch Lomond at this posh hotel I'd been with my family one summer. The place was an absolute sweatbox, coated in condensation wherever your hand rested upon. It was also a den where every single person inside were going off their fucking nuts the whole night and morning long. It felt like the energy inside that one club could've powered the whole of the Lothian and Borders region for the whole weekend.

It definitely felt more intense, more demanding than the larger scale all night and outdoor efforts if that makes sense. Due to the claustrophobic sense of it compared to the open air parties that were set up for thousands attending, there wasn't an escape from it. Wherever you went it remained as loud, anywhere you looked you'd find a mass of others dancing or looking in your direction with a smile and an outstretched hand to you. On the train through Si had told Lisa and I about how there would be a bit more need for adding a wee bit of Sulph to proceedings as we'd need it.

Lisa looked at me with a screwed up face indicating she had no idea what he was talking about. 'Speed, my dear, Amphetamine Sulphate, the cornerstone of any night out and at times even more important than our little friend MDMA' The whole carriage that was a mixture of all kinds of people who, for their own reasons, wanted to get to Edinburgh on a Friday night, would have been able to hear him the volume that he was excitedly talking at. As ever though, Si would not have held much regard for what anyone else was thinking.

He was right though, even Lisa admitted as much. The amount of dancing that we did for hours on end would not have been possible on Eckies alone. It was a house music night with a difference but I absolutely lapped up. It had been my first chance to hear deejays who would play a different version of house compared to what had been going on at the illegal parties.

The deejays Twitch and Brainstorm were playing what I classed as still house but with a darker and harder edge to it, faster too. I'd listened to a couple of tapes that Si had given me of some hardcore deejays and I'd been getting into them. A more faster BPM to the songs, not so many piano breaks but the actual construction of the tracks and then thinking of what they would sound like on a pill seemed like a winner to me. Then again, a pill and Johnny Cash would seem like a winner to me, and I don't even know what Johnny Cash sings!

Si and I popped outside for a joint at one point during the night, fuck knows how he was able to make one when he was inside a place that was a constant sea of moving bodies but he had one ready to spark up as we nodded towards the bouncers on our way outside. The contrast of the cool night air compared to what was going on inside was a godsend. Initially we stood chatting to the two of them, in hindsight it probably wasn't the best policy to smoke a reefer beside the gatekeepers that are there to make sure the patrons are "not" taking drugs but they seemed cool with it.

Compared with dealing with some beer boys I guess a bouncer would take overseeing people like us every time. One of them even took a wee toke when I jokingly offered it to him. Si, steered me over to a wall for us to both sit on and finish it. That's when I was able to tell him about Nora and the gangsters from the week before. I think he had taken two, possibly three Eckies by that point of the night and fuck knows how much speed. When you're just dipping your finger indiscriminately into a bag of powder how really do you quantify how much you're taking after all? In the moment where I told him about the gun to my head, heavily sucking on the last of the joint, the whole harrowing memory of it all came right back to me.

He said that he'd heard of a few stories of what Nora had done to a select few who had left the team but generally most that left would have gotten a kicking and then it was over and done with, if they even got that. They were then history and not worth Nora's time from then on. 'He must've felt it with you though, Zico I mean, you're one of the boys aren't you? I would never have said that you were one of those peripheral figures in the crew. You're one of the boys that the others look out for on match days so if you're missing, it gets noticed. Through that I think Nora felt an example had to be made of you.'

I genuinely didn't even think anyone noticed me on match days but going by Nora and now what Si was saying maybe I was wrong. I took it for granted but looking at it from the outside I guess someone so young who was never shy to get involved was something "to" take notice of. What struck me the most was the almost blasé way that Si processed my news. Like it was a normal reaction. I don't know? I thought that he would've reacted with a bit more of surprise or horror but there was nothing like that.

It was almost like he saw the justification in what Nora had done. It threw me a little but I didn't say anything further on that particular subject and put it down to him possibly being too wrecked to fully visualise how frightening it had been at the time and how real it had been. How it was something that had led to not one single full nights sleep for moi since.

Taking out his skins and attempting to go through the charade I was now accustomed to where heavily under the influence of Class A's, he was going to try and make a joint. He carried on with what he was saying after my protests that I was just one of the foot soldiers on a Saturday. 'Did you never hear about Mikey Harkins?' It was a name I'd heard of from other members of the Utility. He was gone before I started to run with them but apparently he was one of the main boys. Game as fuck and just as hard to back it up. 'Aye, Nora didn't take too well to him calling it a day, gave the poor bastard brain damage for fucks sake, here going to hold this for me for a second' He offered me the three Rizlas that he'd managed to stick together to hold while he burned some Rocky into it.

'Brain damage? How come likes?' I asked .. I'd have wanted to have known in any case but given my present situation it was probably a good bit of intelligence to be in possession of. 'Well, nobody really knows the full story due to Mikey's condition following what happened but the word is that Nora and a couple of other guys, not from the Utility went round to see him. Ran a bath and tried to give him a fright by saying they were going to drown him, kept pushing and holding him under the water again and again only Nora held him down there for too long than was safe and it had some lasting impact to Mikey's brain. He hasn't been the same after that. I don't think Nora meant to do it likes, only meant to scare him but then again who knows. It's fucking Nora we're speaking about here after all.'

'Looks like I got off lightly thinking I was seconds from death' I said only half joking. Before either of really knew it we had entered one of "those" Eckie conversations. The kind where any walls that existed would come crashing down. Si admitted that he had been looking at me and more specifically my reasons for wanting to give up. 'Look, going out with sound as fuck people like you and Shan and having the times of our lives, having an amazing girl like Lisa as my girlfriend, as mad as it sounds I want to be a fucking DJ now I'm getting so much into the music, all that stuff is what's important to me now. I'm going to work on getting a set of decks, it's all I need mate. Fuck running around Aberdeen or Glasgow worrying if you're going to end up in the cells or make it back to the train station in one piece to take you back home again' I could feel myself getting right into it. 'Look, Si, I'm not going to deny what an enormous buzz it is with The Utility on a match day but I've ridden my luck in that arena for two years now and then along comes this fucking Acid House stuff? Has totally changed my attitude towards certain things, likes'

Sucking on the spliff that he eventually got together he sat on the wall nodding in agreement. He came clean and admitted that he was beginning to follow my reasoning and was now thinking about removing himself from the casual scene as well. 'It's not going to be as easy for me as it is for you though, Zico' I said no words .. I think my face in response to him referring that I'd had it "easy" was enough, my eyebrows were momentarily more raised than Roger Moore's.

'No, you know what I mean' Si back tracked when there really was no need to worry. 'I'm not saying you've had it easy but I live in the same fucking town as Nora, I see him when I step out to get rolls and a paper in the morning or when I pop down to the bookies. I cross him then I'm going to have to move somewhere else because life is going to be a fucking nightmare. I've known him for years, well before I started with the Utility' He made a good point. That was one bonus that I'd overlooked all of the prank phone calls and visits from gangsters. That apart from those examples I was fairly protected in terms of where I lived.

'Well look, we'll figure it out, there's bound to be a way that'll get you out of the Utility and get me back on the terraces at Tannadice into the bargain. Right now probably isn't the time for brainstorming though, I think I'd probably struggle with level two on Simon' I said to him. Looking at my Casio, it had just gone past one in the morning. 'For now I think we have more pressing issues to contend with' - Looking like he was still stuck in the whole how he was going to get himself out of the Utility Crew train of thought now that he'd descended into that thought pattern. 'How's that like?' he asked, appearing to have no clue what I was on about. I just nodded back towards the door that was semi hidden by the bulk of the two bouncers standing at the front of it.

His face lit up as he took one last long and lingering toke before passing the joint to me. 'Fucking yasssssss' he punched the air like he'd had the sudden epiphany that he'd now remembered "why" he was sat on a wall in Edinburgh city centre. 'I'll dab to that' he said as he reached into his pocket to fish out his bag of speed. It was like the two of us were getting fired into a Dib Dab only instead of the stick we had our fingers and the sweet tasting sugary powder had made way for some foul tasting chemical compound that had been made in a lab in Holland. Actually, it wasn't much like a Dib Dab at all when I put it like that.

Obviously, Si and I met through him initially offering me a wee dab of some powder so I was no stranger to that side of our friendship but fuck knows where he got this particular speed from or what it even was but it was different from anything he'd offered me before. Better, so incredibly and astoundingly better. At no point did my mood or energy dip. I felt as fresh as I did at any point during the whole of my day when the DJ played the last song of the morning. He looked the exact same, a picture of fucking health if you will. Lisa looked absolutely shattered, she'd taken a wee dab here and there over the night but with moderation. In truth, I think the wee trip outside was what did for Si and moi, I dread to think how much we took of it when we were out there in the dark.

After we left The Venue with myself already vowing to get myself back over as soon as possible, My experience so far had been of parties that only happened now and again with no real regularity but this place was going on EVERY WEEK?! That's fucking dangerous to know is that. Our train wasn't until six so we had the best part of two hours to kill which I wasn't looking forward to as all I could see would be Si and I talking the biggest amount of shite to Shan and Lisa, making complete arses of ourselves in the process, inevitably.

Stood freezing my balls off while ringing wet from the greenhouse that Pure had been like. I was dreading it. Felt like a complete fanny to have even thought that when we got ourselves back down to Waverley to find that some others who had also been at Pure were already down there, with a ghetto blaster already pumping out some similar tunes that we'd all been listening to just up the road all night.

'Wooooooooooh' Shan squealed, grabbing hold of Lisa's hand as the two of them broke into a dance over in the direction of the half a dozen bods that were dancing by the ghetto blaster that was so big it could easily have had its own post code. Si and I followed slowly behind. Him holding out what was by now looking a very much depleted bag of powder. 'Fuck off, mate, I won't be sleeping until midweek as things stand' I replied before completely undoing all my good work within two seconds by adding 'Ok then, just a wee dab eh? Just to keep the wolves from the door eh?' He just laughed as he then shoved his soaked up finger deep into it at the back of me.

The concourse of Waverley Station was the most bizarre mix of all of us types who had been to Pure or similar clubs, and the tramps who sleep rough down there at night. A lot of them didn't seem too happy about the ghetto blaster or the noise that we were all making. Fucking idiots didn't even see the golden opportunity handed to them with us around. If I was homeless I reckon getting money from someone who was under the influence of Ecstasy would be like shooting fish in a barrel.

In my short few months of taking it I wouldn't have put it past me to not only give someone a few quid because they asked but I'd possibly hand them my Bank of Scotland card along with the pin number, my date of birth and my mums maiden fucking name. So suggestible I was when that beautiful MDMA was running things.

You see that though? Half hearted beggars, likes? Couple of weeks ago I was walking along Kirkcaldy High Street and saw this busker. You should've seen the guy. Playing that song by The Doors, Light My Fire on the mouth organ while juggling half a dozen Star Wars action figures. They were all there likes. Luke, Leia, Chewy, Han. Even that camp gold one which I can never get the name right. I never bother with buskers but this boy was top notch.

I chucked him a quid. Wish I'd had my Polaroid on me that I got for my birthday a few years ago cause it was the type of performance that you just knew you'd never see again. Anyway, about twelve shops down and there's a guy sat there, outside Tandy. Not doing fuck all other than sitting there with a blanket over him with a disinterested look on his face with a whippet that was standing there shivering and looking less interested about what they were doing than its owner. I couldn't help but stop and offer him a bit of advice in that if he wanted to get any donations down there he should get himself as far away to fuck from the moothie playing juggler because he was getting killed in the popularity stakes. I still chucked him fifty pence though. Aye, I fucking paid HIM for the advice I'd given him. I'm sound like that though.

The people with the ghetto blaster were waiting on the same train as we were. Most of them were from Inverkeithing which isn't that far from me in the scheme of things. Really friendly bunch likes. Fucking brilliant tunes as well, I must've asked them who the DJ was on this one mixtape twenty times and even after that I still forgot but it was the best mix I'd ever heard. I really wish I'd asked them a twenty first time, not that it would have probably mattered anyway I guess.

Not like I carry pen and paper around with me though is it. No cunt under the age of thirty does that anyway though do they? You could sense the point though where for a lot of the group there had been a chemically influenced "drop" in energy. Instead of the absolutely mental situation of not even a dozen people all dancing around in a train station we were all sitting around with a bit more chilled out style of music playing while we sat sharing stories and spliffs.

It was a good end to the night / morning. The different scenarios for us all following the night we'd all had was so fascinating. You had Si who was now readying himself for a day out fighting. Something I thought was the complete opposite of what must've been flowing through him at that point. On the Inverkeithing crew side of things, two of them, a couple, Fi Fi and G, were going home to pack and then head straight to the airport for a two week stretch in Ibiza.

One of their friends, Lillian was actually going to her WORK for the day? Jesus Christ, how can you have a night of Class A's and then possess enough motor skills to go to work? She did it all the did it all the time she said, and that all her colleagues just think that she's hungover from the night before. It gave me the chills at the thought of having to go into Perry's Bakery right now in the wired state that I was in. Making gingerbread men and stuff like that? Not in this life.

If anything though, all of this was testament to how important this scene was to us all. That we put it first before all other things, that all the other components in life would have to compromise to make way for our need and our love to get on one, or three for the night. It was clearly evident to me that for a lot of us it had simply and effortlessly made its way to the top of the priorities in life. Life was going to go on, of course it was. It was just going to have to go on while following a different path. Adjustments would have to be made, happy mediums reached . Nothing else for it. There really was no walking away from this scene once you had been pulled into it. Once it grabbed you it pretty much then became your legal guardian.

Chapter 28.

Apparently I'd been a bit naive in thinking that having two shady looking gangsters pay me a visit and hold a gun to my head would have been the end of Nora's fun. Within a matter of weeks it wasn't long before the phone calls started up again. Not as regular as they'd been before. They would come sporadically during the middle of the night and on weekends. The fear factor on my side had dipped a little though. I guess that when you're as young as me and you have to go through having a gun pulled on you in the way that I had. It can either finish you off and destroy you or it help you find some inner strength and resilience.

What doesn't kill you as they say? Instead of being scared by these calls I found them more of an inconvenience than anything else. Don't get me wrong, I'm not saying that I was going to go over to Dundee and punch fuck out of him to get him to stop. I'm not stupid, I even dream of doing such a thing I should wake up and apologise to myself for such delusions. As game and fearless that I was while representing the Utility I still knew what a dangerous and nasty individual Nora was and to dance with him would not have ended well for me. The fucking grassing cunt didn't have to tell my auntie what he did the night that she answered though. If I was ever home when the phone would go late at night I would always rush to get it before anyone else could.

It was always assumed who it was that was going to be on the other end of the line. One Saturday night I was at a party on a boat sailing around the East Coast of Scotland (What a night by the way) so I hadn't been in at the time the call came through. He got my auntie out of her bed around three in the morning and when she answered he decided to tell her some cock and bull story where he told her that I was a football casual (stick with me, the bull part is coming) and that I had put him in hospital six months before and it had taken him all that time to fully recover from his injuries. Now that he was fit again he was going to track me down and that he was going to kill me. Just imagine what news like that would do to someone who was getting on a bit in years?

I really didn't need to be walking back home to a conversation like that while stuck in that weird foggy comedown zone that always follows being up all night taking pills? All I wanted to do was slip in under the radar and get up to my room and blank everyone and everything for a while. That wasn't ever going to happen following the call that had taken place during the night when I'd been out. It was probably one of the worst moments in my life and in a weird way much harder to negotiate through than it had been with those gangsters from Glasgow.

I came through the front door in that creeping cat burglar way that I had actually perfected after the numerous parties I'd been to. For some reason I used to have the impression that when I got to my bedroom after a party it would then serve as some kind of a panic room that would protect me from having to interact with the outside world. In reality all anyone would need to do would be turn the door knob and they would be inside the fortress. I didn't even make it to the first step upstairs that Sunday getting home.

It must've been around one or two o clock in the afternoon when I appeared through the door. The boat docked around seven. We then ended up back at an after party somewhere in Dunfermline. Si had got talking to these two girls, Sooze & Jacks during the night and they invited us all back to the house they shared along with, what it turned out, seemed to be three quarters of the people who were ON the boat.

The party was still going strong when we all left at lunch time. I'd tried a Speedball during the night, something I'd asked what actually was and was told that it had a few random things along with MDMA. Almost like the lucky bags I would get when I was a bairn. 'Two things in life that no one will ever know what they're made of, Donner meat and Speedballs' Si said, 'You just know that there's some real nasty shit inside both but you can't help but like them anyway.'

Due to me already being at a disadvantage which was under the influence of a really nice Dove I never even thought twice about taking this new kid on the block. Fucking stupid, could've been anything? Well, technically it was "anything" because I still don't know what was in it and probably never will. It's not like these things have the ingredients on the side of the packet like a Mars Bar is it? Whatever it was I'm pretty sure one of its ingredients was real live rocket fuel. Fucking hell, it wasn't something I was going to be coming down from in a hurry.

The power of any kind of cohesive speech or focused thought patterns had deserted me hours before. Walking into my house and seeing my uncle stood there looking back at me from the kitchen while saying 'Here he is .. we've been waiting on you, you need to get your arse through to the living room, we'd like a word.' Well, it really wasn't what I was looking for in a Sunday afternoon experience.

Walking through into the living room I could see straight away from the look on my aunties face that she'd been crying, was in a bit of a state actually. That sent me into a panic as I was now sure that I was going to get hit with some bad news like a family member dying or someone finding out they were going to die. Something as serious as that. What a fucking thing to lay on someone who's entering a comedown and will do well to last the next twenty four hours themselves I thought to myself.

Immediately I felt like a selfish twat for even having such a thought like that enter my head. 'Sit down, son' he said, taking a longer than normal look at me. The paranoia was completely ripping through me, the last time I'd seen my eyes had been in the bathroom of the house at the party in Dunfermline and they were fucking gigantic. I needed to make as less eye contact with the two of them as possible but by doing so I was then going to look like I was acting a bit strange, I couldn't win really.

'What's going on?' I asked, finding my voice for the first time since coming in the door. 'We had a call through the night' Jimmy said, glancing at my auntie who looked like she was going to start crying again at his words. The words he chose were, for me, classic textbook speak for someone passing away in the middle of the night. I tried to prepare myself for what was coming next.

'Brenda, answered it. It was from some other boy who says you put him in hospital a while ago and is trying to track you down.' Shit, if I thought I was paranoid before then I knew fuck all. I'm there out of my fucking nut on a grand scale and being someone with a violent past like me I'm getting hit with this? I could barely tell you my middle name in that moment and yet I'm trying to remember every single fight I'd ever had since primary school and if any had been serious enough to land the other in the hossie while also trying to maintain a front of innocence to my family.

I was coming up with zero but regardless of that I was obviously going to deny anything I was going to be getting accused of anyway. 'Eh?' I screwed my face up at him like he was talking nonsense. 'Me put someone in hospital? I've never had a fight in my life' I protested. 'He called in the middle of the night, woke us both up, had quite a story to tell about you' - 'Look, it was probably one of my idiot pals drunk and trying to take the piss' I tried to pass it off but wasn't in any state to be oozing confidence with anything that I was really saying. Fuck knows what I must've looked like sat there on the sofa talking to them. My appearance could well have been a different topic of conversation that they might have wanted to revisit at a later date now that I was sat there in front of them in all my less than glory. I hope to fuck not but if anything, I'll be grateful that it didn't take place when I was still out my nut sat there on the sofa.

Even in the middle of this serious chat I couldn't stop myself from zoning out on them and thinking about stupid random things non related to the seriousness of the conversation that I was stuck in. The telly was still on and and one point I found myself starting to tap my feet and nod my head in time to the music on one of the commercials. Managing to stop myself before I really started to blow things. They both noticed the feet tapping though which left me being accused of not taking them serious with their concerns they were trying to discuss.

If I was to be left in any doubt how serious it was. He reached for the remote and switched the TV off completely so as to avoid distracting me from what they were trying to say. It was statement and I knew it. He NEVER switched the telly off. Fucking tore him to pieces when he had to press that red button on the remote each night when going to bed.

'This boy said that you're one of those casuals that go and cause trouble at the football' he continued with a face that was the combination of one half concern, a quarter pissed off at me and the other quarter being the uncertainty which I think was keeping the pissed off part from bubbling over. 'Casuals? I haven't been to a United game in months and you know that' I thought I was onto a winner there but it came to fuck all when I was reminded that this assault happened around half a year ago and that the boy is only now recovering from his injuries. What was I meant to have done to him that it took him six months to recover from? This was making me out to be some Iraqi Elite Republican Guard as opposed to the gaunt, skin and bones excuse for a human being that was there in front of them.

That's when I knew it was bullshit. 'Look at a wee while ago when you came back from the game with your face a mess?' It appeared to now be making sense to him as he continued. At every single second of the conversation I felt like I just wanted to stand up and walk away from it all but also knew that if I did it would only make me look defensive as well as guilty. My head wasn't handling all of the permutations that was open to what might happen in such a situation as this. All I needed was simplicity, to not have to think or say anything. I felt I needed to at least put up some kind of a fight though. Actually I had no choice BUT to. I wasn't caring about the whole me putting someone in the hossie pish. I cared though about this whole me being a casual stuff coming out and was going to fight that as much as i could. Fight being codeword for lie.

'Uncle Jimmy, that was Millwall for fucks sake, everyone knows what they're like, they're notorious and anyway did you see the state of me? Hardly some hard man that would be going around putting people in the hospital!' - 'Steven, language' My visibly unimpressed auntie pitched in. 'I'm sorry, I'm just frustrated because I'm really tired (more lies, I probably wasn't going to sleep until some point the next day the way I was feeling after that Speedball I'd necked at the party) and here I am getting accused of doing something that I haven't done. Have you ANY idea how crazy it all sounds, me battering someone? That's why I think it's one of my pals just on the wind up, probably pished last night and don't even remember doing it' I tried to reassure them.

'Steven? You've not yet heard what this other boy says he's going to do to you when he catches up with you' My auntie chipped in with tears in her eyes and her voice starting to break like she was about to lose it. I was finding it heartbreaking to see her like this. It all felt way too real.

For the benefit of my mental health for the hours that lay ahead of me I really "didn't" want to be provided with such knowledge but I knew she was going to tell me regardless. Well, she tried to at least before getting too upset and Jimmy taking over again. There's no words for the guilt that I felt watching the two of them sit trying to talk about such a subject. This wasn't what their world would ever normally involve and it was evident that they weren't handling it too well. Join the fucking club, folks, I wasn't handling things too easily on my side.

It was soul destroying for me to see how upset, scared and worried they were though.

I just didn't have the marbles to properly deal with it in that moment. If someone had told me what was waiting back at the house in the form of this topic of conversation I could quite easily have never went home again for weeks, if at all. Enrolling with the French Foreign Legion would've seemed like a better prospect than engaging in such a conversation post Class A participation.

'He says that when he catches you he's going to slice your face from ear to ear so that you'll always have a funny story to tell people as you grow up' There's only one person I know who would think that way and the thought of Nora doing that to me as I took in Jimmy's words almost had me rushing to the bathroom to have a whitey. I felt dizzy with a severe hot flush rushing over me and thought that I might well be sick. 'Look, I think we should just try and forget it, it's obviously just a prank call, a bit sick likes but still a prank call' I'm not sure how convincing I was, probably not much. I wasn't even sure what I was going to say myself from one second to the next. Getting out of the conversation wasn't anywhere even close to being as easy as I thought it was going to be though.

'When we let you stay with us the one thing we asked was no trouble and that if the police ever came to the door then you'd be out' My auntie started up which sent me instantly on the defence reminding the two of them that I'd never "had" the police round looking for me. As far as trouble I'd never caused anything more than any other teenage boy growing up. Couple of broken windows through a stray shot when having a kick about. Not exactly stuff that would have me shipped of to borstal, likes.

If they'd known exactly what I'd been up to for the past few years on a Saturday AND what I'd been up to more recently on Friday and Saturday nights then aye, my arse wouldn't have touched the ground. They didn't know, well, for now anyway and I'd be doing all I could to retain the status quo. My uncle who, like I said, appeared to be slowly making some connections brought up the fact that we'd been receiving those silent calls a while back only to stop and now they'd started again so there must've been something in all of this.

Predictably I ended up losing patience, getting defensive and done the teenager thing by getting lippy back and fucking off to my room. I'm going to miss being able to pull that card out of the pack when I'm looked upon as too old and mature to run away. Never fails to get you out of all kinds of situations. I'd tried to talk sense but for fucks sake I was beyond sense by then following all of the chemicals that I'd necked over the previous night. I promised them that I had categorically not put anyone in hospital in my life, which I knew to be true. That was probably one of the only truths that I HAD come out with when sat there with them.

I asked them to not answer the phone when it rang in the middle of the night. If it did then then I'd be the one to talk to him and settle it. 'What if you're not here? It could be someone calling with bad news' My auntie appeared visibly ill at the thought of this. Frightened for the day she'll never see like my uncle always tells her. A woman who almost came out in a rash at the mere thought of leaving the video recorder switched on at the wall each night before bed. Brainwashed by those public service adverts that used to be on TV in the seventies that would strike the fear of death into people. 'We can cross that bridge if we come to it. For now I just want to talk to this joker and set him straight on a few things' I kept getting hit with ifs and buts though and just lost it in the end. Exasperation getting the better of me I left them to continue with a very definite three person conversation with only two taking part.

This had given me something to be thinking about for all the hours ahead of not sleeping. Fair enough, if Nora needs to try and make my life a living misery in all ways then that's up to him but to involve family members like that was uncalled for. He never really was one for playing by the rules though. One nasty bastard who was capable of some sick and twisted shit. This was an unexpected one. He was becoming a right pain in the arse and one that looked like it wasn't going to go away anytime soon. I thought he was letting things go but instead, it looked like he was just starting.

I noticed the irony of me only now classing him as "a problem" after all he'd done up til then. This however was literally a roof over my head that was at stake and without even knowing it, he was putting that at risk. Probably a good thing he wasn't aware of that too I thought to myself as I lay there in bed trying to watch Spurs at home to Liverpool in "The Big Match" on Border, an English channel that my uncle had managed to get us via some extravagant aerial he'd had stuck on our roof years ago. "Trying" being the key word as despite watching the goals fly in at White Hart Lane on the TV I was miles away.

It consumed my thoughts for the whole of the day and night. All I wanted was a chilled comedown where all I had to think about was the night I'd had on the boat and try to remember all the capers that had gone on with Lisa, Si and Shan. I'd gotten into writing down all of my thoughts when I would get back to my bedroom after a party as I knew there was no guarantee that I'd remember them again and precious memories from wherever I'd been the night before would be lost forever. The day after the boat party though was one track mind stuff, Nora Nora fucking Nora. I thought of how I'd told Si that night outside Pure how there would be a way to fix it all but that, admittedly was just MDMA talk. That usual stuff where you feel that anything can be possible in those blissful hours when the Eckies are flowing through you. You've got me, just out of school, no job just making my way into the arena of life experience and Nora, double my age, leader of a feared football crew and someone who can muster a couple of gangsters with guns in one phone call.

The only workable play that I could come up with was that due to all I'd seen him do while we were in the Utility it would be enough to put him away for a wee stretch. He had mentioned to me over a year ago that the police were already sniffing around our team. I'd already seen on the six o clock news about English firms getting their doors kicked in during police dawn raids over their activity on Saturday afternoons. For a while he suspected that one of the new boys to join us actually was a copper. Word is that Nora conducted some kind of "interrogation" in the back room of The Snug after a United game. Turned out he wasn't police but at the same time he never came back the next week, or ever again. In any case, I couldn't have told the police any of that without incriminating myself as I was obviously guilty by association. Put him away and I'd be running the risk of putting myself away in the process.

I could never do that to him though, even if I could be guaranteed to come out of it without any charges from the authorities. Not for a million pounds, a Lamborghini Countach and a diddy ride from Linda Lusardi. Just one of those things that you learn growing up not to do. Doesn't matter a flying fuck that Nora had caused me so much trouble over the past few months. You just don't grass on someone, whoever they are to you. They say snitches get stitches well if that radgey ever found out that I was the one who'd grassed him up then I'd have to emigrate to fucking Saturn before he got back out again. Actually, Pluto. Just to be on the safe side.

Chapter 29.

A friend of mines got himself busted by the Drug Squad the week following the boat party. Can't fucking stand those DS bastards. You look at all of the crime going on and these cunts are bothering with someone who's sitting with a tiny bit of Soap Bar in their house? Especially in a week that I really needed a wee smoke following, without doubt, THE nastiest comedown of my relatively short narcotics taking career. The after affects of that Speedball was the kind that really made you question what "had" been inside them. Maybe some things you're best not knowing?

The Nora situation had dominated things for me and the dreams, once I finally found sleep, were fucking horrendous. I had one where everywhere I went the person I spoke to turned out to be him. The woman behind the counter in the shop had his face superimposed onto her. Billy McKinlay scoring for United had Noras face when you seen him running towards The Shed end in celebration. Fuck? Even Lisa had the bastards face replacing hers while still having her hair and tidy body, THAT was disturbing, actually. I went round to see Jeebs on the Tuesday night in search of a sixteenth as I'd ran out earlier that day. I'm not that big a toker per say but following a party I reckon I could probably smoke Bob Marley under the table.

As I knocked on his door I hadn't noticed that, unlike any other single time visiting, there was no voice on the other side asking who it was. The frosted glass that made up the top half of the door and obscuring who his visitors were had always seen Jeebs look for confirmation before opening up. A sound plan for someone operating their small time drug operation from their own home. This time however, the door opened a few seconds following my knock. It wasn't though, him standing there waiting to usher me. Instead standing there staring back at me was this older man wearing one of those Barbour wax jackets that you see guys in flat caps who drive Land Rovers wearing. That kind of threw me as I'd never seen him before in my life. Why was he answering the door?

'Is , ehhh, Jeebs in' I said hesitantly like I was answering a question on a game show and wasn't sure if it was right or not. That's when he pulled out his badge, flashing it at me and telling me he was from the Drug Squad and would I now like to step inside. I didn't actually see why I should have. Did I even have to? As far as I knew I hadn't actually committed any crime by knocking on someones door.

I didn't think that he had any power over telling me what to do in such a scenario but I'd had enough arguments over the past couple of days and my head was hurting with it all. Adding in the fact that I knew I didn't have any gear on me hence WHY I was even there in the first place. For an easy life I stepped into the house without much of a protest other than a few muted grumbles that barely even registered with him.

By now he had grabbed one of my arms and marched me through from the hall into the living room. Walking in I found a few other officers standing around looking after not just Jeebs but a couple of other lads from the village, Randy and Sleek. They're down there most nights of the week having a toke with him and playing the SNES. Good lads the two of them, you always get a decent laugh with them. Seeing them all sat where they were I was able to picture the scene of when the officers had burst in.

This appearing to have went down only minutes before I'd arrived. If so then it looked like I'd had a bit of a lucky escape. Randy and Sleek were sat down on the floor which I knew meant only one thing. They were sat there by the fire having Spats when their world was about to be completely rocked. For the uninitiated, "Spats" is the practice of heating up two knives to the point that they go red and placing a small piece of cannabis between them and squeezing tight.

This allows the user to inhale the smoke that escapes from between said knives. Oh those two do love their spats, they're notorious for it. I tell you what though I'd love to have seen their faces when the officers had burst into the room! Must've almost shat themselves! Jeebs was sat on his sofa, head in hands. He looked up at me momentarily offering a 'what can you do eh?' look before lowering his head towards the ground again.

I was searched in such a stringent fashion that had me ready to ask the saucy bastard if he thought he should've possibly pondered buying me dinner first before moving up the bases. All my details were taken. I was getting a bit annoyed with them though. I'd done fuck all other than knock on a door. 'So Mr Duncan, can you identify this man on the sofa.' Another officer who had the most cheap and nasty looking black leather jacket on and a haircut that actually looked like there was a percentage of a chance that it was a wig, asked while pointing his finger in the direction of Jeebs. 'Who? Him there?' I asked what was already clearly obvious a question. 'That's Jeebs' With this all taking place in front of my friends and acquaintances I felt I should at least put on a bit of a performance for them. 'What's his real name, if you're one of his friends I assume you know his name?' He continued. 'He doesn't have a full name, he's like Prince or Limahl' I replied which produced a few giggles from the two sat on the floor.

The more I looked at them the more I believed that they'd inhaled quite a few of those spats before it had all went tits up. They definitely looked a wee bit on the wrecked side. Jeebs though, understandably wasn't in the mood for giggles. I could hardly blame him, poor bastard. Sleek, who from what I could see, didn't look like he was all too concerned by matters started to sing Raspberry Beret kind of under his breath but audible enough for everyone in the room to hear until one of the officers told him to stop.

'Oh aye funny man eh?' Wiggy said clearly annoyed at me being wide to him in front of everyone. I said nothing. 'So what was the purpose of your visit to this address tonight?' He continued to probe. 'Who me?' I stalled, the irate face he was staring back at me with was beautiful. Blood starting to boil, he looked like he was about to rip my head off. For being someone who had, by the looks, busted a dealer he didn't seem to pleased with things for whatever reason. Maybe I just rubbed him up the wrong way. I tend to do that with some. I remember my uncle once telling me that, some people will love you in life and others will instantly take a dislike to you. It happens.

'Well, I'm mates with the gentleman sat there on the sofa so was paying him a visit, you know? Like friends do? Catch up after the weekend over a cup of tea and a few Jaffa Cakes, ah, that's a lot of writing though pal, just stick down social visit in your wee book' - 'Sure you weren't here to buy some Cannabis Resin from Mr Jenkins here?' Well that was a shift in the conversation. I'd already clocked all the individually wrapped pieces in cling film sat there on his coffee table. Such a fucking tease, all I wanted was a wee toke before getting to sleep. Sitting there, not even a metre away but it might as well have been still in plant form back in Morocco as I wouldn't be getting my hands on any of it. 'Hash? From him? Nah I think you've made a mistake officer, not him. He's not a drug dealer, and anyway what's

Hash? I've never heard of it.' This drew some more giggles and snorts from Randy and Sleek. 'Oh I think you'll find that "Jeebs" is very much the drug dealer' The Barbour coat one said 'Isn't that right Mr Jenkins?' Jeebs didn't acknowledge him.

'No way' I said to the officer with a look of mock disbelief. 'Surely not, I've known him for years and haven't seen him so much take drugs never mind sell them' - 'Well what's sat on that table there says that you're talking a lot of shite Mr Duncan, although I think we both know that you already know that' He nodded his head in the direction of the table. Knowing I was doing nothing more than being an inconvenience to them, I kept going. 'Well he can't be much of a drug dealer if he's never once tried to sell me any, I'm assuming sales isn't his strong point then?' That was when the other officer who was stood over Randy and Sleek finally found his voice. 'Does he really need to be here, Davie? He's making me tired all over' He asked the visibly frustrated one in the Barbour coat. - 'Yes, I think we're done here, you might want to say goodbye to your mates, you might not be seeing them for a while' he referred to the other three as he grabbed my arm to lead me back out of the room.

I involuntarily laughed at the dramatic tone he'd spoken in. 'Steady on mate, you've only busted a wee bit of Hash. You're making out like you've just collared Pablo Escobar.' I'd watched this documentary recently about this Mr Big in South America who was responsible for most of the Coke across the world. He literally was the one drug dealer who I knew of. Well, apart from my friend Jeebs and even then his career as one was, at that moment, looking sketchy. To be honest I think my sarcastic comment was wasted on them all as I didn't even get any kind of recognition from the officers. They probably didn't even know who Escobar was which is fair enough as they're not exactly going to be trying to catch him in The Kingdom of Fife, Scotland. Can't see it myself anyway.

The Barbour boy was trying to put the shits up me as he escorted me back down the hall to the front door. Telling me about how I was on their radar now and how I better keep my nose clean. This led to a small exchange of words where I asked him about what part of knocking on a friends door was a crime and if so why wasn't I being charged. I cringed internally at a few lines I came out with like 'You don't have nothing on me' that I can only imagine were a product of watching too many episodes of police shows. Should've ramped it up and done a cockney accent for effect and been done with it.

When I started taking Class A's I had entertained some misplaced thoughts that the comedowns would actually become easier once I got used to them. I was to find out though that it wasn't experience that helped you get through the comedowns. It was in fact squarely down to "what" you'd taken. Nothing more nothing less. The week following the boat party and the cocktail I'd had? Truly horrifying, it was the end times and now because of these Drug Squad twats I was having what I classed as my life support being taken away from me. Leaving the house without anything to smoke was the equivalent of having the plug pulled. It was a wonder I'd been able to walk back round to my house since I'd officially flatlined.

I caught up with Jeebs the next day when they released him. His account being, and not something he had any kind of explanation for. They knocked on his door and for the first time since starting to deal he never asked who was outside. Just opened it for them.

It's easier to get into Fort fucking Knox than it is his house and yet there he was, when he had the biggest amount of Hash he'd EVER had inside his house opening his front door in the most cavalier of ways. A team of them rushed him and took over his pad within a matter of seconds. 'All for something that grows out the fucking ground' he ranted at me. Couldn't really argue with him. I was just glad that I'd appeared after the DS had arrived to be honest.

Chapter 30.

Not going to the fitba was starting to get to me. It was ok, for the first month because psychologically I only thought it was going to be for a short while. That's how people find ways to cope with something don't they? They tell themselves that soon it will all be over and they'll be back to normal again. That was how I approached it. Only to then find out it was for longer than first thought, a lot fucking longer. Imagine someone gets slung in the jail and given a couple of months sentence? Aye they'd be pissed off I imagine but at the front of their mind they'd at least know that it was nothing other than a temporary stay. Then, just as they're getting ready for being released, the warden tells them that actually, they're in for life. That's kind of how I felt. United were doing really well too. They'd made a decent start to the season both at home and in Europe.

That in itself only made it all the harder for me to take. Darren Jackson was banging them in, nippy wee cunt, Jackson. I can totally see why all the fans of opposing sides boo him each week. I'd be the exact same if he played for someone else. Still, if he's banging them in each week like he's been doing he can do what he wants in my book. I'd even offer Lisa up to him for the night if he scored a hat trick against Dundee at the weekend. We've got another striker who looks like making this his breakthrough season, Duncan Ferguson. He's come up from the reserves and is starting to get his chance and looks like he's taking to the top level like a natural. And I was missing all of it. It's no good being restricted to something like ten minutes tops of TV highlights each week of seeing your team home and away.

I don't know how armchair supporters can hack that as their lot. I suppose it all comes down to previous experience I suppose. What they've been used to. I was listening to some of the older Indie tunes that used to listen to day in day out the other day and heard Sit Down by James. Hadn't heard it in absolute yonks but there was the one line that stuck out to me. Almost smashed me right in the coupon such was its impact and one that I'd never found when the song was first out. "If I hadn't seen such riches I could live with being poor" - I guess we can all find ways to make that line appear relevant but I definitely associated it with me not getting to go to games these days.

I was taking it hard that it was the Dundee Derby on the coming Saturday and I wouldn't be in attendance. It's the very first matches that you look for when the fixtures get released in the summer. There's a big city rivalry between the teams even if there's not really a sporting one. All due to them being absolute pish. I think they were good in the sixties apparently but considering this was years before I was even born I can only really look on them as being second rate. We've always finished above them in the league as far as I've seen. Well, when we're actually both IN the same league as they're a bit of a yo yo club.

They get relegated then promoted again, relegated and so on. I've seen my team win trophies and appear in a European final while they've never won fuck all in decades. Still it's always a good match. They punch above their weight due to the fever pitch of the occasion. Derby matches can provide that and I think that's why everyone loves them so much. And I'll not be present. I did though, have the prospect of my birthday to come to help take my mind away from me not being on the crumbling terraces of the shit hole that is Dens Park. What better way to celebrate turning seventeen than to jump on a bus with another forty others and head to somewhere in Lancashire, England to join something like another twenty thousand other people in a disused and derelict factory for the mother of all house parties. With my birthday, technically falling on the Thursday. The folks took me out for tea, Lisa and her parents were all invited too.

We went along to this posh restaurant around ten miles away. Decent grub there as well but sadly the night was more dominated by an argument over what I was ordering than it was with present giving and choruses of 'Happy Birthday to You.' Maybe it's more about me and that I've still to learn the etiquette of what to do when someone has invited me for something to eat, with them paying. At least that's the way I was made to feel about it.

Everything had been good as gold. We had all sat having a drink in the bar area while waiting on our table being ready. Lisa gave my my present which blew me away on levels that I couldn't entirely divulge to both mine and her family. The reason being, at the after party in Dunfermline I had found myself sucked into a conversation about how incredibly large space is. Really fascinates me all of what's up there and I had promised myself, during this chat, that I was going to buy myself a telescope the next day, I figured it would be a chilled thing to do, sit there having a reel to myself while looking at the moon, stars and planets. Of course though, Within the hour I had forgotten about all of this telescope business.

That thought and so called serious commitment had gone almost as quick as I'd had it. At the party though I must've mentioned it to Lisa because she HAD remembered which resulted in my present. Fuck knows how she was able to because it's not like she's immune to the affliction of how confused the mind gets on el drugos. It was funny but it took her to actually BUY me one for me to remember I even wanted it. The moment I unwrapped it though I knew I did. The in joke kind of way she winked when I looked at her once I saw this serious bit of nerdish kit looking back at me was priceless.

Aye, everything was going good. then we got called through to the dining room and to take our seats at the table which was now ready for us to sit down. Then came the argument before we'd even had our starters. Look, I'm not sure if there's some kind of code of conduct that you're meant to adhere to when on some one else's roubles but it seems that my choice of meal wasn't cool with some. I'd had a good look at the menu. A few things caught my eye, gammon steak was one, love that stuff, I will never, ever understand though why someone would put pineapple on top of them though. Those type of people need watching in my opinion. I quite fancied the homemade steak pie as well as that's always a winner in small owned restaurants like where we were. Instead and, without ever assuming it would be a problem, I chose the fillet steak with roquefort sauce and these fancy sounding sliced French potatoes.

'Steven, you can't choose the steak' Auntie Brenda instantly corrected me when I gave my order to the poor waitress. Leaving her standing there not sure whether to write it down or not. I heard what she said instantly but for at least the first few seconds I wasn't sure "why" I couldn't choose this particular item of food from the menu. Was the meat off and she'd had some inside information? Had she a premonition the night before that involved me choking on a piece of steak? Before I could ask why, and in more of a controlled tone, she asked me to take a look a the price of what I was ordering. I opened up the menu again, had a quick scan for the steaks and found that the fillet was £17.99. An amount that in my world equated to a couple of pounds away from a White Dove.

Her husband took this as a front to his manhood of course, sat there amongst company and his wife is sitting there saying what he will or won't do with his money. 'You get yourself a steak son, it's on me remember' he said leaning forward in his chair and looking round everyone making sure they were aware of what he'd just said. I know him so well, the worst thing for him would be to think that Lisa's mum and dad would go away saying he was tight with his money or something like that. Brenda's words had gotten into my head though, maybe I shouldn't have been ordering something so expensive? I'd never taken a thought about it but maybe if I had I'd possibly have ordered something different. Still, it was out there now.

'It's fine, Uncle Jimmy I'll just get the gammon steak instead' I said hoping to avoid the oncoming drama that my change of order was going to present but knew I wouldn't. 'You happy, Brenda? It's the boys birthday and you've now got him feeling like he can't have what he wants to eat' he said, either for a second forgetting about the Hopkins family sat there with us, or not giving a fuck that they were there. Auntie Brenda just sat there with her head bowed looking instantly ashamed of herself.

'You get yourself a steak, Stevie boy, get him a steak hen' he said looking up at the girl still standing there awkwardly with her notepad and pen in hand waiting for us to make a fucking decision. 'Nah, it's cool, I've changed my mind now. Just get me a gammon steak, no pineapple though mind, tell the chef please' I made my revised decision. I don't mind admitting that I still wanted the steak but now felt a bit sensitive about it. Didn't think I'd exactly savour each bite of that succulent meat whilst knowing that my auntie was stressing over how many meals through the week the cost of my one main course would've put on the table. Putting his bravado aside, Jimmy was probably thinking the same thing too and I wouldn't have been surprised if there would be more comments later on back at the house. Not a scenario where you're going to enjoy a meal I estimated.

When the girl arrived with the plates I found out that he still had managed to get some kind of communication to her that I was getting the steak. I almost felt like I was being force fed it in the end such was the way this one piece of cow had dominated a birthday tea. The elders got on like a house on fire though considering it was the first time they had really met each other. Both couples knew who they were since we were all hardly living in a sprawling metropolis, I imagine if they'd passed each other in the street they'd maybe say a hello but that would've been that.

They, of course, embarrassed both Lisa and I at a prolific rate in the way that parents generally do. One thing in life I've never quite sussed out is when parents embarrass their kids in front of company. Are they doing it on purpose thinking it was funny or are they really morons? Jimmy, who loves to wind people up at the best of times sat there holding court while everyone was on the subject of Lisa and I and that it must be serious since we were still going strong months later.

'You should've seen this lad here when he first started going out with your daughter' He done this strange move with his hand and thumb towards me that looked like some hitchhiker who hadn't been arsed about attending hitch hiking college. I cringed in advance at whatever was about to come out of his mouth next. With good cause. 'He was walking on air in the house, singing, whistling, couldn't wipe the smile off his face, at first I thought he was on some happy pills or something' Lisa and I exchanged a quick look at each other over his exact choice of words.

No one else would have been able to detect it, we knew though. He continued, It was proper nonsense what he was saying, I hadn't done anything like what he was describing. It kind of backfired on him though, all he wanted to do was embarrass me a wee bit but by doing so he ended up only endearing myself to Bob and Vera. Auntie Brenda then jumped in too. 'And you've been really good for him too, darling' She looked at Lisa bringing out a blush from her. 'He's never in trouble like a lot of the others in the area his age, you know what boys are like these days?'

Ex-fucking-cuse-me? Hardly brings any trouble? She's fresh from talking to a murderous psychopath on the phone, calling because of me. Nah, no trouble at all. And that's without her knowing about the two years worth of organised violence and the copious and varied amounts of drugs that had been consumed over the summer. I wasn't appreciating all of this talk about me at the table, really wanted to say something to steer the conversation elsewhere but after "steakgate" I was practically too scared to open my fucking mouth!

'Aye, he's a good lad' Bob said, looking at me and smiling. 'His choice of a football team leaves a lot to be desired though, Jim, eh?' With that one comment I was parachuted right back into his car the night of that first date. My uncle lapped up that type of patter though. If I had a pound for every time he said 'What are you going to see that shite for?' when I went to the fitba I'd be able to afford a private box at Tannadice AND a chauffeur to get me there and back safe from any potential harm from the Dundee Utility Crew.

There was a bit of an awkward part of the night where it felt like both sets of parents had teamed up. Quizzing Lisa and I on what we had been getting up to at weekends, the trips across Scotland, the fact that we weren't so much coming home in the early hours of the morning but in fact the afternoon the day after. Wisely from day uno and our first party, the both of us had kept things vague with information at the bare minimum for the parentals while in other cases had completely lied our arses off. It would have been naive of us though to have thought that they wouldn't have noticed the change in our behaviour.

The change in routines with us traveling across the country taking strange drugs. How we were for a few days after being away to a night out, the anti social side that they'd see until the comedowns had passed. The change in sleeping patterns. They wouldn't be up to much as so called guardians if they hadn't taken notice of all of that. Lying that we weren't even going to be in Scotland would have been lies on a new level so ahead of Blackburn we'd both told everyone of our plans and this in itself was a great source of interest to them.

Why Blackburn?, what's so good about down there that you're traveling so far just for a night out? That was just two of the questions. Tell you what, the paranoia was fairly kicking in during the conversation. I think it's just the fact that inside I "know" what I'm up to and the fear of being caught can get to me. In truth none of them would know what Ecstasy was if I'd taken one out of a baggie and threw it onto their plate along with their haddock and chips or chicken curry. Between the two of us we managed to give them enough information laced with a dash of fabrication to satisfy them. Couldn't believe some of the shite that was coming out of my mouth at times though.

With them knowing that these parties, which I had sold to them as nothing more than a night out where there was bands and deejays playing. This description in itself sounding no more different than a trip for my auntie and uncle to the local social club. Knowing that they lasted into the next morning I, and without laughing, told them that there was a special chill out room where if people were tired they could go there and have a wee rest, beds and sofas all over the place.

I told them this while thinking about some of the complete mental conversations I'd had while sat in them and that there certainly wasn't any danger of the sleeping part going on. I don't think I done that bad though as much as I talked lots of shite while explaining. When Bob had asked the two of us about why they lasted all night I asked him if he'd ever been on holiday to Spain to which he affirmed that the family were regulars in Lanzarote. On hearing this I brought up the fact that in Spain it's a different culture compared to Britain.

The Spaniards are having their tea at the time Brits have their supper. Most Scots and English are going to their beds at the time where the people are just going out for the night while there on holiday. With a fresh way of looking at it he suggested that maybe we were starting to come round to the European way of thinking here on our Island. I'd never really thought of it in that way but him showing a bit of understanding wasn't ever going to be a bad thing.

'Well you needn't think I'll be going out at midnight for my tea' Jimmy laughed to himself at the thought. - 'Oh I think you speak for the four of us oldies, Jim' Vera joined in as they all laughed along with him. Vera jokingly warned Lisa and I to enjoy it because we'd be boring old farts before we knew it. All in all though the Acid House segment of the night's conversation could have went a LOT worse. I'd be lying if I was to say that I wasn't one step away from being sat there shaking like a shitting dug in front of them though.

For months I'd been taking this drug that being honest, I knew absolutely nothing about other than its name and what affect it had, no one else really did either though. Nobody seemed to question it. They just necked the wee fuckers without hesitation. From what I could see everyone was taking them with no idea what they were putting inside them. Due to how amazing the feeling was, I can only say that taking one was worth the gamble of any nasty twist that may or may not have followed.

Coming back from The Highlands that time. I was telling the rest of the car that I was going to go to the library first thing on the Monday morning to look for a medical book that might tell me something about

MDMA. I never did go, obviously. Me? Going to the library when on a Monday comedown to potentially find out things I'd maybe be better not knowing in relation to my recreational activities? Probably a good thing that it was never followed up on.

Through taking it behind the parents backs though and finding them starting to skate pretty close to the ins and outs of what goes on at the weekend? No fucking wonder I was overcome with paranoia until my talking shite started producing results and I was able to relax a little bit. Couldn't have any spanners getting thrown into the works ahead of Blackburn could we?

It promised to be the biggest and best party we'd ever went to from moment dot. The place itself as a party scene is one that was almost talked about in hushed tones during middle of the night chats with randoms others at some of the events I'd been to. Apparently there had been some really big illegal parties down there that helped kick the whole scene off. Events in warehouses after clubs like The Hacienda had closed for the night. The police trying to get in and stop them, and failing. Throw in the fact that it was only my fucking birthday to coincide with it?! Jesus, my mind body and soul was almost wishing that I would get knocked down by a bus before the Saturday night so that they'd be spared the mental pain and torture of the week that would follow.

Chapter 31.

No one had told me about all of the side effects with the pills. I'm sure this would only be understood by the few but I found that I had become addicted to taking Ecstasy but not addicted "to" the drug. It had never been about the drug itself, more all of the components that made up a night of celebrating this new and exciting culture. The drugs were a part of it though and an integral one at that but no good on their own. So were the consequences though. What goes up must come down/ That Issac Newton boy had it fucking nailed.

After a while I started to notice the side effects, and quite a varied range I had too. I mean, maybe this isn't the fault of the pills themselves but I seem to chew the inside of either side of my mouth throughout the night because by the time I'm back home and coming down, the inside of my mouth looks like a mini Operation Desert Storm has been going on for the previous eighteen hours. Teeth marks, blisters you fucking name it, looking at the inside of my mouth in the mirror while still high is an experience that once sampled is not one that leaves you in a hurry to repeat. That minor eating out of your mouth from the inside issue in itself is not exactly a problem, give it a few days and they're back to normal again. It's the other stuff, the longer term things that seem to stick around, or well, hang about in the background and give you a wee reminder every now and again just to keep you on your toes while messing with your mind in the process.

I've never taken Acid in my life but have heard about the hallucinations that people get from it. I'm not sure if this is the same as LSD but I'd noticed a few episodes of seeing things that upon closer inspection weren't actually there. I couldn't ever remember having such like before so of course it was inevitable that I'd be putting two and two together and pinning the blame on the long term effects of the pills. Obviously a high chance it was because of them though. No joke, I was walking along the road back from the shops a couple of nights after going to Pure and I saw two guys up ahead having a fight, rolling about right there in the middle of the road punching fuck out of each other. I know a lot of people would see that and then change their journey to avoid crossing their paths but I wasn't bothered about that. I was more interested to see who it actually was having a swedge more than anything.

Felt a bit of a twat when I got a few yards closer and saw that it was actually a big black bin liner rolling about the road, blown by the wind. I had another moment a few weeks before when sat in my uncles car while he had nipped into Ladbrokes I thought someone across the road in a car was staring at me. You know? Like proper not moving their heads or closing their eyes or fuck all. Like they were completely obsessed with me. Once he got back from collecting his winnings from Haydock and drove off I was able to look across into the other car and see that it was just some extravagant abstract design of a seat cover. No one was even sat in the car.

I even went to get my eyes tested after the first month of seeing odd stuff but it didn't matter, I still saw them. All of this only ever followed a whole nights session of consuming various Class A narcotics. You can see where it was easy to make the connection.

Then there was the weight loss. I wasn't exactly someone who was ever going to be seen at the latest Weight Watchers meeting to begin with. My Uncle Joe once told me that I had a good metabolism because I ate anything I liked but it didn't matter in terms of what my weight was. Then came MDMA and suddenly I'm having to look for sharp objects to make extra holes in my belt so that I can put my fucking jeans on and make sure they stay up.

I'd noticed the same with Si the last time I saw him. I can't speak for anyone else of course but personally, following a night out on the mixture of pills and Speed I would not eat for two days straight, the first twenty four hours? Just forget it, I wouldn't even attempt, I'd tried and failed a few times before I got wise to how the game went. Then I would go through the whole pantomime in the following day where I would convince myself that I was now actually hungry.

Getting the food into me however wasn't as easy as it normally is. Just couldn't stomach it, you know? Would only really be the Wednesday before I was eating normally again but I can only imagine those few days of not eating in addition to sweating myself through whatever party I was at were enough to have a visible impact on me.

Paranoia though? Definitely the worst side effect as far as what I saw. I'm not exactly someone who has ever been backwards at coming forwards, wouldn't say I was Mr Confident by any means but still, you can definitely file me in the "not really giving a fuck about anything" category but once again. A heavy narcotics session and I was beginning to experience certain feelings that I'd never had before. Just wee things but still really noticeable, uncertainties all over the fucking place. Going into the chippy and thinking that there were people in there who in reality are, like you, just in there to collect some food, who were talking about laughing at you.

Mishearing what a person has said to you but due to your state of mind you're then questioning .. aye but did they "really" say what they assured you they'd said? Getting something in your head and even if you recognise yourself that it's stupid you still can't stop it from affecting you. Obviously, having had to endure some of the shit these past few months that had come my way, that is a bit of a dangerous cocktail when mixed with the after effects of some unknown drug.

If I think that there is someone sat in a car staring at me for example, there's probably a chunk of good cause attached to it considering the Nora problems and the fact that as much as I'd like it to be finished with, it's not. That's the thing though. Normally you get some pills there's a fucking message on the bottle for you - DO NOT DRIVE-DO NOT DRINK-DO NOT WORK HEAVY MACHINERY You know where you stand with that, you can't say that you weren't warned, I've seen a few who have ignored the do not drink part and aye, they should've done what they were told!

Another thing with those drugs is that you get told what possible side effects may come through taking them which I assume through fear of being sued, the company lists basically every ailment known to man as a potential. I took pills once and read the small print and my personal favourite was "may cause irregular behaviour" You're not beating that. Does that mean I can do something like try to rob a bank and then when I inevitably get caught I can use the fact that the doctor had me on radge pills that had me not in control of what I was doing?

Still, though, they come with an information sheet as such. Eckies come with absolutely ride all. No idea what's inside them and where they've come from. I heard that most of them are made in Holland but I never know what to believe as most of the intel I come by is during conversations when all parties minds are not as they would otherwise normally be. Lots of shite gets spoken, lots. From me especially. We just get given this pill and take a leap of faith that the "chemist" who assembled it knew what they were doing. No instructions, no advice.

If you called the NHS and asked them for information on Heroin I bet they'd be fucking full of advice. Ecstasy though? It's not on their radar but from what I've witnessed so far in this musical movement, they better "start" paying attention.This is only going to go one way and through word of mouth is going to become bigger and bigger. It would be nice to keep it as the amazing underground scene it is right now but it won't stay that way for long, nothing does like that. People simply aren't going to be able to keep their mouth shut.

It's a scene that's only going to grow and grow and at an alarming rate, that much is obvious. With the passion and enthusiasm that those driving the scene already possess it's going to be impossible for it not to go just the one way. Despite the side effects that evidently come through partying it doesn't come anywhere close to having me question what I'm doing with myself. I'd already decided that I wanted to get even more into it.

As wrecked as I've been all of the nights we've had when the four of us have went out I've still found a bit of time to really pay close attention to the DJ. To watch how he mixes the records, the reaction of the crowd when he brings in one of the tunes they've waited all night long to hear and the adulation he receives that follows. The star treatment, the money, the fame? For me, reason number one would be simply to get closer to everything, to be a bigger part of it.

Everything else would just be perks in my book. I can't really see any downside to being a DJ, I bet they even give you free drugs when you're playing. I personally have, at times, wanted to offer a pill to a DJ purely on the strength of him playing a certain record that had grabbed me in an almost spiritual way for the three minutes or so that it had played for and that's me alone. I bet they're getting drugs thrown at them from everywhere. Girls as well, not that I'm bothered about that side of things. I'm sure Lisa would be ok with me having a few groupies each time I played, eh? Aye fucking right she'd be!

Crazy to think that, unlike the past few years when I've had a wee bit money, instead of thinking what clothes I could be buying I'm thinking that the money can go towards a set of decks. When the scene inevitably went overground and the explosion began I wanted to be "in place" because soon it was going to be a case of, like De La Soul predicted in that unbelievably cool and game changing 'Three Ft High & Rising' album last year. "Everybody wants to be a DJ." I had it all planned in my head as well. I wasn't going to be happy to get a wee gig here and there playing at the illegal events I'd been to so far.

Having seen Pure over in Edinburgh, how raw, how full on, how it appeared like it was everyone in theirs first night ever out on pills while knowing that it probably hadn't been … and that this was an EVERY WEEK club? it wasn't hard to see an opportunity in it all. It was a scene, that for me I felt that anything was possible because we were all, every single one of us, at the ground floor of a lifestyle, a cultural explosion, a rebellion and one that was going to go on to become a monster once it blew up. It was a chance for anyone who wanted to make something of the opportunity put in front of them to grab it with both hands.

I'd spoken to my cousin about it one night in my bedroom when he'd started to quiz me about what I'd been up to. The way I described it all to him and in a way that I couldn't have done to his mum and dad sat downstairs. He told me that it sounded like punk all over again. a scene that had everyone wanting to be a part of it. Cunts that couldn't even play two chords of a guitar were picking one up wanting to learn how to play so they could start their own band. I knew he'd get it though. Quite a bit older than me, but he definitely knew the score. Bit of a party animal himself and ironically a DJ too although nothing like in the way I want to be. He's famous round here for his nights that he's put on while on the decks. One night down in Leven when he was a DJ at a nightclub, a mass brawl broke out. Tables and chairs going flying all over the place. Punches and kicks in all directions. So what did he do? Kill the music until it had all settled? Nah, he only went and stuck on that Eye of the Tiger song from the Rocky film which played over top of all of the fighting!

Perhaps just a pipe dream of mines probably but In life I reckon we all need them, even if they're shoved right into a pipe never to be released. If we didn't have our dreams then we'd probably never get out of bed in the morning and civilisation would grind to a halt. The world would spin off its axis and everything, we'd be fucked, all of us.

Chapter 32.

Blackburn though? I think I could best describe the events from over the weekend in just two words - FUCKING + HELL! Two more chaotic, badly behaved, unforgettable, incredibly messy and mind blowing days you simply could not find. Truly spiritual stuff.

The birthday boy overdoing things in the narc stakes as he approached celebrating his birthday in what could only ever be classed as "proactive." A night where, while three pills strong and in deepest la la land I experienced a chance meeting that immediately became something bigger than Blackburn and the party itself.

We'd managed to secure four seats on a bus that was running from Edinburgh. Laid on by one of the promoters responsible for some of the parties we'd already attended up in Scotland. The atmosphere on the journey down the road was electric, almost like a pre party of sorts. There seemed to be an endless supply of mix tapes that were being blasted out the stereo at the front of the bus. People were dancing in the aisle and getting thrown all over the place with not one single fuck given. I can't even begin to imagine what anyone passing us on the motorway must've thought.

Some on the bus were visibly already dipping into some of their drugs on there which, now that I knew the score a lot more. I didn't think would be the best idea with regards to the long night that we all had ahead. Their decision I suppose. Me personally didn't want to be coming up until I was in line to get into, well, wherever we were going to. Timing is everything. Fuck, one of the previous parties, we thought we'd had the timing down, popped our first pills of the night while outside only for the line to take about double the time for it to go down than we'd thought. This inevitably meaning that we were all magnificently fucking spangled by the time we got to the entrance. Fuck knows how I got past the security that night. Could barely stand such was the rate I was going up. You live and learn.

The journey took over eight hours due to the bus stopping for toilet breaks then invariably taking double the time to try and find half of the zoomers who were wandering around motorway service stations out of their minds. Apparently one of them, some boy from Livingston had been found sat inside one of those kiddy car rides that you stick ten pence into and it goes for a few minutes, playing music with flashing lights. Sat dancing inside it he had refused to come out of it again. Pumping ten pence after ten pence into it every time it stopped. He fucking shat himself when he saw the bus pulling away without him though. I watched out of the bus window as he come tearing out of the services entrance, the panic on his coupon was priceless!

Talking of priceless? then there was Lisa. She was looking her cool self traveling down, sat next to Shan with the two of them in front of Si and moi. She was wearing a pair of jeans and a skinny t shirt with some sixties American band called CCR on the front of it. I'd never heard of them in my life likes, to be fair Lisa admitted the same and that she had only bought the t shirt as she liked the design of it. Only she would buy a top for some unheard of ancient band to then wear and look cool and sexy as fuck in it. She'd even look gorgeous in a Dundee top but that's definitely not something that's going to be happening, ever. Even just to test out the theory.

It was what she had to wear for while at the party though that was the most brilliant and unique thing I'd ever seen. Like me, she'd really taken to the scene in all ways. Once sampled she was snared in a big way. It's funny how quickly the two of us, as a couple had matched each other every step of the way since that first party in Ayrshire. Step by step, drug for drug. Well, apart from the sneaky wee extra pills and dabs of speed I'd had over those nights that she wasn't around for. Saying that, what's to say that she'd not been doing the same? Shan, her partner in crime was hardly a Girl Scout.

She's an absolute fiend and I swear she could probably be the last one standing if the four of us were to ever take leave of our senses and have a drug taking competition. You know? Like you see with drinking? The scene in Raiders Of The Lost Ark for example when that bird that Indiana Jones hooks up with is having a wee sesh with that other "person" who even to this day I'm not sure if it is a man or a woman. I've fucking watched that film hundreds of times as well and still don't know. If we done some kind of last one standing drug competition I reckon Shan would win. We'd all be dead though so I'm not sure her newly crowned title would be the biggest priority for her though.

One of the undoubted best parts of all of these people, loved up and in a field etc is the silliness. The sense of fun, camaraderie and mischief. The feeling that standing there surrounded by everyone else, regardless of them being strangers, you always feel like you can wear, do or say anything you want. There's no judging, just a sense of acceptance. They just aren't like your archetypal night out. It's what set things apart from what the rest of the world are doing when trying to have a good time. So with that, Lisa had been telling me that she was planning something a little different for Blackburn. An outfit however, that she was nervous about what she'd look like in it and that only when her first pill of the night was kicking in that she reckoned that would feel comfortable wearing.

She'd enjoyed teasing me all week long about it while not showing or telling what it was. Telling me that it was a bit revealing which led me to believe that she was planning some short dress or some scantily clad type of outfit. It was only on the Friday night that she actually provided a sneaky peek.

I'd been down to visit Jeebs for a catch up before making the journey up to spend the best part of the night up at hers. He ended up getting several bongs down me during the visit which is normally all fine but even though she says it doesn't bother her I pretty much can guarantee that me turning up to meet her while stoned DOES bother her. Which in turn then has me paranoid while I'm high. That in itself kind of ruins the whole point of it. I'm not saying that he'd held a gun to my head and I'd "had" to smoke the two bowls but his offer in the first place was obviously the catalyst to it all.

Sat on her bed she told me that the outfit was through in the other room so she'd go change and come back through in a moment. I was sat there with all kinds of designs running through my head, most with the length of it being something that more resembled a belt, other designs were coming to me that involved the front being low cut and showing off some cleavage. One thing about Lisa was that as far as I could see she definitely had larger tits than the average size for girls her age. Which again, is one of the many things I love about her, obviously.

When she'd teased earlier on the week about it being revealing I found myself conflicted by that thought. Aye, she's really hot so to see her wearing something sexy and suggestive, sign me up for that. On the flip side though, she's looking that way around thousands of men who have all had pills and are by default "touchy feely." This set off a whole chain reaction of thoughts. If Lisa was going to go looking in "slut mode" like I'd had in my head then this was going to change the dynamics of the night for me.

Despite the fact that we always go out in our group there's always a few moments where we'll go off on our own adventures and then meet up all in the one place again. I say moments, but some of my adventures have taken as much as two to three hours before reappearing due to having no understanding of the concept of time. These disappearing acts would not be possible as I'd now need to act as her bodyguard. Me a bodyguard while Eckied? Jesus H, I don't think I'll be able to do any guarding while I'm on the celling for a couple of hours.

'Ready' she said from behind the door, stood there in the hallway. I actually wasn't sure if I was but at the same time couldn't wait to see what she'd been teasing me with. 'Get your arse in here now' I said, which I suppose was a way of saying that yes, I was ready. I said I was but definitely wasn't prepared for her walking in and instead of wearing some sexy little outfit like I'd imagined, well? I fucking kid you not, you know those car seat covers that are made of brown beads that help people with sore backs to drive? Well she had MADE A FUCKING DRESS OUT OF A THEM! It was, BRILLIANT. It basically looked like a dress the way it sat on her. You could see quite a lot of her skin but that was though the many gaps between the beads . She had her bikini on underneath it to hide her vitals from being on show. I got to my feet and gave her a standing ovation before then asking her how in the fuck did she come up with that as an idea.

Her dad had started using one recently, she said and some of the times she'd been sitting in the back seat while he drove and looking at the cover it had come to her. An outfit that was going to grab the attention of so many people without a doubt. That would be the only thing that will be getting grabbed though because as she stood there modelling it for me I moved in and gave her a cuddle, slipped my arms around and tried to grab her arse and found out that due to the assortment of beads I couldn't get any kind of a grip on her, same with her tits. The dress was like some fucking medieval fortress of an outfit. Chainmail but for the nineties!

On the journey down, Si pulled out that all too familiar baggie of white powder. 'This'll help give us a wee boost, make the journey that bit quicker, eh?' he said with that infectious grin of his whenever he's up to no good. 'Nah man, 'I'm not wanting to start on the Sulph so early in the day considering what's going down my neck over the night, cheers though' I turned him down before he even really offered me any. It was almost a bit presumptuous of me but if there was one thing I knew about him it was that he wasn't going to keep whatever he had for himself. In any case I felt it was too early for such capers and was comfortable in saying so.

He just laughed at me and shook his head while fishing into his pocket for something other than the bag that he was holding, finally producing this wee metal instrument. I wasn't really sure what it was initially until I then recognised it from a few episodes of Miami Vice. Almost like the Guinness book of Records worlds smallest ladle.

He plunged it into the baggie bringing out a heaped amount. 'Mon, move your head forward, ya daft cunt' - 'What did I fucking say, Si' I said to him completely missing what he was actually doing and getting pissed off at him for not listening to me in the process. 'Zico, it isn't Speed ya wee fanny, mon Tony Montana, get it fucking up your konk' The penny was just dropping on me that it was actually Coke he had in the bag right at the moment he fucking jammed it under my nose and once more told me to get it up me.

I'd never taken it before. I'd seen others using it at the after parties and if I'm being honest it made a lot of them look like they were dicks. Maybe they already were in the first place though? I definitely wasn't in the business of wanting to be a dick. I'd never really even fancied taking it despite me being slap bang in this experimental phase of my life. Coke seemed to be, like Heroin, a drug that people would just "take" there didn't have to be a special occasion for it. That's not the life I wanted for myself, taking something mostly everyday? That's what I loved about what I have seen termed on the news as "recreational drugs" I liked the fact that as awesome as taking them actually was, they weren't something that you wanted to do everyday. That, they weren't something that you "needed" to take.

Obviously if you did you'd have psychosis before you'd even got past year one. The fact that there's no dependency, they're just, to me, something fun do to now and again and that when you do you always have the time of your life because of how special it is. Then again though, what harm could a sniff do plus Si can be like a dog with a bone at the best of times so without any more thought I hoovered it all up in one go. 'Good lad' he said approvingly before taking the spoon back into the bag for himself.

I'm not going to lie, it was fucking good, REALLY good and within a few seconds I was seeing how that one drug had captivated millions of people all over the world for decades. Unlike an Eckie, where you could in all probability watch an episode of Sportscene before things really started happening. Coke was a case of sniff to WHAT THE FUCK IS THIS quicker than you can utter 'say ello to my leedle friend.' I was instantly alert, remarkably so, I really did feel fucking amazing.

By now the girls in the front had cottoned onto what was going on. 'Push that wee baggie forward to us when you're done' Shan, said smiling while making the international sign language for "gimme gimme gimme." When her and Lisa were then having a go themselves I felt a weird twang of regret, almost sadness about it. I know this will sound hypocritical but seeing Lisa sniffing the Ching, I felt responsible for the fact that this truly beautiful, inside and out, person who is kind, smart, sexy, caring and loving, this person was, through me, sitting sniffing Cocaine when only months before they'd have ran a million miles from drugs. I'm not sure why with it being that specific drug that it felt so symbolic, it just did. I felt more aware of things while buzzing off it, just really on top of my game. I don't know for sure but had the impression that it was probably responsible for some of the sharp and clear thoughts I was having. It was a world away from MDMA. You felt unbelievably amazing yet retained all of your self control.

Without any surprise whatsoever she loved it as well. Turning round to me when it started to hit her with wide eyed amazement on her face looking back at me saying 'wow.' Fair dues to Si, that wee baggie of his made sure that the journey flew right in. All I had been used to for motorway driving entertainment was being bought a copy of Roy of the Rovers or shoot at a service station. Was almost scary how quickly the time passed. On a cocaine related subject though Simon was telling me on the way down that Nora had been hitting the white stuff in a big way and that it had been now starting to show. He's being a complete prick with a lot of the boys in the crew and is destroying the morale amongst everyone.

He now had a lot more cunts talking about him behind his back than ever before. Friends being lost all over the place while he's acting like some dictator who's trying to cling to power when the people aren't as scared of him. DICKtator if you fucking ask me! 'Good' I said, 'hopefully he keeps going and ends up with a fucking mutiny and I'll get back to the fitba again then eh?'

'You any closer to getting yourself out' I asked while we were on the subject. Shan hearing me and turned around for a second in a moment where I sensed a wee bit of tension when her and Si. Locking eyes before she turned around again and continued talking to Lisa. 'Aye, it's not easy, mate, told you that before. He still refers to you now and again and that was a few months ago now, doesn't say you by name but makes it obvious when he starts talking about those who don't have the bottle to run with the team anymore and have went AWOL. He's bitter as fuck about it, me and him go back a lot longer than you and him as well Zico so if you think that he's upset with you, think about it from my point of view'

'Aye, you're pretty fucked eh? We both are, actually' I laughed in that way that you laugh at a shit situation otherwise you'd cry. I was quite comfortable with this topic of subject since, unlike the early days when we were all out, Lisa knew all of that side of things now. Well, minus the gangsters with guns stuff as well as the physiological war that Nora continued to wage on my family and I.

As we found ourselves getting closer to Blackburn, the excitement on the bus started to build more and more. Everyone seemed to know each song that came on during the mixes that had been the soundtrack to our journey. I could hear them name checking the artists and songs amongst all the excited chatter. I'd been a fast learner since diving into everything and already knew a lot of artists by now. I'd already settled on my own preferences of which kind of house music in what was, musically, splintered and diverse.

I wasn't close to the standard of knowledge compared to those on the bus though, you could tell that most of them had been around the scene a while. One tune I did recognise though was Promised Land by Joe Smooth and joined in with everyone including Lisa, Shan and Si singing along to it. "WHEN THE ANGELS FROM ABOVE FALL DOWN AND SPREAD THEIR WINGS LIKE DOVES. AS WE WALK HAND IN HAND SISTERS BROTHERS WE'LL MAKE IT TO THE

PROMISED LAND." The whole bus was belting out. I sat there singing along while looking out the window, nudging Si when I saw the sign welcoming you to Blackburn up ahead. A sight that helped provide a sudden wave of adrenaline filled butterflies flying up from my stomach as I thought about what lay ahead over the night and morning that was to follow.

Due to all the toilet breaks we'd had, it was already dark outside as we pulled to a stop. It was hard to see too much outside but I was still sure that there wasn't any venues that looked capable of holding thousands of people outside waiting on us. That's when the boy down the front, the promoter or whatever he was, who had been using one of those mobile phones you see those yuppies using. He had it practically glued to his ear anytime I looked down the front, came off the phone again and told us all that we were going to have to walk the rest.

'A mile and a half?' 'This had better be worth it' Lisa grumbled to no one in particular. It was. And some. Obviously she had not bargained on having to walk over a mile while dressed like a car seat but gallant me came to the rescue and gave her my cagoule which came down so far on her you could barely see any of her costume. Once we dealt with the formalities, the balancing act of necking the first pills of the evening while hoping we'd be through the door before they completely kicked in, getting our bearings once inside.

Having got through all of that the night just went completely ballistic. The location was the most surreal yet for me. A fucking disused factory, absolutely massive building. I'd love to know what products used to be made there but I'll never find it out so should just drop it. There was even big pieces of machinery still attached to the walls in some areas.

Definitely not a place that looked like it would ever pass a health and safety check before it was to attempt to hold a pubic gathering of any kind. Not that any of the thousands of people crammed inside on the three levels of the building looked like they cared in anyway about potentially slashing their hand on some sharp piece of metal inches away from their fancy dance moves that they were pulling.

It was a great experience meeting so many different people from all areas of Britain. The Scottish parties I'd only ever spoke to other Scots and a select few English but this was on such a grand scale that it had attracted boppers from all quarters of the UK. The vibe of the place was truly special, all these individual groups of people who were, under normal circumstances, generally popping pills and partying in their own corner of their country. Everyone all thrown together for the night yet left with the unmistakable feeling of "normal service resumed."

This night though was one of all coming together and it was an unbelievably magnificent sight and an exceptional feeling to be in there amongst it. Scousers were dancing beside Mancunians, Cockneys beside Glaswegians. At one point of the night when I was looking around and taking it all in, I'd climbed up onto one of the machines to get a better look. I thought of that film where those New York gangs all have a meet up in Central Park without kicking the shit out of each other. All sharing a related interest in the same scene they made up. Fucking good film though even if a little unbelievable. Imagine a gang that can't go out the house until they've put their make up on? Those cunts decked out like baseball players as well? Too radge, that!

It was priceless seeing peoples reactions to Lisa's dress when they stumbled upon her while just going about their night. Well it was until I stopped really clocking it when I reached the inevitable part where at least for a few hours I wasn't going to be noticing fuck all! A loved up smiley nonsense talking talking fanny and nothing less. Lisa and Shan had made friends with these sound girls from Burnley so, fancying a wee look around the place, Si and moi went for the obligatory wander.

I had thought that the venue was just one huge room but in fact that was just the production line part of the factory. As we explored further we found that once you left the huge hall where the action was taking place there was then a series of rooms where I guess the office staff must've all worked in previously. We eventually ended up in what looked like had been the staff canteen due to all of the tables and chairs that were bolted to the floor. The place looked like it was serving as some kind of chill out / smoking room. All of the tables were taken, people were sitting around, toking, chatting and laughing. I don't think I had ever been in a single room that produced so many different accents out of it. Si took this as the green light to get involved himself and fetched his skins out and got to work. You could tell that whoever it was that were organising this all had thought it through. While the factory didn't have electricity they had still made plans for things like lights set up in the canteen from a generator for people to go to and escape the madness. It was when we were standing around in there that we met Mikael.

Now this individual was a real topper. I'd clocked him earlier on in the room before he first started speaking to us. He wasn't hard to miss, likes. Black leather trousers that he looked like he'd probably had to parachute into before he could wear them, so tight they were, a white shirt completely open through not even having any fucking buttons to fasten in the first place alongside these big flappy sleeves. He had what looked like around thirty leather necklaces hanging loosely around him and shoulder length hair, slightly curly.

He wasn't on the young side either by the way, looked like he had to have been between forty and fifty. I'm rubbish at judging ages though but he definitely looked well older than most of the other people in the room. Fuck it eh? Good on him, if the boy wants to look like Michael Hutchence then fucking let him. I wasn't for judging or pointing at him. My girlfriend was here dressed as a car seat.

He struck up the conversation with us through the t shirt that I had on. In the preparation for Blackburn I had got myself this cheeky wee "in joke" of a top when I was over shopping in Edinburgh. No mad or fancy designs or nothing. Just two words written tastefully and discreetly on the front - Narcotics Officer. Mikael, who was standing close by having a cigarette pointed at me when he saw I was looking in his direction and in an accent that I really wasn't prepared for, almost like Dutch but maybe Scandinavian instead, was really hard to pin down, said 'Love the shirt my friend, very good.'

Within minutes Si and I were talking away to him like we were old friends. I could tell that he wasn't in any kind of a state that could've been compared the both of us. I wasn't even sure if he'd "had" any Eckies at all and if he had then he was handling them a lot better than our sorry arses.

He was spending half of the time laughing at the two of us, I don't even want to know what we must've looked like, it was specifically after we'd dropped our second of the pill while with the girls and now they were starting to really take hold. Regardless of how he looked and sounded he was definitely into the spirit of how things were inside these places.

'Whoa ya fucker, how good are these pingers, Zico lad?' Si, shouted a bit too loud for the room we were in. His words drawing more than a few nods and glances from those sat around our vicinity. 'mon, Mikky lad, here get one to yourself' He offered our new friend one of his own stash. 'Maybe later, Simon' he replied in a way that reminded me just how older he actually was. the way he said maybe later was almost like when you were young and you asked your parents for something and they'd say "maybe later" .. Which usually meant NOT fucking later!

He'd told us that apart from a few lines he'd not had anything as he was here on business and wanted to take care of that before he let his hair down, of which he had a lot to play with. Right at that moment I didn't really have any kind of a logical thought process going on so never really questioned why he was doing business in the middle of an illegal house party.

As he took the joint from Si, taking a long draw on it, some smoke was still escaping from his mouth when he began to tell us that he'd been in the VIP area since getting here but had wanted to pop his head out and have a look at the place. Fucking VIP area? In this place. I looked at Si and we both couldn't help but laugh at him. He looked a little confused by what he'd said to have us laughing.

'What is so funny?' He looked like he was preparing himself for the fact that we, possibly were starting to be dicks with him or something. 'Just you saying about VIP, mate we're in a factory that looks like it's not been used in decades so I get your sarcasm' I tried to explain although when you have to explain the humour in something it's never good. - 'No, but there really IS a VIP room, free alcohol, all the best girls, complimentary Cocaine' He insisted, his face lighting up again on seeing that there had been a bit of confusion but nothing nasty on our part.

'Come, I'll show you, I wanted to take you anyway as my friend and business partner is going to love your t shirt Zico, private joke, yes?' Mikael said, already making to leave the canteen and take us to what even then I was skeptically looking on like we might have well been heading towards the lost city of Atlantis or some equivalent.

Of course though, there really WAS a VIP area. Two bouncers stood outside it, they were like super bouncers, with an aura of being twice the size of the regular ones who had been outside the factory letting people in. There was a line of around a dozen people or so outside waiting but Mikael said not to worry and to follow him. This drawing a few dirty looks from some stood there frustratingly waiting to get in, if they were lucky. The moment the bouncer clocked Mikky approaching he just respectfully nodded and cleared the path to let him in. 'These two are with me' he confirmed while we filed in behind him past the two brick shit houses.

I could hardly believe my eyes when I saw the Hampden roar in there. Was quite a decent sized area with what looked like leather sofas plonked all over the place. It even had its own DJ stuck in the corner playing some mellow ambient house. Mick wasn't fucking joking either about the "complimentary gifts" either. There was a table over near the makeshift bar which was a case of helping yourself. Almost like the fucking pick n mix sweetie section in Woolworths.

Sat on the table was a big bowl, the type that you'd put a trifle into only this was full of white powder. Cunts were just going up and scooping a wee bit out with their bank cards and then hoovering it up over at the tables they were sitting at. There must've been thousands of pounds worth of it on the floor that people had accidentally dropped. At that point in the night, Coke was the last thing we even wanted but we both agreed that before we left we should at least get our share and take a wee doggy bag of sorts away with us.

The MDMA crystals though? There was a smaller dish with that in it which made sense as most of the people in the room didn't really look like they were here for getting themselves into a sweaty stinking mess back out in the main room. They seemed to have a different attitude and look. Almost like they had different reasons and motivations for being in there. It appeared that the people inside the VIP were of a more grown up vibe. Si and myself stuck out a wee bit because of that I guess. Probably because they had all been taking Ching they all looked calm and composed, reserved where it would not have been difficult for the two of us to have been clocked as the two that's out their nut on E.

The MDMA in front of us looked dangerously good. There was a dirty brown colour to the crystals, not too dissimilar to brown sugar which I have always hated although call it a hunch, call it whatever, I had a feeling that this stuff was going to be a lot better than the brown sugar that people put in their tea and coffee.

I had no concept on how much I should've taken so played things safe, as far as I knew by shoving my wet finger tip in until it got past my nail and shoved it right into my mouth to be met with what was the most foul taste I'd ever come across in my life. I was almost sick on the spot which I assume would have seen us making as quick an exit from the VIP as our arrival had been. I managed to keep it down, saved by a bottle of Budweiser that I had hurriedly grabbed from the bar.

What a novice, it's pretty fucking obvious though when you think about it. You are basically shoving a chemical that unlike, a kids medicine which has been modified to taste like strawberries specifically so that kids will take it, is instead going to taste as disgusting as mother nature intended. When you shove chemicals into your mouth don't be surprised when they taste like. Well, chemicals. It really was the worst taste ever in the world. Think Brussels Sprouts and times it by a billion and you're still way way off. Truly horrific. Si, didn't take as much as I did which I found a wee bit concerning. 'I'm not convinced about how much you took, going to play it safe' he said before trying to reassure me that regardless of how much we'd both taken we were both going to have our arses kicked by it. Prophetic words indeed.

We were still stood there doing our best to try and wash away the lingering taste from the MDMA when Mikael called us over to meet the friend and business partner that he'd mentioned back when were standing outside with the rest of the unwashed. Now I don't know what it is with these fancy VIP types and their idea of what to wear on a night out because while you had Mikael standing there looking like a mix between a pirate and the front man of INXS.

Sitting down on the comfy sofa beside him was a guy in a full blown suit. Looked like he'd come straight from the office or wedding. He was sitting with his head down looking at the two humongous lines he was knocking up on the table in front of him. 'Pedro, I'd like you to meet Stevie and Simon' Mikael said in that, what I'd now learned, weird as fuck Finnish accent. The other man looked up from his lines. As spangled as I was in that moment my initial thought was ... Fuck, I knew him.

Looking at Si first, he stood up and flashed him a huge smile and shook his hand. Si in the state he was ended up giving him a hug which I noticed only went the one way. He then turned to me and it was one of those moments where all that was required was the DJ in the corner to provide the obligatory scratch with the needle going off the record.

The big smile he'd had on his face evaporated when he set eyes on me. It was like his face completely dropped. Without any shaking hands or pleasantries being exchanged between us but still standing there looking directly at each other he said, without showing any emotion whatsoever 'Mikael, please can you give Simon a tour of the party favours table' Which was such a blatantly obvious euphemism for "can the two of you please fuck off for a while and leave us alone." Si wasn't seeing it though, 'nah it's alright pal, Stevie and I have just been, fucking first place we went to eh, wee dab of MDMA as well, likes. Top notch by the way top fucking notch'

Mikky could see exactly what his friend was hinting at though and gently grabbed Si's arm to steer him away to the other side of the room. 'You alright staying here, Zeec?' He asked, still completely missing the point that I was stood exactly where the situation was dictating me to be. I watched the two of them head off in the direction of the table that boasted enough drugs to keep Ibiza going for summer season. I was glad to avert my eyes elsewhere other than in front of me and all the awkward vibes that it was giving me.

'How are you, son? There hasn't been a day in the past four years where I haven't thought of you.'

Did he even have the fucking right to call me that? I wished he hadn't, why didn't he just call me Stevie? Was calling me son strategic? Was it a gentle reminder from him that just in case I had forgotten, this was my FUCKING FATHER standing there in front of me? So many questions inside a head state that was never going to turn up any answers. The crucial question though and one that justifiably I kept asking myself in my head was WHY THE FUCK, HOW THE FUCK, AM I STANDING FACE TO FACE WITH MY YEARS GONE AWOL DAD IN THE MIDDLE OF A FUCKING ACID HOUSE PARTY IN A FACTORY IN BLACKBURN?

It was the biggest head fuck in my entire life. I wanted to be angry yet couldn't. I didn't want to be happy, but was. fucking Ecstasy eh? What can you do? I wanted to let rip at the cunt, give him both barrels like from one of those sawn off shotgun you'd see criminals using in bank jobs on The Professionals, pair of women's tights over their heads as well! Classic. I wanted to go radge at him but I just didn't have it in me. Make no mistake though, these two people bump into each other during any other circumstances that does not involve one of them having MDMA running through their veins then the exchange would have went down a completely different way. Instead of scowling or sneering and calling him all of the names that I'd dreamed of, I just couldn't.

Sat there, jaw swinging all over the fucking place, feeling the MDMA crystals starting to come on. bobbing my head to the tune the DJ was playing. Little Fluffy Clouds by The Orb, one of those chilled ambient house tunes that you never hear played at an event but always do at the afterparties when things are slowing down. Fuck knows what he thought of his long lost son who was a world away from even underage drinking the last time he'd set eyes on him before his life took an unpleasant turn and had ended up incarcerated.

The last time he saw me I was a fresh faced kid who was only interested in playing fitba with my pals. It's all I wanted to do, morning noon and night. I had to get dragged in once the streetlights came on, always protesting "just another half an hour" - If anyone asked me what I wanted for my birthday it was always the same answer, football tops. Not just the latest Dundee United top, English teams, European and International sides. I fucking lived in the things most of my life as a kid.

A young boy with one dream, to play for Dundee United, then Barcelona whilst of course playing for his country along the way. That "Stevie" would really be all my dad had as a point of reference when thinking of me while stuck in his cell, well, if he did at all. Now though, he was looking at me, not even having reached my eighteenth birthday and there in front of him, verging on concentration camp thin and wearing a t shirt saying he was a narcotics officer while laughably looking like someone who was anything but a stranger around nar-fucking-cotics. Still, who was he to judge?

He pretty much hadn't changed a bit. Almost like he'd been cryogenically frozen since the last time we'd seen each other before he went inside. Actually if anything he looked BETTER despite being older. His slick gelled hair was more fashionable than that stupid as fuck Charlie Nicholas / George Best side flick that went in his right eye that he used to sport. Unlike most dads his age he hadn't put on any weight in the way that those in their forties tend to do when they start giving up. He looked tanned, healthy. Like he had a glow about him. The fucking suit was like Michael Douglas in that Wall Street film from a few years ago. He looked good.

I tried to find my voice but due to the MDMA my mouth had completely dried up. He sensed it and reached down for his glass of champagne to give it to me to wet my whistle. Check the cunt out though, snorting Colombian marching powder in VIP areas with a bottle of this stuff called Dom Perignon on the table. Considering what I'd known myself coupled with what others had told me during him being "away" it looked like he hadn't changed a bit. Had now gone up a few levels in showmanship if anything.

This all felt a bit like fucking Cilla Black and that Surprise Surprise show she presented where she reunited poor bastards who hadn't seen each other for years (if at all) under the most emotional circumstances. My auntie would need the tissues out every single week when it was on. Only I was now in some completely twisted eighteen certificate rated version of the show minus the ginger Liverpudlian presenter. I bet they never filled any of the cunts on that show up with Class A drugs though then pushed them on stage and let them get on with it.

It's actually pretty sick to subject someone like me to something like that and then ask me to handle it with any kind of consummate ease. Which I was never going to manage. I simply was not in a position and certainly not at that stage of the night, for any kind of logic or cohesion to be present. That didn't stop me from trying though. Once I finally found my voice I never stopped. I had no conversations skills that was going to see me through this heart to heart conversation however and to be fair, he recognised that straight away and was pretty patient with me from what I was gathering.

I tried to ask him, find out, what had happened? Why he hadn't got in touch with me? Did he realise what disappearing in the way he had would do but these things are not easy to articulate as much as you might like to think when you're feeling like these MDMA crystals are going to take your head clean fucking off. The rate that I could feel the rushes coming on was astonishing. As far as all I'd learned since that first night in the field in Ayrshire it now felt like I was right back on the first day of school again. These brown crystals were astonishingly much more stronger than pills.

Right at the beginning of what I felt at the time was a deep serious question I got this almighty rush that stopped me dead in my tracks and once passed left me sat there silent with my dad asking me what I had been trying to say. Embarrassingly, me then having to reply that I couldn't now remember even if it had only been eight seconds previous. I was pissed off at myself because of how friendly I was being with him. Automatically putting this down to me being so full of a drug that made you naturally want to express good vibes and friendship to others.

I was finding out just how much the drug followed that ethos to the letter of the law. Still though, even sat there I was feeling a nagging doubt that it wasn't because of the MDMA and that it was possibly my true feelings surfacing. Feelings that I'd masked behind the resentment that I'd held, and THAT pissed me off even more because I "wanted" to be angry, he deserved it as far as I was concerned. Well, apparently.

'Why didn't you come and see me when you got out' the very first thing I asked him. One of the only serious questions I managed to put to him before those fucking crystals started their capers and took away any hope of much in the way of meaningful out of the conversation. 'I wanted to, Stevie, surely you must know I'd have wanted to?' he said looking dead convincing while the voice in my head was telling me that 'aye he "would" say that though, wouldn't he?'

'Your, mum warned me off, it was Janice that told me to stay away, left me with no option, Steven' Pish excuse if you ask me, if everyone did what their mums or wife, ex wife even said then no one would get anything in the world done. As far as I'm concerned he had a right to see his son so if this was all true why did he not just tell her to fuck off and come and see me anyway. I let him know it. Must've been fucking bizarre for him to have this conversation where someone is asking them questions like this, possibly tough questions to answer yet the boy who's stood there asking has a big stupid grin on his face looking like the world is his.

'Wasn't as simple as that though, son' he tried to explain. 'Obviously you know about me getting caught with that Skag in my warehouse?' Seriously though, how many teenagers will have their mum or dad ask them a question like that? Too fucking mad, likes. I nodded although I then thought that maybe he just took that as a normal nod. The kind that I'd been doing along to the music while sat down with him, he continued anyway. Evidently through the appearance of his son who was without question out of his fucking tits, he wasn't exactly shy about the way he went about telling me the story.

'Well what I got caught with wasn't exactly too much in quantity, luckily one of the couriers had just been that same afternoon and taken the most of it away otherwise, well I wouldn't be sat here talking to you right now and would be still stuck in Barlinnie. I got off lightly in the scheme of things, I'm not saying it was a pleasure living at Her Majesties pleasure but things could've been far worse, lot lot worse. I got out in no time and "because" I never grassed on anyone connected to me I came back out with my stock even higher with everyone than it had been before I went away.'

It was pretty fucking surreal to sit there listening to your parent tell you stuff like this, especially in the down to earth and matter of fact way that it was being put across. 'Thing is, there's quite a bit that your mum knows' This had me instantly thinking that my mum had been part of this as well, which would've been stupid to think but you get to the point you're not sure you know ANYONE. He stopped that thought pretty much by telling me that she had various "things" on him and had issued a warning that she was going to go to the pigs with the info if he didn't stay away from me. If true, poor form from my mum for threatening to be a grass likes.

I wanted to ask him what information she had on him but you know what? I wasn't sure if I even wanted to know. I'd already had my mind blown over the night on many different levels and wasn't sure if I could really handle any more. It helped that he understood exactly what was going on inside my head there and then, lets face it, most parents wouldn't. 'I can only imagine how you're handling all of this right now' he laughed with a knowing look. A knowing look alright, he's sat there sniffing what will be primo Colombian marching powder and sat completely in control while his son and the other participant in the conversation is the exact fucking opposite of "in control."

It was actually cool as fuck in that I was able to talk to him in the way that I'd have done with any of the "what's your name where you from what you had" crowd populating the space on the wrong side of the velvet rope. It's like the whole issue about me taking drugs had been discarded with. Who knows? Maybe he'd wanted to have a go at me for being on something but knew that he couldn't possibly be so moronically hypocritical by doing so. I laughed back at his observation 'Handling really isn't the word for it. Si and I had some of those complimentary crystals over there to top up the pills we'd already had tonight. I'm handling fuck all I assure you, tonight hasn't been one for holding back though and now you see the results of it sat beside you'

I laughed again. That's when I had the sudden reminder about why we were down in Blackburn. 'It's a special day of the year for me after all so you have to go for it don't you?' - I wasn't giving a fuck that he'd forgotten my birthday, he hadn't seen me in years and I didn't even KNOW when his was so I wasn't exactly expecting him to sing the birthday song to me the first time he set eyes on me there in the VIP area. It took him a few seconds but he got it 'Happy birthday, son. I'm sorry I never realised' he gave me a wee hug which was fine by me, not a chance we'd have hugged at the start but I'd definitely thawed a little towards him.

He reached into his suit jacket and pulled out his wallet, it could've choked a horse. He opened it and peeled a few notes out of his stack and handed them to me, pressing them into my sweaty palm when I didn't accept straight away after showing a bit of reluctance through my pride. I looked at them, fucking hell it was three, hundred pound notes. I'd never even SEEN a hundred pound note in the flesh before and now I had three, one for every Eckie I had for Blackburn. Fitting.

'Nice one, dad' it just slipped out, I never meant to call him it, I just did 'Don't see you for fucking years and then when I do you sort me out with all my birthdays that you've missed in one go.' I laughed while doing that stupid fucking thing where, when on pills, I kind of massage one half of someones shoulder when I've put my arm around them, don't even known I'm doing it. 'Oh that's not all your birthdays, just todays one. I'll sort you out with all the other ones later. The way you're looking, I wouldn't be surprised if you lose the three hundred I've given you before the end of the night anyway!' He winked at me leaving me not sure if he was joking or not but leaning towards the fact that he wasn't. With good cause I would readily admit.

He probably knew that he was already risking things to put that amount of money in the hands of someone who was so far out of it that there was an extremely high chance of them not seeing the night without either losing the notes or more likely, exchanging them for more drugs. It just wasn't the way this "conversation" was meant to be. It was meant to involve shouting, emotions and lots of tears and potentially violence. It had none of that. Mikael and Si, appeared while I was still clutching the three notes in my hand talking absolute shite to my dad. Si, spied the notes straight away. 'Fucking hell, Zico, what have you done to earn that wedge when we've been away? Suck his cock?'

'Well considering this is my dad, nah not really. I might be a lot of fucking things, Si but incestuous isn't one of them' I said back sharp as a tack. The three of them burst out laughing, the fact that Peter (Now Pedro) Duncan and his friend from Finland "did" laugh was probably a good thing for Si, even if he didn't quite know it. I noticed a moment between my dad and Mikael where no words were actually spoken but could see that he was checking if it was cool for him and Si to rejoin us. My dad flashing him a brief smile while making the OK sign with his hand which led to Mick ushering Si to sit down with him on the empty sofa that was sat facing the two of us.

'Wow, Pedro .. Your, son?' Mikael said, looking quite amazed by this in a way that, I don't know? Felt like he was reacting more than a business partner would really do at news like this. It left me feeling that he knew of me in whatever way he did. Si on the other hand had heard not one word about my dad. Thinking about it, he'd never mentioned his either to me at any point during our fighting, dancing and generally arsing about since becoming friends. Due to this he wasn't aware of the importance of this all. The only thing he wanted to know was why the fact my dad was at the "must not miss" Acid House party of the summer.

To spare my father any embarrassment over what he'd done in the past I told Si that I'd tell him later knowing that the chances were, if he was going through the same as I was, he was going to forget this topic within the next ten minutes anyway. I needn't have bothered. Wasn't long before him and Mikael were telling us some of their tales from their experiences they'd had in South America. Peru being where they'd first met each other.

During the whole "where have you been and what have you been up to" chat that took place before the other two had joined us he'd told me that when he was released. Having kept his mouth shut and done his time he had been given a series of welcome out "care packages" from some of the major boys in the game that he had been doing business with before going away. I can only imagine when he got huckled they must've been shitting it that he was going to give them up to get a better sentence, kept quiet though and they apparently displayed their gratitude on his release. This set him up enough for him to get out of Scotland altogether.

This allowed him to move to Amsterdam to get away from it all and start a new life. He kept details to a minimum but was open enough to tell me that he became pals with this Turkish guy who owned a series of windows in the Red Light District. Some pimp cum wholesale dealer of all drugs you could ever want and some you didn't even know existed. This took my dad to Istanbul for a stint and that was where he started working with these brothers from Bogota in Colombia where he eventually relocated to and still lived today. He told me it with the caveat that it would be better if I didn't know much more of the details. It sounded quite heavy so I was happy to go along with him on that.

From what the two of them were telling Si and moi, South America sounded out of its tree, completely lawless and a continent that I wouldn't want to be setting foot in by the sounds of it. Si was loving the stories he was hearing without, I felt, really grasping "why" the two of them were in that part of the world. Fuck knows what he had been up to when him and Mikael left us for the half hour but he was definitely in a lot worse state than I was in, and I wasn't exactly looking like I was ready to go on Top of the Pops with those Grange Hill pupils and perform a rendition of 'Just Say No.'

'So, you still supporting Dundee then?' I knew he was only trying to mean well and show a bit of interest so I broke with my tradition and didn't correct him. I never even got a chance to answer before Si, butted in 'Eh, Pedro … It's Dundee UNITED.. do we smell like Dundee fans?' He tried an in joke that was never going to work on a person who didn't realise the significance of omitting the "United." - 'Sorry sorry' my dad laughed holding his hands up like we had a Kalashnikov pointed at him.

275

'Well, dad, I'd say I was going to see them as always if it wasn't for some serious issues that I have at the moment' With a loaded statement like that he really would have had to have been a self serving insensitive prick not to ask which issues they were, he wasn't. Immediately asking what was happening with me. This produced a high tempo drug fuelled rant from both Si and myself as we took him through everything. It was not an easy conversation to conduct at times due to the effects of the crystals. We kept losing our threads and forgetting what we were trying to say at times

Telling him about the intimidation of both myself and my elderly aunt and uncle (who of course, in a previous life my dad had known) to the gangsters to, what for me, was the worst part, my "ban" from going to see United. Apart from a few non committal tuts and looks between each other there wasn't much forthcoming from either my dad or Mikky. It really was hard to gauge though. Fucking hell those crystals really were something else.

I could've sat there the whole night talking absolute shit to to both my dad and Mikael and probably would've done had it taken for Si to get a little impatient. He reminded me what were were missing outside in the main part of the factory and suggested that we should go back in again, politely adding if that was ok with everyone. And OF COURSE there was the not so small matter of us leaving our girlfriends alone for fuck knows how ever many hours it had been. Lisa was going to fucking kill me.

We tried to get the two of them to come with us, me saying how they needed to meet Lisa and Shan but they weren't having it. Mikky ambiguously telling us that they were waiting on some associates arriving who were already on route from Manchester Airport. Due to this they had to stay put. Sound cunt that he was, he invited us to help ourselves to what we wanted from the table by the bar before leaving. 'tuck in boys' my dad joined in. 'A wee doggy bag be alright Senor Duncan?' Si didn't hang around to ask 'cause if I have any more of anything right now I'll probably die or something but, later on though eh? That fucking Coca is going to come in handy once the sun comes up. We've got a long bus journey back up the road to come once this has all finished'

'Help yourself, the pair of you, actually' My dad trailed off as he looked across the room before finding what he was scanning it for.

'Katie' he gestured while doing that kind of whistle that takes your thumb and index finger inside your mouth to pull off, which I've never been able to do in my puff, gave up trying years ago. Whistling is kind of fading away these days though, can't even think of anyone I know that whistles. Anyway, he managed to get the attention of one of the girls who was working in there, serving drinks, taking peoples coats from them, that kind of thing.

She was well tidy likes, short black pencil skirt, and white blouse. Long blonde hair down to her arse almost. She came over and gave us all a confident smile, it looked like she was familiar with my dad and Mikky especially. 'Can you please get these two gentlemen a gift bag before they leave, no scrimping' It must've been all in the way he said the words to her because she came back a few minutes later with a ziplock bag each for us that were a mixture of colours inside. The white of the cocaine inside its own wee bag, brown of the MDMA, green from the grass and dark brown from the Hash. It was a beautiful medley of colours.

Si bounced up and down on the spot like United had scored a last minute winner in a cup final. 'Your dad is the coolest cunt in the fucking world, you as well, Mikky' he announced for anyone interested in hearing, and there were many. The two of them just laughed in what was nothing more an attempt at humouring him. As trolleyed as I was inside the VIP area (and I left a whole lot fucking trolleyed than I was when I entered, by the way) I'd never lost sight of the fact that we were just two daft teenagers out their mind on chemicals while the other two were serious cats, and by the looks, successful businessmen. Never more was that evident than in that moment.

I mean, they'd made sure that we walked out the place with enough drugs to keep us going until fucking Christmas without batting an eye. It was a weird feeling to say our goodbyes and, despite all of the uncertainties I'd had for years regarding him, leave this time knowing that he'd keep his word and would remain in contact and make up for lost time. I'm not sure where the confidence came from, it was just there.

As we walked away and left them to it we got as far as the door before one of the other girls working in there came running up to catch us, looking for me specifically. 'Mr Duncan would like to see you for a quick minute before you leave' - 'I'll just hang around up here' Si said which I sensed, saved the girl the embarrassment of telling him that it was just me who she wanted to come back. 'Long time no see, Dad' I joked when I joined them back at the sofa they were on.

It was met with, well nothing. The smiles that the two of them had been sporting most of the time we sat with them had been replaced by a more serious appearance. 'Listen, Stevie' My dad said while putting his hand out for Mikael to pass him a rolled up note before then leaving me hanging as he hoovered up a worrying looking sized line that had been knocked up in front of him. I then had to wait a second or two until he got himself together from it before he began to continue.

He then handed me the note while pointing it towards one of the other equally psychotic sized lines on the table. I was listening to him as best as I could but it's hard to concentrate while on MDMA, your mind goes off elsewhere and you almost always forget what the person was even saying from the start of the sentence to the end of it. I was also distracted by the sheer magnitude of the size of the line I was imminently going to be putting up my hooter. I was listening though, as good as I could at least.

It was only really when I took the rolled up note and started to trail it all the way down that white line, the contents disappearing and providing a welcome refreshing feeling to combat just how strong those MDMA crystals were that I was able to "truly" hear what he was saying. Halfway along the line I heard him say the words 'we know who Nora is' I kept going along the line, resisting the urge to lift my head at what I'd just heard him say. When I finally reached the end of it, taking it clean up my nose I lifted my head back up in time to catch him and Mikael both sitting looking at me and my dad saying 'We think we can help you.'

Chapter 33.

Words don't even come close to describing just how royally pissed off I was at Stevie when we were down in Blackburn. What kind of a boyfriend takes you to another country, (which even though we didn't need passports to get into, technically it still was) and then abandons you for over three hours? He said he was only going for a look around and would be back soon with a bottle of water for me. 'I'll be back before you know it,' he said. Just as well I wasn't dying of thirst, that's all I'm saying. Si and him left us two on our own in the middle of this big factory that was absolutely heaving with people.

What was, for me, the biggest crowd of people that I had ever been part of in my life. Packed into that derelict disused factory in the middle of that cold, desperate and grim looking English industrial estate. He knew how much of a complex I had over the "dress" that I had chosen to wear, that I had wanted him to stay close to me as a result and what does he do? Goes missing for even LONGER than he had ever done at any of the other nights we'd been to. What unthoughtful kind of a man does something like that?

It wasn't even the fact that he deserted me that annoyed me the most. It was that after a while I genuinely started to get worried in case anything bad had happened to him. Trouble with some other guys in there? Perhaps he'd had a health scare through all of the chemicals he'd been knocking down. I told him that just because it was his birthday he didn't have to overdo things but with Si egging him on he never listened to me. By getting worried about him I was starting to then get annoyed at myself because through the worry, the logical side of me just knew that there was nothing wrong with him. Logic pointing towards him having the time of his life and not even giving me a seconds serious thought. If he even remembered that I was there with him, of course.

That's not to say that I spent those three hours weeping inconsolably in the corner at my loss. Shan and I had a crazy brilliant time, danced our tiny asses off for the most part. Mike Pickering, DJ from The Hacienda in Manchester was on the decks performing a set that the crowd wouldn't let him end. Tune after tune just got better and better, my arms were getting sore from being in the air so much. Every time he dropped another big track Shan and I would just look at each other and excitedly scream right into each others faces.

I have to say, my choice of dress got a LOT of attention. Then again, deep down I knew it would.

One guy even came up with a polaroid camera and asked if he could take a picture of me with his girlfriend! I didn't know the two of them in any way but of course I agreed. It was quite flattering all of the attention I was getting. I had other girls coming up to ask where I got it from while most of the guys were just smiling and nodding their head in approval. One came up to me and said that it was genius and that it was the best dress he'd ever seen in his life. It was a garment that I felt certainly stirred the imagination and was a little worried about encountering some horrible pervy guys but in reality nothing came close to that. It's actually mad that I'm even calling it a dress because it wasn't really. Two car seat covers sewed together does not make a dress as far as I'm concerned but hey, I pulled it off. It really displayed the attitude of the whole scene though that someone can turn up wearing something like that and not be laughed at.

Apart from all of the brief exchanges with people from the crowd I actually ended up making friends with this really nice girl called Jana, a fashion student from Liverpool. She even spoke like Jackie Corkhill from Brookside and everything! I don't think I've ever met a scouser in the flesh and was fascinated by her accent. She was really pretty, had this combination of straight AND curly long hair that I would swap my next birthday and Christmas presents for! Like so many others she had struck up a conversation with me purely down to the fact that I, as she eloquently put, was wearing a dress "similar to her nan's Mini Metro seat covers."

She had me giggling right from the off at that statement. Normally whatever I have on me could never be compared to anything remotely to do with an OAP but there's a first time for anything I suppose. She explained to me that she was really into fashion and was studying to be a designer and the second she set eyes on me she had to come over to talk. I laughed at her dead serious assumption that I too was a designer and had to tell her that I wished I was doing something as cool as that. Instead I was still at school and had simply stolen my dad's seat covers and used a friends sewing machine to attach them together while making some minor tweaks so that I could wear it. She told me that was a head fuck because it was the type of dress that you'd see one of those models wearing at Milan fashion week in one of those shows where they all wear clothes that cost thousands of pounds but in reality you'd get laughed at if you wore outside the house.

We actually got on so well that we swapped phone numbers and our address', saying that we'd write to each other and hopefully catch up at the occasional party if she was in Scotland or vice versa. I know it probably looked like nothing more than two people on Ecstasy who in the moment were promising all of these things but she seemed pretty sincere about it and for what it was worth, so did I. At one point she said she was going to find the rest of her girls and bring them back over to meet Shan and I. It just felt so amazing, just everything.

The feeling of the couple of pills I'd had which "were" strong but not enough as to spoil the fun. There, in a position of being able to meet beautiful and friendly people like Jana. The overwhelming fact that we were all in this together, that what we were doing was "right." Yeah, we were breaking the law in more ways than one at times but never, ever felt that we were the ones in the wrong.

It was when we were waiting on Jana returning that finally emerging from the sea of dancing bodies. I saw the two of them. Way before they saw Shan and I. The two of them looked completely out of their tree, big time. What on earth had they been up to? Stevie especially. I wanted to be so angry at him, he'd left me for such a long time on my own and just look at the state he's been getting himself into while away. Obviously he wasn't thinking too much about me when gone. Si didn't look like he'd been missing Shan either by the looks of him. It was the grins on their faces and the state of their eyes that I couldn't get past. You really do have the most random of nonsense breeze into your head while skied on pills but looking at both of their eyes it made me think of answering machines you get for for phones as the two of them had this "I'm not in right now" look about them!

I already knew trying to get any sense out of either of them was going to prove difficult, for a few hours at least and by that time they would have probably forgotten anyway. I couldn't be angry at him though. I was more happy to see him than anything else. He's just a lovable rogue at times, he does things with an air of cheek that always seems to get him off the hook with me. Love can be so complicated and I hope that as I get older I'll start to understand it more. When he finally did see me, well, after having to do that fucking pirate eyepatch thing with his hand to make sure he could focus looking at me, his face lit up, pulling on Si's arm with him looking in a completely different direction to Zico.

As he approached close enough for us to hear, Stevie pulled out this big ziplocked bag announcing 'MDMA crystals for all' - Si pretending to play a trumpet or something to provide the fanfare for such an announcement. 'FUCKING WHAAAAAAAT' Shan reacted in a majorly enthusiastic way at this development and was already licking a finger and dipping it into a bag Stevie had produced from within the bigger bag. It was hard to see with the way the lights were flashing all over the place. Sometimes you could see something and then the next moment it was darkness that you were looking into. When the lights were flashing our way though it was pretty clear to me that he was holding a pirates booty of all sorts of stuff, more than he could ever afford. Then I saw Si, pulling something similar out of his pocket before promptly dropping it and not being able to find it even though it was clearly right beside his foot.

The poor boy was getting confused by the fact it wasn't there and started to stress over losing so much drugs. I picked it up for him to settle him down and put him at ease. Really though, what had the two of them been up to? I would get my answer but only after the matter of Stevie and Si dishing out these crystals which, I'd taken it they'd already sampled some. This being proved by how much the two of them seemed to be completely rocked, I wasn't sure if I wanted to take what was in the bag.

This was new ground. I admit, since that scary moment when taking my first pill and the worry that I was going to actually die or at best have a horrible time seeing monsters all over trying to eat me, I had never had any fears or any hesitation when it came to necking a Dove or a New Yorker or any other name you want to give them. This stuff though that Si was offering me? Once he managed to get both bags opened, this was meant to be strong, super strength stuff.

You'd hear people speak about it like it was the holy grail of Ecstasy. Some said it was five times more strong than a standard Eckie, others said ten. As far as I was concerned it was as real as the Loch Ness Monster in the sense that everyone speaks about it but none have ever seen it. I wasn't up nor down about it as I never thought I'd ever come into contact with any. Of course, these two appear with two full to the brim bags of the stuff?! Despite his clear lack of awareness Stevie told me that I "really" was going to want to try this stuff. That's all he had to say, I was obviously intrigued and "wanted" to try it but was still scared it would be too much for me. If a plain and simple pill is as strong as some of the ones I'd been taking since starting out, how much more stronger could it really get? Or in fact, did I really want it to get?

There really was only one true way to find out. 'One thing though, just take a wee bit, at least to try it. It's not the kind of stuff that takes prisoners and will completely rock your world indiscriminately' Stevie told me and considering he was obviously a man speaking with experience I was happy to heed the warning when I tentatively dipped my finger into the bag he was holding out for me. Shan? To hell with this softly softly approach, she'd dipped her finger in up past the knuckle and pulled it back out sucking on her finger like a baby. Well she did for about one second at least until her face screwed up and immediately started to gag. Suddenly I wasn't so keen on it.

Si and Stevie were no better in this situation. Si especially. His girlfriend looks like she's had a bad reaction to these strong crystals and he's standing there laughing right at her? I thought it was pretty rude. He was supposed to be better than that. I was about to tell the pair of them what dicks they were behaving, until 'Fucking hell, darling, you went too quick,! Jesus, the bag was just opened and your finger was right fucking in there, what if Stevie had got mixed up and opened the one with the Heroin in it?' Si said, casual as you like.

Shan who avoided being sick was standing there screwing her face but not at Si. I still wasn't sure if she was in a lot of pain or what. I'm pouncing on Si's words. 'Heroin? Smack? - He just laughed at me like it was all some joke. 'Nah, we've not got any Smack, Leees, only joking .. Well, I don't think there's any in there at least' before he started trying to look inside it in a way that I really didn't know if he was going along with the joke or being deadly serious.

Closing the bag again he looked back towards Shan, who after having a few swigs of water, appeared to be looking a wee bit better and was smiling again 'Had you waited, you absolute drug fiend, you'd have given your boyfriend the chance to warn you that MDMA crystals were THE most foul tasting thing you will have ever encountered in your life and that you should think of an alternative way than to just lick clean off your finger but then again, you know that for yourself, now' - I obviously got why the two of them had been laughing earlier at her which put me at ease as it was confusing me why they were being so mean to her.

'We tried it in the VIP area earlier on and almost lost our stomachs, that stuff should come with a health warning' Stevie said, validating what Si had said about the taste of it when in truth there was no validation needed. Shans face was enough of a warning for me.

Fuck the MDMA, I'd just heard my boyfriend say something about having been in VIP?! 'I'll tell you all about it ONCE you take a hit from Si's wee bag' He promised me. 'Well you seriously don't think I'm going to dip my finger in and repeat Shan's tactics which were so obviously a resounding success' I sarcastically said to them all. Her method hadn't exactly sold it to me. I'm not sure really how he did it but within about a minute, Si had managed to pack some of it inside a cigarette paper, sealing it shut which allowed me to pop it like a normal pill and wash down with a drink of water, no taste no stress no fuss.

It took around half an hour to start but when it did? It was like nothing on earth while being heaven ON earth, absolutely unique. Even when on it I was weeping for the fact that this was not going to be an every party occurrence. It was, special. Simply better in every single way over an ordinary E but oh how it was strong. Before it all started to take hold however and we partied until the sun came up, Stevie and I had some time out to ourselves.

He'd knocked up a few joints inside the factory and we went for a walk around the grounds outside. The nippy cold air felt incredible. Offsetting just how insanely hot it was inside the factory with all these bodies crammed inside. Those crystals themselves had left me burning up. Switching temperatures in such a noticeable way was clearly going to be a combination that could leave me with a cold but for how refreshing the feeling was, it was more than worth the risk.

The tale he told me of what he'd been up to when he went missing left me without any real words. His dad was someone that he'd not really spoken too much about to me. I'd tried a few times to find out about that side of his life but Stevie would always just react angrily and clam up. I knew he wasn't his dads biggest fan, that much was obvious. Put it that way. So for them to not see each other in years then have a random meeting here in Blackburn at an illegal house party? I can't even begin to imagine what it would be like talking to my mum and dad while on a few pills.

How could that even be a series of moments that could end up coming together to make it possible? Well, as he went onto explain, it all "did" make perfect sense as much as I never thought it would or could. I found it really sweet that despite all of previous negativity and resentment, Stevie looked genuinely thrilled and happy that he'd met him even though I'm not entirely sure that his head was fully capable of dealing with it all there and then. It was like he was barely believing it all himself never mind trying to tell someone else about it.

You could tell by the way he told the story though and the words he chose, he never once referred to his father in a bad way. Who knows? Maybe it was purely because this person had given him a big bag of drugs for free before leaving but I detected more than that. Going by some of the things that I was being told there was definitely going to be further talks on what had happened. Preferably while I wasn't going up on a, questionably "small" sample of MDMA. I was questioning whether Si's quality control on me receiving a small amount had been up to scratch. Si and or Stevie were visibly not exactly the best people to be left in charge of anything never mind dispensing a safe amount of super strong MDMA.

It really was a pretty mad turn of events to happen though, especially under the circumstances. My boyfriend goes off for a walk and to get me water and comes back having gained a father and a family sized bag of drugs. Only him I suppose, that's reason number 2843645 why I love the guy.

There was evidently lots to revisit with regards to what had taken place over those missing hours but for now all we wanted to do was be back inside with our friends, sharing the love and the laughs. We still had many hours to go and the feeling that was coming on me from those crystals, I wanted to milk every single second for all that it was worth out of the night and morning. In no time we'd be back on that bus and making the long journey home to Scotland with all the others. "That" was not something I was looking forward to by any stretch of the imagination. We had hours to go yet and in those moments that is always the most important thing of all.

Chapter 34.

I decided not to tell any of the family about bumping into dad. To have done otherwise would have only meant having to spin an industrial strength web of lies and after Blackburn I was doing well to even keep my head above water just in a general day to day existence type of way. To then have to add layers of lies into the mix, lies I already knew I wouldn't have had even a remote chance of keeping track of? Some things are best left alone. It would have only been a matter of time before I ended tripping myself up over and getting caught out.

Ignorance is bliss as they say so I kept my trap shut. Fuck, I can only imagine the reception news of me meeting him would have brought. It would've been questions on top of questions. Would've made the Spanish Inquisition look like everyone had been too scared to open their fucking mouths. A week later and I could still barely even believe it myself that he was back in my life and in the most outlandish of ways. I spent the whole journey back from Blackburn, when everyone were all sat having their own private quiet time, replaying and replaying what had happened. Well, as much as I could remember of it, as it were. Despite how wrecked I was on the night I'd certainly grasped the headlines of it all though. He seemed to be doing quite well for himself for someone who, had been in jail. In my mind, you go to jail and life is pretty much fucked from that point on.

Even when you get back out it's like you've been marked for life, cunts will look at you different and as far as getting yourself a decent job? Aye good luck with that. Him though? Must've been a Hugo Boss or Armani suit or something he had on, he just had to click his fingers and he had people coming over and doing his bidding. His mobile phone seemed to ring half the time I was with him, some calls he would look at before ignoring, others he'd answer either in English or Spanish. I was secretly impressed. The stories he told and the way he delivered them. He was different than I remembered from before. Don't get me wrong, he always was flash and cocky at the best of times but he seemed to have this air of superiority that, while I should've thought he was a fanny for acting that way, I almost admired it. He was likeable.

It's most definitely wrong and goes against everything I thought I'd feel about him. But seeing him sat there, namedropping all of these exciting cities that he'd travelled to and lived in. Hearing him talk about all of these notorious criminal organisations that he'd done business with like the Russian mafia, Irish paramilitary groups and Mexican and Colombian cartels. I felt proud of him in the way that someone is proud of a family member or friend when they do well for themselves. Local boy done good and all of that stuff.

Of course though, it would have to be in connection with a subject that I couldn't really talk to anyone about and DEFINITELY not my immediate family. He hadn't called me since Blackburn but that was cool with me, I hadn't called him either. I wanted to but told myself I'd wait a while before doing so. Pretty fucked up state of affairs to find myself in too. I found it similar to when a girl gives you her phone number and you feel that you have to wait an acceptable amount of time before calling them. You of course "want" to call but stop yourself through fear of looking too keen or needy. Yet I was finding myself feeling that way with my fucking DAD!

In any case, it wouldn't have exactly been ideal for him to have called me at the house. Speaking to him I was going to want as much privacy as I could get. Not like I could have called him from the house even if on my own either. The number printed on his business card which was for some ceramics firm, had more digits than a fucking maths jotter, all these extra codes added on before the main number even began.

I'm not stupid, I call a radge exotic number like that from the house there's going to be a fucking riot when uncle Jimmy opens that phone bill the month after. Would be quite funny to be a fly on the wall though when he opened it. 'Brenda? Have you been calling Bogota? Actually, where the fuck IS Bogota?'

I waited just over a week in the end before calling him, reverse charges as well by the way, too fucking right. He told me to do that anyway and even if he hadn't I'd still have been doing it. Took fucking ages to get connected to him, rang for ages in this strange ringing tone that was different to when you called someone else in Scotland. Then I got connected to some woman speaking Spanish at a fucking hundred miles an hour, not one lick of the lingo I understood. I spoke back to her in Scottish, she listened only to start speaking in Spanish back to me again.

With my mum staying in Spain and me spending a bit of my youth over there I "did" know a wee bit so managed to pluck out 'hablo English' which as far as I could remember was something like 'speak English.' This probably sounded rude as fuck from me if that was the direct translation. She's there doing her job and suddenly she's got some arrogant Brit telling her to talk his language! It went quiet to the point I thought she'd hung up on me only for a man to come on the line asking if he could help me.

Fair enough he could speak my language at least but someone being able to speak the English language and be able to "understand" someone from Scotland are not two of the same things. It was quite the struggle. Subconsciously I resorted to that talking slower and louder way that UK citizens are famed for when they're talking to someone from a foreign country and they experience a difficulty communicating with them.

We got there though, eventually and soon he was connecting me to the number that I had given him. When the phone answered I heard the sound of some kind of salsa music playing, trumpets and some high pitched man wailing over top of it. Eventually my dad spoke "Pedro Alvarez hablando' I honesty didn't know if he was fucking about for my benefit or being serious with that introduction as I assumed that he already knew who was on the phone to him because of the reversed charged call.

'Hola Papa Pedro' I replied. 'Ahhhhhhhhh my bambino' He said reverting to a mix of Spanish English. I could tell he was smiling as he said this although the way he seemed to recognise that it was his son on the phone left me thinking that possibly he'd been serious with the way he'd answered the call initially. If so, someone should tell him that calling yourself Pedro Lopez kind of doesn't work when you've got a Scottish accent. 'How's the head after your trip to England? recovered yet' He asked showing just how much knowledge he had on such matters, probably already well aware of how hard the following days would have been after the whole Blackburn and take as much drugs as possible and use your birthday as an excuse thing.

'I'm just about getting back to normal now' I confessed, feeling a wee bit embarrassed and conscious of the subject we were talking about. I wasn't giving a flying fuck at the time due to how incredibly high I had been but now, stood in a phone box round the corner from my house? It felt exactly how it should've really done when a father and son are talking about drugs, awkward.

That VIP area meeting had been too natural, way more natural than the subject of drugs should be with a parent. This, I felt was reality biting. 'Ach well, I wouldn't have been able to look myself in the mirror if I hadn't celebrated my birthday to the very limits of possible' I justified myself for whatever state he really had seen me on the Saturday night / Sunday morning.' - 'You're a chip off the old block, I'll give you that' he conceded. 'Christ I hope not,' I thought to myself.

We engaged in a bit of small talk, but even so I enjoyed it. While it was only small talk it never felt forced on either side. I asked him when he had flown back to South America. He told me that Mikky and him had went down to London the day after Blackburn to another party to take care of some more business. I definitely wasn't going to ask him who all these business partners were that he was meeting on his whistle stop tour of Britain. I figured he'd tell me that stuff if he wanted me to know and I didn't want to risk embarrassing him or myself by sticking my nose in where it wasn't welcome.

He told me that I had just caught Mikky and him heading out on a trip up into the Andes to meet an associate who ran an operation up there. The small talk aside, there was that elephant in room and not one called Nellie but Nora. He must've sensed this too because just as I was building up enough courage to ask him about it he took control of things. 'So this problem of yours then?' - It was without a doubt the one thing that had dominated my thoughts since Blackburn.

It was pretty fucking surreal to bump into my long lost pops while I was completely wired at an illegal house party but to do so and learn about his involvement in the drug game and not in a small time way either. Aye that was all, understandably a lot for a teenager to deal with. Finding out though that he knew "exactly" who the square route of all of my problems in life was and that he could help take care of them? Well that's just the type of thing that "would" dominate ones thoughts.

How could he help me with it though? My mind had run amok with it all. Lets face it, I didn't really know my dad. I'd never spent any length of or quality time together to connect and find out about each other. All we'd ever had together were the basics and due to this it had my mind running through all kinds of scenarios. I assumed that it was not going to be the case where a parent steps in when there's a problem and talks it over like when a kid smashes the next door neighbours window with a stray shot when playing fitba. One dad talking it over with another.

This obviously was light years from those kind of situations. One of the places that my mind had taken me to was that he would have him killed which regardless of what had gone on before with Nora and moi would have been way too far. It was completely mental that I was even having thoughts like that but well, we can't choose what pops into our head, can we? I just wanted him off my case and me getting back to see United again. Just get the fatwa cancelled and we'd say no more. No need to kill any cunt over it eh?

Like any parent though when they feel their kid is experiencing problems I could tell he wanted to help. As wrecked as I was it wasn't too hard to notice him visibly react when he heard about the gangsters that came through to visit me. He had appeared as shocked as he was angry. In a strange way, despite the circumstances of it all I felt a swell pride that he felt that way about me. Obviously I had bottled up a lot of stuff inside over all of the years we'd been out of each others lives so to be validated that he still loved me, still cared. It felt good.

'Aye, I never got a chance to ask you how you know him' I asked showing how ignorant I was to this whole different way of life he was living and completely not getting the fact that he was never going to talk about such matters. 'It's not something I can go into over the phone, Stevie but what I can say is that during recent times he's someone who has gotten into the habit of pissing off the wrong type of people' he replied which had me ironically laughing while I agreed with him that Nora most definitely had a talent for pissing people off.

'One of my contacts in Newcastle did some business with him a while back and it didn't go well, one of those types of men that you don't get a second chance with. You come the cunt with them and your card is marked from there on in, heavy people to get mixed up with' - My mind was flooded with all kinds of scenarios. I'd always known there was more to Nora than we were all seeing on match days. As far as I'd heard, he didn't have a job but was never skint. I never seen it but had been told that he had a top of the range Mercedes and lived in one of the posher areas of Dundee. Doesn't take a brain surgeon to work out that if someone with things like that doesn't have a job then the cashish is flying in from somewhere else.

He continued, 'There's been a couple of times where something was arranged but then called off again. I can't really go into that right now. Bottom line though is that he won't exactly be missed by a lot of people if he was to disappear' By now I had picked up about the need for careful thinking before opening my mouth and speaking. Jesus, my head's full of paranoia at the best of times anyway when it came to the immediate days that would follow a drugs binge. I could really have done without having a conversation on the phone while worrying that the fucking DEA or someone were listening in as well.

I knew deep down that I was overplaying who my dad was and that he wasn't as powerful as to be on the radar of anti drug agencies but still couldn't stop my mind from going down that path. When he'd mentioned about Nora 'disappearing' it's fair to say, whether wrong or right, I took that as being killed. Now that was way too heavy for me to even be contemplating. The last three to four months had been a bit of a mind fuck with all that had gone on and all I wanted was for it to go away, not like that though. 'Look, the boy's put me and some of the family through hell at times recently, even when I was on his good side I still never lost sight of the fact that he really is a nasty bastard and he probably does deserve whatever is coming to him but I can't have that over my head dad.'

Even by saying that I was stood there in the phone box worrying that it was enough for to get me in trouble in an incriminating way. That was stupid though and I knew it. After all, I was standing there saying I "didn't" want him killed. I continued while hoping that I wasn't going to use any wrong words 'He's caused a lot of trouble to me and the family and I could just do with it all going away, let me get back to normal. It's not right that I'm banned from Dundee United matches' I could feel my temper rising, it always did when I got thinking about the fact that I wasn't getting to the games.

It's not like he was the fucking manager or owner of the club, that I could actually accept. The cunt makes himself out like he owns the City of Dundee and all that is in it.

My dad just laughed back at me, which left me feeling embarrassed, then resentful at myself for feeling that way. Little more than over a week before I was firmly in "my dad's a prick" mode and yet now here he is with the ability to make me feel stupid. 'I wasn't suggesting what you're thinking I am ya daft wee bastard, although I wouldn't rule that out happening to him at some point. Like I said earlier, he has no idea how close he's already sailed to that particular wind, if it does though it won't be of my doing.' He left me questioning if that last part was said for effect just in case someone "was" listening. It was actually pretty fucking frustrating to be having, what was probably one of the most vital conversations of my entire life and not be able to speak freely. I wanted to know exactly what was going on but instead it was all a bit cryptic. The fear of saying something wrong, the paranoia that my dad was on some watch list or something, it almost had me to the point of being scared to open my fucking mouth.

'Look, to simplify things, son, you want your problem to go away. I can make that happen' I decided to stay silent and let him continue, reasoning that I'd know when I had to offer some input. 'The less you know about it the better anyway but when there's any development you're going to know about it.'

'Now, Stevie this is muchos important here but since Saturday night what have you told anyone when it came to you and I chatting?' He got me thinking back though, what "had" I told anyone? Family? Absolutely fuck all never mind telling them that we'd spoken about the inner workings of Colombian cartels. Lisa? I'd obviously told her about meeting my dad in the VIP area, just as well as how the fuck else was I going to explain to her why I'd left her for three and a bit hours?!

That aside, I'd kept a lot of the Nora stuff from her to save any worrying on her part so it wasn't ever a subject I'd have told her about. When it came to Si though I genuinely didn't know what I'd told him. I couldn't remember the moments that followed me rejoining him after going back to speak to my dad and Mikky the second time. Did he ask why I'd been called back? Did I tell him? I didn't have a fucking clue. This was right at the time where those mental crystals were starting to really grab hold of the pair of us so there wasn't much in the way of memories from that half hour period. There was so many permutations to the possibilities. It wouldn't exactly be out of the question for him to have asked me what my dad had said and me tell him only for Si to then forget anyway!

'Nah you're good on that, dad. I haven't told anyone about meeting you at the weekend apart from my girlfriend but wasn't as radge as to tell her half of what we spoke about' To the best of my knowledge when she'd asked where all of the drugs I'd brought back from VIP had come from. I'd told her that they were just lying there on a table, which was actually the truth. 'I haven't told any of the family, you saw the nick of me on Saturday night so you'll know that there is no way I'm going to want to deal with all of the questions they'd have had for me.'

'Good, just keep it to yourself, the less people who knows of any connection between you, me and our third party the better' - This was something that we were without a doubt on the same page as each other. Once we'd started to speak about Nora and I saw where the conversation was steering towards I had found myself getting this really horrible feeling in the bottom of my stomach. Wasn't the good one you get when you're excited about something, I think it comes from adrenaline or something like that. No, this was, I don't know if it was dread or whatever but I just had the feeling that I was dipping my toe into a world where I had no right to be in.

One of those worlds that exists right under the noses of everyone else and one they never come into contact with while living their ordinary lives. Back when I'd started to question me running with the Utility boys, one thought that I'd had was that I was growing up too quickly, getting exposed to certain stuff that a fifteen year old shouldn't. Things that people who live their whole life will not see. I leave the Utility hoping that I can have a crack at being just a regular teenage lad and how does that work out? I have a gun put to my head with the trigger pulled and within months am speaking to an international narcotics wholesaler based in Colombia about making people disappear, or something to that effect. That was the thing, I was discussing having something bad happen to someone without even knowing what it would be, or what the definition of "bad" really was.

Bizarrely, yet also while feeling weirdly natural, we changed the subject completely, and enjoyed a regular chat. He switched from organising underworld moves to how much he missed a cold tin of Irn Bru and a Tunnock's Teacake like it was nothing. I joked that I'd send a care package of all the traditional Scottish delicacies over to him, providing he paid in advance of course! He said he might take me up on that offer. He asked me about some of the TV shows that were on

British telly these days, reminiscing about some of the comedy shows he loved like Fawlty Towers and Rising Damp.

It felt good to talk like that and left me with a completely different feeling compared to how I felt when we were talking about the serious stuff. I asked him about Colombia and what it was like. I told him how I'd watched the Escobar documentary and the country looked completely mental, they even said unofficially the country was called 'Locombia' as it's that fucking loco. He joked about how sick and tired he was of the constant sun and heat for most of the year and missed the Scottish cold and rain. The dick!

He admitted that the country was completely unhinged and in lots of areas pretty much lawless considering how much the police and politicians had been bought off. As far as a tourist board rep, he wasn't much of one and in fact only confirmed some of the stuff that I'd already seen on the telly. Obviously he had a good reason for being there and the mess that the country seemed to be in was something that certain people were going to take advantage of.

We were still talking away (fuck knows how much the call must've cost him, by the way) when I heard that unmistakable unusual accent of Mikael in the background speaking to my dad, automatically distracting him for a minute. I waited on the other end while noticing the fact that he had covered up the phone while speaking to Mikky. I could still make out my dads voice but not in any way that was clear enough to hear what was actually being said. Eventually he came back and said he'd now have to get going.

He advised that he was going to be stuck somewhere in the fucking mountains for the foreseeable so would be out of contact for a while but for me to give him a call in around a weeks time again and he'd possibly have some more news for me. He hung up after that leaving me there questioning what I'd now put in motion with that one phone call. It was the very same question I would spend the majority of my waking hours thinking about on a loop until the next time we would speak.

Chapter 35.

I'd started to look further into the whole DJ side of things, how much all the equipment was going to cost. Where I'd get records to play because with House it wasn't like I was going to be able to stroll right into Woolworths and ask them for the latest tunes Carl Cox or Grooverider had been heard playing. There "was" a shop in town that had a small selection to offer each week but it really was more of an afterthought than anything else. Plus, I'd heard that one of the staff was the type to keep all the rare twelve inches to himself.

Nah, once I got my decks, which incidentally, the Technics SL 10's along with mixer were going to set me back the best part of a grand. When I finally had them it looked like if I was going to be serious about things I'd have to be making a regular pilgrimage to Glasgow so I could visit 23rd Precinct for my vinyl. This sound lad I'd got speaking to down in Blackburn was telling me about the place, he was from Motherwell himself and one of his mates was just starting out trying to be a DJ and that was where he went for his vinyl.

A shop pretty much built on dance music. Unless the boy was talking some Ecstasy induced shite. He told me that when you go into 23rd, you tell the shop assistant the specific type of dance music that you are looking for. They then pick out a big pile of vinyl for you and, get this, give you your OWN fucking turntable and a pair of headphones to listen to them?!

In amongst all of the shit that had been going on recently this whole DJ thing was something that kept coming back to me. It was like I had become obsessed with it. I had continued to study the deejays at the parties I'd been to, see how much attention they had to pay to both tracks that they were mixing together. The Technics themselves had the ability to speed up or slow down the beats per minute of the records, enough for them to match each other beat for beat.

I could already see that any respecting deejay didn't just play any old song into another. They had to have a flow to and as far as I could see, these deejays I had been soaking in over all of the months since starting. They had really thought about which songs they were playing. Weren't just reaching into their record box and taking random ones out to play. I actually had a brief chat with one of the Pure DJ's when we were over in Edinburgh that night. I had popped out for a wee breather, desperate for some fresh air through what severe sweatbox Pure was.

Minding my own business having a puff he came over and asked if I had a spare fag to give him. He could've been anyone asking for one as far as I knew but as we stood chatting I was raving about the DJ that had just been on for the past few hours and how good he was. He just laughed before telling me that HE was the DJ and had just now finished his set for the night and was gasping for a smoke.

I know he would have just looked at me as someone who was off their tits on chemicals and talking pish, regardless of how sure and sincere I was in that moment. You know what though? Even if he "did" think I was just some dreamer he was cool enough to answer all the questions I had about getting more involved in the scene. I told him that being a spectator was the best thing to happen to my life but now I wanted to be a participant. There's no accounting for the amount of words per second someone can get out when high like that. I told him about the whole casual side of things and how I was now looking on the house scene as some kind of salvation.

He gave me some really good advice although some of which left me with the impression that it was more down to luck than anything. I guess that's the same in all areas of life? I bet there's been some fucking amazing fitba players across the world who just never got the break they needed and gave up instead with the world none the wiser the talent they missed out on. Same for musicians, I can imagine that there are some bands who never got the record deal they needed and we missed out on someone that might well have rivalled The Beatles or The Stones.

It makes perfect sense that it would be the same for anyone looking to become a DJ. He told me to develop my own style of mixing and choice of records because it would help me stick out from the rest. Also to practice like my life depended on it. Once I felt confident enough to get some mixes recorded and then fucking bombard my tapes to all the promoters and those who owned the clubs and outdoor events. If I'm going to an allnighter to party then take some with me and seek out the promoters. Never to leave home without a couple of tapes in my pocket as you never know who you're going to bump into. That was how he got his break so it was pretty sound of him to pass on a few tips.

I joked with him that within a year we'd be both on the same bill, he laughed along with me. Well, I presumed it was with rather than at.

I'd made my decision though, I was fucking going for it. I was going to hit my dad for a couple of thousand to get me the decks, mixer and a big pile of records. With that I'd be off and running. I'd worked out that I'd probably only really need maybe two, three trips to Glasgow for tunes before I had enough to play with when it came to making up a few varied mixtapes with me showcasing some of the current house tunes out there. Oh aye, I had it all worked out, likes. Was going to hit him up for the money under one of those "I'll pay you back" kind of deals that would involve me doing absolutely fuck all paying back in any shape or form.

He'd have to be the first to admit that he'd gone missing during some vital years in his sons life. Now we both found ourselves going through the whole building bridges and healing process as son and dad and if he wasn't willing to spring for a fucking pair of Technics SL's in support of his reconciled sons dreams then there had to be something wrong there eh? Going by the size of the lines of ching he was putting up his nose when I seen him, he's probably spending the equivalent of a pair of decks on cocaine every day anyway. Then again, I don't know how much he's paying for it, if he's even paying at all.

My family had been pure nipping my head over the whole work situation. I'd told them that I was waiting on the whole job with my cuzz coming to fruition but I'm not sure if they were really buying it. Being honest, I was fucking dreading the day coming around when he told me that the position was now available. Don't get me wrong, I fully understand the need for an adult, even a young one, to make money. Without money then life wold be kind of shit. You'd never be able to go anywhere, do anything, buy anything and that sounds like a kind of life that I don't think I'd be able to get behind.

I wanted to earn money under my own terms, however. Not putting a shirt or overalls on five days a week and being chained to an office space or factory for most of your life. Aye, of course I wanted money but I wanted to make it in a different way from most people out there.

I'd decided that where I was in life and the attitude that I was brimming full of. A standard nine to five just wasn't going to cut it.

I'd already had that little taste of work at the bakery and there were cunts working there who had done that same job for over twenty years?! Decades worth of making cakes and pastries, getting up at an obscene time of the morning just so they could make cakes and savoury snacks. Was that their dream when they were growing up? I'm assuming not, if so then they must've had a fucking screw loose.

I didn't want to be one of those people. Do a shitey job all of their life and get given a gold carriage clock at the end of it then spend a few years wondering why they wasted the best years of their life only to eventually die. Fuck that, I had seen that life was full of opportunities if you had the balls to go against the grain and reach for them. I'm not sure that many adults had realised this or not but I saw that it "could" be possible to make money but have a good time with it along the way. To earn while feeling that you were making your mark in life. Making a difference but not in the way that you'll hear a member of the emergency services say. To make a difference, culturally.

As soon as all of this shite with Nora was done and dusted I was going to be hitting papa for a "loan" and launch myself head first into it. I really felt like a man in a hurry when it came to that although, with the possibility of "normal" work starting to hang over me I WAS in a hurry. What with the Nora stuff though? Had something happened already and I just didn't know it? Was it already planned and yet to happen? Was it going down right this minute in time and that fuck knows what was happening to him? Well, that was the thing. I didn't know and despite it being a subject that wasn't leaving my mind, I knew I was only going to know when it was time for me, and not a minute before.

Chapter 36.

'Strathclyde Police have reported that last night they seized over a hundred thousand pounds worth of heroin in the Easterhouse area after a raid following an undercover operation. The drugs were recovered from a house in Duntarvie Crescent in a raid that brought the Glasgow street to a standstill. Two men who were found at the scene are said to be assisting the police with their enquiries.'

The plump newsreader who I always laughed at because of the industrial strength amount of make up she always wore, sat there at the news desk taking the STV viewers through the evening news. You got the usual wee bit footage to go with it which never ever amounted to more than a few seconds of the house where the raid took place before moving onto a very pleased with himself looking copper with a shit eating grin standing there with the Smack laid out on a table that looked nothing more than one of those fold up ones you see cunts using when they're wallpapering a house. During the brief interview he was banging on about how vital it was for the community that they stop the flow of hard drugs getting onto the Easterhouse streets and that whilst considered a major bust it really was only the tip of the iceberg and that the war on drugs would continue.

I was sitting having my tea with my auntie and uncle and just as I was about to slag the officer for being a bit dramatic I managed to see sense and stop myself before any words came out of my mouth. Just as well considering Jimmy was about to go off on an anti drug rant in response to the whole subject of people selling and taking drugs.

'See those druggies? Nothing more than a waste of oxygen, what they wanting to be putting that filth into themselves for? Bloody lucky they're even born and then they put it all to waste by taking drugs' - There was so many things I could've said back to him but it really wouldn't have been wise. I wanted to ask him if he'd ever considered that it was maybe "because" of what their lives were like that they were even taking drugs in the first place.

Any talk like that though would only have put a spotlight on me. Something that I'd much rather have avoided. I know the way his mind works, if he was to even guess that I was offering sympathy towards people in the drug fraternity then it wouldn't be long before he was getting out his calculator and putting two and two together. For easiness sake, as well as my dislike of that brown stuff and what it appeared to do to people and all of those in their lives that it ruins. I was happy enough to vocally agree with him. 'I just don't see the fascination for it, that Heroin stuff? They take it once and then they're hooked forever. Next thing they know they're living in filth and breaking into houses and cars to help feed their habit, slaves to a drug, that's all they are.'

He was quite pleased to hear me back him up with such passion. Fuck, even people that smoke are the scum of the earth to him and he'd always said that if he'd found any of his kids smoking then he would sit them down and make them smoke the whole packet, one after another right in front of him. Christ, I really hope that he would not apply that same way of ironic punishment on me if he'd caught me taking an Eckie. There would be a bit of a problem if so!

'Aye well someone's not getting their fix tonight by the looks' he said, all chuffed with himself at using the correct term. I looked down at the meal that we were eating for tea and made a joke about the irony of us sat eating hot turkey with roast potatoes and veg while some over in the Weeg would be having COLD turkey. Fell flat on its arse mainly through him and my auntie not being aware of the term. It was a bit of a shame as it was a killer line too.

If you have to explain the joke to someone then that's never the way to a successful wisecrack. I left it. 'Tell you what though, I wouldn't want to be in the shoes of those the police caught with the drugs, that sounds an awful lot of moneys worth, they'll throw away the key on them, good riddance' - He had a point, I'd always worried about what would happen if I was to be caught holding just a couple of pills when I was out wrecked somewhere but getting caught with dealer quantities of any hard drug and it would never end up being just a slap on the wrists.

I hadn't actually sat down the stairs with them at tea time for quite a while, too many comedowns being nursed to be socialising with family, the other times I'll have had a smoke with mates and felt too stoned to sit and chat with family. It wasn't like I didn't like sitting with them, we always had stuff to talk about when we did. The tea itself was brilliant, that's one thing about my Auntie Brenda, the woman can cook, likes. The turkey was almost melting in your mouth it was so succulent and the fucking gravy she made? I'm not sure what she puts in it but it's the best you'll ever taste. I ask her what she puts in it and she always shrugs her shoulders and says 'just Bisto.' There has to be more to it than that. She's not fooling anyone.

After that she came through with home made apple pie with ice cream, fucking SCORE! Greedy bastard me but I was just finishing off a second helping of it when Lisa arrived at the house. My auntie and uncle were really pleased to see her as it was rare that she was ever down due to me generally going in the opposite direction. The reason that we spent more time up at hers was due to the fact that we got more privacy in her room. I'd been too embarrassed to tell her about the time I got caught having a pull in my bedroom that time when my auntie came in but had certainly put the point across that we wouldn't get much privacy down at mines. Most insistent I had always been, understandably.

Lisa was barely there though before we were heading back out again. I left her downstairs blethering to the two of them while I quickly changed my polo shirt and trainers before heading back down the stairs again. We were heading through to Kirkcaldy to go to the cinema. We hadn't even looked to see what films were on, just wanted to get away from everyone for the night.

She looked like she was sat there quite the thing and not someone who knew that they had to get their arse into gear if they were to catch the vital pre screening bus that would get us in on time. Sitting there eating a Wagon Wheel with a cup of tea that seemed to have come out of nowhere, I was only away for a couple blinks of the eye and in that time she's been sorted out for tea and biscuits! That's aunties for you though, always wanting to sort everyone out and not happy unless they're doing so.

'We need to get going if we're going to catch this bus, babe' I said to Lisa while standing impatiently but trying to appear the opposite of that. Straight away my uncle was offering to give us a run in but I wasn't having it. I knew he was only dong it to impress Lisa anyway and show how good a host he was. If it had been me on my own I'd like to see how quick he'd be offering to taxi me.

'No no, it's cool' I assured him, 'besides, you've just had your tea, you'll be due for a wee kip anytime now once you get settled back into your chair' - Everyone laughed, even him. I wasn't even trying to crack a funny. I was only stating an undeniable and inevitable fact. Lisa and I left them to it which within the half hour would see him sleeping and my auntie catching up with her Emmerdale Farm on the telly. Can't blame him for passing out with that shite on the TV either by the way.

The film though? Well first up it was as symbolic as it had been impacting. When I say "impacting" I pretty much mean the best film that I'd ever witnessed in my entire life. That first date Lisa and I had we'd sat and watched the trailer for it before Total Recall came on. I'd joked with her about if she had wanted to go with me to see it. At that point though I really couldn't have dreamed that it would have been possible, didn't really have the right to be thinking so far ahead down the line.

After all, it was only our first date together and there was going to be so much water to go under the bridge before we would be reaching the point of the year where Goodfellas was going to be seeing its general UK release. I had no fucking idea that the two of us would still be together by the time autumn rolled around. Truth be told, I wasn't even sure that I was going to get a second date with her at that stage of the night sitting there in the ABC cinema. Yet there we were, still together, by now every inch a "couple" sitting watching the opening scene of the film with Robert De Niro, Joe Pesci and Ray Liotta driving along that dark road listening to the sound of someone or something inside the boot of their car trying to get out.

Three hours later we were walking back out into the chilly October night after what hadn't so much as been a film than a journey. I hadn't seen a Martin Scorsese film before but man does he know how to tell a story. I think it says it all that you can sit through such a long film and barely notice the time that you've sat there. Almost the equivalent of two games of fitba put together. I mean, there's not many people who enjoys the beautiful game more than I do but even I don't think I could sit and watch two games of football in a row.

Goodfellas had everything though in what was the true story of the rise and eventual fall of a gangster in New York. Fair enough, I probably hadn't watched enough films in my life to give such an assessment but a film hadn't touched me in the way that it did. While being worlds apart from each other so much so that the main character could've been on Jupiter and I on Saturn I couldn't help but find similarities with "Henry Hill" when it came to us both seeing the glamour of being part of a gang. Seduced by the lifestyle only to find that it can end up becoming a living nightmare. I'm not trying to say that being a soccer casual and being in the Mafia are apples to apples but seeing him join them as a kid and how easily he was pulled into things was something I felt an obvious connection with.

The only part that I didn't like about the film I suppose was how Hill grassed on everyone at the end to save his own skin. Aye, easy for me to say not having the threat of being "whacked" hanging over me from the Mob I guess. Not that I'd been completely free of any threats though. I wonder what life is going to be like for him from now on though. Anticlimactic with high levels of daily apprehension. Every single day of his life looking over his shoulder wondering if "today" is the day they're going to find him. I can't see the Mafia forgetting about what he did anytime soon. Definitely going to check out more Scorsese films in the future now.

As we would always do after the cinema we went for a burger and sat talking about the film. It was weird but I'd never had a girlfriend remotely long enough to find myself slipping into certain rituals like this. It was only through meeting Lisa that I was starting to experience such repetitive behaviour. Was only something that I could ever look upon as a good thing that her and I were so settled together that we actually "had" certain things like that together. Without sounding like a complete sad sap of a boy we were now into a third season as boyfriend and girlfriend although that pretty much 'does' have me out as a sap.

We only met at the tail end of the Spring and it really was just the beginning of Autumn. Still though, three seasons it was, technically. Not like I was ever going to marry her at our age but I might have well as because I really did want to spend the rest of my life with her. Found myself thinking what the pair of us will be like in our fifties and stuff like that. we obviously won't be taking pills and dancing all night by then, surely not eh? Then again, who knows these things because if this age group of mines are doing things like drugs and all night parties at this stage of their life then that might well reflect on their whole attitude to life as time goes by.

That stuff fascinates me, like how one generation had a certain attitude and carried that on as they got older. Then you've got younger generations who look at things differently with a fresh pair of eyes and as such, attitudes will change accordingly as the decades pass. Can totally image that in around fifty years time years you'll be seeing pensioners covered in tattoos and all having had experience of taking drugs. If that's the case then the kids of those times will have it a lot more fucking easy than the ones right now.

Imagine getting caught with a joint by your grandad and instead of him giving you a slap before grassing you up to your parents, he tells you to pass him it so he can have a toke himself? How fucking cool would that be? Who know's maybe "I'll" be that grandad?

I wasn't in any rush to get back home but Lisa had school the next day so I had to respect that as she'd be up early the next day so we made sure we got the earlier bus back than usual. We finished our burgers as we walked along the high street on the way to the bus station to catch the 9.50 to Anstruther. I got her back safe and sound and left her to get ready for bed. The alarm would be going off soon enough for her the next morning. I wasn't exactly feeling that tired myself so thought I'd swing by and pay Jeebs a visit on the way home for a wee nightcap joint but his place was in darkness. Either he wasn't in or he was crashed for the night. Wasn't risking knocking on the door anyway as he's a bit of a prick that way. Woke him up once before when he was working shifts and he went fucking radge at me. Almost came to blows as he took it too far and I reacted. How was I supposed to know he'd be sleeping at two in the afternoon? Not like he'd sellotaped his fucking rota to his front door eh?

Instead, I ended up watching some of the highlights from across the European cup tournaments over the night. It was when we were sat watching Manchester United easily dispense of some Welsh side that Jimmy finally let me know that Si had been on the phone looking for me when I was out at the pictures with Lisa, three times he'd called.

'Brenda, told him that you were out for the night but he phoned back an hour later, she told him the second time around that she'd said you weren't going to be in until the end of the night and you know what? He bastarding phoned back another forty five minutes later. You need to tell him that he can't be doing that, son' The only concern he seemed to have was that they were being disturbed while trying to relax and watch the telly. For me I was immediately alerted to the fact that he must've had a good reason for calling me so many times.

By that point it was the back of eleven and definitely not a time of the night to be calling anyone. Knowing Si, he'd have still been awake but I was hardly going to try calling his house since I'd have to talk to him there while my uncle was in the room. I briefly thought of going back outside and taking a wee walk down to the phone box to call him. I decided against it as I didn't have a clue what kind of an excuse I'd have been able to come up with that would explain away me going back out of the house at that time of the night without it looking a bit suss.

I "was" intrigued why he was in such an urgent rush to catch me. My guess was that he'd found out about another party that was happening and had let his excitement get the better of him. Figured that he was checking if I was wanted to go which if he already knew me, which he did, then he'd have known I wouldn't be missing it for all the Ching in Bogota. I tried to play down the fact that he'd called the house so many times in the one night. 'Aye, he gets excited about the slightest wee thing does Simon' I said non committing anything further before we went back to concentrating on the rest of the ties before the end of the show.

Chapter 37.

'Have you heard the news about Nora?' Si's voice excitedly travelled down the line to me.

You've got to hand it to him, he's a persistent cunt, likes. After all the times that he had phoned me when I was out with Lisa at the pictures he never even gave me a chance to get out of bed before he was calling me again the next day. I was already awake as whoever was last out the door between the other three in the house had slammed the door when leaving which woke me up. I wouldn't put it past being my cuzz though. Doing it accidentally on purpose to wake me up for the day while he's off to earn a crust pissed off at me lying about in bed with no commitments to speak off. Eating coco pops while watching Australian soap operas, smoking Hash and masturbating didn't exactly count as commitments to him.

I lay in bed and heard the car start up and drive off knowing that was me safe for the day The house to myself to get up to whatever I wanted for another day. King of the fucking castle, guvnor. I still had the three hundred quid that my dad slipped me when we came face to face in Blackburn. It was guilt money, nothing more but if he was thinking that I was going to stand there full of pride not accepting it and all that then he would've been in for a shock. Fucking hell, I was out my tree on pills and crystals and someone was offering me a stack of cash. What else was I going to do other than take it. Was quite funny though hours later when I'd completely forgotten about him slipping me the notes and I was sat on the ground outside the factory having a smoke and found myself looking for a lighter and ended up pulling out hundreds of pounds from my pocket.

I hadn't trusted myself not to squander it so had left it with Lisa for a while but had gotten it back when walking her back home when arrived back from the cinema. With the world my oyster I had been contemplating getting the train through to Glasgow to go and have a wee look at this 23rd Precinct place. Maybe buy a few tunes while there and get started on the whole DJ ball rolling?

I wanted to have a wee chat with the guys in the shop and see how everything worked. Like I'd experienced with certain clothes shops, if you're a regular. Through time the staff begin to recognise you and before you know it you're all on first name terms. They're then giving you discounts and keeping limited edition pieces of clothing back just for you as they get to know what type of stuff you like.

I was assuming that it would be the exact same with record shops. Makes sense stuff like that, a customer is regularly looking after them so it would be mad not to show some love back in their direction to ensure that you keep them coming back. It would be a case of one bus and two trains to get me there though so I'd need to be getting up sooner rather than later. You know what it's like though eh? You're not long awake and the bed always seems at its optimum stage of comfiness at that point.

Even the phone going off downstairs wasn't immediately enough to have me springing out of bed. I let it ring out as it wasn't going to be for me at that time of the morning anyway. It was only when it rang again seconds after stopping that I then remembered about Si trying to get hold of me so many times the night before. Just in case it "was" him I jumped out and ran downstairs bollock naked to answer it before it stopped again.

There was none of the usual sentiments we'd go through on the phone. The second he heard my voice he asked me the question while I'm stood there realising that with the way things are, I'm standing in front of the main window looking into the living room and am needing to be closing the blinds double quick. Either that or I'll be getting lifted for flashing at all the neighbours outside.

The way he asked it, the tone of his voice. I could tell this was big. My guts immediately started to churn and I felt like I needed to sit down. I wanted to know the news, of course I did but in the way that I guess, someone wants to know their test results for a serious illness like the Big C. I knew that there was a chance that what he said next to me was going to leave me smiling or extremely troubled.

'Nora? Nah, last time his name even came up was when he was pished a few weeks ago and phoned to let me know that he was going to slice my face up from ear to ear the next time he saw me, how? What's up?'

Si laughed back at this although it was one of those forced and put on laughs that someone will do just for the benefit of what they're about to follow up with.

'Aye, well he's not exactly going to be slicing up your face now, mate'

My heart was about to jump out of my body. The reply from him left me impatiently waiting on the beef. I remained silent, he was the one with the news and he obviously wanted to tell me about it considering all the calls last night.

'Get this, Zico. Nora was through in Glasgow a couple of nights ago doing some deal with some Weegies and when he was stood there in the boys house the fucking Drug Squad knocked the door down and caught them in the middle of the trade.'

I felt like screaming my head off and dancing a fucking jig but the superstitious in me was worried that there was some kind of sick twist still to come where Nora had escaped and is now going to try and kill me as part of some urgent "things to do" list before he finally gets taken in by the DS.

'So he's been lifted then' I finally found my voice, asking Si while crossing my fingers on what was coming next.

'Aye, you could say that. Another way to describe it though would be that when they busted in through the door, Nora's grabbed the Skag and tried to escape through the back door in the kitchen. That didn't go too well and ended with him grabbing a steak knife from the cutlery drawer in a stand off with the coppers. You know what he's like eh? He was never going to go quietly in a situation like that?'

As he described how it had went down I could totally see it all taking place. Not a fucking chance Nora was ever to be one of those that was going to say "it's a fair cop" and stand there with his hands up in the air. Doesn't matter a fuck if he was trapped in a small semi detached house or not, the mad cunt wasn't going to give up until he knew he was completely fucked and out of options. I couldn't work out why he grabbed the Heroin though. Not that I'll ever be in that same position as him but I'm pretty fucking sure that if I'm face to face with the Drug Squad like he was, the last thing I'd be doing would be picking up any fucking drugs in front of them! What the fuck was he thinking of?

309

'Unless I'm missing something here if it had stayed out of his possession then with it being someone else's house, they'd have struggled to pin the drugs on him? No?' I asked Si, finding myself starting to shiver, still standing there with nothing on, scanning the room in case there was even a blanket or something I could grab from the sofa.

Once again, Si laughed at me but this time I could sense the sincerity. 'Do you fucking know how much the stuff was worth?' Best part of two hundred grand, mate. If Nora had managed to escape from the house but not with the money or the product then his life was going to be pretty fucked anyway. Wasn't his money but an investors, some heavy people likes, I guess it was a chance that Nora would have had to take in that moment'

It made a lot of sense the way he put it. I'm thinking of it in the kind of way where I'd toss a couple of pills to the ground if I saw the police and just walk away from them. Walking away from a debt of two hundred thousand to some seriously dangerous people isn't as easy as saying goodbye to two White Doves.

Walking away from a couple of pils? At that moment of 8.47am on a Thursday morning I felt like I was fucking GOING UP on two fucking Eckies. It felt too good to be true but what Si was telling me was going hand in hand with what I'd seen on the STV news the night before when eating my tea with the folks. I'd obviously never made the connection. I'd not really had any reason to do so, you see news of drug busts all the time on the regional news.

I was still waiting on something to show me that while it "was" looking like all of my dreams had come true, they weren't. There was none forthcoming though. Si was telling me how it was the only thing that anyone was talking about up his way. That's the thing with wee cities like Dundee though, everyone knows your business, sometimes before you truly know it yourself. It didn't take me long in the conversation before I found myself thinking of my dad although for obvious reasons I had to keep them to myself.

Had he been anything to do with it? Possibly it was just a coincidence? By all accounts Nora had been riding his luck with all the wrong people so maybe it was just a case of it running out, eventually. It would be naive though for me to think that there I was having a conversation with my dad where sorting out Nora had been the main agenda only for days later all of this to happen though? Some eggheads don't even believe in coincidences. I do, but the more I thought about it the less coincidental I was seeing it all.

The rest of the conversation with Si had me thinking about the Wizard of Oz film as the phone call between us definitely had a ding dong the witch is dead vibe about it. Apparently, due to the volume of drugs that he was caught with as well as the fact he was threatening officers with a kitchen knife, bail was never going to be an option for him and right now he was stuck in Barlinnie. No hope of getting out until at least his next court appearance. The things that you think about in such a moment and I had fucking plenty to consider, more than most. The first thing I thought of was ... Who the fuck do United play at the weekend?

'That's me done with the Utility now' Si confirmed which made me smile but, weirdly at the same time, it also made me sad. I thought about how the two of us had met and all of the madness that we'd been involved in, how exciting it had been. The laughs, the chaos and lots of fun. We'd lived a certain life and saw things that most others will never come close to seeing. It was hypocritical of me if anything considering I'd been the one that had given it all up months before him but with Si saying he was done that officially signalled the end of an era. It was almost like a sign that we were maturing which, in itself was stupid considering none of us were even in our twenties yet. It, if anything though, gave an indication that for as young as we were we'd done a bit of living already.

Whatever had happened and however it had transpired I couldn't help but feel that the biggest of weights had been lifted from my shoulders. I felt a strange sense of freedom. Almost born again, like a Christian. I wanted to call Lisa but couldn't as she was probably in fucking higher geography for all I knew, definitely not at home. Even if so I couldn't call her anyway considering I'd played down the whole Nora stuff for her benefit. As far as she was concerned I didn't "have" anything to now be celebrating.

I wanted to tell my auntie and uncle that they wouldn't have to worry about anything but once again, they were otherwise disposed. Fuck? I wanted to telephone Maurice Malpas, the United captain and apologise to him for my prolonged absence in supporting the boys but that, due to the sinister of intentions of a total psychopath I wasn't exactly feeling welcome in supporting Dundee United from the terraces each week.

I wanted to tell him that now that things had changed I would be there at three o clock next Saturday. I had the great need to tell anyone and everyone. We chatted about other stuff, most importantly things like meeting up at the football and even more importantly, the fact that there was an all nighter at Motherwell Civic Centre in a few weeks time and preparations had already begun. Jesus, between Si and moi and what we had left over from our lucky bags from our trip to the VIP area down in Blackburn we weren't exactly in a position of struggling for any party favours for on the night through in the west.

We said ciao for now, he was starting work at lunch time due to some rotation cycle of a trio of shifts and he needed to chill for a bit before getting ready. He left me there, still fucking stark naked, feeling like whatever I wanted to achieve from my day that it was there for the taking. 'Fuck it,' I thought to myself. I'd get myself out of the house and away through to Glasgow for the day, even if just for the pilgrimage properties of visiting the city where Nora met his end, at least for a few years anyway.

Of course, the fact that I would get a chance to see what clothes I could maybe pick up in Dr Jives in addition to what I could discover inside 23rd Precinct would be nothing other than a Brucey Bonus. I'd definitely need to speak to that International man of mystery that was my papa too.

Whether it was or it wasn't his doing it was something I really needed to find out. It was weird but once I'd experienced that feeling of being free of this lunatic I couldn't have cared less "who" was responsible for it. If I'd definitely found out that it was the work of Allah I'd probably have converted to Islam on the fucking spot, so thankful that I was. I still wanted to get my dads take on things, regardless. If anything, we had a chat about a pair of Technics SL's to be taking place.

Chapter 38.

Most of the day though was spent with my mind inside the walls of HMP Barlinnie and what was going on at Nora's end. Having never been inside a prison in my life all I'd had to go on was the usual take you got from films and TV. I imagined how he was taking to his first day inside. Not very well, without a shadow of a fucking doubt. How he was taking to his new surroundings and the "friends" he would be shacked up with. Just as pertinently, how were THEY taking to him?

I almost pitied the inmates and screws in there. By the very definition of things it was a prison, not a holiday camp so I can imagine that it would've been on the grim side at the best of times but now having a Nora, no doubt angry at the world. Having him in there with them, things were bound to far worse for all concerned. As far as whoever was going to have to share a cell with him? They have my condolences but as selfish as this might sound. Rather them than me. Poor cunt, whoever they are.

23rd Precinct was a novelty, an absolute trip. I couldn't find the place at first and in fact I walked past it three times before I eventually sussed out that the shop was sat BELOW street level. I'm walking about the street like some doss cunt looking for a shop that as far as my line of vision was concerned, wasn't there. Which was down to the fact that it actually wasn't! Could've almost headed straight back to Glasgow Central and got on a train home through sheer embarrassment when I realised I had been standing right beside the place all along with a clueless look on my coupon. The basement location I felt quite fitting for the operation it was running. Songs from the underground sold from beneath the ground.

It was everything I'd been told of and a lot, lot more. As I walked into the place there was some techno playing, this heavy bass tune that had a haunting vocal with this creepy voice repeatedly saying, 'Ecstasy Ecstasy' I'd heard it played down in Blackburn with many a wink and a nod exchanged across the place when the vocals kicked in. I'd managed to convince myself that it was a ghost that was saying it on the record. Then again, those MDMA crystals really didn't take any prisoners. I'm sure Pickering had played it but don't quote me on that as it came during that part of the night where you were never quite sure what was going on. The shop was quite dead which left me a wee bit more intimidated than I should've been considering I was there to see about handing the shop assistants some business their way.

All eyes were on me from the three guys behind the counter when they clocked me coming in. I knew instantly that this was an establishment that was doing things under their own terms as two of the assistants were standing there openly smoking fags. It's not something I'd ever really seen inside a shop before and to me, screamed that it was an outlet that didn't need to follow all of the usual principles of running a business. They knew that their patrons needed them, weirdly, a lot more than the shop needed them.

This theory was blown out of the water in seconds though when I saw the big smile on the boy nearest to me when he asked me if he could help. With this tune from Blackburn still playing, almost without realising I'd done it. I turned around in the direction of the giant speakers on the wall and replied - 'You can start by telling me what that is' - His face lit up, 'fucking belter eh' which I could tell was nothing more than rhetorical as he continued. 'Joey Beltram, Energy Flash.'

I'd never heard of Joey Beltram although chances were I'd probably heard some of his other stuff and just hadn't known it. I faked it by nodding my head and taking a chance by saying that he was never a disappointment with what he brought out. I don't know why I felt the need to immediately fit in. I'd never felt that way in any other shop but this all felt different. It felt much more than a simple case of paying for goods.

'Aye, we just got ten white labels in today, not easy to get at the moment, Pickering was only playing it last week' I'm not sure if this was all just some sales pitch from the boy but he seemed sincere enough so I was sold. 'Actually, I think I heard him play it down in Blackburn' I replied which at least was something that actually "had" happened as far as I could remember. The guy behind the counter just rolled his eyes at the mention of Blackburn.

'We were all down there as well, what a night eh? There were a few sore heads coming back up the road the next day, that's putting it mildly' What he said had caught the attention of the other two and before long they were all joining in talking about the party in the factory and the capers that had gone on down there.

This was brilliant! I'd actually found a shop where the staff were all of the like minded to me, clearly having a passion for house music and all of the things that came with it.

Once we got down to business though he asked me what specific style of music I was looking for. I fucking loved the place instantly. Just saying "house music' "really wasn't going to leave the boy any further forwards in what to recommend me. Alongside, of course, a freshly procured copy of Energy Flash. Since I already knew he was on the same page I took him through some of the parties that I'd been to, how aye, I liked a bit of Italian House but added that going to Pure that night in Edinburgh and seeing DJ's playing a harder stuff, faster than Italian and containing a lot of fucking mad and dark techno noises had been turning my head.

The boy obviously knew his stuff because before I'd realised it he'd picked out a good twenty five to thirty records for me and sorted out a mini stereo to listen to them on. I can't even explain how special it all felt, how exclusively exciting. Most of the records actually had a smell to them that suggested they had only just been pressed recently. The anticipation of each record when I would take it out of the sleeve and put it onto the turntable? Words could barely even come close. Not having a scoobie what it was going to sound like until the needle dropped down onto the vinyl.

I soon got into a system of listening to the intro for around thirty seconds before lifting the needle and seeing what it was like by the minute stage and then onto the middle and so on. A fair percentage of the records had Dutch scribbled on them, it was like a lottery with each one listened to. I was soon starting to notice certain label names pop up again and again as I went through the pile he'd given me. R&S Records being one that I was seeing regularly come up.

As I was approaching the end of the pile I felt that in such a short time I'd gained in experience simply by having access to all of these tracks. I'd already picked out twenty from the pile as keepers when I got to the last record which had the, by now, unmistakable R&S logo which for some reason reminded me of the Ferrari badge. They're probably fuck all like each other but that's what I thought anyway. I didn't even bother listening to it on account of how many I'd already selected from the label and simply added it to the pile of twelve inches I was buying.

I listened to it when I got back home, it was shite, of course. Good experience though for an aspiring DJ. Listen to every record before you agree to purchase it which when I think about it was kind of obvious. After my trip through to the weeg though, that was me now with enough records to start practicing with and get a mixtape knocked up. The fact that I'd gotten all of these newly released white labels hot of the press it would give me a decent time scale to get practicing and then get the tape recorded and allow me to start pestering cunts with it.

Still needed the fucking decks and mixer though, mind. As far as I was concerned they were as good as in the post as soon as I spoke to El Papa in Locombia. Impatient as I was through the news about Nora I planned to give him a call later in the night. Given the news Si had began my day with there was NO fucking way I was going to just phone my dad "some time" and had it not been for the time difference between the UK and Colombia I'd have phoned him straight after coming off the phone from Si early that morning.

When I did eventually manage to pull myself away from all of the vinyl I'd bought to go and call him I both A. Caught him free to talk and B. He wasn't so hesitant with his choice of words unlike the previous time we'd spoken. I didn't feel like I could ask why but I yet noticed this was a lot different. He seemed more carefree, somehow. The things he was saying during the conversation were the exact type of stuff that would get you pinched if the police "were" listening in on things.

'So you've heard the news then' he asked upon hearing my voice on the other end of the line. 'Oh, what news would that be?' I tried to play it cagey but was obviously underestimating the man that my father really was. - 'Don't fucking work yourself sonny Jim' he laughed back. I giggled in an embarrassed kind of way. 'So, it was you then? I asked, immediately regretting the choice of words I'd went with.

'Well, considering I'm sat here in Bogota right now, of course it wasn't me' Fucking wide cunt, he knew full well I didn't mean it like that. 'Buuuuut I might've had a wee hand it somewhere along the line.' I could practically see the smile on his face over the phone. The bastard was enjoying teasing me like this but I was happy enough for him to do so. I already had been provided with the best of news in any case so he could've said or done whatever the fuck he wanted. 'I found out this morning from a mate, been on the telly and everything likes, from what I heard he's not getting back out again, no bail or fuck all.'

As I told him this I could hear him having a line. As hypocritical as this will sound that was one thing I wasn't too happy about with my new found dad. I guess it would be a bit of a head fuck to anyone having to watch one of their parents blatantly taking Class A drugs but then throw in the mix that he's seen me out of my tree too. I'd never seen myself while I'm on pills but can only imagine the fucking state I must look with my eyes and all of the facial expressions and "that" fucking swinging jaw going all over the place.

Anyway, hypocrite or not it still felt weird to know my dad was a regular Cokehead I just didn't want him to end up like Tony Montana or something. I know it was only a film but lets face it, Coke is fucking amazing. I'd only tried it for the first time on the way down to Blackburn but I couldn't help but notice how outstanding it was as a drug and could easily see why cunts would want to take it all of the time. It's not something for kids like me of course, teenagers who are doing well to scrape together forty pounds for a couple of pills for a night out once a month never mind having to pay for a habit day in day out. I just didn't want it to go tits up for him. All those feelings of resentment I'd held towards him were now gone. I actually liked him, he was one of those people that you just "liked" after five minutes in their company and to be fair. He was doing nothing but living up to the stories that I'd heard from people in the area who knew him.

'Bail? Do you know what he actually did inside the house?' He replied leaving me now questioning how much of the truth Si had been told in what had bound to have been a game of Chinese whispers that had swept across Tayside. 'Well, he tried to escape and was waving a knife at the police to try and buy some time' I said, kind of hesitantly in case this had all been a lot of bullshit. 'That and the fucking rest' He replied laughing at what was still some kind of a private joke.

'Son, he hid from a women police officer who was coming in the back door and the next thing she knows he's got a knife to her throat holding her as a hostage. He's shouting all kinds of nonsense at the rest of the Drug Squad about getting a plane ready for him at Glasgow Airport, the boy's evidently a few cans short of a carry out. Stupid cunt is going to get more for that than he would've done for the half a millions worth of Heroin that was in the room and I assure you, he was seeing double figures for that alone, it couldn't have worked out any better.

You just needed him gone for a while and he goes and puts a big fat cherry on top for you.' Nothing he told me was really any news in terms of how mental, Nora was but fucking hell, I didn't think he was as stupid as that either. I suppose who can predict what you'll act like in a moment like that. Desperate times calls for desperate measures and all that I guess.

'So look, I appreciate it if you can't go into it with me, especially over the phone but I could really be doing with knowing how it all happened and what you might've had to do with it, actually dad, I'm curious as fuck to know' We both laughed before he told me that he was fine to talk and proceeded to give me a bit of an education of how the drug game actually works.

'Well, all I really needed to do was make one phone call which would've meant that someone else would then have had to call someone else and eventually the message would have been passed down through the chain to have it set up for your pal to be traveling through to Glasgow to pick up a delivery of H from one of his usual suppliers. Only, I'd made sure that it wasn't going to go like all the other times he'd came through. Look, son, I know you won't be thinking about it when you've got a pill in your hand but there's a LOT of stuff happening in between before you get that disco biscuit inside of you.'

I was fascinated by all of this, aye, he'd used the term disco biscuit in a non ironic sense which I'd have expected better from someone who knew about drugs, I'd have assumed that from a reporter from The fucking Sun or something like that. Still though, I wanted to hear what he had to say. - 'There are many rivers to cross before it gets into your grubby little palms, laddie' I let papa continue as he told me about all of the intricacies, the ducking and diving and dodging and weaving to get the product out and into the market. All of the palms that had to be greased to get things from A to B. Police were in on it, dodgy coppers topping up their inadequate salaries who would play nice with the main players in the local drug scene. 'Everyone's for sale' he said in such a cocky way that I didn't know whether to be in admiration of who he was or be repulsed by it.

As he continued, he told me about how one of his connections in Scotland has a paid mole in the Strathclyde Police Drug Squad. The two of them work in tandem sharing information that will benefit the other. Just the usual stuff, if there was a bust headed his way his man on the inside would get the word to him in advance while my dad's connection would share news on his competitors to the copper.

Oldest trick in the book according to my dad and a good way to stay out of jail while putting your rivals IN there. In the process making you even richer. 'So anyway' My dad tried to get back on track, I was loving hearing all of this stuff. It wasn't exactly the type of stuff you hear someone saying in your day to day life and I was sucked in.

He probably didn't know it, to him he was just nonchalantly stating facts but it was, exciting. 'Nora was heading through to Glasgow to meet up with a regular through there, Donkey Jack Ferguson. They'd done business plenty times before so there was no reason for your boy from Dundee to be apprehensive in any way. Childs play as far as Nora was thinking.

That probably would've been the case were it not for the fact that my associate had already experienced several issues with Ferguson recently. There had been an argument over a missing twenty five grands worth of Coke that neither party had backed down over. Ferguson's not exactly a mug. He knows he's got a bit of clout that can back him up when going up against my associate from through in Edinburgh who himself, is the biggest importer in the whole of Scotland, that I know to be fact' I really didn't want to speak, I wanted him to just keep talking and tell me more of all of this stuff, he came to a stop. Long enough for me to but in and ask 'So what happened with Donkey Ferguson and Nora then?'

This was met with playful exasperation from him. 'Have you been fucking listening to me son? My man in Edinburgh has had a falling out with Ferguson, although they're still working together all be it strained, at best. You follow that part, aye? Patronising prick I thought. I answered him with a simple 'yes.' 'Throw into the mix that I had a relative axe to grind with the other person taking part in the transaction along with Donkey Ferguson , the axe also known as YOU, still with me?'

Just keep talking I was thinking to myself. I could tell that the line he'd taken had started to take hold with the way he was talking to me. Reason numero uno for avoiding taking Ching ... It turns you into a full of yourself twat who doesn't realise they're being a, well, full of themselves twat. I was happy to let all of this pass. In my eyes he was a fucking GOD if he'd played any part in getting this psychotic mentalist of a man out of my world. 'So you add myself and then my associate and remember that we both have a stake in it ... thhhhhhhen you add in the fact that my Edinburgh man has the connection with the DS in Strathclyde annnnnnnnd?'

He was actually looking for me to offer the next part of input like it was some fucking murder mystery and the audience were to guess "whodunnit." Now I guess to any free thinking person who didn't have a hundred levels of stuff going through their head like I did from what was coming out next from R&S records to exactly how my dad had managed to help engineer a psychopathic football hooligan and drug dealers incarceration.

It was obvious that the DS officer had played a part in all of this. It just wasn't obvious to me, that's all I'm saying. I think my dad's pretend exasperation had shifted to actual when he found that he STILL had to explain to me that Donkey Ferguson had taken a serious amount or product from the wholesaler, and fathers contact, in Edinburgh .... this information had been passed onto the DS through in The West. From then it was a case of the Drug Squad staking out the house with it all set up for Nora coming through to collect and hand over the money. Orders apparently being that once he was in the house along with Ferguson it was go go go, mallet through the door type deal.

Ferguson was gone as a result and solving the problem he was causing the dealer through in Edinburgh, Nora was out of the picture and well, enough said about that cunt already eh?, The Drug Squad boy got himself a big half a million pound seizure that, "suspiciously" had reduced in size from half a million to a hundred grands worth by the time the STV news had ran the story. I asked my dad about the fact that the news said a lot less Heroin had been busted. He just laughed back at, what I took to be my naivety. I left it at that.

If I was to be trying to absolve myself of any guilt over it all then I could easily have adopted the fantasy that all of this was going to happen anyway however, without really saying that much to me, I had started to join a few dots. My dad had given me the lasting impression that he had driven it from minute one and that the rest of it had fallen into place because he had steered it in that particular direction. He explained how, now that Ferguson was locked up away along with Nora, his man in Edinburgh now had a larger catchment area to move into through in The West. Of course, there would be some from through there who would have a go at it but he was already in place, had all the connections and infrastructure and as always, the most important thing of all. He had the product, ready to go. The way that he explained it all to me it almost felt like "I'd" been the one that had been used (although I'm pretty fucking sure that Ferguson & Nora would debate that) by falling on the wrong side of Nora purely so someone could then take advantage of the things and turn my situation into a profit for themselves.

Aye I was just being paranoid but I had this wee suspicion that my dad, amongst others in his circle were going to end up benefiting from Nora's demise a lot more than I would. I don't know? it just felt like that there had been more to all of this than just a father looking out for their boy. Almost like my part in the story hadn't been as much of a driver in the situation and I was nothing more than a peripheral figure. All that while my father "made it out" that he was doing all of this to help me. When I started to think that way I almost felt duped. Like he'd used my perilous and incredibly fucked up life to to help himself out.

You know what though? Good on them whoever made what out of it. It was a life I didn't understand never mind wanted to be part of. I just found myself in a world of shit that, were it not for the most random of circumstances I wasn't getting back out of again so aye, beggars and choosers.

Dad asked me how I felt now that it was all over with. Well first of all I told him that I felt I had my life back again and was going to grab the chance that I'd been given with both hands. All I could say to him was that, like him, I wanted to do things different. I wasn't up for that whole nine to five stuff that the "others" engaged in. I shared with him some of what I wanted to do in life, it felt pretty weird to be honest, having a conversation with that exact person that you should've held those same kind of chats with all of your life from the moment you could speak.

I ended up going emotionally deep at times. Told him my feelings over not growing up with either him or mum. I probably stretched things by saying that him and mum may well have been the reason why I had ended up embracing such a group like the Utility. Where my feeling of "belonging" had possibly come from. Aye, I hammed it up just to give it in his direction, he could see where I was getting at though. I'm not sure if he had appreciated, beforehand, but stood there with my head against the glass and leaning against the inside of that red phone box, told him that how I felt now was that with Nora gone I was going to get on with things, get on with "life." I was going to go back and watch that team of mines but also .. I'd found a new passion, music and how I'd been buying records and now needed decks and mixer and of my grand plan to become a DJ. I tugged at his heart strings. 'Like you, dad in our own individual ways. I want to be different, life's for living at the end of the day.'

He didn't even seem to take a moment of pause at this, instead answering in that confident and cocky way that he'd projected at all times since we had gatecrashed each others lives again. 'Don't you worry about it, I'll get Danny Rampling himself to hand deliver those Technics and set them up for you' he laughed. - Hearing the words I was more impressed at the fact that he knew who Danny Rampling was rather than the fact that he'd agreed to sort me out with what was over a grands worth of electronic goods and something, left to myself was a galaxy away from ever being achievable.

We left it at that. We'd spoken for almost an hour, in that time I'd had to deal with a selection of cunts standing outside the phone box waiting on me finishing my call. Some had given up and walked off again pissed off at the inconvenience of not getting to make their calls. A few ignorant women had actually opened the door to the phone box mid call when their patience had eventually snapped.

Asking me how much longer I was going to be. Both times had been met with the same reply from me of 'I'll be finished when I'm finished' - Fairs fair though, I'd hogged what was one of only two phone boxes in the village and besides, I could only imagine what other stuff my dad was needing to be attending to on his end. I left him with my bank account details before hanging up with him telling me that the money would be with me in a few days.

Lying in bed at the end of what had been, all things considered, a truly amazing day for various reasons. I couldn't help but notice that the same day I find out about Nora's arrest I'm then in Glasgow starting out in attempting to chase my dream. Those two being on the same day wasn't a coincidence. That bastard had ground me down over all of those months with his threats and mind games. I'd questioned if this was the norm for sixteen year olds to be so knee deep in shit and if life would never get any better for those that found themselves in positions like that at such a young stage.

Unable to sleep, I took myself from that day on the Haymarket platform years back when taking a kicking from the ASC and Nora and crew appearing to the rescue while fulfilling their own agenda. Nora sitting talking to me having a fag, how impressed he'd appeared over someone as young as me. How excited I was to be part of such a group, how impressionable I'd been, taken under his wing. How in a matter of years I'd done such a mad amount of growing up while within the group which ironically, led to all of the "unpleasantness" directed towards me, as well as the family. End of the day it was all my fault, I was the one who fucked up by agreeing to run with a gang of hoolies and you know what? Regardless of how it turned out I regretted nothing about running with the lads home and away. Aye, of course I messed up but I fixed it in the end didn't I? Having done so, still only seventeen with most of my life ahead of me. As I dropped off to sleep for the night I don't think I'd ever felt more positive in my life. All bets were back on.

Chapter 39.

6 months later ......

It's amazing how much life can change over the course of a year. 1990 started with me directionless. Thinking that all there was to life was designer clothes and soccer violence. 1991 began with me having a girlfriend that I would do anything for, a deeper and more meaningful connection with my family than ever before and a sense of knowing what I wanted to achieve in life and what I wanted OUT of it. Free to live exactly as I wanted to, my relationship with Lisa and friends like Si and Shan had only became stronger and stronger. Still under the radar to the rest of the family, dad and moi's relationship had progressed with us both in a good place with each other despite the less than normal life we both lived.

Despite the earlier years worth of heartache I really liked him and appreciated having him in my world. Doing so while trying to stay as grounded about it as I could. The facts were that the knowledge I had what he was doing in his life, each time we spoke might've been the last before he "disappeared" again. From the moment I got those Technics courtesy of pater I barely went a waking hour of my free time without being stood over them with a headphone stuck to my right ear and my right hand on the crossfader. House music was starting to become the behemoth that I had predicted it would. The music was breaking off into all different kinds of directions. Italian House, Garage, Hardcore Techno, Acid and Breakbeat. Mini scenes were springing up in all ways

The snowball that had been pushed down the hill in 1989 was now traveling at pace and I felt I was in a good place for taking advantage of it. The trips to 23rd Precinct had become such a fixture in my life that before long I was on first name terms with all of the staff who proved to be, as contacts inside the scene, invaluable. It didn't take long before my mixtapes started falling into the hands of the right type of people in the industry and the bookings followed as a result. First of all strictly through in Glasgow at a few clubs in the city centre and outdoor parties but as things began to build and word of mouth spread I was getting gigs nearer to home and occasionally even further down in the North of England.

I was following my dream while LIVING it and you know what? It was beginning to look like I was going to make something out of it. I had one foot in the door and wasn't going to be stopping until both feet and the rest of me, for that matter, were firmly THROUGH the fucking thing. I definitely wasn't making what could ever have been classed as a fortune but at the same time I was making enough of a wedge to get by and more importantly, to be able to contribute to the household in terms of digs and getting everyone off my back when it came to hassling me about taking a job.

Small steps I told myself but the direction it was all going in was exactly where I wanted it to be. After one appearance in Newcastle during the build up to Christmas and New Year I'd chatted with a promoter from London with connections to the legendary Amnesia in Ibiza. Having heard my set he asked if I'd be interested in taking some work there the next summer. Details were exchanged, for what, I felt would be the greatest experience of my life. Playing records on the infamous white isle for thousands of people. Life was beautiful and as far as I was concerned it was just going to get better and better. Well, that was my grand plan anyway.

Plans change though, don't they?

Also by Johnny Proctor

Ninety Six

Six years on and following events from 'Ninety' ... When Stevie "Zico" Duncan bags a residency at one of Ibiza's most legendary clubs, marking the rising star that he is becoming in the House Music scene. Life could not appear more perfect. Zico and perfect, however, have rarely ever went together.

Set during the summer of Euro 96. Three months on an island of sun, sea and sand as well as the Ibiza nightlife and everything that comes with it. What could possibly go wrong? It's coming home but will Zico?

Noughty

Noughty - The third book from Johnny Proctor. Following the events of the infamous summer of Ninety Six in Ibiza. Three years on the effects are still being felt inside the world of Stevie 'Zico' Duncan and those closest to him. Now having relocated to Amsterdam it's all change for the soccer casual turned house deejay however, as Zico soon begins to find. The more that things change the more they seem to stay the same. Noughty signals the end of the 90's trilogy of books which celebrated the decade that changed the face, and attitudes, of UK youth culture and beyond.

Available through DM to help support the independents.

Twitter @johnnyroc73

Instagram @johnnyproctor90

www.paninaropublishing.co.uk

Also available through Apple Books, Kindle, Amazon, Waterstones and other book shops.